Willing Sacrifice

Joey W. Hill

An Ellora's Cave Publication

www.ellorascave.com

Willing Sacrifice

ISBN 9781419969959
ALL RIGHTS RESERVED.
Willing Sacrifice Copyright © 2013 Joey W. Hill
Edited by Briana St. James.
Cover design by Syneca.
Cover photography by Artem Furman/Shutterstock.com and iStockPhoto.com.

Electronic book publication May 2013
Trade paperback publication 2013

With the exception of quotes used in reviews, this book may not be reproduced or used in whole or in part by any means existing without written permission from the publisher, Ellora's Cave Publishing, Inc.® 1056 Home Avenue, Akron OH 44310-3502.

Warning: The unauthorized reproduction or distribution of this copyrighted work is illegal. Criminal copyright infringement, including infringement without monetary gain, is investigated by the FBI and is punishable by up to 5 years in federal prison and a fine of $250,000. (http://www.fbi.gov/ipr/)

This book is a work of fiction and any resemblance to persons, living or dead, or places, events or locales is purely coincidental. The characters are productions of the author's imagination and used fictitiously.

The publisher and author(s) acknowledge the trademark status and trademark ownership of all trademarks, service marks and word marks mentioned in this book.

The publisher does not have any control over and does not assume any responsibility for author or third-party Web sites or their content.

Acknowledgements

When it comes to writing about the U.S. military, especially an elite force like the SEALs, it's really easy on one hand to overdo it and give them the qualities of superheroes (because some of the things they do are exactly like that), and on the other hand to screw up the more specific details about their service, with its plethora of regulations, ranks, ratings, acronyms...you get the point.

So I send my fervent thanks to Lynn and Lauren, both of who provided me invaluable resources to research Max's background and attitudes and probably kept me out of ninety percent of the trouble I would have found without them. The ten percent I screw up is likely due to my own creative stubbornness. For that, I ask their forgiveness—as well as the forgiveness of Navy SEALs. I hope I err on the side of praise, because these guys really do the impossible, pretty much behind a curtain where we'll never know all they've done to help and protect others.

As a side note on that, I also thank Lynn for the idea of including a "camo quilt" in Max's truck. These quilts are a volunteer project, started in 2006, whereby small camouflage-colored quilts are provided to servicemen and women throughout the world. Search on "Camo Quilt Project", and learn all about this awesome effort that's provided thousands of serviceable quilts to our military folk.

Thanks to the incomparable author Mary Wine, who initially started me down the road on my SEAL research. In addition to that, she gave me some great hand-to-hand tips for Max to share with Janet.

Another thanks to Emily, who told me about the foot problems a ballet dancer could experience.

My gratitude to Mark, who provided me the insightful "cat in a box" idea, one I understood immediately, given that I have a handful of beloved feline family members.

A big shout out to Michele for helping me with the prologue. There is no way I could have written that accurately without the insight of an ob-gyn nurse who has seen things that would give me nightmares. Yet she calls that horrifying process "childbirth" and considers it a natural and lovely thing (laughter).

As always, my thanks to all the readers who have made the KOBR series so popular with their enthusiasm for these men. My deep appreciation goes out as well to my Ellora's Cave editor and beta readers for making every manuscript shine.

Finally (but always) to my husband, for giving me the support and love to keep pursuing this crazy passion.

Dedication

80

This book is dedicated to the Navy SEALs and the families who support them. Thanks to my research on Max and Dale, I now know a little bit more about this outstanding group of individuals. One of their guiding mottos is "The Only Easy Day Is Yesterday". Yet they still get up every day and honor their code, wherever it takes them, and whatever sacrifices it demands.

My thanks to them for walking the path they do, and for the willing sacrifices they and their families make in the hopes of doing the highest good.

Prologue

"All right back there, Mrs. Kensington?"

"Yes, Max. If you ask me one more time, I will make you stop the limo and shoot you with your own gun."

"Yes ma'am. That's clear thinking, having me stop the car before you shoot me."

"I'm pregnant, Max. Not mentally defective. Now, at the risk of sounding like a rich and powerful woman with minions to indulge my every whim—shut up and drive. Or raise the glass and annoy Janet."

Max pressed his lips together, as if hiding a smile. "Yes ma'am," he repeated.

Sitting in the front passenger seat, Janet shifted onto her hip so she was facing him. While it helped her sort through the paperwork she had in her lap, it also served the purpose of keeping an eye on their very important passenger.

Savannah Kensington was in her eighth month and had been put on bed rest five weeks ago for pre-eclampsia. Because of that condition, as well as being in her late thirties and having other physical factors that concerned the doctor, she had to go in for regular diagnostics to monitor the baby. Today she had one of those appointments, but she'd called Janet early, before Matt arrived at the office. Janet had to hide her own smile, recalling the conversation.

"Janet, when Matt gets there, please ask him if he could send the car to the house a couple hours early so I can go for a drive. I was a complete bitch this morning and I know he's likely to walk in and tell you he's cancelling his Baton Rouge meeting. If he does that, I swear to God I will lose it. Tell him I called to wish him a good day and to apologize for being cranky. Make it sound as though you suggested the drive, and I'm very happy about it. Reassure him that we women know what we're doing, the universe is in balance, and we'll handle things. He can go to his meeting."

"Is it just a cover, or would you really like to go for a drive?" Janet asked.

Though the man was a six-foot four-inch female fantasy, Matt Kensington, head of Kensington and Associates, was overprotective to the nth degree. As well as being his pregnant wife, Savannah was CEO of Tennyson Industries and a remarkably independent and self-contained woman. Sharing some of those same qualities, Janet understood the woman's state of mind, the frustration Savannah's weary sigh revealed.

"It's utterly pathetic," she confided, "but I would love a drive. Maybe go to one of the parks and sit by the water for a little while."

"It's not pathetic," Janet assured her. "And I'm glad you meant it. It's very difficult to get a lie past him."

"Try impossible." There was a smile in Savannah's voice now. "I owe all of you an apology. I know he's been coming to work agitated, and Matt agitated is like dealing with a wounded bear. Much like dealing with me, I expect. The only thing that's kept this pregnancy from triggering a double homicide is the innocent life we'd be sacrificing."

Janet chuckled. "Peter dropped Dana off at the church this morning, so Max may have come in early. I'll check and see if he's available."

"Give him my thanks and my regrets beforehand, since I'm sure to be highly ungracious when he picks me up."

"They're men. They like it when beautiful women abuse them."

* * * * *

When she'd disconnected the call, Janet had realized she had some paperwork that needed to go to the airport for signing by their private charter company. She could easily courier it, but with Matt and all the others heading out of New Orleans to go to Baton Rouge today, it was going to be relatively quiet. From Savannah's tone, she might appreciate having a woman along. Plus, if Max was driving...

So here she was. Savannah had insisted Max take them out to the airport first, and the women had chatted along the way, Janet bringing Savannah up to date on K&A business matters she would find interesting, and any other tidbits about business district gossip and politics. Max put in a word now and then, but mostly he drove. Even so, Janet was far more aware of him than she knew she should be.

She could dismiss it as mere sexual attraction, because the former SEAL kept his body in the kind of shape that gave even the most practical woman salacious ideas. But since every one of the five-man K&A executive team, including Matt, had the face and form to turn a woman's head three hundred and sixty degrees if necessary to secure a proper view, she was usually immune to that. However, there was a steady core to Max, a quiet mystery, that kept drawing her attention. Several vital issues made them incompatible, but even so...there was nothing wrong with thinking about it, was there?

They stopped at the park for about a half hour. Janet walked Savannah the short distance to a bench and stayed with her while Max relocated the car to the street, eschewing the more remote parking area provided off the road. He obviously had no intention of letting them out of his sight, even though Janet could buzz his cell.

"It's like they all take a class," Savannah muttered. She waved Janet off once she was settled. "Why don't you go take a stroll? I'm just going to sit here and watch the ducks a bit."

While her tone suggested she'd be fine if Janet and Max jumped in the lake and drowned, Janet took no offense. Max had looked a little concerned when Savannah insisted on walking to the bench. Janet had given him a slight shake of her head, stopping him before he tried something admirable but misguided, like offering to carry Savannah, or driving the limo over the green and only stopping when the bumper was within a hair's breadth of the bench.

If the whole world was hovering over her while she felt like an overinflated balloon, Janet expected she'd be just as cranky as Savannah. She chose a bench about twenty-five yards away, making a show of checking her email on her phone. When she glanced over her shoulder toward the car, Max nodded to her, holding eye contact for an intriguingly long moment before shifting it back to his primary charge.

Janet was amused to find her cheeks warmed from the attention. Yes, definitely something fascinating about the man.

Savannah was gazing meditatively into space, oblivious to passing joggers and cyclists, the ripple of wind on the lake. Janet knew they didn't have to worry about her overdoing. No matter how hormonal or frustrated Savannah was, she and Matt were equally protective of their unborn child. Being downwind of the woman, Janet could hear Savannah humming a lullaby, all while keeping her arm curled beneath her belly, holding what would surely be their only biological child, given the difficulty of this pregnancy and Savannah's age.

Janet lifted her face to the wind, closing her eyes. She didn't do enough of this, simply taking a moment to relax. She wondered what it would be like if it was just her and Max, and he was sitting next to her. He'd likely be as quiet as he always was. She imagined reading next to him, his arm along the back of the bench, fingers sliding along her upper arm as he gazed up into the branches of a live oak spread over them. He would be like that tree, a powerful, comforting presence.

Maybe Max was her midlife crisis. She could do far worse.

Once back in the car, Savannah said little. She instructed Max to drive around the city, making loops through different districts until it was time to head for the doctor's. Then she laid her head back on the seat as she studied the passing terrain. Glancing over at Max, Janet noticed him checking his rearview mirror. He'd been doing it even more frequently these past fifteen minutes, and now she realized he wasn't watching traffic, but Savannah. Taking her legal pad, she scribbled the question, turned it in his direction. *Problem?*

He shook his head, checked the mirrors once again. Janet followed his gaze. Savannah's thick-lashed eyes were half closed. Her long blonde tail of hair fanned out over her shoulder. The woman was stunningly beautiful on a normal day. Despite the changes to her body, pregnancy had enhanced her attraction, making her blue eyes more vivid, the golden hair even softer and thicker. She projected ice princess calm, but it came with a physical delicacy that drew men to her. Her designer maternity wear was a tailored pale-green creation with pleats and slashes forming soft folds from the empire waist. Janet noticed Savannah had her hands on that expanse of cloth, pressing her palms against her stomach here and there. Perhaps she was having cramps or gas pains. She wondered if that was why Max kept checking on her.

"Just a feeling," he murmured. "I'll take you back by the office and then run her home. Maybe hang around a while."

Janet debated whether to ask him for more details, but then—unfortunately—she didn't have to ask.

There was a sudden indrawn breath from the back, followed by a sharper, startled gasp. When her head snapped around, Janet saw Savannah had gone from a relaxed position to one where she was hunched forward, both arms curled around her belly. "*Janet…*"

From Matt, Janet knew Savannah was stoic about pain, barely made a whimper about anything. Now a cry wrenched from her lips, strangled back with the greatest of effort. "Oh…Oh God…this…"

"Get in the back," Max ordered, flipping the console out of Janet's way. "Now."

Janet was already in motion, abandoning her heels so they wouldn't slow her down as she navigated between the front seats. The moment she was seated next to Savannah in the roomy back area, the limo leaped forward. Max was buzzing the office, using the steering wheel controls to activate his hands-free.

"Randall, I'm en route to the hospital with Mrs. Kensington." He glanced at the GPS, and Janet saw the ETA was approximately thirty minutes with traffic. His jaw tightened. "Her ob-gyn needs to be contacted."

"Her pager and cell numbers are on my desk, right next to the phone." Janet jumped in immediately. Max's gaze caught hers in the mirror. "Tell them she's experiencing constant pain and..." Janet laid her hands over Savannah's, gripping her stomach. The area was hard. Really hard. *Oh God.* "Her stomach is rigid."

"In short, prepare them for an emergency, in case that's what this is." Janet was impressed by how calm Max sounded, looked. There was no doubt it was definitely an emergency, but he had the presence of mind to make it seem like anything else was a possibility. She'd never seen Savannah look frightened before. It flipped the same switch for Janet, taking her to a cool place in her head, a place where everything else shut down.

"Max is going to get us there," she said firmly. "Hang on."

"It hurts. Oh God...this doesn't feel like labor. There's no...end...to it. Oh God..."

"I'm here. Hold on to me." Feeling wetness, Janet looked down, bit back an oath. Blood was dripping down Savannah's legs. She pulled off her trim suit jacket, balled it up. "Open your legs, honey. It's okay. Let's just press this here."

"My water?"

"Yes. No." She changed her mind. Matt Kensington could scent a lie, but his wife's radar was just as sharp, perhaps even more so in this state. The kid wouldn't get anything past either one of them. "Savannah, you're hemorrhaging. Let's see if we can get that slowed down. Press your legs together, tight. I'm going to lay you down, get your hips propped up. I know it hurts, but try to stay as still as you can."

Thank God the limo had backseats like wide couches. Janet had no idea if the change in position would help, but she couldn't imagine Savannah being upright when blood was dripping out of her would be helpful. As she helped her maneuver, she saw Savannah's gaze latch on to the front of Janet's blouse. In changing her grip on the coat between Savannah's legs, she'd smeared herself with a liberal amount of blood.

"No." Savannah's jaw firmed. Shuddering with pain, she curled her arms tighter around her stomach. "I'm not losing you, angel. You stay with me. Matt..."

"Randall will call him first thing after the doctor. He'll be on his way. It's all right. Women can handle everything, remember? By the time Daddy gets there, the universe will be aligned, everything will be in balance. We'll be sharing a latté and cooing over your new baby." *God willing.*

"Unh..." Savannah's cry wrenched everything inside Janet, but she quelled it, keeping her hands steady over the woman's. Her stomach was like a stale egg, no sense of movement or life, and she knew Savannah registered it as well. Janet met her gaze. "It's going to be okay. The baby's in there fighting. You can't be scared. You don't want to scare her."

Savannah nodded. She closed her eyes, tears of stress on her face, her lips pressed together tight. She tried to hum a little, like she had when she was on the park bench, and Janet joined her, smoothing her hands over her stomach, very lightly, since everything seemed to be causing Savannah pain.

As she did that, a part of her stayed aware of other things. The world was flashing by, the limo moving in a zigzag pattern that was remarkably smooth, though constant. Constant movement didn't happen in New Orleans traffic.

When she tuned in to what was happening, she felt like she was perched on a roller coaster car, careening through a minefield.

Max was maneuvering the limo between cars as if they were orange cones on a professional course. He never touched the horn, knowing New Orleans drivers were cantankerous enough to slam on brakes at such an insult, but Janet suspected he didn't need the warning signal. All they had to do was look up in their mirror, see that black behemoth bearing down on them with no intent of stopping. If they weren't fast enough to shift out of the way before he got there, he was already around them. He barely braked at the stoplights, not checking green or red, merely whether he had an access to get through them.

She'd heard that Max knew combat driving, part of his SEAL training, but she'd had no idea what it meant until now. Though she was a pretty adventurous driver herself, she wondered if it was the better part of valor to keep her full attention on Savannah. The decision was made when he dodged a traffic snarl by roaring up an alley, narrowly missing an officer on horseback. The cop shouted, but Janet would be surprised if he got anything more than two letters of the back plate before Max screeched around the next turn.

"So...did Matt make you come with me today?"

She looked back down. Savannah had gritted out the words, though she appeared to be concentrating for all she was worth on something deep inside of her. Though she'd never been one comfortable with intimate gestures, intuition had Janet stroking the woman's hair back, then locking her hand with hers once again, all while keeping the other hand busy pressing the compress between Savannah's legs.

"No. You gave me the perfect opportunity to make my move with Max. I was just about to jump him in the front seat before you interrupted us."

"Damn it, I thought it was my day to jump him. Dana shouldn't have all the fun." Savannah gave her a grimace that passed as a smile, then she jacked forward over Janet's hand "*Oh...*"

"Hold on, honey. You make any noise that helps."

Savannah shook her head, but the moans kept vibrating in her throat. Janet hummed the lullaby, rocking with Savannah, tiny movements that might help mitigate the pain, but not nearly enough.

"Dr. Rosen's on the other line," Randall barked through the speakers, because Max had kept the connection open with him. "She wants to know—"

"She's bleeding badly, and her stomach is still hard. The pain is constant, going on six minutes now."

Janet leaned forward to be sure Randall could hear her. The coat was getting heavier, telling Janet blood was soaking it. She could feel it trickling down her arm. When Max's eyes coursed over her bloody blouse, his expression reflected her own reaction. "Fuck," he muttered.

She heard garbled voices, Randall communicating with the doctor on another line, then he was back. "Max, where are you?"

Janet saw the GPS had realized what kind of driver it had. The ETA was now ten minutes out, even though for a normal driver it would be twenty. Max merged onto the interstate, the limo shooting into the middle lane. As he did, the speedometer tipped past a hundred. Janet was aware of the cars flashing by outside, but that wasn't her concern. Everything was blood and pain, Savannah gasping.

"About eight to ten minutes," Max responded.

"What—" Randall began.

"*Matt...*" Savannah's cry of agony blasted through the limo, bringing the security chief up short. Randall's stomach had probably jumped into his throat, same as Janet's had.

"Has Matt been called?" Janet asked sharply, squeezing Savannah's leg. *Hold on, honey...*

"He was already on his way back. He left the meeting early. He's about thirty minutes away. Don't crash into each other in the hospital parking lot."

"He knew... Janet..."

"Of course he did. The man's omniscient. You know that. It's okay. It's okay. You just focus on breathing, and getting you and that baby there. Dr. Rosen will make it right. Matt put the best baby doctor on the Eastern seaboard up in a penthouse apartment, just for you. Remember? He's not going to let anything happen to this child, or to you. *Savannah.*"

Janet sharpened her tone, bringing Savannah's attention back to her. "He takes care of you. You're *his*. He'd expect you to remember that."

It was something they never talked about directly, but of course Janet knew that Matt Kensington was a sexual Dominant. All five of the K&A top management team were. Their wives, including Savannah, were strong, fascinating and accomplished women, and every one of them was her respective Master's submissive soulmate. Now, in this moment, where pain threatened to take away Savannah's strength and courage, Janet reminded her she'd surrendered herself to Matt Kensington, trusting him utterly.

Mission accomplished. Savannah's blue eyes flickered as if Janet had thrown her a lifeline. The pregnant woman was wearing the delicate collar he'd given her, and her fingers went to it now, bloodying the rose quartz and silver. Her eyes closed against the pain, but the words she spoke were fierce.

"I won't let him down. I won't let either of them down."

"He knows that. They both do. We've got you. You keep thinking about that, honey."

Savannah's eyes opened once more. Janet saw the strength of character that either impressed or scared the hell out of everyone who met Matt's wife. "I'm going to fight, Janet, but if something happens, you tell them to save this little girl."

"I will, but a baby needs a mother. You fight, honey. Fight like you've never fought before. You survived over thirty years with that brute of a father of yours. This is a piece of cake."

"You always...know...so much. I'm glad Matt...has you." Savannah's head jerked back abruptly, her body contorting.

"I'm here, I'm here." Janet clung to her. "You listen to me. I'm not taking your place, I can damn sure tell you that. Working for him's bad enough. Doesn't matter how much money he has or what he can do to a woman with his dick. So you better not go anywhere."

Savannah was well beyond smiling, but Janet's resort to the shocking language made her strangle on a chuckle. "Can't wait...to tell...him you said that."

"I'll deny it. Tell him you were delirious." Glancing up, Janet was relieved to see the hospital sign flash by. The limo skidded to a halt at the emergency entrance. Underlining how serious the situation was, Dr. Rosen was already waiting with a gurney and a small army of medical personnel.

Before Max had brought the limo to a full halt, the ob-gyn surgeon had her hand on the door handle. Janet backed up, squeezing Savannah's hand with one last reassurance before the medical staff swarmed into the limo like ants. She found the door behind her open, Max helping her out of the way, his hand on her elbow. He had his eyes fastened on what they were doing, the shocking pool of blood on the seat and floor.

Seeing it herself, her knees started to wobble. No, she couldn't do that. She had to listen to what they were saying, do what needed to be done, be ready to tell Matt everything he needed to know when he arrived. There would be paperwork to handle inside, because there always was. Most important, she needed to stay as close to Savannah as she could, as long as they would let her.

"Go with her," Max said, reading her mind as the medical team got Savannah out of the limo. "I'll park and come find you. I'll take care of everything. Go."

She nodded, following the gurney and Dr. Rosen. His sudden absence felt like an amputation, as if what had happened in the limo had fused them together. Savannah was whisked away, the staff headed for the surgical wing. It left Janet swaying in front of the ER admitting desk. The stout, silver-haired nurse she faced looked like she regularly handled the worst that NOLA could deliver. Now she gave Janet a once-over. "Let's get the basics, then we'll get you some scrubs and a sink."

Janet glanced down. Things had gone far beyond that initial smear to her blouse. She was soaked in Savannah's blood. On her clothes, her hands and arms. It was probably even smeared on her face. Oh God, if Matt...

"Janet."

She closed her eyes. Damn the man's timing. Giving the nurse a look she hoped conveyed the possible need for a second gurney, she turned to face Matt as he came through the emergency doors. Had he conjured a winged horse to get here right on Max's heels? It wouldn't surprise her if he had. Matt Kensington's abilities exceeded that of a mortal man's. Most of the time.

His piercing gaze took in her appearance. In the next moment, Matt Kensington turned pale as a ghost, his face gripped with an anguish and fear that tore her heart from its framework.

Once, a long time ago, Matt Kensington had stood between Janet and the loss of her soul. She'd do everything she could to return the favor now. *Fight like a tiger, honey. Fight for him, because he needs you so much more than you realize. And we all need him.*

Or maybe Savannah did realize it. The way she'd looked at Janet, her gaze practically boring into her. *I'm glad Matt has you.*

Closing the distance between them, she put her hands on Matt's forearms, despite the blood she transferred to his white shirt. He'd shed his jacket and tie in the car. In that uncertain moment before she spoke, when he didn't yet know what had happened, she thought she might be holding him up.

"They took her to surgery. The uterus wall detached, Matt. They have to operate now to save her and the baby."

* * * * *

In certain situations, time really had no meaning. It was simply one task after another, lined up to keep the cold knot of fear at bay, the knowledge that everything might be brought to a screeching halt by a doctor's somber face, the resigned gaze. By the time she and Matt were in the surgery waiting room, Max had joined them. With barely a glance, Max understood what she needed. He sat down with Matt, beginning to relay additional details in that direct way that helped her usually unflappable boss. Information. Men always thought it could help solve things, change them.

Max had pressed her cell phone into her hand, along with her hands-free earpiece. When he did, he'd tightened his fingers on her briefly. She kept him and Matt in her sight but out of hearing range as she started her list of calls. Matt hadn't given her any guidance, but then he rarely had to do so for any situation. She wouldn't be seeking any for this one. Now that the initial shock was wearing off, he was practically vibrating with suppressed fury and frustration. Savannah and his child were behind a closed door somewhere, going through an indescribable trauma, yet he couldn't help them, couldn't be at their side.

Her first call was the most important, yet the one she hoped would be least necessary. "Yes, may I speak to Reverend Dana? Thanks... Dana, this is Janet. Savannah's in surgery. Something went wrong." When her voice quavered, she stopped herself, forced it to calm before continuing. "You need to come right away. Matt may need you. I'll have Randall send a car. Call Jon and have him come straight to the hospital as well."

Dana would call all of them, all four of Matt's executive team and their wives, not just Jon. However, if the worst happened, Dana and Jon were the ones Matt would need most. The worst simply couldn't happen, however. Janet refused to accept that. She thought of Savannah's jaw firming, the determination in the pain-racked features. She would fight. No matter her pain, no matter her exhaustion, angels would have to drag Savannah Kensington's soul screaming from that room to take her away from the child and husband she loved so much.

"Ma'am?" She turned to see an orderly, a gentle black giant with the brown eyes of a deer, standing by her. He held a set of scrubs and a pair of disposable booties. It was the first time she realized she was walking around in her stockings.

"You look like a size small to me," he said kindly, indicating the scrubs, "but I brought a medium as well, just in case."

He directed her to the bathroom, fortunately placed right across from the waiting room. Max acknowledged her gesture, letting him know where she'd be, then she disappeared behind the wooden door.

She knew it was a mistake, but after she closed the door, she turned and looked at herself in the mirror. With the next breath, she was somewhere else entirely.

Another bathroom, very different from this sterile environment. There'd been a gilt-edged mirror, gold fixtures, a marble floor and countertops, but blood didn't care about such things. She'd had it in her hair but hadn't remembered when it had gotten there. It had also splattered across her face. She remembered that. That was what happened when you hit an artery. She'd stood in the bathroom, holding the knife and meat cleaver in her hands. For endless moments, she'd simply stared at them. The rage that had kept her going, made her incapable of stopping, was draining from her like blood itself. Her legs ached, an incomprehensible irony...and vindication.

No. Stop it. That's over and done. No time for that shit right now.

"Janet."

She came back to the present like she'd been shot, with a jerk and wide, staring eyes. Max was standing right behind her. She hadn't locked the bathroom door. She'd pulled off the shirt, was standing there in her lace bra and her skirt, her stockings. The blood had soaked through the thin blouse, so she had a stain on one of the bra cups. Fortunately, he'd closed the door behind them so passersby couldn't see her. Or Matt.

"Matt..."

"Lucas just got here. He's with him. Apparently the meeting finished earlier than expected. They're all headed back into New Orleans now."

She was still gripping the sink, and the blood had created pale pink rivulets on the white tile. "Okay. All right."

Picking up one of the washcloths the orderly had given her with the scrubs, Max ran it under a stream of warm water. He gave her a look, making sure she was okay with it, then rubbed the cloth over her shoulders, down her sternum, over the tops of her breasts, her upper abdomen. He took away the blood, left warm, clean dampness behind. Balling up the blouse, he jammed it in the biohazard can, no question that she could ever wear it again. She had her hair in a twist on her head, but some pieces had come down. He moved them out of his way to run the cloth over her neck. Then he rinsed out the cloth, picked up a clean one and did it all over again, covering the same terrain.

She stared at his face throughout. No thoughts in her head, though she should be thinking of a hundred details. His face wasn't expressionless, not exactly. It was like staring at one of those old concrete statues tucked in the corner of a garden. Something that had been there forever, seen everything come and go, and still it stood, just as strong. "You did good," she managed.

"So did you. You could be a combat nurse." Those steady gray eyes held hers in a lock as intimate as a physical embrace. "You with me now?"

She nodded. He picked up the scrub top, offered it to her. If she didn't pull it together, he'd probably help her take off the skirt, dress her in the drawstring pants like a child. She cleared her throat, resisting the urge to let him do just that. "I'm okay. I'll be out in a few minutes."

"All right." But before he turned away, he did something remarkable. He put his arms around her. Despite her surprised stiffness, he closed the step between them to hold her close. The contact with his body sent a current through her, waking up frozen nerve endings. As he cupped the back of her head in one large palm, his heat and strength surrounded her. She once again remembered the way he'd navigated through that traffic, never showing panic or lack of control. Neither had she. He was right. They'd both done damn good.

"Sometimes, after something like that, human touch helps ground you, brings back your focus." He spoke against her hair.

It did. "It does," she said into his chest. "Thank you, Max."

* * * * *

As she expected, all four of his team came, with their wives or significant others. She leaned against the wall, watching the way they formed a protective circle around Matt, supporting him. All of them waiting.

Jon Forte sat in a chair at Matt's back, a deliberate choice, Janet was sure. Though in business Jon was Matt's engineering genius, with a secondary but no less significant talent for finance, that wasn't the reason she'd felt it was as imperative for him to be here as Dana. The other men, more traditional

Southern males, routinely teased Jon for his philosophical studies of ancient texts and the advanced yoga practice that gave his leanly muscled form a tensile strength, but their respect for his sincere and solid spiritual core was obvious in difficult situations like this.

Rachel, Jon's wife, had just brought another round of coffee from the cafeteria. After she distributed it, she took a seat next to Jon, her hazel eyes serious. Because Rachel's blonde hair was pulled back in a ponytail, Janet clearly saw the strain in her face they were all feeling. There were so many connections in this room...that had to mean something, didn't it? A sense that things happened for a reason, that truly bad things couldn't happen when bonds were this strong and fated?

For instance... Rachel was a physical therapist, but it was her second job, that of yoga instructor, that had brought her across Jon's path. When he learned about the PT, that had connected her to Dana. Dana was an Army veteran who'd needed Rachel's skills. Peter Winston, Matt's operations manager and a former National Guard captain who'd served two tours in the Middle East, was her husband. He'd retired to care for Dana when she came back from Iraq so severely injured she lost her sight and most of her hearing. Fortunately, cochlear implant surgery had helped her regain much of the latter.

Janet shifted her gaze to Peter, his powerful body squeezed into a chair next to Dana. Since Max was Dana's primary driver, the men often teased the big man about how similar he was to Max in build and coloring, with his storm-gray eyes and dark-blond hair. Nobody was teasing anyone right now, however.

Thinking about the men's similarities, she turned her head to locate Max. He was standing at the corner of the waiting room, ready to help. He met her gaze briefly as she turned, then Janet's attention was pulled to more pressing matters.

"Fuck this." Matt surged up from the seat and moved toward the hallway. "I'm going to her."

Peter was already in motion, but it was Lucas who was closest and intercepted him, shifting a step ahead of Matt.

"You can't, man. You know that. She's in surgery."

"She needs me. They need me." But the emotions beneath the rage said the words Matt was too much of a traditional, stoic male to say. *I need them.*

"I know that. But you don't want to distract them from what they're doing. They're doing everything they can for her, and you don't want them to spare a single second from that, right?"

Lucas, the voice of calm reason, Matt's CFO and best friend since college. As an amateur cyclist who regular biked to work, the gray-eyed, sandy-haired, athletic male took his share of ribbing over stretchy shorts and compressed testicles, but his success in the sport reflected the focus and calm thinking he exercised now. He knew Matt so well...they all knew one another so well. The bonds they'd formed, through laughter and tears, were unbreakable. Janet's fervent hope was the former, or something in a similar positive vein, would prevail by the end of this day.

She saw Cassandra, Lucas' wife, link hands with Rachel. The way their fingers tightly intertwined reflected the anguish they felt for Matt, the worry for Savannah. They were all so used to Matt being in total command of himself and everything around him, the undercurrent of agony in his voice twisted something in all of them. Including Janet.

Ben joined Lucas now, on the opposite side of Matt, a subtly strategic move in case he bolted anyway, but Janet could tell her boss knew Lucas was right. He was simply a man of action. The waiting was killing him. And Ben knew it.

"Tell you what. Let Marcie go stake out the emergency room and see if she can get somebody going in and out to tell her anything. Best if you stay here, though, in case someone from admin needs anything from you, or if the doctor slips out a different door and she misses her."

Ben was legal muscle for K&A. With his devilish good looks—green eyes, dark hair and silver tongue—he was quite capable of convincing anyone of anything, but Janet understood why he was sending Marcie. Marcie, Cass' younger sister, worked in corporate investigations for Savannah's company, and no one was better at convincing people to inadvertently give up confidential information. And the attractive blonde with chocolate-brown eyes was only twenty-three, with a fresh-faced beauty and deceptive innocence that only enhanced that ability.

When Matt gave a grudging nod, rubbing a hand over his face, Ben glanced toward Marcie. No words needed to be exchanged for her to understand her task, and not just because she was just that intuitive. She and Ben had been an item for less than a couple months, but with such a bonded intensity that they all expected an engagement announcement any day now. She disappeared down the hallway.

Connections, bonds, fate. Janet repeated the thought to herself. The five men had supported one another through loss and gain, as well as when each man found the woman of his dreams. Those shared experiences, as well as the traits they had in common, like sexual Dominance, had made their relationship far beyond that of simple friendship. It was an unconditional brotherhood. As Janet looked around at the women, seeing faces that reflected a fear of the worst but also a complete commitment to support Matt and their men, whatever the outcome, she knew the women had become part of that inner circle as well.

She thought of Savannah, the grip of her hands, the fear in her eyes. Whatever happened, Matt would have these people. His link to them would help him survive. But Janet knew what kind of road that was, and she wouldn't wish it on anyone.

*****

Marcie returned with a report that Savannah was holding her own, but that the outcome for mother or child was still in the balance. Janet could tell Marcie wished she had better news, but she delivered it with painful honesty, knowing Matt wouldn't settle for anything less.

He nodded, taking a silent seat in his chair once again, staring straight ahead. Ben touched Marcie's face, gave her a reassuring nod and the girl returned to Dana's side. The vigil resumed.

In some ways, Janet knew the news made things worse for Matt, but now he'd lapsed into a raptor-like stillness, staring at something beyond all of them. Just waiting. For the next hour, less than a dozen words were exchanged.

Finally, Dr. Rosen arrived in the waiting room.

She looked exhausted. Yet when Matt pushed up from his seat and faced her with the fixed expression of a man locked in stone, she gripped his hands and told him the thing he most needed to hear. "They're both fine."

Lucas put his hand on Matt's shoulder as a hard shudder ran through the man's large body, the stone cracking. The doctor proceeded to explain Matt had a healthy, six-pound baby girl, and that his wife, when she woke from her surgery, would want to see him first thing.

But Janet had been right. This would be their only birth child. They had to remove Savannah's uterus, a full hysterectomy, but otherwise she was going to make a complete recovery. Amid the tears and congratulations, Dr. Rosen added, "Whoever your driver is, Mr. Kensington, he saved your daughter's life, and very likely your wife's. Ten minutes later, and we'd have lost both of them."

Janet turned toward the entrance to the waiting room. Max had remained at that far wall like a soldier on watch duty, prepared for anything, but now he was gone. When she peered around the corner, she saw him striding down the hall toward the elevators. Mission accomplished, right? Though in a far less intense context, it was the same when she planned a major event for K&A. She didn't usually stay for the event itself, only long enough to confirm she'd exceeded every expectation Matt had for it. For people like her and Max, having accomplished their mission was the victory. They didn't need to stand around for the parade.

However, when Max reached the stairs, he stopped and looked back, as if knowing she was standing there. A muscle flexed in his jaw, and he lifted a hand, acknowledging her. Then the fingers curled and his face changed. The flash of regret told her he'd hoped to escape when he had the chance. A blink later, Matt touched her shoulder, passing her to move down the hall toward his employee.

She didn't hear what her boss said to Max, because his voice was low, and got lower. She saw him gesturing, then Matt's hands fell to his sides, conveying a helpless inability to express what was beyond words. Max's expression transformed, reflecting the empathy a strong man felt when another strong man faltered. He stepped forward, putting his arms around Matt's broad shoulders. It was a good thing they were a like height.

Janet had to slide down the wall, her eyes filling with tears. Her legs simply gave way at the unlikely sight of Matt Kensington, the most indomitable man she knew, weeping. Max's face had that aged granite look as he held Matt. But his gray eyes shifted, locked with hers. Throughout the next few memorable moments, he didn't look away.

Neither did she.

Chapter One

Six months later

"Randall, is Max in yet?"

"Yes and no, ma'am."

She paused by the security desk, arching a brow. The head of K&A security pressed a button on his console, calling up the needed camera angle on the top covered level of the parking deck. "He's not on until noon, but most mornings, this is where you'll find him. He won't mind doing anything you need, as long as you don't mind he's not in uniform. Want me to buzz him? He's wearing his pager."

"No. I need to stretch my legs. I'll go to him."

Randall nodded, waited until she was a safe distance down the hall, then murmured, "And fucking fantastic legs they are. Ma'am."

Janet paused at the elevator, a good fifty feet away, and glanced back at him, a glint in her eye. Randall cleared his throat, paid close attention to his monitors and didn't let out a breath until he heard the elevators close. Jim, the desk guard, gave him a grin. "You're a brave man. Mr. Kensington says she can hear through concrete walls."

"Why do you think I added the 'ma'am'?" Randall responded wryly.

"Should we give Max a heads-up she's coming?"

Randall shook his head. "The moment she steps into the parking-deck elevator, he'll hear it engage. He'll be tracking where it stops."

Jim studied the video dubiously. "He looks like he's asleep."

"Trust me. He can tell you how many bugs have scurried across the parking deck in the past half hour, *and* give you their current coordinates."

"Since she can hear through walls, sounds like they're made for each other."

Randall pursed his lips. Imagining Janet Albright, Matt Kensington's terrifying admin, and Max Ackerman, his head limo driver, as a couple wasn't as unlikely a vision as he'd expected. In fact, it might be a mighty interesting combination. 'Course, an explosion was interesting — if you were outside the blast zone.

* * * * *

Janet stepped off the parking elevator, careful not to snag her heels on its metal threshold, and headed toward the back corner of the parking deck. Her glossy brown pumps made a crisp echo on the concrete. Glancing over the wall at the New Orleans business district, she drew in the faintly smoky air, pleased to detect the cool scent of fall beneath the city smells. But as she made the turn toward that back corner, other scenery captured her attention.

Randall had said Max wouldn't mind running her errand as long as she didn't mind he wasn't in uniform. She wasn't sure there was a red-blooded woman alive who would mind that. He looked handsome in his various uniforms, everything from the traditional chauffeur's suit to the more informal black dress jeans and crisp black placket shirt with the embroidered K&A insignia. However, in the blue jeans and dark-blue T-shirt he wore now, he was pure sex.

He had his muscled arms crossed over his broad chest, his back braced against his windshield in his reclined position on the hood of his battered Ford Ranger pickup. The jeans were classic Wranglers, worn down to that soft cling that drew the female eye to all the right points of groin, thighs and ass. Despite the covered parking deck, he wore sunglasses, which made it impossible to determine if his eyes were open, but she knew they were. She suspected they'd opened as soon as she stepped off the elevator.

Max had been working for K&A for over six years but had taken over management of the fleet after less than two years with the company. He oversaw maintenance of the vehicles and management of the rotating staff of eight drivers. One of his important secondary duties was being Dana's driver, taking her to and from her job as assistant pastor at one of the local churches. Peter and Max looked enough alike that the other men teased Peter, telling him he'd provided his wife a surrogate for the frequent times he had to be out of the country, dealing with their Central American plant operations.

The physical features of the two men were remarkably similar, dark-blond hair and gray eyes, both over six feet and possessing a large-boned build wrapped in a lot of military-trained muscle. However, to Janet's way of thinking, their respective personalities gave each man a unique stamp. They both had the discipline and strong moral code of many servicemen, but there was a silent core to Max, seemingly impenetrable. When he met her gaze, she felt pulled into that silence, and it wasn't a bad place to be. A gray, overcast day, no break in the cloud cover, somber but comforting, like a blanket being wrapped around the earth.

She'd dreamed a lot about those eyes in the past six months. They'd gotten in the pleasant habit of interrupting her occasional nightmares, driving them away with their tails tucked between their legs.

The limo he usually drove was parked in its spot along the back wall, pristine and gleaming, the way he made sure all vehicles in the fleet were kept by the team he supervised. Though his older-model pickup truck had seen some fender benders, it was equally clean and polished. His sturdy, thick-tread work shoes were crossed at the ankle but projected over the edge of the hood, not making contact with the paint. He not only took good care of what he was paid to maintain, but his own belongings as well, no matter their age or condition. A woman noticed such things.

Music was wafting out of the truck window, and the selection surprised her. *I'll Never Find Another You* by the Seekers. The poignant, innocent sound of it made her think of waltzing across the concrete with him, her hand curled on his neck, a faint smile in her heart.

Ever since Savannah had given birth to sweet Angelica, the idle fascination Janet had with the limo driver had grown far stronger. The man had been positively heroic, getting Savannah to the hospital under trying circumstances. It would have made any woman's heart trip faster. But Janet knew he'd intrigued her for quite a while before that. That day, as now, she reminded herself she'd kept her distance for several intelligent reasons.

Yet here she was, seeking him out for something any of the other on-duty drivers would be happy to do for her. It told her she'd reached some kind of decision in her mind. It was an intuitive thing, not fully formed, which wasn't the same as being impulsive or rash. She'd mulled it over for well beyond those six months, yet recently realized the reason she couldn't get a clear sense of her intent with Max was because she needed more information to sift. So this was a planned direction, even if the road ahead was murky.

Matt had told her Max was a former Navy SEAL. After looking up considerably more specific information on it, she'd learned that meant he'd left the SEALs before reaching the twenty-year retirement mark. Even so, she wasn't sure if the term "former" or "retired" truly applied to a SEAL. The quick reflexes and cool nerve he'd demonstrated the day they had to get Savannah to the hospital had underscored it. It was also why she knew his eyes were open behind those glasses, though he hadn't yet moved. Not until she turned with purpose in his direction. Then he slid off the hood in one powerful motion, taking off the glasses and hooking them in his shirt. She waved at him with the folder she carried.

"No, don't come to me. I'm coming to you."

She issued it as a command, and he simply nodded. "Ma'am." But he still took a couple steps toward her, showing he wasn't entirely comfortable waiting for her to do all the work to get to him. She really needed to sit in on hiring interviews one of these days. She was fairly certain Matt Kensington had the HR department subject all male applicants to a super-secret chivalry test handed down since Lancelot's days.

"Were you sleeping?"

"Just a short nap, ma'am." He nodded at the folder. "Do you need me to take that somewhere?"

"No." Though it had been her excuse for coming to him, she decided then and there she would send the documents to the bank with Wade later today, when he took Matt to his lunch meeting. She didn't dissemble when it suited no purpose. "Max, do you dance?"

He wasn't expecting that. She experienced a small spurt of satisfaction at the flicker of surprise, and amusement when it turned to wariness. "Not really, no."

"I'm on a break. May I join you?" She nodded to the hood of the truck. "You made that look very comfortable."

Actually, she visualized using his body the way he'd used that truck, leaning back against his chest, her body ensconced in the cradle of his thighs, her hand caressing one as she put her head back on his shoulder and they gazed at the rectangular panorama of the city. He'd be warm, she was sure, a good contrast to the touch of cool air wafting over the business district. She wouldn't miss the sweater she'd left on her chair.

There was a reason she connected so well with the K&A men. She herself was a sexual Dominant, one who regularly enjoyed playing Mistress to willing submissives at Club Progeny. As such, she was direct with men, in or outside a club. Her senses were tuned to evaluate how they responded to the unexpected. Max glanced at the hood of his truck, then at her pale-pink silk suit, his gaze lingering on her stocking-clad legs revealed by the just-above-the-knee hem. The short slit in the back offered a glimpse of her thigh, which she knew was what had caught Randall's eye. She dressed for business, but she also thoroughly enjoyed being an attractive middle-aged woman. She had no problem highlighting her better features within the tasteful boundaries of professionalism.

"I'll need a boost," she said. "And you'll need to take off my shoes once I'm there so they don't scratch your truck. Of course, you still haven't said whether you mind ten minutes of company."

"I'm just trying to keep up, ma'am." He had a little bit of a Texas drawl, just like Matt. It was entrancing. "Why did you want to know if I dance?"

"I teach a ballet class for teenagers at the community center. We don't have any male dancers at the moment, and the girls want to learn some basic lifts. When a dancer first starts learning lifts, confidence in the strength of your lifter helps you focus on your form. You seem more than capable of lifting teenage girls. But it does require some grace and agility, which is why I asked about the dancing."

She gave him a critical look. "You move well, though, so even if you don't have any dance training, I think it will still work. If you're willing, it pays nothing, and it will take up a night of your time. Given your looks, I'm sure it will also gain you the slavish adoration of a dozen underage girls. While I promise not to give them your social networking links, I can't guarantee they won't find them anyhow. A fourteen-year-old has ways of ferreting out information the CIA only wishes they knew."

Putting the folder on the hood, she held out her hands. "Want to prove you can lift something heavier than a teenager?"

"If I see something that is, I'll do that, ma'am."

She chuckled. "Charm serves a man well, Max." She kept her arms out. She knew he couldn't let her stand that way for long without it becoming awkward or embarrassing for her, at least to his way of thinking. Sure enough, within a blink, he stepped forward to close the distance between them. When his hands settled on her waist, he met her gaze. If he'd wanted to keep it more impersonal, he wouldn't have done that, so that alone gave her another intriguing piece of information about where this might go.

First intentional physical contact was a critical sensation, where she logged her own reaction as much as his. Heat swept out from where his hands closed over her waist. She felt the strength in his restrained power, saw the biceps flex as he tightened the grip and prepared to lift her. Then he stopped himself. "Hold on a moment." Releasing her to open the truck's door, he twisted his upper torso to reach behind the front seat. He came back with a rolled-up quilt in a brown-and-green camouflage pattern. He untied the straps, folded it into a rectangular cushion and put it on the hood where he'd been about to place her.

"It's clean enough for me, but not that." He nodded to the pastel color of her suit. "I don't want you to get anything on it."

She didn't think there was a speck of dust on the truck, but she appreciated the consideration. Now he lifted her. She'd expected his display of easy strength, but her reaction when it swept through all her nerve endings startled her. During that effortless suspension, short as it was, she was catapulted to a memory of lights, a crowd's breathless attention as she bounded lightly across the stage, leaping into the capable hands of her partner, who lifted her high above his head.

Jorge had given her that moment. She couldn't deny that gift. He'd also been the one to take it all away.

"Ma'am?"

She opened her eyes, realized she'd simply gone away, too much like that night in the hospital bathroom. Her hands were gripping his on her waist, nails digging into his skin. He'd put her on the truck hood, on the quilt. His hard abdomen was pressed against her knees as he held on to her, obviously not wanting to let her go until he was sure she was all right. Maybe for other reasons too, but it was a little too soon for that. She wasn't given to fanciful romanticizing. Then she thought about how she'd imagined lying inside his embrace on top of the truck and realized he'd already taken her down that road. Men didn't usually do that to her. Not anymore.

"Yes. You did that very well. In fact, now I'm not sure the girls will be able to focus on their form at all. You'll make them think they're swans, about to give flight. Which is actually what it feels like, when it's done right."

"You dance too?"

"I did. Now I teach." She gave his hands a functional pat, a signal to let her go. They reflexively tightened, a brief squeeze, then slipped away, leaving her tingling. "Thank you. Please remove my shoes. You take very good care of this truck. I don't want to cause any scratches."

"It's had its share of those." He paused. Wondering if he would kneel to take off her shoes, she played with that fantasy, but of course the truck was too high to make that necessary, and he wasn't that type of man. She already knew that much about him, one of the intelligent reasons she hadn't pursued anything with him. She liked her men submissive, and limited to a club setting. At least, she had, until Max started visiting her waking thoughts as much as he did her dreams.

He slipped off one of her pumps, his fingers sliding along her arch. She quelled her visible reaction to the arrow of sensation that went right up her inner thigh, but she savored it behind a neutral expression. When he touched the other arch the same way, she was sure he was testing her reaction, because he looked up at her, meeting her gaze once again. Setting the shoes carefully by the front tire, he leaned on the hood next to her, propping his elbow by her hip. He laced his fingers together, but his knuckles were a tempting distance from the modest section of thigh her seated position revealed.

When she glanced down at that small space, a weighted pause drew out between them, inundated with sexual awareness. She'd introduced it by requesting a personal favor, suggesting physical contact, both of which encouraged a new level of intimacy between them. Now she waited to see what he would do with those signals. Studying her leg, his head bent so she could gaze upon the dark-blond strands across his crown, Max loosened his fingers. He allowed one to slide along her stocking, to the hem of the skirt and just under it, encountering the lace top of her thigh high. He stayed within that short range, his finger going still as he lifted his head to meet her gaze.

Nothing so sexy as a man who didn't doubt himself. She thought of the cameras, but where he was, his broad shoulders were blocking the lens. To Randall or anyone watching, Max was leaning against the truck, talking to her. Perhaps they were closer than the usual personal space boundary, but he'd just lifted her onto the hood.

She had no doubt he'd shifted into this position to ensure their privacy. It made her ache for more contact than just that casual fingertip. As a general rule, she wasn't impulsive when it came to desires. She might be guided by intuition, but it was disciplined and directed to enhance her own pleasure and that of the man she was controlling. However, this time her intuition was taking her down a path where things were far less calculated. "You always call me 'ma'am'," she said. His finger might be motionless, but since it was still beneath her skirt, resting on the lace top of her stocking, her leg was in danger of catching on fire. "Whenever I tell you to call me Janet, you just nod and say, 'Yes ma'am. Janet'."

His expression was somber. Though his attention returned to her leg, it wasn't as if he'd lowered his gaze, not the way she was used to a man doing around her in a sexual situation. It was as if he was absorbing everything happening beneath and around his touch, sensing the simmer of her blood, the delicate ruffled shape of her clit swelling to ripe reaction. She thought of his mouth there and nearly shuddered.

"Just the other day," she continued, "I overheard you leaving Ben's office. Alice asked you something and you said, 'No problem. See you later, Alice'. You call Alice by her name, Max. Yet you call me ma'am."

"You prefer ma'am. You like it when men call you that." His gaze lifted then, and there was a heat in those gray irises. "Your eyes get more focused, like now. It reminds me of a hawk. I like it. I think that's why you and Matt get along so well. You're both birds of prey."

She blinked. "Will you join me for the ballet class?"

"When is it?"

"Next Thursday, seven to nine."

He nodded. "I'll drive you, if you like."

"We'll see." She should meet him there, keep things on a controlled footing. Letting him drive might be relinquishing too much, sending the wrong message, but it took more than one detail to upset her balance of power. "I'd also like you to consider coming to Club Progeny one night, as my guest."

He straightened, taking his hand away to hook his thumb in his jeans pocket. He braced his other palm on the truck hood. A polite withdrawal. "I don't know much about that world."

She lifted a brow. Matt, Lucas, Jon, Ben and Peter regularly took their women to Club Progeny, as well as Club Surreal in Baton Rouge. Despite her religious vocation, Dana was the most hardcore submissive of all the wives, and would be until Ben and Marcie decided to marry, since Marcie even eclipsed Dana in that department. Rachel was a close runner-up to Dana. Savannah and Cassandra were softer in that regard, but still very much in tune with their respective husbands' Dominant sides.

"Given the places you've taken Matt and the others after hours, it doesn't say much about your eye for detail."

A smile tugged at his firm mouth. "There's seeing a world and knowing it."

"Are you interested in an inside look?"

"Not so much. Except when you talk about it." His gaze slid over her, then back up to her face. "I might like to see how you see it. But I don't do so well with getting more personal with people."

"Neither do I."

"We could start with coffee," he suggested.

"There's a nice coffee shop on Progeny's viewing deck. It even has a separate entrance and exit for those who want to observe but not participate. Street clothes only allowed. It's like being outside an aquarium, where you get to watch all the exotic life swim around." She cocked her head. "But you already know that. Lucas says you've hung out there some nights, watching the public sessions, until they're ready to go home."

He didn't say anything. He didn't ask the obvious, if she'd been checking up on him by fishing for information from Lucas. He just waited her out, probably to see what other information she'd volunteer. He wasn't a nervous talker. That silent core, she reminded herself. It impressed her. As a result, she was willing to give him an idea of where her interest in him had been taking her.

"I've been reading about Navy SEALs. One thing that caught my interest was a description of what it was like to be down range, on a mission, in enemy territory. The SEAL who wrote the article said it was like being on a different plane, everything high intensity, hyper alert, every detail mattering." She glanced down at her leg, recalling for them both that single touch, his close attention to it.

"It made me wonder if you like watching the public sessions because a Dom and sub are exploring that intense immersion in detail. Their mission is this one focused goal, a goal the Dom always has to keep in sight, yet the journey to that goal is indescribable. The immersion itself is a drug, something you miss when you no longer have it. No matter how brutal or bloody it can be, how it tears you open or pushes you past your boundaries, you always want to go back for more."

She had his full attention now. Interestingly, that was all she had. Everything else had closed up, reminding her of a coiled snake, so close his fangs could reach her if he chose to strike. She could vividly imagine what it would be like if Max struck. Passion was a form of controlled violence, and she expected Max did controlled violence very well, if the quick shift from gray cloud to molten steel in his piercing gaze was any indication. Though he hadn't moved, he felt much closer, the way something did when it became far more dangerous.

"Why haven't you tried it, since you like watching?" she asked.

He lifted a hand toward her face. She intercepted it, a simple lift of her hand. When she pressed her knuckles against his palm, her long nails gleaming, she didn't push it away, just held enough pressure against it to keep him from touching her face. He let the hand stay there though, hovering near her lips, her lifted chin.

"You want to play it out this way?" His voice was a rumble.

"Do you?"

He closed his hand, put it back down on the truck hood next to her leg. "I'm not the Master type. I'm protective enough, but I couldn't tie up a woman or strike her. Even spanking. It's not how I roll."

"Yet I'll bet you've psychologically dominated every woman you've been with. Just taken her over with that alpha vibe and made her surrender. You've got the conqueror in you. Of course, sometimes you find that in a sub as well."

He chuckled at that. "I definitely couldn't be on the other side, ma'am."

"Most of us could be on either side. And you'd be infinitely fascinating either way." She closed her hand over his thick wrist, the one attached to his braced hand. "Notice when I touch you like this, everything between us gets still, focused, intent. What am I about to do? What are you reading from me, and me from you? There's an intensity to it. You're trusting me to care for you, watch your back, no matter what. And I'm trusting you to do the same for me. Because whichever one is holding the reins, we both hold one another's souls, even if it's just for a short space of time."

He lifted his gaze, locked with hers. It recalled the night at the hospital, when he was holding Matt, yet the two of them couldn't look away from each other. That was really what she'd been unable to forget or dismiss, wasn't it?

He put his other hand over hers, fingers sliding over her knuckles, a lingering caress. Then he squeezed it, stepped back, taking both his hands away. "Maybe I'll come in sometime when I'm bringing Matt or one of the others. Just see if you're there and go from that point. It feels like it needs to be that way. More unplanned."

"Less controlled."

"Is that a problem?" She detected a hint of challenge in his tone, and met it with a cool gaze.

"Not for me." She glanced at her shoes, bemused when he immediately understood her desire. He retrieved them, sliding them back on her feet, his fingers once again sending those lovely ribbons of sensation spiraling around her calves and inner thighs.

When she put her hands on his shoulders, she indulged the desire to slide her fingertips from the broad span up closer to his neck. His grip on her waist increased, his thumbs caressing her hip bones beneath the skirt, which sent a definite arrow of reaction between her legs. Her nipples tightened beneath the lacy bra. This man would be a thorough, overwhelming lover. That wasn't usually what she was seeking, but maybe her tastes were evolving.

"I still have your shoes," he said as he put her on her feet. "From that night at the hospital."

There were only a few inches between them, and he hadn't let her go. With the truck behind her, she was pleasantly enclosed between two very masculine, large objects. Lifting a brow, she slipped out of that narrow crevice and tapped him with the folder she retrieved from the truck hood. She wondered what he'd do if she swatted him on his very fine ass with it, and expected he might swat her back. It almost made her laugh. Then she registered his words.

She pivoted to face him again. The intensity of his expression made her feel like she was flush against him. "And you haven't had the opportunity to get them back to me in six months?" she asked lightly.

"You haven't asked me for them."

They studied one another. "Max, I want my shoes."

He cocked his head. "There it is. That female hawk look."

She understood what he meant. She knew the feeling when it took her over, that sense of command, exercised over a male eager to experience her power. She didn't feel that eagerness from Max. More like intrigued curiosity, another type of raptor perched on a different branch, watching her with abiding interest.

He moved to the limo, opening the front door. Oblivious to what viewing the stretch and bend of that powerful body could do to her, he leaned across the seat, withdrew her shoes from a side compartment. She noticed he'd wrapped them in a towel to protect them, and he took that off now, bringing her the dainty pumps, the sheen of the white-gold insoles a contrast to the polished outside walnut color. The shoes had ankle straps, but he carried them under the arches, rather than letting them dangle.

When he brought them to her, she closed her hands over the straps, pinching the back of the shoes between forefinger and thumb. As his hand slid away from the soles, her arches tingled, remarkably. What did the man wear? He had a scent like sea water and cotton, plus that musky heat that was distinctly male. Looking up at him, she saw he was staying put, less than a foot between the rise and fall of her breasts and his chest.

He lifted his hand, but this time she didn't stop him. He didn't reach toward her face. He slid beneath her bent arm and pressed his palm against her back, just below her shoulder blade. As if he was about to begin a proper ballroom waltz. She was always aware of her body's movements, particularly in relation to the give and take of a man's, and the way he eased them together was like clouds, a drift that seemed effortless.

As he bent toward her, he kept his eyes open. So did she. When he put his mouth on hers, she saw the flicker in the gray, a reaction to how her lips parted, releasing a soft sigh into his mouth. He held the contact there, a bare touch, then he drew back, pressing his lips together.

"I was wondering if that gloss tastes the way it smells. Like honeysuckle. It does. There was a honeysuckle bush behind the house where I grew up."

She imagined him plucking a blossom, drawing out the threadlike inner stem, bringing that single drop of honey to his lips. Her body responded in the same manner. She felt the tiny blot of cream dampening her panties.

"I have other flavors as well. But honeysuckle is my favorite." Turning, she moved back toward the elevators, making sure she kept her steps efficient and even as always, the sound of the heels against the concrete just as crisp. She'd had twelve-hour rehearsals that required less effort than such nonchalance took.

She lifted the shoes out to her side, not turning. "You better not have stretched them out. And I hope you wore them with proper stockings."

At the elevators, she looked over her shoulder to see him leaning against the truck, watching her, one foot hooked around his ankle. The position made the most of every inch of his hard, powerful body.

His gaze sparked with humor. "Yes ma'am."

Chapter Two
ဢ

With grim amusement, Max noticed he let out a breath after the elevator door closed. "That woman's a handful and a half," he muttered, but of course that just piqued the interest of his overachiever side. A side that embraced the SEAL maxims of *be better than your best* and *the only easy day was yesterday*.

Actually, he expected she was two handfuls. Two very nice handfuls.

Before the day in the limo with Mrs. Kensington, he'd known pretty much the same things about Janet that most of the K&A workforce did, though his study of it might have been a little bit more in-depth. He was a good listener, and he'd kept his ears peeled for details about her. She was Matt Kensington's terrifying administrative assistant who demonstrated cool efficiency and an exemplary work ethic that made all their lives easier. To his recollection, the woman had never once screwed up a detail, and Max found that intriguing. Matt Kensington trusted her implicitly, and he didn't do that with anyone, really. Max had seen him check Lucas' numbers or Ben's legal work, but Janet could be riding in the limo, put a stack of papers in front of him, and he'd sign them with a cursory glance.

When Max was hired, Matt had taken him around the office to introduce him. Though he and Matt had a personal connection, the HR guy could have done the task, and Max wouldn't have felt slighted. Instead, it kind of flustered him, the CEO himself doing the intros. It had earned him a second look from a lot of people. But it was Janet's second look he'd remembered.

She had a way of examining a person as if she was noticing a lot more than most people did. He'd been around enough special ops guys to recognize someone who evaluated strengths and weaknesses right off, cataloging a man's abilities. He'd taken a good look back, no sense denying that. She'd been wearing a pretty butter-yellow suit combo, with silky white stockings covering a pair of excellent legs. Under her thin blouse, he could see the lace of a camisole top. She was small-boned, small-breasted, but all well proportioned.

In his time working this close to the executive level, no one had ever mentioned she was a dancer. But on that very first day, he thought of a ballerina, because that was what she looked like, the way she kept her dark hair pulled up on her head, the fine lines of her hands and body. How she moved.

He remembered what she'd said to him today. "Now I teach." When he'd put her up on the hood, taken off her shoes, her toes had fallen naturally into a graceful point as she crossed her ankles.

Her face intrigued him. She was a handsome woman, her facial features not delicate enough to be called pretty. Cheekbones and nose cut in sharp planes, brown eyes direct. The way she kept her mouth glossed in that tempting sheen disguised the thinness of her lips, but that thinness fit her face, like the slim, elegant lines of her dark brows. It was the force of her personality beneath that radiated her confident sexuality, the unmistakable aura of a woman who regularly donned the clothes of a Mistress and indulged that side of herself at Club Progeny.

He'd seen her at it a couple times, though not close up, because she tended to choose a corner of the public floor at a distance from that coffee shop she'd mentioned. She'd restrain a man with nothing but commands or nominal restraints, but he'd stay locked in the proscribed position as she took a whip to him, wielding it with skill. He'd noticed she didn't wear the high break-neck heels a lot of the women did. During a break in her sessions, sometimes she'd sit down, zip open her modestly heeled boots to rub her calves, as if she had cramps there. He'd imagined doing that for her, bringing ease to her expression as he enjoyed the feel of her toned limbs beneath his fingertips. He supposed whatever troubles she had with her legs might be the reason she no longer danced.

Be that as it may, it didn't explain her attention toward him. She was smart enough to know he wasn't interested in being dominated by anyone, let alone by a woman. Of course, maybe the reason she was interested was as inexplicable as the fact he returned the favor, in spades. Even before the terrible day with Savannah, he'd thought about her more than he should. She'd been featured in some pretty outstanding fantasies during his early morning post-workout shower. In his mind, he put her up against the wall, thrusting into her from behind. In reality he pressed his forehead hard against his fist, closed against the slick tile, his other hand working himself to jetting climax beneath the pummeling spray.

Despite that, he'd kept his distance, knowing he couldn't give her what she wanted. She gave him a few appraising glances now and then, but he chalked that up to the fact that women noticed a guy who kept military fit. Didn't mean they were compatible enough for more than a one-night stand.

That wasn't something he made a habit of doing, and he sure as hell wouldn't inflict it on a coworker. Particularly one so close to Matt Kensington. He'd never do anything to cause Matt problems. Beyond that, he couldn't see Janet as the impulsive, regret-it-like-hell-the-next-day, one-night-stand type. Outside her sessions in Club Progeny, she didn't seem to date or indulge in any kind of relationships. Inside Club Progeny there were far more stringent, clear-cut rules for those things. Manageable. Maybe that's why she kept it there.

His impression was that she didn't offer her body or her heart freely. She took pleasure, offering a fair, intense and often affectionate-in-the-aftermath exchange with her chosen subs, but vulnerability didn't appear to be part of that offering.

Her armor was lovely to experience, to touch, but that was as far as the men got.

Going over all this in his head, he wryly concluded he'd done more intel gathering on her than he'd admitted to himself, and the rate of it had increased since that day in the limo. She'd probably chastised herself for her meltdown in the hospital restroom, but that would have been unjustified. When it counted, she'd been as firmly in control as she was at command central—what the staff called her desk, set smack in the middle of the top floor between all five executive offices. She'd kept Savannah focused, moving them forward toward a common goal. As far as how she'd been with him, they'd clicked together as seamlessly that day as SEAL members who'd trained together. That didn't happen unless there was a solid connection there.

He recalled her standing in the bathroom, the imprint of the blood on her skin, her bra. When something triggered a memory that took over everything else, he knew what that looked like on a person's face. She'd been staring in the mirror, but her eyes had been a million memories away, a whimper stuck in her throat, her fingers clutching the sink to keep herself from being whirled down the rabbit hole, back to whatever awful thing all that blood had summoned to her mind.

As he'd washed it off her, he'd noticed the softness of her skin, how firm her body was beneath it. Not too firm though. The woman was in good shape, but her ass had a nice roundness to it. He liked that about women in their forties, when only the most fanatical workouts in the gym could keep the curves at bay. She was a few years older than him, but not enough to be a cause for concern for either of them. Women were more worried about that than men, anyhow.

When he'd lifted her up onto the hood, he'd wanted to keep his hands on her. He'd wanted to see if she closed her eyes when she kissed, if the sharpness of her face softened, if the rigid, straight line of her body would become more curved, melt into his. She hadn't closed her eyes, and her body hadn't softened, but the lips had, and he'd felt her quiver under his touch. The day he'd held her in the bathroom, she hadn't relaxed either, but today he'd felt the hint of what it would be like if she fitted herself to a man's angles and curves, let him palm that sweet ass and pull her closer, against a cock that was more than eager to show her pleasure.

Was he ready for such a step? It'd been awhile for him. Yeah, he'd indulged the occasional sexual release with the right woman in the right moment, all fun and games, no harm, no foul, but this wouldn't be in the same realm, he was sure of that.

What he was contemplating might go so bad, the mission should be aborted before it even started. It seemed like they were both interested enough to give it a try though, so he'd take responsibility. If it went sour, he'd be the one who'd leave. It was clear she had a family here. Max viewed them that way as well, but he could maintain that without the work itself, whereas he perceived she needed that structure to stay connected. He'd back off, move on, if needed. He wouldn't shit where she lived, so to speak. Or if he did, he'd clean it up by clearing out.

He had a weird urge to seek Matt's permission to court his secretary, but he saw no graceful way to do that. Plus, Janet would likely jam her stapler up his ass if he tried. Wondering if K&A's generous benefit package covered such an injury, he grinned.

*****

Friday night. There was no doubt in Janet's mind about going to Club Progeny. Her body had been on turbocharge since her visit with Max in the garage earlier in the week. That faint brush of lips across her mouth had stuck with her, as powerful as if he'd lifted her up against a wall and fucked her brainless, so she needed some perspective, some balance. It was like they were engaging in a rumba, everything powerfully suggestive, filled with overwhelming potential, but still confined within the careful boundaries of the dance.

He was being just as cautious as she was, which meant they both understood the consequences of taking it into uncharted territory. She hadn't realized a man who evaluated things so thoroughly beforehand could be so damn sexy. She guessed it was because of the barely restrained passion behind it. A powerful warrior more than ready for the heat and passion of the battle, but he was going to make damn sure he had it won before he even stepped on to that ground. Brawn and intelligence—how could a woman resist?

Tonight would be helpful to clear her mind, figure out a counter strategy that would be an adventure for both of them. She had no doubt the ballet class would provide an intriguing neutral ground for them, full of more pleasurable innuendo. So far her interactions with him had been like the slow consumption of a flawless chocolate mousse, made perfect by the defined, precisely spaced experience of its taste and texture.

Pulling into the club parking lot in her red classic Mustang, she was intrigued to see Max's truck. She could hardly mistake it, because there were very few older Ford Rangers maintained in such pristine condition. As she circled closer to it, her lower extremities coiled up in anticipation.

Maybe I'll come in sometime...Just see if you're there.

Getting out of her car, she locked it, shouldering her garment bag and makeup case. Once inside the club, she didn't look around. She showed her membership card and went straight to the women's changing area. She had a different goal tonight. If Max was in the coffee shop and happened to see her, that was fine, but it was too soon to engage. In fact, maybe she should use a private room tonight. She needed to focus, balance. But that was weak. Finding her focus in a public arena was a challenge, requiring discipline, and she liked to stay sharp.

Slicking her hair back with sculpting clay, she made sure her topknot was secure. She'd chosen a pencil skirt that zipped up the side, the zipper starting at the top of the high slit. A tight black blouse went over the skirt, the blouse sheer enough to show the black bra beneath it. She pulled on tight boots that etched out her calves like a second skin, as well as a pair of elbow-length gloves that had the same supple fit. She took a look at herself from all angles before locking up her personal belongings. Carrying the bag of items she might desire to use on her chosen sub, she headed out to the public floor.

She remembered the first time Matt had brought her to this type of club. After what she'd been through, she thought he was insane for thinking such a place would intrigue her. She'd been tense, only her trust and respect for him keeping her sitting on the bar stool rather than heading back out to the parking lot. Then he'd told her to close her eyes.

Listen, Janet. Really listen.

She knew what it sounded like, the thud of objects hitting flesh. Fists, belt...baseball bat. It made the bones in her face ache. *I broke my doll, but see...I have the power and money to put her back together, make her beautiful again. That's why I know you're mine,* querida, *my sweet ballerina.*

Matt had brought her back from that with another touch, repeating his gentle admonishment. "Hear the differences."

And finally, she had. With a Dom and sub, there was a rhythm to it, one that was wholly absent when the striking was done in violence. That kind of beating was more chaotic, like white noise. This was like a mesmerizing piano concerto, the rise and fall of emotion, of action and reaction. It made her open her eyes. She'd rested her attention on a Mistress flogging a male who was on his elbows and knees before her. When she bent to lay a kiss on the reddened expanse of one quivering buttock, he'd begged her to let him press his lips to her shoe.

What seemed an act of humiliation on its face had been anything but. Janet had registered the absorbed look on the

Domme's face, the adoration on the sub's. She felt a sudden desire to be standing in that Domme's shoes, to prove...what wielding power should be. To feel what it could be like to wield such power. She hadn't had much luck in getting close to men since Jorge, but maybe this way, she could. Within prescribed boundaries, holding the reins, she could find something her body still ached to have. The arousing, respectful touch of a man. Maybe she wasn't ready for passion — it was too close to violence — but this she could have.

That feeling brought her back again and again to this environment. A sense of being safe, of being at home. Max or no Max, she could anticipate what the night would bring like a kid at a carnival, no worries that any of the monsters would follow her home.

She saw several of her regulars here, occasional playmates. Harris came to her with a smile, dropping to a knee before looking up at her with pleased affection. "May I serve you tonight, Mistress?"

"I'm in the mood to be harsh, Harris. Over your limits. Maybe another night. Who would you suggest?"

He covered his disappointment with a respectful nod, glanced toward the floor. "Thor."

"A sub with the name Thor?" She shook her head. "Does he know how that sounds?"

Harris gave her a grin. "Like a slave needing punishment for getting above his station. You said you were in the mood to be harsh."

"Good point." She touched his hair in fond acknowledgment. "Send him to me, and I'll look forward to taking you in hand another night."

"I'm always eager to serve you, Mistress."

As Thor came toward her, she studied him critically. She'd seen the brawny male before. He was pleasing to the eye, well-muscled and clean shaven, with dirty-blond hair trimmed in a military cut. She hadn't played with him directly, but had seen he straddled a good balance. Not too willing to please, because he sought a Mistress with a firm hand, but once he found one, he accommodated what both Mistress and sub were seeking. That level of subtle cooperation was something she enjoyed. His powerful form, height and breadth reminded her just enough of someone else. Yet he was different enough she wouldn't get confused, depriving him of his just due by getting lost in her head. The sessions were about an equal give and take, and she was a fair Mistress.

Of course, fair or not, no matter who she chose tonight, a great deal of her energy was going to be driven by the memory of another man's hands, his mouth. Well, if the sub got a pleasurable ride from her frustrated desire, she expected he wouldn't complain. Such was the nature of her restricted interactions in the club. They knew what they could expect from her—and what they couldn't. Until a few days ago in a garage parking deck, she would have said that was enough for her.

That was when she looked up and saw Max. He was sitting by the rail in the coffee area, and he had his eyes on her, his face in that expressionless mode that fascinated her, because of all she sensed behind it.

In that moment, she changed her mind about the private room. "Thor, please secure Room Six for us. I don't think anyone is using it. Wait for me there."

"Yes, Mistress."

As she crossed the floor to the narrow catwalk that passed directly beneath the coffee area, Max's eyes never left her. She felt like he noticed everything, how the snug clothes fit over her breasts and thighs, hips and legs, how she moved in them. That regard made her stride become more pendulous and provocative. When his gaze sharpened on her, she wet her lips.

He was wearing a white dress shirt and black slacks. Ben had had an afternoon meeting that required more formal attire from his driver, but she was surprised Max hadn't changed before coming here. He'd shed coat and tie though.

She stopped below where he was sitting. He'd scraped back the chair as she approached, and amused her now by sitting down on the floor by the chair, letting his legs dangle over the wall. She pressed her upper body against his calf, gripping his knee to stretch up and be heard over the club's boisterous noise. Accommodating her, he leaned down, his fingers settling high on her rib cage, the other hand braced on the rail by his head. His ear was now close to her lips and she indulged herself, nuzzling the short dark-blond hair behind it, smelling that sea salt smell.

"Waiting on one of the guys?" she asked.

He shook his head, gestured at the table. "Coffee's good here. Just got off work. Dinner deal with Ben and the Michigan steel plant folks. He got them hammered, had them agreeing to all sorts of things that'll put their company in Matt's portfolio before Christmas."

"No doubt," she said, already imagining the research workload on her and Alice's desks on Monday.

Max tangled his fingers with hers, lifting her hand to examine the sleek fit of the glove, his thumb rubbing the thin fabric over her palm. "I dropped them off at their hotel. Figured I'd stop here before I went home."

So there were no restrictions to dictate his reasons for being here tonight. She was tempted to drop Thor, try to coax Max to take his place, but she had a code of conduct when it came to her subs. Plus she knew Max wouldn't do it. But he was here, wasn't he?

"I'm taking a private room tonight, but you're welcome to come watch. Thor's a public player. He won't mind. Room Six."

He shrugged. "I'll be here with my coffee. Why don't you come join me when you're finished?"

A standoff. She withdrew her fingers and stepped back. "If you get done before I return, don't stay up past your bedtime on my account. My invitation stands."

He nodded, rising to his feet and taking his seat again. When she reached the archway that led to the private rooms, she glanced back to see him sipping his coffee, still watching her. Being the center of his focus could unsettle a woman, for certain. In a lovely way.

Room Six had mirrors on one wall, a bench and steel frame in the center of the room that provided various restraint options, and several comfortable chairs along the non-mirrored wall. Those were for a Master or Mistress to rest or view their sub from a detached position during a session, or to hold that same sub during aftercare to ground them with a soothing touch. A small closet bathroom ensured that comfort breaks or hygiene needs wouldn't disturb the flow of the scene with a trip back to the public restroom or locker area. There were erotic photographs on the wall, stark black-and-whites against dark-red paint.

The room was functional yet atmospheric in a direct, unpretentious way she liked. Thor was kneeling by the bench. He still wore his clothes, a white T-shirt and jeans. He hadn't assumed she wanted him naked, but he had set out lubricants, restraint options and other tools to save her time. She appreciated a man who anticipated without second-guessing her. Picking up a riding crop, she tapped him on the shoulder. "Take off the shirt."

He complied, revealing a tattoo of a mermaid in the embrace of a dragon on his back, though it looked like the mermaid had the dragon fully under her control. She traced it with the whip. "Beautiful work."

"Thank you, Mistress."

She stepped to the wall, entered her membership number in the panel there, and called up his profile to be sure she knew everything she needed to know. "Your safe word is Zeus."

"Yes, Mistress."

A mythology fan, for certain. She liked him though. He was confident, strong, accepting of his craving for submission, yet he didn't seem like the type to follow a Mistress around like a puppy, pouting if he didn't get enough attention. She was somewhat surprised he wasn't already taken tonight, but there were always far more unattached subs on the floor than Dommes. It was a powerful woman's paradise, unless she was looking for something in particular. Or someone.

"Stand up. Keep your eyes down."

When he complied, she circled him, trailing her gloved hand over his shoulders, then his chest. She wondered if she'd told him to keep his eyes down to test his manners, or if she'd known not seeing gray eyes focused on her might disrupt her concentration.

Getting into a scene was a process, requiring the right energy. She stopped herself, thinking it through. If she couldn't give a hundred percent tonight, the best thing was to cut Thor loose with a straightforward apology, not give him half-assed attention. He deserved better than that.

Before she could make that decision, there was a light rap on the door.

Chapter Three

Her fingertips stopped on Thor's pectoral. His back was to the door, and with him between her and the entrance, she was mostly screened by him. "Enter," she ordered.

Max stepped inside, his attention touching on the half-naked man not more than a few feet in front of him. She shifted, met his gaze. He held on to that enigmatic expression but looked pointedly toward the wall that had the three chairs lined up along it. She nodded.

"Thor, your profile says you enjoy being watched, by men or women. A friend of mine is going to observe tonight."

"Yes, Mistress." When Max moved into Thor's line of sight, Janet noted the visible hitch in her submissive's gaze as he registered just how virile and appealing a man had joined them. Her twinge of possessive irritation surprised her, but she kept it out of her voice. She hoped.

"Eyes back down. He's here to look at you. You don't have my permission to look at him."

Max's expression, and the direction of his gaze, said he had no interest in looking at Thor at all. There was only one person in the room holding his attention. It made her far more intrigued by the scene that would play out here than she'd been a moment ago, charging the energy in the room tenfold. From the increased tension in Thor's body, the arousal swelling against the fit of his jeans, he'd picked up on her increased response as well. He was well-tuned to a Mistress's desires.

Max seemed capable of stoking those desires by doing nothing more than taking a seat in one of the chairs, stretching one arm out along the top of the other two. He crossed his ankle over his opposite knee, settling back.

Janet put her back to him, but she wasn't ignoring him. Everything inside her steadied, helping her find the center that had eluded her before he'd come into the room. "Thor, remove all your clothes. Take your time with it. Make me notice your ass."

The large man pivoted so his back was to her. As he began to unbuckle his belt, she savored the tightening of the denim over the superb buttocks before the jeans loosened and he pushed them off his hips. He wasn't wearing any underwear, so the jeans clung to the curves. He removed them with an inadvertently sinuous effort that made her want to heat her palms against the firm flesh, score him with a sharp bite of her nails.

He'd removed his shoes, so once he got the pants to his ankles, he bent, all that muscle shifting and rippling as he pulled the legs free. His feet were far enough apart she saw the heavy weight of his testicles swinging free.

"Knuckles on the floor, head down. Eyes closed. Straighten your legs, but don't lock your knees."

He obeyed. Stepping up behind him, she ran her hand over his ass, and down, closing her fingers on his balls, her grip tight enough that he grunted. He more than filled her hand, suggesting the size of the erection in the front. She stroked him, letting the crop she held slide along the inside of his thigh, tease the back of his knee. When she reversed it in a deft one-handed move, she pushed against that bend in his leg with the handle, taking him down to one knee.

"Forehead to the floor, baby," she murmured.

She sat down sidesaddle upon the arch of his back as he did that. It put him in a pose similar to Rodin's Thinking Man. Laying the crop on her lap, she stroked his thick hair with one hand, running her gloved palm over his buttocks with the other. In this position, she could turn her head and look at Max easily, so she lifted her gaze in that direction.

The look on his face made her part her lips. His gray eyes were the color of an impending storm. She wondered if he'd even looked at the other man. Everything in his expression said he was noting every infinitesimal detail of her reaction to mastering the male sub. The concentration evident in her glittering eyes, the tension of her facial muscles. Beneath her black lace bra, her breasts were full and aching, the thong beneath her pencil skirt already wet. Delicious tingles of heat kissed her throat, her jaw line.

She wished Max was wearing jeans. They were unforgiving, such that a man had to reach into them, straighten himself when he became erect, or else he'd be bent at an impossible angle. Slacks like he was wearing now gave way before that pressure. His cock would be stretched up along his lower abdomen, below the hold of his belt. If he had been wearing jeans, would he have adjusted himself in front of her? From the riveting power of his gaze on hers, the sexual heat pumping from him, she thought he would. She had no idea what to call this, but it made her want to take Thor on the trip of his life.

Rising, she turned away from Max again. "Thor, make the proper adjustments to the bench and lie face down on it. Guide your cock into the spacer that's one size short of comfortable and then grip the handholds."

The bench was broken into a long and short piece, the long piece for the upper torso, the short piece for the pelvis, with adjustments for different body lengths and heights. It essentially supported the torso while a sub was on hands and knees. Thor made those adjustments now, and as he did, she noticed he was rigid, his cock slit already wet with semen. Good. He was enjoying what was happening in this room as well. No matter her attention to Max, Thor was her first priority while under her command. She believed in doing a job well. And thoroughly.

As he laid himself down, he guided his cock between the opening of the long and short piece. There was a rectangular stainless steel frame there with different hole sizes that slid along a track. He didn't cheat his Mistress. He centered the hole that was a size too small for his already turgid cock, working it through carefully. When he made it all the way through, he was flat on his stomach on the bench, his knees and hands on the floor. His testicles were pressed against the lower piece of the bench, his cock captured and pointing toward the floor. From her view behind him, his testicles were an intriguing, vulnerable nest of flesh on the bench's vinyl surface. He locked his large hands around the handles provided beneath the bench.

"As far as you are concerned, your wrists are manacled to that bench, your thighs tied down, a strap over your shoulders and forehead. You are glued to that bench. Tell me you understand."

"I understand, Mistress."

She never tied them down, not in a way they couldn't easily escape. Thor was far physically stronger than she was, but it was her will and his desires that held him helpless. She inhaled that aphrodisiac, the energy swirling between her and him. The power emanating from the man watching was a solid, pulsing wall at her back.

She'd hung her toy bag by the sink. Now she returned her crop to it and withdrew her paddle, a half-inch thick oak rectangle with three holes cut into it to add a sharp bite to the sting.

Setting it aside, she slipped the buttons of her fitted blouse, sliding it off with a roll of her shoulders. She sensed Max shifting, but she didn't look at him now. She eased the side zipper of her skirt up, all the way past the curve of her hip, and then unhooked it. The fishnets she wore tonight shimmered with tiny sparkles. A garter of sleek vinyl held them up. While her black thong would reveal a toned ass, her upper thighs weren't perfect. Middle age and a job where she sat on her ass in front of a computer made that unattainable. Men liked soft strong thighs, though, ones that could lock around their shoulders. She could hold a man to her pussy until he ate her out to her satisfaction. Those soft thighs could also lock around his hips as he pounded into her.

It had been quite awhile since she'd indulged that fantasy in reality. She was imagining it quite vividly right now, but not with Thor.

She pulled her strap-on from the bag. It was a glossy black rubber dildo, six inches in length and thick, curved to ensure good contact with the most responsive areas. She buckled it over the thong, adjusting the clit stimulator to its proper place. As she did that, she slid her fingers over her mound, teasing herself with her own touch. Thor's left cheek was pressed to the bench, so he could see what she was doing. Though she maintained an indifferent tilt of her head, her body angled away from him, she watched him in her peripheral vision to catch the involuntary flex of his hips as his cock jerked, expelling another drop of fluid. She heard the needy sound in his throat.

Though she didn't look toward Max at all, the sense of being near a dangerous animal on a breakable tether had increased exponentially. She reveled in the attention of the two men, picking up on the growing electricity arcing between all three of them.

Pulling out two condoms and a blindfold, she crossed the room to Thor, enjoying the weight of the dildo pressing against her clit as the phallus moved in a lifelike way with her stride. In the mirrors, she saw the female sway of her hips, a provocative contrast. Max was motionless, a dark potent blur outside her range of vision. When she reached Thor, she swung her leg over his buttocks again, rubbing herself against the seam between, the movement similar to the way she'd thrust into him. The phallus curved up over his back. He pressed down in reaction, a groan breaking from him.

Tearing open one of the condoms with her teeth, she lay down on his back so she could reach beneath him, wrap her fingers around his shaft. As she explored the shape and weight of him at her leisure, she made a sound of reproof that kept him still. When he was quivering like a restrained stallion, she stretched the condom on him. Then she did the same to the dildo, making sure the lubrication on the outside was adequate for what she desired. Taking off one glove, she reached behind her, traced the dimple between Thor's buttocks and went lower to tease his rim, pushing into the puckered entrance to confirm he'd already oiled himself up. She drew a playful circle between his shoulder blades with that slick substance, then rose, putting her glove on again, working it up her arm, past the elbow. She loved the close fit, the supple feel of it.

She always loved the pacing of a session. She could take her time, run her hands up her arms, feel how the tight fabric molded them. She could enjoy her own body, knowing Thor was watching her, suffering, lusting. The greater his anticipation, the more explosive his reaction would be, the more violent his climax. He would give her everything for one touch.

When she rose, she was well aware of what she looked like, one hip cocked as she displayed herself in the strap-on, black thong, matching bra, garters and knee-high boots. She wore a delicate silver chain with an onyx pendant and matching earrings, her dark hair in the slick bun. The heavy blush along her cheekbones would increase their severity, the piercing intensity of her dark eyes. She'd chosen an almost black lipstick that had a hint of rose color. She imagined what it would be like to fuck Thor senseless and then, as his sides were still heaving with exertion, straddle Max's lap, grip his face, and kiss him with a vampire's hunger with her rose-black lips.

A nice visual. As much as she hoped she was tormenting him by not looking at him, she knew the effort not to look his way was only driving her own hunger higher. And Thor would reap the benefits of that.

Moving behind Thor, she put her hands on either buttock, one finger at a time, so he felt the press of each of the ten digits. "I'm in a bit of a butch mood," she purred. "I want to fuck you hard and fast, like a man would. If you don't please me, I'm going to give you a sound thrashing with my paddle, make you sore inside and out. Think you can handle it?" She trailed her fingers up his spine, leaning forward as she did so, such that the strap-on pressed between his buttocks. She gave him her full weight, savoring the flex and shift of his body beneath her as her breasts mashed against his back. She gripped his nape, holding his head to the bench, a reminder of the power she held over him.

"Anything, Mistress. I'm all yours. Fuck me hard. Please." He corrected himself quickly enough, but her lips curved.

"You'll pay for that one."

He didn't apologize. Instead, his body quivered under hers, a much more pleasing response. He was enough of a man that he would forget himself in a moment of lust and make demands, enough of a sub that he relished the idea of being punished for it.

She was lying full along his back, her legs draped on either side of his hips. Now at last, she turned her head to look at Max, tilting her chin down, since he was to her left and somewhat behind her. He still bore that same hard-to-fathom expression, but the gray irises remained iron and fire. Stretching her arms back, she cupped her buttocks, arched her back and sat up using only her stomach muscles. She rolled her body in a lithe wave, rubbing the dildo against Thor's crack and making his fingers tighten on the handholds.

Max's eyes followed her every movement like the flow of water over her skin. He hadn't moved by so much as an inch since she'd taken off her shirt. His hand was still curved loosely over the second chair. She found that incredibly erotic. Had he been a sniper with the SEALs, such that he'd had to sit motionless, waiting on a target to materialize, while staying intensely alert the whole time? If so, she had a feeling she was seeing that skill in action now.

She slid back off Thor, standing between his spread thighs. Now she removed the other glove, loosening the fingers then capturing the middle one in her mouth to tug it all the way off. She slid the garment along the small of Thor's back, dropped it there. Then she did the same with the other. Putting both hands on his fine ass, she fitted the head of the dildo to his rear entrance. That tight opening convulsed, anticipating her.

His profile said he was highly experienced with ass fucking, but given that this was her first time with him, she wouldn't slam into him first thing, as she might with Harris, whose ass was much more familiar. She preferred hands-on verification. The delicate tissues of the ass could be torn as easily in a man built like a brickhouse as one made out of straw. She was a female wolf that preferred to keep either type of house intact. As she eased in, the sphincter muscles released immediately. She pushed in to the hilt, and let out a sigh of pleasure. Thor didn't exaggerate his abilities, and she'd reward him for that. Pulling back out, *now* she let go, slamming back into him.

Thor let out a fervent curse, but she was just getting started. She wanted the fast and quick hits on her clit, those tiny explosions of sensations that would keep her working Thor hard but wouldn't spiral her toward climax too fast. It also gave her enough headspace to keep in touch with everything happening with Thor, how often he swore under his breath, the clutch of his powerful hands on the steel handles beneath the bench. The lift and drop of his hips, the trembling of his thighs. He was biting down on the corner of the vinyl, his gaze rolling wildly toward her, hungry and fierce. He wanted to see her come. That would never do.

Slowing her pace enough to accommodate her intent, she pulled free the blindfold she'd tucked beneath her garter.

Elongating her upper torso enough to put it over his eyes, she made sure it was secure. "Just feel me," she whispered, taking a sharp bite of his earlobe. "Feel me fucking you and know you're helpless. I am going to make you come, keep you completely under my control, and you're not going to want to be anywhere else."

"Yes ma'am. Yes…Mistress. Oh…fuck." She'd straightened again, and now started rocking in and out in a sawing motion that had him nearly foaming at the mouth. Okay, getting close now, but she wasn't yet ready for him to come. The energy was swirling hot and tight around her, so she closed her eyes, slowed it down once more. In deep, work the tip of the dildo in a rubbing, pressurized motion that made him cry out, then withdraw, leaving him shuddering on that cusp as she stroked his channel, dug her nails into his ass.

When the hand touched her shoulder, she didn't jump. Not for a moment had she forgotten Max's presence. It was what made her so demanding, so involved in her session with Thor. Those watching gray eyes, witnessing what she could do to a man. How she could summon him to her will.

His touch didn't startle her, but that didn't mean she'd expected this, or knew what he'd do next. As she kept up the pumping rhythm with her hips, Max put his body against the back of hers. She'd wanted to see his erect cock, pressing against the fabric of his slacks. Now she got to feel it, the heated steel of him through the faint scratchiness of the wool fabric against her bare buttocks. He shifted forward, so her movements into Thor became smaller, deeper. The man under her command cried out, bucking at the sensation. It also rubbed the clit stimulator over her in shorter, more intense movements.

Max put his lips on her shoulder. In that position, he'd be gazing down at her breasts, the strapless bra allowing them a lot of give and wobble, despite their small size. His left hand slid over her shoulder, fingers wrapping around her breast. As he held the bra cup, he traced the bare upper curve. His teeth pressed into her shoulder and she breathed a moan of her own as he brushed her nipple with his thumb.

She was still moving inside Thor, but she'd once again slowed her rhythm, inflicting pleasurable agony on her captive while Max explored her body, making her aware of nerve endings she'd never known could be so sensitive. He sucked on her skin, nipped it, moved up under her ear to breathe on her there, sending tendrils of heated air down her spine. He pushed his hips against her ass again, rotated so he was rubbing his turgid cock over her buttocks, pressing in between them.

As she leaned forward over Thor, she did a similar provocative circle with her hips, working the dildo in creative ways inside her sub as she teased Max's cock. That steel organ pressed the wet crotch of the thong and the strap of the dildo into her folds. Max captured her buttocks, his fingers almost bruising.

"Mistress…I'm so close…may I…"

"Not yet. Another few seconds. Or you'll get more of that paddle than you're going to want."

She was proud of her ability to talk, but when Max tugged at the thong and dildo straps words deserted her. He found his way past them, two fingers sinking into the wet heat of her pussy.

"Fucking honey," he muttered, just as Thor cried out again.

Max moved with her in perfect sync, fingers sliding in and out as she fucked Thor to the very edge. Then Max put his mouth on the other side of her neck, cruising along the artery, delicate tongue touches, followed by a heated, open-mouthed, sucking kiss where his teeth latched on to her once again.

"Come now," she gasped to Thor. "Come, baby."

The powerful sub let go with a pleasing roar worthy of a thunder god. In some distant place in her mind she knew that meant she'd done what she was supposed to do, but she was still spiraling up and up, worked by Max's fingers, the simple touch of his mouth on her throat. He kept the weight of his body against her so Thor's cries intensified, because she kept plowing him in those deep, short strokes. Her legs shook, her body shuddering as the clit stimulator hit her just right, the rhythm Max setting inexorable. Thor's ass kept rising up to meet her, increasing the force of their threefold impact.

"Stop," she whispered. "Stop."

Max shook his head, his dark-blond hair brushing the back of her neck. "Come for *me*, baby," he murmured into her ear. "You're driving me fucking crazy. Trust me with it."

It was a plea and a command, and she couldn't deny either. Her clit hardened, her pussy rippling tight around Max's fingers as her body went over that precipice. She arched, thrusting forward with her hips as she dropped her head back against his shoulder. It pushed her breast farther into his large hand, and when he pinched the nipple, she gave a strangled cry, her nails scoring Thor's back. He reared up against her in spasmodic aftershock as she shoved in even deeper, her body going rigid, caught up in the pleasurable waves.

She wanted those slacks out of the way, wanted to feel the heated steel of Max's bare cock against her flesh. Though this wasn't the moment for that, he at least kept moving with her, that additional sensation driving her to full, mostly satisfied repletion. When she came to a slow halt, Thor's chest was expanding like a bellows, his mouth beneath the blindfold alternating between tight and slack, his body shuddering, fingers clamped on those handles. She'd pushed him hard, and he would need care to ground him. The problem was, she might need it as well. Holy God. She really hadn't expected that. Not just what Max had done, but how she'd reacted to him.

Max kept his arm around her, his mouth at her ear. "All done with him?" he asked.

She nodded, and he backed off, but he took her with him. He eased her out of Thor's ass with surprising gentleness. He loosened the dildo straps as she swayed with a pleasurable dizziness in his arm span. Setting the strap-on aside, he picked her up, put her on the chair he'd vacated. One robe hung on the back of the door, part of the room's standard supplies. Max plucked it off its hook now, slipping it around her shoulders before he squatted before her, touching her knee. "Tell me what to do for him," he said.

She blinked at him. She wasn't a woman to be swept off her feet, but her body was still vibrating from that orgasm, as well as how smoothly and capably he'd lifted her to move her less than three feet. She let her gaze glide down his body, to the obvious, mouthwatering arousal that looked like a heavy lifting job. "It's what I want to do to you that should be discussed."

The gray eyes were heavy-lidded, the pupils large and black. "We'll get there. I want to help you with this."

She considered it. She also wasn't the type of woman who turned her aftercare responsibilities over to another, but she wasn't in the habit of being this weak-kneed by the end of a session. "Usually I'd have him crawl over here and bring me to climax with his mouth, as soon as he felt steady enough to do so. But I think you've taken that away from him." Her gaze shifted to Thor's still twitching body. "I think he'll be okay with that this time."

"I expect so."

"If you can do for him what you just did for me—get him to a sitting position, get him warm—I can take over at that point. Touch helps ground them, but I expect that's not really your thing."

Max put a hand on her knee, gave it a light squeeze. When he rose, going to Thor, he touched the man's back, letting him know it wasn't her before he gripped his flank and shoulder to help him push up. She opened her mouth in warning, but Max was already ahead of her. He'd tightened his hand on Thor, slowing him down and murmuring. Thor nodded, fumbling between his legs to guide his now-flaccid cock out of the ring, preventing tender flesh from being snagged.

"Take off his blindfold," she murmured and Max nodded, pulling it free. He steadied Thor until her captive could straddle the bench in a seated position, facing Janet. Whether deliberate or not, it gave her the pleasure of seeing the naked, dazed sub in all his aftermath glory, the damp cock resting on the slick upholstery of the bench, his broad chest still expanding as he caught his breath. When Max stretched out to get him a bottle of water from the convenience bar provided for that purpose, Thor swayed, but Max gripped his shoulder with the opposite hand, holding him. As he came back, he straddled the bench behind Thor, bringing the man back against his chest, snug inside the line of his thighs. Max's arms were draped comfortably around Thor as he opened the water and offered it, supporting Thor's hand. Thor kept his head turned to the outside of Max's shoulder, stealing looks at Janet.

She'd recovered enough she was sitting up straight, her knees together, legs demurely folded like a debutante, but she was watching him closely. His eyes were getting more focused. Max was stroking his hair, a hand lying on his hip, keeping him upright. She got no gay vibes from Max at all, yet he was remarkably comfortable handling a naked man, cosseting him in this way. She'd always assumed he just watched the public sessions the way anyone did, with a voyeur's surface interest, but he seemed quite familiar with the warning signs important for proper aftercare of a sub.

Underscoring it, when Thor turned his head inward, nuzzling against Max's throat, Max kindly but firmly drew out of his range, gripping Thor's jaw to turn his attention back toward Janet. "I don't go that way, man," he said. "Just here to provide you a prop and take care of you for the Mistress."

Thor accepted that easily enough. After all, he'd come to her for a physical experience. The emotional, intense as it was, was intended to be as temporal as the session itself. Janet rose, moving to her clothes. Under the gaze of both men, she put her skirt back on, following it with her blouse, straightening it tidily. She could have gone into the bathroom and dried the slickness between her legs with a towel, but she wasn't yet in the mood to do that. She was still feeling Max's fingers there. When she met his gaze, she saw a flicker that made her wonder if he'd read her mind again.

Thor shifted with a grunt and glanced back at Max. Her sub for the evening had recovered enough there was a spark of challenge in his eyes. "React that way again, dude, and I'll start doubting the whole 'I don't go that way' thing," Thor said.

Max snorted, shoved the other man's shoulder. "I think you're good." Rising from the bench, he nodded to Janet. "He's all yours. If you don't need me for anything else, ma'am, I'll see you at the coffee shop."

And just like that, he slipped from the room.

Chapter Four
ಬ

She finished up with Thor, thanked him and cut him loose. Even though she had no further plans for club play tonight, she didn't change back into her street clothes yet. She did retrieve them though, putting them in her carry-on before wandering back out to the floor. She found Max in the same spot at the coffee place. As she came to him, she saw his eyes covering the intimate areas he'd touched. Her neck was still throbbing, and she thought it might be bruised blue and red tomorrow from the force of that hot, demanding mouth.

By the time she arrived on the catwalk below him, the spot where they'd spoken before her session with Thor, he'd stood up. Leaning over the rail, he reached down, took her bag. She was already raising her arms, so he caught her beneath them, brought her up to stand on the lip of the coffee house floor. Then he put his arm around her waist, scooped her up beneath her knees and lifted her, guiding her legs over the rail and down to the opposite side.

The coffee house manager gave her a quick once-over, but Janet knew her clothes weren't too outrageous to fail the street-clothes-only requirement of this part of the club. She also recognized Janet as a regular, nodding in friendly acknowledgement.

Max pulled out her chair for her, helped her scoot it up before taking his own seat, aligning his feet on the outside of hers under the small table. When the waitress came, Janet ordered a black coffee and a croissant. Then she folded her arms on the table, fixing her gaze upon him. She'd left the top three buttons of the blouse open, her breasts on a shelf-like display with her arms crossed under them. His attention naturally went to that, but then fastened on her pendant.

Reaching out, he toyed with it, but she closed her hand on his wrist, drawing his eyes back to her face.

"How did you know how to take care of Thor?"

He shrugged, hooking a shoulder on the back of the chair. His thighs were casually splayed, his other hand lying loosely on the table. Did the man realize he oozed testosterone?

"During BUD/S, you're cold. A lot. The boat work, surf torture. If you and your team come out on top during the boat exercises, you might get rewarded with a few minutes on the beach, not having to be in the water. We sit like me and Thor did, folded into each other, back to chest, to share warmth. It's a way of grounding and settling as well. Physical contact like that with another human being when you're going through a lot of stress, it's pretty basic."

The words echoed those he'd spoken at the hospital that night. *Sometimes, after something like that, human touch helps ground you, brings back your focus.*

"Surf torture?" Her brow lifted.

"The instructors have us link arms and lie in the surf for about fifteen-minute stretches. It's fifty-some-degree water. You start thinking Hell is polar caps, not a fire pit."

"That sounds a little inhumane."

He chuckled. "It's not just to torture us, though there are times you think so. On missions, they know we'll be in some pretty cold waters. Traveling in SDVs—SEAL delivery vehicles—especially the underwater ones, sucks rocks. By the time you get out, you feel colder than an ice cube."

He leaned forward, tapping her knuckles, then stayed there, his finger resting on top of one of hers.

"Why don't you tie them down?" he asked. "Most of the Mistresses I've watched seem to prefer that."

She knew what it was to be tied down, unable to escape while the blows came. Rationally, she knew this was different, but the first time she'd tried to tie up a sub, pushing her own boundaries, the blood had come back, the thud of blows, the straps cutting into her flesh as she screamed and tried to get away...

A moment later, she realized her croissant and coffee were there. He pushed the plate toward her. "Maybe eat a little. You look pale," he noted.

"Is this a game to you, Max?" she said, staring at the food. Her gaze snapped back up to him.

His brow creased. "No ma'am. I'm just figuring out the terrain. Determining where the land mines are."

She tucked her hands around the coffee, warming them. "Call me by my name, Max. Please."

"Janet."

He brought his chair closer to hers, which kept her between the rail and his body. She didn't feel trapped though. Instead, she was enclosed, a blanket on a cold night. He slid an arm around her waist, threading it between the chair and her body, and his palm wrapped below her hip, his fingers curving over her ass as he brought her up toward his mouth, his head bending to her.

She didn't wait for him. She met him halfway, and dove headfirst into the sensation. He met her, fire for fire. She wasn't on the chair anymore. He'd hooked his other hand under her knee, turned and pulled her onto his lap, her buttocks pressed solidly down on his erection as he pushed his fingers into her hair, gripped hard, the sculpting clay not a deterrent. Their mouths stretched and strained, tongues lashing, wet lips rubbing together. She clutched his shoulders, the warmth of the coffee that had lingered in her palms replaced by the solid heat of his body. She wished she hadn't worn this pencil skirt that kept her from straddling him, though she knew they were pushing the boundaries even now, probably back under the scrutiny of the coffee house manager.

As if Max figured it out at the same moment she did, his grip tightened, but to pull her back, even if only a few inches. "Time to get out of here," he said. "I want you under me.

Those gorgeous legs wrapped around me. I want to taste your cunt."

Her breath shuddered out, her fingers tracing his lips. He licked them, drawing in one to suck on it, hard, give it a sharp bite. The need pulsing from him was pure animal. No rules, no patience to talk about who was in charge. Unlike what most outsiders thought of it, BDSM gave civilized rules to uncivilized behavior. Right now, the pure instinct that predated it drove them both.

Rising, he dropped bills on the table, picked up her bag. He offered his hand, but when she put hers out, he closed his fingers around her wrist, drew her up to him, against his side, and they moved toward the exit that way. His hand dropped to her hip, then lower. The man enjoyed fondling an ass, and had no compunction about doing it in front of others, though in all fairness, he wasn't exactly in a place that disapproved of blatant sexual expression. He seemed fascinated with the tightness of the skirt, fingers following the way the fabric hugged and curved under her buttocks. He stroked, explored, interrupting himself only to open the door and guide her through it, so they exited to the parking area.

The parking lot lights were a light sheen on the truck's flank. His hand was back to doing that distracting pattern across her sensitive buttocks. But two could play it that way. When they reached the truck, she put her hands on his chest, pressing him up against his door. As she leaned into him, he dropped the bag and shifted his grip to her hips, bringing her even closer to him. He bent for another kiss she was sure would cause her brain to explode, but she tilted her head down, denying him. Those provocative lips slid across her temple instead.

Her hand moved up his chest to the base of his throat, then to his jaw, curving around it before she tightened, digging her nails into his neck enough to make him understand the wordless demand. As he turned his jaw away from her, he took it an extra step, understanding her desire. He laid his head back against the window glass, exposing his throat fully to her.

Power and pleasure flooded her, and she put her mouth on that strong column, suckling and biting it as he'd done her, wanting to leave those same marks on him. In answer, he gripped her ass in a two-handed hold so aggressive her boot heels left the pavement. The skirt was too tight, too stiff a fabric to give way before his sizeable erection, let it push into that valley between her thighs where she could feel that sweet pressure against her clit. Now she wished she had changed into her street clothes. But she took what the moment could offer her.

She yanked at the dress shirt, not caring when buttons came loose. Such a properly dressed gentleman, he had the thin white cotton T-shirt beneath, and she clawed at it as well, pulling it loose from his waistband, bringing the hem up to his throat. He kept his hands on her hips, letting her do as she wished, inflaming her further. He was restraining himself. Catering to her needs, her wishes. Her nature. Yet she could feel the power and response building in him, stoked by her actions. Eventually, it would be too much. He'd tear loose of his self-imposed control and sweep them both away.

It was an unspoken give-and-take, an intuitive power exchange so erotic because of the lack of defined boundaries and words, its unpredictability. She felt as free as a wild animal in truth. She could desire and demand anything from Max. He was strong enough to handle it, and her, and still make her feel safe. At least in this moment.

Hard muscled flesh. Manna straight from heaven. She put her mouth on his pectoral and went right for sensitive places, closing her teeth delicately around his nipple, her tongue swirling around it. He was silent, but his body was a full orchestra, arched into that latch point, abdomen muscles taut beneath her other hand, her thumb caught beneath his waistband as her fingers splayed across the defined ridges. His heart beat rapidly beneath her other hand, pressed against his chest. The hand he had on her hip gripped hard, and he'd brought the other up to cup her head.

Normally she'd have snapped out an order to keep both hands down, but what he was doing, fingers digging in then stroking, moving down to grasp her nape, felt too good. He was following the line of her neck to her shoulder, a motion that sent tingles of sensation down her spine to her tailbone, and from there into the deep crevices of her body, creating a bittersweet yearning.

She ran her tongue along the crease between pectoral and upper abdomen. This man's body was sheer fucking perfection, developed to fight, to serve. And all hers at the moment.

She noticed he'd managed to catch hold of the skirt zipper and ease it up way past mid-thigh. The breeze touched her skin, replaced by the solid heat of his hand, sliding up the back of her thigh to cup her ass, bared by the black thong. She bit down on the nipple, and he pinched her in reply, his other arm circling her waist to band her closer to him.

"Excuse me. Sir, ma'am?"

Max shifted the hand he had on her nape to her jaw, her cheek, keeping her face pressed to his chest, averted from the man who'd approached them. His hand came out from beneath her skirt, smoothly working the zipper down in the same motion so she was covered.

"No disrespect, but the club doesn't allow sexual play in the parking lot. You can take it offsite or back inside."

"Understood. My apologies. I got a little carried away."

"No worries." The security guard's stern tone eased, the man recognizing he wasn't going to be dealing with a belligerent guest. "Can't blame you a bit. The two of you were hot enough to make me think about waking the wife up when I get home tonight."

Max chuckled, pressing a kiss on the top of Janet's head, an idle caress as the man moved away. She straightened, pushing away from his grip, though her fingers stayed latched on his T-shirt. He put his hands on her elbows, keeping her in his grasp as well.

"I think we need to slow this down. Time for me to call it a night." She met his gaze squarely, though saying the words, removing her hands from his body, was like pulling frozen hands away from a warm fire. "Will you walk me to my car?"

He shook his head. Giving his T-shirt a casual tug downward so it covered his rock-hard abs but leaving his shirt open—no choice, given that she expected several of the buttons were under the cars around them—he fished his keys out of his pocket and shifted to unlock his vehicle. Pulling open the door, he picked up her bag, put it in the back and then extended a hand. "Get in the truck."

"The mating call of the Southern male," she said lightly, but her pulse had leaped at the command. His gaze had fastened on it, making her think of his mouth there once more. "Where are we going?"

"To a place where you can look up at the stars while I put my mouth between your legs."

They held gazes for a long moment, then Janet lifted a shoulder. "More sure of the terrain now? No land mines?"

"The reward balances the risk."

She sidled back up to him, pressing thigh to thigh deliberately. When she reached up, stroked through his hair, he obligingly brought his head down, put his lips on her shoulder, held them there while a single, hard shudder ran through her. He wasn't a Dominant. He was simply...overwhelming. Different. Unclassifiable. She should go home. It was time to evaluate where she was going with this. Where he was taking her.

He rubbed his lips along that bare stretch of skin between blouse collar and throat, making her fingers curl deeper into his scalp. "Janet. Truck. Now."

"All right, Tarzan," she whispered, a smile flirting in her heart, on her lips. He put his hands on her waist, lifted her into the truck. He'd made it an order but waited for her consent before proceeding. He was the oddest mix of things.

He'd lifted her into the driver's side. The seat was a long cushion, no console, the gear shift on the hump between the floorboards. It reminded her of an old farm truck, and when she scooted over so he could get in, turn over the ignition, the powerful roar of the engine enhanced the impression. She hadn't moved any farther than necessary to get her legs over the gears, and he pleased her immensely when, once he put the truck in gear, he settled one arm over her so she could lean against him. It helped with talking over that engine noise as well. She propped her chin on his shoulder to speak into his ear as they pulled out into traffic.

"You're Texan, aren't you, Southern male?"

He glanced at her, amused, and when he lifted his hand from the wheel to shift, she was already on it, smoothly changing gears as he worked the clutch. Her Mustang was a straight drive as well, a dying breed. The light in his eyes said he appreciated her ability to coordinate with him. And she appreciated that he didn't indulge in any adolescent comments about her ability to handle a stick. "Yes ma'am. I thought you knew everything about everyone at K&A."

"Contrary to rumor, I don't routinely scour personnel records. I rely on intel from office gossip."

"You should have gone with the personnel records. You would have known I left my last job because they objected to my side hobby. Taking women out into the swamps to cut up their bodies for the gators."

"Are we going to do the watching the stars thing before the murder thing?"

His arm tightened around her, fingers sliding under her buttock to take a firm grip. "Count on it."

"Well then. That will give me time to think about my escape plan."

"I doubt you'll be thinking much."

She laughed then, a throaty, sultry sound that drew his gray eyes to her in a way that sobered her. She traced his mouth with her nails as he turned his attention back to the road. "How did you know something was going to go wrong? That day with Savannah?"

"It was a gut feeling. You develop it in the field. A tickling sense that something's not quite right." He shrugged but then gave her an intent look. "That's not what I want to think about right now."

"What do you want...right now?" She felt the give of the light layer of hair beneath his T-shirt as she trailed her fingertips down his sternum. His chest hair was dark blond, like what was on his head. She wanted to see all of it, not just what was visible from the scoop-necked collar.

Keeping one hand on the wheel and his eyes on the road, he nevertheless lifted his arm from around her shoulders and reached across her to the zipper of the skirt. He pulled it up a few inches from the slit, but he needed a second hand or her help to get it higher. She put her hand over his.

"Tell me what you want, Max."

He gave her that glance again, then he made a turn on to a service road. "I want you to put your fingers inside yourself. I want to taste you while I'm driving." His gaze went to her face, then higher. "And I wish you didn't have that stuff on your hair. I think about your hair all the time. What it would feel like, all soft on my chest, my stomach."

She could follow that track in her mind, see herself going down on him, opening up her mouth and sucking on his cock. She fantasized about tying him up while she did it, watching every muscle fighting his bonds. No, she never tied up her subs like that, but fantasizing was a safe indulgence. Though with Max she wondered if she'd be tempted to cross the line into reality, see if he could keep her mind out of the clutches of the past.

Lifting her hips off the seat, she worked the zipper up so she could put her fingers beneath the pencil skirt. Nudging the thong aside was easy enough. He slowed the vehicle to turn down another road. She helped him shift to lower gear, and they bumped down a dirt road. He'd opened the window and she could smell the water, hear the nighttime wildlife. Fortunately, it was almost cold tonight, meaning the bugs wouldn't eat them, and the stars would be bright in the sky. Such thoughts didn't help her coordination.

Her pussy was soaking wet, no surprise there. Her fingers went in easy and deep, with a quiet sucking noise that she wasn't sure he'd heard, but when she glanced up and saw he'd brought the truck to a halt, those intense eyes glittering in the darkness, she suspected he had. She pulled her fingers free, brought them up between them. They'd stopped in front of a dock and what looked like someone's private boat access. One dim light on a pole illuminated a small gravel parking area.

Curling his fingers around her wrist, Max sucked in her two fingers, glistening with her honey. She stretched out the other fingers, stroking the five o'clock shadow, the cleft in his chin. Superman's chin, a strong block that went with the strong face and powerful body. A man with a chin like that invariably lived up to it, a genetic indicator of character, courage. She noticed things like that, how often the physical feature appeared on police chiefs, career military men. The man who worked two jobs to support his wife and children. The lone homeless guy who dove into an ice-cold river to pull kids out of a car that had spun off the road.

Max took his time, stroking each finger with his tongue, caressing her palm with his thumb, holding her in that firm grip that did all sorts of things to her lower belly. He seemed to understand the complicated mix inside a Domme—at least this particular one. How the exploration of that intimate interplay of restraint and power could tease her senses, especially if approached with the delicate precision that he'd thus far demonstrated.

Squeezing her hand, he opened the truck door, then reached behind his seat, withdrawing a duffle bag and a thick blanket. "Stay there a minute."

Moving to the back of the truck, she felt the dip as he stepped onto the wheel well and did something, probably arranging things for her comfort. For their pleasure. She slid behind the wheel, turned so she had her boots propped outside the truck on the running board, and gazed out at the dock. There was a bass boat tied up there.

"Whose property is this?"

"A friend's. He's in Afghanistan right now. I take his boat out sometimes, keep it maintained."

Max jumped out of the back of the truck, came back to her. He leaned against the open door, studying her with those intent eyes that made the crisp night much warmer. "Why were you going to leave me?" he asked. "At the club?"

"Control. I don't like to rush. Or take a step down the wrong path. This is a little like a roller coaster. Once you go over the crest of the hill, there's no turning back."

"There's also nothing like the thrill of that ride." He caught a lock of her hair between two fingers, massaged it between his knuckles. "What is that stuff?"

"Sculpting clay. It holds the hair in place, gives me a more severe, scary look."

"Like you need to be more scary. Even Matt Kensington won't cross you."

"You don't seem all that scared."

His lips quirked. "Do you want me to be? I don't think that's the rush for you. You just like things done right, and you don't tolerate sloppy work. Carelessness. Or inappropriate behavior. Just like him. You look at something and know how it's supposed to look or act, how the picture is supposed to be framed. Structure, the way you do it, is how it's supposed to be. You know it, and you don't have patience for those who don't get that."

Reaching behind the seat, he unzipped her bag. As he leaned over her knee, she put her hands on his waist to feel the way his body moved, a simple pleasure. He came back with her street clothes, her casual skirt and cotton shirt. To her amusement, he'd left the panties and bra in the bag but retrieved her socks and canvas sneakers.

"I'll go take a walk on the dock," he said. "Why don't you put those on? They'll be more comfortable." At her quizzical look, he added, "Control, right?"

He was a rather remarkable person, all in all. When she glanced around, he touched her face. "You're safe here. It's private. And I'll know if anyone's coming long before it's an issue. All right?"

At her nod, he squeezed her knee and left her, headed down to the dock. Janet watched him, a tall, broad-shouldered man with a casually powerful stride. His head turned this way and that as he took in his surroundings. She noticed how deliberate he was in his movements, as if aware of the placement of each foot, the angle of his body, his position in relation to everything around him, including her.

Janet slid out of the blouse and shelf bra, pulling on the cotton stretch T-shirt. Without a bra, her nipples and small breasts were blatantly obvious, but she decided to indulge his less-than-subtle attempt to influence her clothing choices. She ditched the pencil skirt and put on the less restrictive one. She removed boots and stockings but left off the canvas sneakers and socks for the moment. She put all the rest neatly back in her bag.

Seeing her hair brush, she smiled. Unpinning her hair, she tossed it forward, running the brush through her dark tresses as they unraveled to their full length. The brush broke the hold of the sculpting product, making her hair soft again. As she straightened, she tested it, running her fingers through the strands, imagining Max doing the same.

When she looked for him, she found him sitting on the rail of the dock, watching her now. Putting the brush back into her bag, she braced herself on the running board to put her other bare foot on the wheel well. Then she swung herself over into the back of the truck. He'd unrolled some type of cushioned mat there, covering it with a blanket, then put the camo quilt on top of that. There was even a serviceable travel pillow.

"I don't think this is the first time you've entertained a woman in the back of your truck," she called out, taking a cross-legged seat on her bed, as dignified as an empress.

"Thanks to that prior experience, I've learned that women do not like lying on the steel slats of a truck bed, nor do they care for being naked when they're cold." As he came back toward her, she watched the lithe, sexual promise of his body like the gift it was. "A man's lovemaking skills," he continued solemnly, "as extensive as they might be, have no hope of impressing his female companion if her basic needs are not met. It's not really fair, but that's the other thing I've learned. Women don't really care about fairness."

"No, we don't. It's highly overrated." Janet couldn't suppress her smile as he leaned his elbows on the side of the truck bed. When he touched her hair, a look of deep pleasure capturing his features, she was ridiculously pleased with her decision to brush out the sculpting clay.

"Lie back for me," he said quietly. "I want to see you. Pull your skirt up to your waist, let me see your beautiful legs. And everything else."

She reached out, tugged at his T-shirt. "Only if you get rid of this. Every woman in the office wants to see you shirtless."

He grunted dubiously at that. "This better not show up on YouTube."

She would have smiled again, but that energy was returning, swirling around them, drawing things tighter. He shrugged out of the shirt she'd ripped open, then pulled the T-shirt over his head.

Oh my. She'd been right. The way he moved, the obvious power he held, was mapped on the body. All smooth, rolling muscle, the gleaming dark-blond chest hair arrowing down between the sectioned stomach muscles. The angled muscles from hip to groin became even more noticeable when he pulled off the shirt, because his upper body lifted, dropping the slacks lower for a vital, pleasurable moment. He had a couple scars, she noticed. And a tattoo. She shifted to her knees, curling one hand on the edge of the truck so she could touch his muscled arm with the other, a demand to let her see.

He lifted his arm, revealing another amazing stretch of layered muscle and a soft patch of curling underarm hair. The tattoo was inked vertically on the stretch of rib cage under his right arm. Three skulls held on a trident. The top prong of the trident went through the crown of the middle skull, whereas the two side ones came out through the skulls' eye sockets, their position angled accordingly. *Brothers in Hell* wound in a spiral along the trident's handle.

She trailed her fingers over it. "A SEAL thing?"

He nodded, and she saw the shadows in his gaze. A brooding darkness, but one that enhanced this moment, sharpened it toward his intent as his gaze slid down her throat, lingering on her breasts, delineated so provocatively in the T-shirt. "Come here," he rumbled in that husky tone. "I'm hungry."

She was already up against the truck side, but understanding, she rose off her heels, standing on her knees. He snaked his arm around her, palming her ass to hold her in place as he closed his other hand over her right breast. Squeezing it firmly and pressing his thumb beneath the nipple, he tilted it up as he closed his mouth over it, through the shirt. Janet gripped his shoulder hard, her other set of fingers clinging to the side of the truck to give her an anchor as he suckled her hard, almost as hard as he had her throat. He knew she liked to feel the demand, no tentative brushes of lips or tongue. She liked to devour, so she wanted to be devoured.

He released her abruptly but held on to her hand as he put his foot on the wheel well and joined her in the back. Kneeling on the bed he'd made them, he caught her about the waist again, but this time to put her on her back, settling himself between her legs, his muscled shoulders and back beneath her grasping fingers as he cupped her breasts in both hands and got down to the business of suckling, biting, licking and generally driving her insane. She writhed beneath the press of his body. With her skirt rucked up to her waist, she discovered his washboard stomach provided sweet friction to her clit.

"I want you to come from this, and then I want you to come with my tongue in your pussy," he muttered.

"Well, if you insist..."

When he chuckled, the vibration against her nipple made her cry out. It wasn't a lighthearted laugh, but the sound of an incubus, knowing exactly how to pleasure her and where, dragging her down into the sensual darkness with him.

He gripped her thigh, encouraging her to wrap her legs around his body, rest her crossed heels on his ass, which flexed with his movements against her. "It's all about your pleasure, Mistress."

The whisper fired her blood. She raked her fingernails over his shoulders, tightened her legs on him, working her clit against him at her own pace. Meanwhile, he teased and nursed her breasts, squeezing and kneading, making the nerves ripple and ache, scream for more, sending out floods of sensation that drove pulses at all her erogenous points, and even beyond that, creating new ones. The track where she worked herself against his lower abdomen had become slick with her juices. If she lay on his stomach later, she'd smell herself on him, a feral marking.

He opened the slacks, shoved them and the briefs beneath off his hips enough she could feel the rise of his bare ass beneath her calves, but more than that, she could now rub her pussy all the way to his groin area. She didn't feel the blunt stab of his cock, so she knew he must be keeping it pressed downward, out of the way for this part. She expected it was somewhat uncomfortable. The fact he was suffering for her just made her hotter.

Then he began doing something with his tongue, a quick lashing thing, alternated with the squeezes of his hands. When he followed with a deep sucking, punctuated by hungry murmurs in his throat, she was lost. She climaxed, a short, deeply intense wave, where she ground herself against him, crying out her pleasure to the night, all those stars becoming like shooting stars because of her glazed vision.

He kept suckling and squeezing, though she could tell his buttocks were pumping in rhythm with her, as if they were fucking in truth. But he didn't push that agenda. He kept to the mission he'd described, waiting until she was shuddering with aftershocks to slide down her body, push his arms under her thighs, cup her buttocks in his two large hands, and put his mouth fully over her exposed cunt.

She screamed, the aftershocks pulsing against his lips. The tissues were so sensitive, but he slowed way down, making tender, slow licks along the labia, soft nuzzles on her clit that made her shudder. He was going for the slow build, so slow it was like a simple teasing aftermath, except his hands remained firm on her, his body taut with the desire he kept in check as he gave her pleasure, ramped up her desire again.

She wanted him in her arms, wanted to explore every inch of him, take his cock in her mouth, make him lose his mind as he was making her lose hers, but for now, this was also what she wanted.

All about your pleasure, Mistress. So much of what she did as a Domme was calculated, holding the reins, watching the sub get more and more aroused while she figured out what slight adjustments would affect his reactions. It was an aphrodisiac all its own, but this... This was somehow a different form of service, where she had to calculate nothing, not worry about the reins at all. He knew what she wanted from him.

When she had a brain to think about it, she would be considering this carefully, but she had to give him his due. He'd said she wouldn't be able to think much, and he was delivering on that promise.

Shuddering, she stared up at the stars, floating in a lull between the climax of a moment ago and the one he was taking her toward now. Her heels rested high on his back, and her hands, now that he was between her legs, had caught hold of the netting at the top of the truck. She assumed it was to keep things from sliding around. It helped her bear down against his mouth, a very pleasurable feeling. Looking down her body, she found he had amazingly thick dark-blond lashes, fanning his cheeks. He stayed intent on his task, rough stubble abrading the tender insides of her thighs in a way she loved. She hoped the redness would be there tomorrow.

She'd never thought about wanting to be marked by a man. Or even about owning him. She owned her subs, commanded them, at the club, but outside, she was Janet. She stood alone, confident in that solitary strength and power. She told herself this was want, not need, but she couldn't deny the sharpness of the one was such she could easily mistake it for the other.

He pushed his tongue deep inside, stroked her silken tissues while suckling her clit on the outside, then started lashing that tiny bud of swollen flesh, a concentrated flogging that had her rising up to his mouth. His hands were strong on her legs, her hips, the muscles taut along his shoulders and back. She let go of the netting to reach down and grip his short hair, hold him to her, tug, convey her desires. He growled in response.

She arched back as he did something else that changed the waves of sensation, making it a spiral, then a staccato pressure, then a slow glide. She was moaning, and it didn't matter, she didn't want to rein back her response. She wanted him to know how much pleasure he was giving her.

His fingers bit into her buttocks, beginning to knead, press the cheeks together, massaging the sensitive area in between with the pressure, and that arrowed right down into her pussy. Her legs tightened on those broad shoulders, and she imagined what he must look like from a view above, his ass likely moving in that instinctive coital rhythm with hers, even though their joining point wasn't cock and pussy, but his mouth between her legs, his hands clamped on her body, so she twisted and writhed within the span of his glorious hands.

Another rolling wave of sensation, and she felt the crash coming. She lifted up to meet it, her arms spread wide, clinging to the net again, her breasts lifted up with the arch of her body. She caught a glimpse of him looking, taking in the sight of her, and when he thrust deep with his tongue, pulled even harder on her clit, she knew he was monitoring everything, how close she was. When to take her that last step and then cut the lines, let her fly.

This time it was twice as intense, and not short at all. She cried out, long, moaning wails as the orgasm gripped her. Her fingers gripped the netting so fiercely it cut into her flesh. She could feel everywhere he touched her, mouth, fingers, his shoulders against the inside of her thighs. She wanted him on top of her, wanted to feel him.

The climax was ebbing, and she let go of the netting, clawed at his shoulders, telling him. He slid up her body and met her mouth with an impact that pushed her head back, his fingers framing her face, delving into her hair, elbows planted on either side of her shoulders, holding her down with the length of his body. Her hips jerked, still reacting to the climax, rubbing against him. The change in position had let his cock stretch into its intended upright stiff position, and the thick, rigid weight of it was against her abdomen. With his slacks and briefs pulled partly off, it would be a simple thing, that one last step.

But he merely kissed her. All that sweet need in her met the raw demand in him, their bodies melded together, quivering, held in a powerful stasis. When he at last lifted his head, his face was all harsh planes, eyes dark slashes in the night. She lifted a hand to him, and he closed his own around her wrist, pushing it back to the truck bed, holding it with her pulse battering against his palm. "Let go of me, Max," she whispered.

He took his time thinking about it, nuzzling her throat, rubbing his jaw against her hair. But then he released her, and she put her arm around his broad back, tracing the lines of muscle. He worked his way back down her body, gentle kisses that brought her back to earth as if she were borne on the wings of butterflies. She turned her head to the foam mat, eyes closed, merely feeling.

He kissed his way down her thighs, then put his mouth on her cunt, cleaned her, slow licks and teasing kisses, small sips to take away the fluids from her climax. She made soft sighs in response, and then he was kissing his way down the inside of the opposite thigh.

When he reached her ankles, he straightened onto his knees to adjust his slacks and the boxers beneath. He brought them both back up to his waist but left the slacks unhooked. Then he settled onto his heels and ran his hands up her calves. Learning her curves, enjoying her body but giving her enjoyment as well. His strong hands caressed areas many men forgot to tease and seduce as much as their more preferred parts of a woman. He ran his touch all the way up her legs, covering knees and thighs, then came back down to do the same thing all over again, starting at the arches of her feet.

Max grounded her and sent her floating at once. Eventually he unfastened the skirt so he could slide his hands unencumbered from her hips to her rib cage under her thin cotton shirt, give her the sensation of that same, strong rubbing glide, both a caress and a massage.

The cool night air was starting to seep into her skin, but he anticipated that as well. Bracketing her rib cage with both hands, he slid her up and worked the camo quilt out from under her, sandwiching her between that and the covered padded roll beneath. He joined her under it, pulling her close so she could wrap around his heat, lay her head on his chest. He stayed propped up against the netting, stroking her hair.

Her hand rested on his abdomen. When she let it ease downward, wanting to touch the sizeable erection available through the unhooked front of his slacks, he closed his fingers over hers, bringing them back up to his mouth. She tilted her head to look at him.

"Max, I want to touch you."

"Just let it be this tonight. Let it be all about you."

She arched a brow at him, tapped his lips with her nail. "Me touching you *is* about me. I did say *I* want to touch you. Should I make it a command?"

His gaze kindled, reminding her that he was still a very aroused male who'd not yet been sated. Not by a long shot. "Give it a try," he encouraged, his voice low. "It'll make me harder."

"Shut up while I touch you," she said. Though he bit her finger, he let her hand go.

Sliding back down that same terrain, she was aware of his heated breath on the back of her neck as she bent her head to her desired task. The advantage of slacks was the same thing that had made them a disadvantage at the club, when she wanted a better look at his reaction. The fabric had enough give that it wasn't difficult to get her hand back beneath them. She worked her hand under his boxer briefs, not content to settle for merely feeling the shape of him through cloth. "Unzip them the rest of the way," she said shortly, not willing to remove her other hand from where it curved behind his lower back.

He reached down, complied, and she helped, holding the fabric taut with two fingers as the teeth parted over the impressive mound. As she pushed her hand all the way beneath the briefs, his fingers caressed her forearm, then withdrew. When she closed her grip around that steel heat, his thigh muscles flexed, his heart ramping up its beat beneath her ear. She'd handled a man's cock plenty of times before, but the first time could be as potent as a first kiss, if approached in the right frame of mind. She hadn't put any thought or preparation into it. She'd just wanted to touch him, and as a result it was like having a hunger sated—or discovered—to grip him now.

Glancing up, she saw him watching her. Under her gaze, he deliberately stretched out a long arm, hooked his free hand in the netting. His other hand remained against her back. When she twisted her head, giving it a look, then glanced back at him pointedly, he didn't immediately respond, obviously weighing what he might do.

"Max," she purred. "Do it."

He moved the other hand then, both sets of fingers now hooked in the net, letting her do as she would. She kept her eyes on him as she slid her grip up to the head of his cock, rubbing her thumb across his wet slit. She wanted to taste that fluid and she did, lifting the finger to her mouth. His jaw got tighter, his eyes hot.

"All about me," she murmured. "Why is that, Max?"

"You know a better way to be sure I get a second date?"

She laughed, though there was a bite to it, a showing of her teeth, that conveyed she wasn't relaxing the terms of the moment. She liked seeing him restrained by her words, though still free to pounce. She preferred to be a lion tamer, letting the deadly animal make his own choices, held back only by her wits and words. She liked the thrill of being caught between his hunger for her, his own natural instincts, and a thin veneer of control, so blended he couldn't tell what was hers and his.

"Is it that difficult to get a second date with me?"

"Yes ma'am. You haven't had one date in the time I've known you."

"Perhaps I'm a very private person who doesn't let anyone know my personal business."

He didn't say anything, just looked at her. She hadn't denied it, so it confirmed what he already knew. A very smart lion indeed. It hadn't been just in the time he'd known her though. It had been far, far longer. In that time, nothing had ever been offered to her that would give her more than what the club sessions and her own vibrator could.

She used the point of her wrist to hold the slacks down so she could see her fist, wrapped firmly around his base. His cock jutted well above her grip, showing he was a good length and thickness. No woman would have to ask if he was all the way in when he was seated inside her. The flesh between her legs, still sensitive and moist, rippled at the thought. She loosened her grip enough to slide up, bringing some of that velvet skin with her, rubbing her thumb along the sensitive area beneath the head, and his breath drew in.

She knew how to get a man off, for certain. Now she entertained herself with a few slow pumps up and down, dragging her palm over the skin, not holding it too tightly, teasing the corona with her nails, giving him the sharp tip of her thumb nail in the slit once, making him quiver. She'd like to see him naked, see the veins in those well-muscled thighs become more prominent as he resisted movement.

Turning her attention to his face, she shifted farther forward so she was still resting on her hip, still holding him, but her breasts were pressed against his chest, nipples prominent through the thin fabric of her cotton shirt so he'd feel their tautness against his own flesh. She was close enough to be kissed, but she held there, that small space between them as she constricted her grip, did another firm glide upward, downward.

His breath rasped out, fingers digging into the netting, which made his biceps bunch, the muscles of his stomach get even more rigid. "So," she purred. "Since it's all about me, if I decided I have all I want for tonight, would you go home and jack off to Internet porn?"

"No." He bit his bottom lip, dropping his head back against the truck's rear windshield, just above the netting. It exposed his throat—not deliberately this time, but that didn't make it any less inviting. She restrained herself though, wanting his answer. Another tease of the ridged head with her nails, a sharper scrape this time.

"I'd be lying there in the dark, fantasizing only about you. Thinking of your mouth on my cock. Your cunt closing around it. Sitting on top of me, while I held your breasts, still in that shirt. I love the way that looks, no bra." He groaned as she tightened her grip. "I'd bite your nipples through the cloth when you came again."

God, this was like a drug. It always was, but in this different environment, with this different man, it was the contrast between a one-drink buzz and a much stronger proof. Perhaps not a substance manufactured by man, but natural, uncut arousal, emotions mixing with the physical to make it even more addictive.

"But what if I don't want you to come like that? What if I want you to keep your hands away from yourself, give me that pleasure when *I* decide I want it?"

He brought his chin down. She'd shifted close enough now it followed the line of her nose. When she adjusted so they were eye to eye, she bit his lip but drew back before it became a kiss, leaving that tempting flesh swollen from the pressure she'd put on it. The look in those gray eyes now was unmistakable. The lion was deciding if it was time to leap. She was on the fence herself, not sure if she wanted him to take her down, or rein himself back at her command. Both options had an appeal.

"I'd say..." He closed that inch, too quick for her to withdraw, and caught her lip in a sharp nip. Then he leaned back with a challenging, heavy-lidded look, holding on to the truck webbing with strong fists. "When can I pick you up for that second date?"

Chapter Five

Janet sat on the roof of the K&A building, her lunch open next to her, untouched. The potted ferns surrounding her waved in the breeze. A trio of tiny bells, hung from a stake in the soil of one of the plants, chimed softly. From this height, she could see the Mississippi, the boat traffic coming and going. This little spot was all hers. She'd discovered it during her first year at K&A, when she'd brought some maintenance men up here for roof repairs. Over time, she'd designed her own space, importing a couple of lounge chairs, an umbrella for shade, the plants.

When she didn't care for company at lunch, she came here. If it was an early spring or fall day, when the weather was irresistible, she might forward her phone and bring her laptop up here to work a couple hours. If Matt decided a contract needed another minor revision after the hard copies had already been sent out and filed, or rescheduled a meeting at the last minute that involved twenty people in four different countries, she'd come up here for five minutes. He probably had no idea how many times her ability to do that had saved his life.

Today, however, she wasn't seeking solitude to avoid homicide. She had a lot on her mind. She also wanted to finish a task she didn't particularly care to explain to anyone.

Adjusting her reading glasses, she focused on the shirt in her lap. She kept a button jar in her desk, stocked with buttons that would match what was on most men's dress shirts. She'd found several that could replace the ones on Max's shirt, the ones that had been lost in the Progeny parking lot. Wetting the thread with her lips, she peered through the glasses to thread the needle and then tied it off, shaking out the shirt over her knees. Up here by herself, she could do the girly thing, put it to her face and inhale his scent. She'd kept it neatly folded in a bag under her desk all morning, yet had barely resisted the urge to take it into the bathroom and do just that, several times. She shook her head at herself.

He could have tried to fuck her. Demanded to do so. But he hadn't. On one level, he'd served her almost like a sub, bringing her pleasure, giving her release multiple times. But usually in a session, her focus was on putting a sub through his paces, getting him so wound up, he'd beg for anything, including the right to come. Max had been so hard that it had been difficult for him to get his trousers fastened again, to position himself behind the wheel when it was time to take her back to her car, but he hadn't demanded anything from her. Moving slow, letting her hold on to control. Yet she wasn't really controlling anything, was she?

He'd assured her at the dock that no one would come up on him unawares, and she'd believed him without question. When he dropped her off, walked her to her car, he'd taken her keys, opened her door for her. She'd noted his visual sweep of the interior, making sure she was the only occupant of the car. Gestures like that, as automatic to him as breathing, inspired a woman's instinctive trust. She knew the dangers of that, but she'd learned those dangers from a much different kind of man. Since then, she'd grown up, gotten better judgment, though having confidence in it had been a hard-won battle. When one made such a series of terrible, horrifying mistakes, it took years to believe in oneself again. She'd made it, and she wondered if a man like Max was the prize for such a journey.

Before he'd let her get into her car, he'd slid an arm around her waist, his fingers stroking her backside through the thin skirt. She hadn't ever put on the panties. Though he didn't linger, it was obvious he desired strongly to do so. The cock pressed against her hip was still more than ready to serve her. He put his mouth to her ear.

"Next time you put your hands on yourself, think of me, Mistress. I'll be thinking of you. And suffering like hell, because I won't be touching what's yours."

She couldn't figure him out, and that would keep her going back for more. Neither Dom nor sub, yet elements of both that conflicted with and complemented her own skill set. So what did that leave?

Despite the bright sunlight, Janet shivered. The nip was still in the air, because the sun kept coming and going. She'd known that before she came up, but she'd left her sweater downstairs. It proved her level of distraction.

She hadn't set a second date with him. Not just to torment him, but to give her some time to think. However, today was Thursday, the day he was going to come with her to the ballet school. There she'd be, supervising a bevy of hormonal teenage girls, who'd be thinking the same things she was thinking about him. Only whereas he was beyond their reach, he was solidly under her fingertips, everything offered.

The access door to the roof opened with a metallic squeak. It irritated her mildly, but she expected it was one of the maintenance workers who sometimes came up to tweak one of the heating and air units. On the rare occasions their visits coincided with her lunch time, they didn't usually speak to her beyond a cordial greeting.

When she looked up, anticipating such an exchange, she was surprised to see her boss.

Matt Kensington's height and breadth spoke of his father's military and football background, but the dark hair and eyes, the rugged beauty of his face, were a combination of his father's Texas roots and his mother's Italian ones. His full name was Matthew Lord Kensington. Occasionally a business rival would make the cutting joke that Matt preferred to go by Lord Kensington. The joke wasn't made too often, however, probably because the honorific fit him so well no one could argue with it. The sheer authority that emanated from him said it wouldn't matter his era or circumstances of birth, he'd always end up leading men. Not from fear or intimidation—though he was quite capable of those traits—but out of respect for his leadership abilities.

He asked for a hundred and twenty percent from those who worked for him, and he gave a hundred and thirty percent of his own effort to lead by example. He had the prescience of a demigod and an uncanny ability to see a situation in full spectrum, even while he tracked details like a medieval monk working on an illustrated manuscript. As if that wasn't enough, the four men most loyal to him augmented his strength with equally impressive capabilities of their own.

Her lips curved in a rueful smile at the small but significant evidence of his capabilities. He'd brought her sweater. As he reached her, he shook it out, swept it around her shoulders, snugging it up around her collarbone. As he did, he touched her cheek in an affectionate caress and then lowered himself into a sideways seated position on the lounge chair across from her. As he opted to stretch his long legs out beside her crossed ankles, rather than staying flatfooted and having his knees up to his chin in the low lounge chair, she made a mental note to bring a chair up here more suitable for him. He'd never come up before, but she wasn't surprised he knew about the spot, or that he'd known to find her here.

If she had a chair up here that could accommodate a larger man, perhaps another man, one of a similar size, might one day join her.

"Did you need me for something?" Automatically, she checked to make sure her phone was still on forward.

"No, the universe is spinning adequately without either of us today." In a surprise move, Matt turned so he was stretched out on the lounge, adjusting the back so he was only slightly reclined, his feet braced on either side of it. He lifted his face to the sun as it re-emerged, closing his eyes. "Nice day."

"Hmm." She bent her head back to the shirt, focused on the button she was sewing. "How many times have you visited Angelica's webcam today? Or do you just keep it on full time now?"

"I've managed to limit myself to ten minutes every hour. Our nanny probably feels like she's under a microscope, but I just want to see her play with her fingers and toes."

"I hope Katherine is doing her job, not playing with her fingers and toes. Or any other part of her anatomy."

Matt snorted, didn't reply to that. He kept his eyes closed, one set of fingers casually resting on his thigh, the other holding the frame of the lounge by his head. He'd left his jacket below, so he had the sleeves of his white shirt rolled up. Pulling the needle through the similar shirt in her lap, Janet smiled, remembering the week Savannah had returned to work. It had taken awhile, Savannah needing to recuperate from the C-section and hysterectomy, and then on top of that she'd opted to stay home several months with Angelica, coordinating her workload with her executive staff from the house.

After several days of catching up at her office, Savannah had come by Matt's on the way to a lunch meeting. While the couple was talking in his office, Janet had overheard Matt teasing his wife. He was trying his best to convince her to turn on the webcam in her office, so he could watch her throughout the day, just like he did Angelica.

"Unlike you, I don't have four minions to run every aspect of my company," Savannah retorted. "And I refuse to indulge your twisted fantasies." There'd been laughter in her voice, however.

"Maybe I'm trying to indulge *your* twisted fantasies," Matt suggested.

"You just want access to proprietary information, and even offering to striptease for me in front of your computer isn't going to work. Now, if you have Lucas do a striptease, I might consider it."

Janet had glanced up to see Matt drawing his wife between his long legs where he had his hips braced on the edge of his desk. Savannah kept her arms stubbornly crossed until he snagged her wrist, pulling her all the way to him.

Always anticipating her boss's needs, Janet had pressed the button beneath her desk that closed the double doors with a silent whoosh of air. He only had ten minutes before his next meeting, and Savannah was just making a brief stop, but there were things other than sex that required privacy between a bonded couple. The tender way he drew her to him, the soft, knowing look in Savannah's eyes, despite her teasing, told Janet it was one of those times. Matt had almost lost his wife and child a few months ago, and he was still coming to terms with that, figuring out how once again to hold on tight out of love, not fear. A person had to risk freedom with the one he loved, to enrich the relationship with the qualities that came with standing alone as well as together.

She mulled on that. "Matt, did you know Max before he came to work for you?"

"For about a year or so, though most of our contact was as part of my interactions with other friends I have in the service. One of them sent him my way when Max left the SEALs."

She tied off the one button, snipped the threads with her small scissors. One down, three to go. Matt's eyes had opened, and he was studying what she was doing. She kept her attention on the shirt. She was *not* going to blush. She was not a blusher, even if there were very few reasons a man's shirt could have several buttons missing. Matt had seen her at the club, knew her Domme tendencies. For all he knew, she'd ripped the shirt off a sub as part of a session. That would make sense. But the tender, intimate act of sewing the buttons back on for said sub, when she could order him to do it and inspect it the next week as part of the ongoing game?

Not so much.

"You know, when SEALs go through training, they do uniform inspection. If a shoe isn't shined properly, or a button is loose, they lose points. Which means that every one of them knows how to sew a button on a shirt, probably as well as my tailor."

"That's an interesting factoid," she said, not faltering over her sewing in the slightest. "Why did he leave the SEALs?"

"You know I'm not going to tell you that." Matt straightened and turned, bringing his feet back to one side of the lounge again. He leaned forward, toyed with the button she'd sewn. "Tight and even. Maybe I should have you do my mending."

She swatted at his hand, making him draw back. "Right after I stab you in the eye with this needle."

He grinned, a devastating expression that could dribble a woman's heart in her chest like a manic basketball. Fortunately, she took daily inoculations against the charms of the K&A men. But Matt could affect her for reasons far beyond female hormones, and he proved it now, sobering.

"You've been distracted this week," her boss said, no censure in his tone. He understood her work ethic, her personal pride in perfection. He wasn't here to chastise her for sloppy work, because she hadn't done any. He just knew her.

"Somewhat." She nodded, pulling on the thread. "I'm working it out."

"Is he treating you well?"

"Probably better than I deserve."

Damn it. The jerk of reaction caused her to prick herself with the needle. Why had she said that?

As a drop of blood welled up from her forefinger, Matt picked up her hand, put it in his mouth. He sucked the blood away with a swirl of his tongue, then put his thumb over the tiny wound, his other fingers resting on her wrist, holding her in place. Most men, she'd pull away if they held her restrained like this, but not Matt.

"I didn't mean that. I shouldn't have said that."

"No, you shouldn't have. Because nothing is further from the truth." His dark eyes held hers.

"You're right. It's not true." She straightened her back, but she let her hand stay in his grip. "I'm all right."

"Better than." But his expression stayed serious. "He has some significant demons of his own, Janet. The difference is, he was trained up front to deal with them, and you had to learn on the back end. You both handle them damn well. They don't rule your lives. But like yours, his are still there. If he's vulnerable, if he lets his guard down, they can attack."

His expression became more thoughtful. "Throughout my life, because of my father and the contacts that continued after his death, I've been exposed to people in various branches of the military. SEALs are a unique breed. They're trained to keep everything close. They don't share with outsiders, not only because most of what they do and endure is classified, but because it's part of who and what they are. Keep that in mind.

"On a different note," he glanced at her, "a SEAL would make a hell of a Dom or sub, one because they're ambidextrous in a sense—trained to lead and follow. Also because they're machines, the way they process details. As a sub, he'd notice everything about a Mistress; how she feels, what she wants. He's not anticipating; he's actually in the now, watching the details, while another part of his brain is planning how to handle it. When the guy in charge tells you what to do, you stop what you're doing and do it, so he's immediately responsive."

Well, that was obvious, and why she got several different vibes from Max—Dom, sub and something that was neither.

Matt lifted his thumb, verified the blood had clotted and there wasn't anything that could get on Max's shirt. She thought of her boss's warm mouth on her skin. Her immunity to the K&A men's considerable sexual potency notwithstanding, her body was vibrating, every nerve ending now alive, because the touch of Matt's mouth had reminded her of Max's, between her legs. "That was a little unsanitary," she managed.

"The best treatments usually are." Matt gave her a wink, another brief touch on her cheek. "I better head out for my one o'clock. And yes, I opened the documents you sent me on my tablet, and they're all there. I have what I need, thanks to my infallible admin."

"Remember that at Christmas bonus time. The Mustang needs new tires, and I want to get her special rims."

Matt chuckled. "Those rims can come out of the exorbitant-but-worth-every-penny salary I pay you, but if she needs new tires, charge it through my expense account. And you'll still get that Christmas bonus." He moved toward the access door but paused with his hand on the latch. The look he gave her reminded Janet why very few crossed Matt Kensington.

"Don't cut yourself down like that again, Janet. I won't tolerate anyone treating you badly, and that includes yourself."

* * * * *

Max took the overpass walkway from the parking deck to the main building, then hit the stairs. He was between tasks and figured he'd do a pass by Janet's desk to see if she needed to go by her house before the dance class, so he could adjust his departure times accordingly. He'd be picking Dana up at the church at four, giving him plenty of time to get her home and swing back by, since Janet rarely left at five, due to projects Matt and the guys had had in process these past few months.

Since their night at the dock, he hadn't seen much of the woman who'd been uppermost in his thoughts. When he left her at her car at the club, she'd pushed his dress shirt off his shoulders, tucked it into the Mustang without explanation. He'd had all sorts of fantasies about her wearing it, only those one or two remaining buttons holding it closed over her bare body. She'd felt superb under his exploration, firm and soft in all the right places, arching up into his touch.

Because the limo drivers often doubled up as security during slow times, he had the same access to K&A as Randall. As a result, Max had come by her desk early that next day, before anyone else arrived. Only the dim security light had illuminated her command central area, and Matt and the other guys' offices were all locked up.

It felt right, leaving her a token. Nothing extraordinary, just a four-piece box of handmade truffles from a local chocolatier, and a handful of wildflowers from the dock area. He'd threaded them into the vase of white and yellow roses on her desk. The executive level always had fresh flowers, part of the ambiance, and he was pleased to see the ones he left complimented the roses. Would she notice? Thinking of how carefully she'd watched his every reaction the previous night, he expected she would.

That same day, she'd sent him a text. *Chocolate and flowers? Still angling for that second date?*

Always. Name the time and place, baby.

He'd added the teasing endearment on purpose and was rewarded with an emoticon in return, the one with the tongue stuck out. It kept him grinning, but true to what he'd expect of a woman of her nature, that had been their last interaction that week. He'd deduced she was going to hold off taking it any further until after the ballet class, both to torture him and to keep things slow, in control. That was all right. Of all people, he understood the value of timing, planning, strategy. It gave him time to plan his own.

As he stepped off the elevator, he detected a hint of tension in the air and found the source of it quickly enough. Janet was standing behind her desk, her fingertips resting on top of a stack of folders, her steely gaze fixed on Ben

O'Callahan, who was shrugging into his suit jacket with an impatient motion. Max recalled today's schedule, the details mapped in his head like a desk calendar. Wade was dropping him at Jackson Square for a lunch meet with the lawyers from Bally, Winslow and Martin.

"This isn't about that," Ben said, a hard edge to his tone. "I need to change my five p.m. appointment today to a different date. Jenkins and I—"

"I already spoke to Mr. Jenkins about that. He said he can meet you in the morning, and I moved your nine a.m. with Ellen Watkins to ten a.m. She said that worked better for her anyway."

"If we handle it tonight, it keeps the workload for tomorrow—"

"Exactly the same." Janet's jaw was set, though she didn't emanate any temper. Simple inflexibility, like a brick wall. "The decisions you made tonight wouldn't be typed up until tomorrow anyhow, and I'll make sure the paralegals put it top priority so it's all done before the end of the workday." She held out a handful of slips to him. "Here are your messages, none of which interfere with your five o'clock."

Ben approached her desk, eyes narrowed. Max wanted to take a few more steps into the area, be the knife to cut the tension, but he checked himself with effort. It would be foolish to defend Janet from a mere verbal assault, and one that came from a difficult man she handled regularly.

"I didn't authorize you to do any of that."

"No, you didn't. Aren't you glad I'm here to anticipate your needs?" Janet arched a brow.

"What if I decided I wanted my meet with Jenkins right back where the hell I wanted it?" Ben asked in a deceptively pleasant tone.

"I'd say he's probably made other plans by now, being just as busy and important a person as you are."

"Let me guess. You'll tell Matt if I skip my bloody five o'clock?"

"No." She held his gaze. "Are you asking me to do so?"

The lawyer pressed his lips together, the clash of wills going on for another ten seconds. Max reconsidered his idea of moving into the room, because for a moment Ben did in fact look like he might reach across and choke her. But Janet had that stapler close to hand. She'd brain him with it in a heartbeat.

"You," Ben plucked the pink message slips from her hand, "are Satan's Mistress."

"Flattery will get you everywhere." She gave him that ice-cool look, but her hand closed on his, squeezed briefly. "Go to the five o'clock, Ben."

That gesture evaporated the tension between them. The rueful twist of Ben's lips said that, whatever had happened, he knew she was right. His Irish temper was hot, but brief, and he didn't usually let himself off the hook for it, which he proved now. "Sorry, Janet."

She shook her head, tapped his wrist. "Give Nancy Adams a call on your way. She's the message on top. She just wants to know the projected filing date, and she's not a talker. If you know the date, I could do it."

"No, I'll do it. I need to charm her a bit for what I'm going to want from her in the future."

"Well, lesser miracles than you and charm have been known to happen."

"Nice. Tell Satan to send up some demons to give you a hand, so you can get out of here on time."

She gave him a suitably disdainful look in answer to that, and then he was headed to the elevators, shouldering his laptop bag as he went through the message notes.

Max noted the slight tension leave Janet's shoulders as Ben left her area. Then she noticed him and her gaze cleared, a smile curving her lips that warmed him from head to toe.

He sidled into the room, leaned against the corner by her printer table. Ben didn't take a limo to that five o'clock meeting, but his attitude toward it, and how regularly it occurred, made it pretty clear what it was, to a discreet staff that paid attention. It was a therapy session.

Ben was the most streetwise of the group, with a volatile Irish temper yet a fierce loyalty to all of them. Marcie, Cass' little sister, had been in love with him since her teens and just this year had gone to great lengths to prove he and she were meant to be together. Her stubbornness had convinced him. However, earlier in the year, when Marcie had come back into Ben's life, the man had been struggling with some nasty issues from his past, trying to drown them in alcohol.

Max had had a ringside seat when Ben's past and present had collided, and had witnessed the collateral damage it had caused. But the result was Ben was now getting help and seemed to be doing better. Of course, Max had buddies who'd had to get treatment for PTSD, and knew no man enjoyed the serious mind probing needed to get back on track, let alone one used to being in authority. Ben was the most hardcore sexual Dominant of all of the executive team, with serious control issues. Max wondered if his therapist took Valium before their sessions.

He liked a lot of things about Ben and wished him well, but he couldn't deny the knot of tension that had risen in his chest at the exchange between him and Janet. If Ben had reached across that desk in any way Max interpreted as a threat, he wouldn't have hesitated to put him on the ground. Hard. He wasn't going to let anyone touch her.

Okay, maybe he needed to step back, get his emotions under control. Anger and passion had their place, but not in executing a mission goal. He still hadn't really decided what his mission goal was with Janet, but the strategy had to be carefully thought out, not driven by reckless emotion. Then he thought about how she'd climaxed, crying out to the stars. Maybe reckless emotion had its place as well.

When he approached the desk, he couldn't help reaching out, touching the hand resting on the files. She had thin hands, elegant, but the knuckles were a little prominent due to the thinness. "Okay?"

She nodded. "Yes. Ben and I regularly lock horns."

"That was a little less good-natured than I've seen in the past."

"Yes. I think they're hitting some particularly rough areas in his sessions right now."

He appreciated that she didn't bother pretending he didn't know Ben was in therapy, even as he was impressed that she recognized how in tune he was with the comings and goings of his main charges. He supposed they shared that trait.

"I keep it marked on all their calendars," she continued, "which he doesn't know, but as a result, no one makes any meetings for him during that time, just like when Dana was doing physical therapy and Peter was going with her. They watch out for each other."

"And you watch out for them."

"It's what Satan's Mistress does," she said.

When she sat down at the desk, smoothing her skirt beneath her hips, he realized it had flustered her a little. He knew Ben didn't intimidate her, so that suggested something in Ben's struggle had resonated with her. He didn't comment on it, simply filed it away as he let her choose which way to go to regain her composure.

"Have you decided teenage girls terrify you and you're here to back out of the class?"

"Yes, teenage girls terrify me, but no, I'm not here to back out." He smiled at that. "I wanted to know if you need to go to your house beforehand."

She considered him with a bemused look that instantly made him wary. "How early can you take me?"

"Five o'clock. I need to run Dana home. You've been pretty slammed here though. I don't mind waiting around if you need to work later."

"No, I told Matt I'd be leaving on time today. There's something I want you to do beforehand, at my house. And no, I'm not going to tell you what it is."

Okay, wary moved right into alarm, but he covered it with a shrug. "Whatever you need."

She gave him that thoughtful look again. "Do you live here, Max? You never seem to leave."

He made a vague grunt. "I go get food. I never miss a meal. And I expect you know my home address already."

"I've got it on my stalker board at home. I'll show it to you."

"I'll bet." He let his gaze drift over her face, pause on her lips as he recalled their last kiss. "You're wearing a different gloss today." A different scent.

"Yes." Her look challenged him to try to find out what it was in exactly the same way he had last time. Matt's door was open. The man was sitting at his desk twenty feet away, on a call, but he had a clear shot of Janet's desk.

Max thought about meeting her challenge anyway, but they both knew he wouldn't take it further than that. That was part of the charge. But he better head back to the elevator, or his typical male reaction to such a challenge would become way too obvious.

"I'll see you at five, ma'am. Looking forward to it."

Her snort followed him to the elevator. When he stopped there and looked back, she was giving him a thorough appraisal. She didn't look away when he noticed, not embarrassed to be caught looking. From the direction of her glance, the way it shifted upward at her own leisurely pace, he had a pretty good idea she'd been studying his ass. He was wearing slacks and the K&A dark embroidered placket shirt, no sports coat over it at the moment. When he lifted a brow, she shrugged.

"That's sexual harassment," he muttered.

Despite the distance, she offered a seductive smile and picked up her pen. "Report me," she mouthed, and gave him a wink.

He grinned all the way back to the parking deck.

* * * * *

Matt decided to leave with Janet, as he was meeting Savannah in the French Quarter for an early dinner with Peter and Dana. They'd all been working long hours, so Max could tell Janet was pleased they were taking some time as couples. However, since Matt walked out with her when Max pulled the limo out to the front, there was no immediate one-on-one time.

Max kept an eye on her in the mirror, but she was still in full work mode, switching out papers with Matt for him to sign, their heads bent together as Matt showed her certain things he needed adjusted. He wanted them by tomorrow afternoon at the latest. With the dance class tonight, Max wondered when she would get any sleep. But she didn't seem concerned at all, merely agreeing it would be done.

As Matt exited the limo at Jackson Square, he gave Max a nod. "Take care of her." Those dark, hawklike eyes held his a moment, then Kensington turned and was striding across the street, a tall, powerful man who always drew attention. He crossed in front of one of the carriages, gave the dappled horse harnessed to it a fond pat on the nose before he cut through the park.

"Home, James," Janet said from the back. Max glanced up at her amused face in the rearview, then pulled away from the curb. "I notice you didn't ask for my address," she said.

"Because it's on *my* stalker board."

"Ah. I figured that was you outside my house this week, scratching on my windows. I'll leave some Windex out there so you can make yourself useful."

"Sounds like you need a gardener to cut back branches."

"Hmm. I prefer to do it myself. I like yard work."

"If you want, I can come help you do it this weekend. I'm pretty handy with pruners."

"I'm sorry. Bringing me to screaming orgasm in the back of your pickup is one thing. Helping me with yard work is moving way too fast. I'm feeling smothered. We may need to back off this relationship for a while."

He snorted. "You want to come sit up here? It might save your life, because I keep looking in the mirror to see you."

"Then I'm ordering you to stop looking at me." She slid out of his view then. A moment later, she was leaning against the seat directly behind him, her voice so close her breath touched his ear. "Just drive, Max."

She slid her hand around the side of the seat and found the open collar of his placket shirt, her thumb caressing the light layer of hair there. He was taught to focus on more than one thing at once, so he didn't have to tell her to stop to get her home safely. Not unless her hand dropped to his cock, in which case they might have a real problem. They didn't really cover cock teasing in combination with combat driving.

He couldn't resist covering her hand, though, interlacing his fingers with hers. "I've thought about you a lot this week. Missed you."

She was silent a moment, her fingers going still beneath his touch. He sensed a pressure against the seat, almost as if she'd rested her cheek against it. "I don't really do easy when it comes to relationships, Max. I prefer chess to checkers. Is that going to be a problem for you?"

"No ma'am. Not so far." To his way of thinking, learning the way his opponent played the game was to anticipate and get out ahead of them, make them play the game on his terms.

He sensed some of that between them, but something else too. Something that was more like checkers and chess mixed. He stroked her fingers. She was very responsive, every inch of her skin so aware of contact. He felt her concentration on that one stimulation. It made him want to touch a whole lot more of her.

Her Garden District house was built in the eighteen hundreds. It was a two-story with floor-to-ceiling front windows, large black shutters and an elaborate wrought iron railing on the second story. The front porch was flanked with a lush potted garden. He noted what she'd mentioned, that some of the surrounding vegetation and trees were growing a little wild, but in an appealing way. On the side of the house, vines twisted around the light post, which threw illumination along a cobbled garden path. She told him it led to a screened gazebo and porch in back. Two big concrete pineapples on either side of the front walkway welcomed visitors.

It was a nice place, and though Max was sure Matt Kensington paid her well, this type of home was beyond a secretary's salary. Perhaps an inheritance? For all that he knew about her at work, he realized there was little he knew of her outside it. She didn't speak with an accent. No Southern or Texas drawl, no Midwest flavoring. She spoke with precise, perfect English, like someone raised with a strict, disciplined education. Whether intended or not, it fed into the Domme side of her, making it easy to imagine her as a stern schoolmistress or haughty queen. From what he'd seen of her performance with Thor, that was just an element of the whole, genuine package. She was a woman who enjoyed control over a man, and could make him enjoy it as well, even if it wasn't necessarily a part of his nature as it was with Thor.

She pointed him to an alley to park the limo, and chose to walk with him rather than have him drop her off in front. She took him up to the house through a back cut-through, so he saw the garden space she'd created in her small backyard. It was obvious that, when in season, fresh vegetables and herbs grew in pleasant disarray next to more carefully designed flower beds and shrub groupings. In addition to the gazebo and porch, there was a screened pavilion in the yard so she could enjoy her garden at ground level without being eaten by the bugs. The porch had a saltwater spa she explained converted to a hot tub in the colder months. It was nine feet by six feet, a rectangular small pool.

She took him past it to the back door. Handing him the keys, she let him open the door. He stepped in, taking stock of their surroundings, then gestured to her to step in and lead the way.

Janet gave him a curious glance but said nothing. It wasn't the first time he'd seen her making note of his personal security detail training, but she was apparently like him, filing it away rather than bringing it up. At least not until it would be useful to their interactions.

Her interior layout was what he expected. Quality furniture choices, a little eclectic, but they worked together. She added touches of color with flowers and pillows as women did, but kept the walls a simple, clean white, accenting them with pictures. Over the sofa in the living area was a large oil painting of a ballerina. Her back was to the viewer, but she was stretched out on the floor of a dance studio, a bevy of milling ballerinas behind her in their gauzy white skirts. She was on her hip, one leg pointed and bent over the other, her back arched and hand gracefully lifted behind her head.

A matching painting on the adjacent corner showed a ballerina leaping in the air, that white flowing skirt making her look like a bird in flight. The leotard she wore was cut low between her small breasts, accenting the slim grace of her body. Her face was to the camera, but his attention returned to the one that wasn't. It was the central feature of the room as one came into it, meaning it had the most significance to her.

The space was comfortable, a haven for the woman who lived here. He could imagine she did some entertaining, but likely small groups of intimates. She wouldn't invite strangers or business acquaintances here. He'd bet money on it.

"Follow me upstairs." She touched his arm, moved up the steps, her fingers trailing the banister. She had her hair twisted on her nape, accentuating the delicate ears, the slender bones of her neck. It reminded him of the ballerina in the painting. His gaze followed its desired track down the trim lines of her suit where it nipped her waist, clung to the swell of her hips and ass, accented those gorgeous legs. She had on a slip beneath the skirt. He could see the edge of lace through the modest slit, a strange vulnerability that made his heart tighten. She'd stepped out of the shoes before she went up, and carried the low-heeled pumps in her hand.

He put his hand on the banister and followed her.

She turned the corner and vanished. When he reached the top of the wooden steps, he saw there was a side table in the hallway, holding a vase of flowers. Two small paintings flanked them, probably bought from the art district. They were New Orleans Blue Dog paintings, one where replicas of the dog lined a railroad track, and the other showing four images of him in a grid pattern. The whimsy of it reflected the woman herself. Controlled beauty with touches of the unpredictable, hints of the chaotic passion she could display as well. He was willing to put a lot of effort into making that last one happen again.

There was one photograph on the table as well. A young woman who looked like Janet, likely a sister. She had a soft prettiness that Janet did not, but Max saw it as a difference, not a shortcoming. Janet made up for it with her mesmerizing charisma. They shared a love of dance, because in the posed shot, the photo's subject reached for the ceiling, leg stretched out behind her, neck arched as she cast her gaze toward the stage. She wore the gauzy long skirt, her upper body clad in a brief top of satin and glitter.

"That's Nelle," Janet said, something odd in her voice. "She's not part of this."

When Max looked toward her, she was leaning against the doorframe of a room at the end of the hall, and she had something in her hands, a black piece of cloth with strings trailing from it. He decided to leave that peculiar statement alone, for now. He came toward her. Through the open doors he passed, he saw a guest bedroom, an extra bath and what appeared to be her home office. The rail followed the hallway, open to the foyer below.

"Stop there," she said, when he was about three feet from her. He would far prefer to close the distance between them, because he could feel her intent need and wanted to taste it, but he complied. There was a tranquility to the house he liked, a hushed presence that suggested it was a good space, a place guests would feel welcome, when she chose to make them so. What was swirling between them in the hall had a biting edge of the unknown, of risk and danger, but the kind that engaged his senses, sharpened them.

"I've been doing my homework," she said, "and learning more about your training. What they'll share online of course. The one that intrigued me was 'ditch and don'. Do you remember it?"

Where a SEAL was required to ditch his gear underwater and then put it back on, all without surfacing. If even a strap was out of place, he had to redo it until he got it right. Guys who made it through Hell Week sometimes didn't make it through the water phase, discovering they couldn't handle that sense of drowning, of lungs burning and still having to think, to stay focused on the task, the mission.

"I remember it."

While she threaded the black fabric, some kind of satin, through her fingers, he noticed she'd changed her nail polish to a deep burgundy. It matched what was on her lips beneath that gloss. Strawberry. That was this week's scent. Not a sickly sweet teenager's gloss. Just a faint fragrance that made him imagine her biting into the fruit, licking the juice from her lips, the red deepening the color of her tongue.

"I've come up with an exercise somewhat like that. I want you to help dress me for my class." Now she lifted the piece of fabric. "You'll wear this blindfold, so you have to do it all by touch and intelligence."

He extended his hand. "Let me see the mask."

She put it in his palm, her fingers whispering over it as she withdrew. It would cover his face fully, a hole for his mouth and nose, and lace down the back curve of his skull to ensure that he was fully blinded, no chance of cheating and catching a glimpse. He grimaced. A SEAL wasn't above cheating if needed to achieve the objective, because the point was winning. A fair fight, while an exciting challenge, always made that more difficult. He had a more important concern, however.

"If it's laced up, I can't get it off fast."

She pushed away from the doorway then. Even in her bare feet, she was as much a temptress as Medusa, making a man want to look at her, no matter the consequences. She put her hand on his wrist, moving the hand holding the mask out of her way to press against him. He'd donned his jacket for the ride, and now she slid her arm under it. Her fingers caressed the nine millimeter in the shoulder holster, then slid down his rib cage, to the pocket of his khakis. Dipping in there, she stroked his upper thigh and came back with a folded knife. He caught hold of her wrist as she brought it up between them, anticipating when she depressed the spring and the blade snapped out, wicked sharp, between them.

"You could cut the laces pretty quickly with this, but there won't be a need. This is just you and me. No threat, no danger. You'll be giving up control to me, obeying my will, performing this task to my satisfaction. Much like you did for your instructors. Giving them everything to earn their pleasure, their respect."

Imagining his hard-edged BUD/S instructors as Dominatrices, complete with boots and corsets, was an image he didn't necessarily want planted in his head, but it did loosen some of the tightness in his chest. He saw a smile flirting around her lips, a reassurance with the demand.

"I want something in return." He folded the knife, returned it to his pocket. She kept one hand light on his chest, her other hooked on his belt. She was so close, but he could feel that dense energy between them, a wall she wasn't yet ready to let down. It was intense, being this close to her and yet feeling held back by her will alone. He could shove through it, but he knew which doors were to be kicked down and which ones worked better with a knock.

She cocked her head. Waited, those dark eyes a seductress's tool.

"I want you to let your hair down. I want to see it before you blind me."

"Samson and Delilah." But she hesitated at the thought, glanced up at him. "I won't betray you, Max."

"I know that." He touched her hair. "I've often thought there was more to that story. I think she loved him, and they forced her to betray him, or tricked her into it. It probably destroyed her as much as it did him, in the end."

"I won't be tricked or forced. Not ever."

"No. Not you. And not me either." He gave her a significant look, and her lips curved in response. It made him want to bite her bottom lip. Instead, he waited, his fingers tightening on the satin face mask as she reached up, drew out the clips that held her hair. It tumbled down, a lovely set of waves and curls, all the way to her waist. He threaded his fingers through it, drew part of it over her right shoulder. He brought it to his face, nuzzling it with his lips. Her fingers tightened on his belt, and her head dipped, her crown brushing against his cheek, a gesture of intimate affection. Taking a deep breath, he resisted every urge he had to kick that door down, and gripped the hand at his belt, transferring the mask to her other one. Then he stepped back. "Will you leave it down?"

She nodded. "At least until we go to class. I need it out of the way for that."

He was tall and she wasn't, so it didn't take much thinking to decide what to do to make it easier for her to put the mask on him. But he well understood the significance of him doing so.

He dropped to his knees.

Chapter Six

The expression on her face was overwhelming, overpowering. Sometimes, like this, he felt as if he was standing inside her. Her reaction to his willingness to surrender was something that stopped his mind, made him accept—at least in this moment—that there were things they drew out of one another that couldn't be defined, classified. Things he hadn't considered ever giving to a woman. For her part, she'd taken the time and care to research a significant aspect of who he was, tied her own desires to things familiar to him, challenges he'd met. It was diabolical, unexpected…and entirely impossible for him to resist.

She moved behind him. In bare feet, she had the walk of a ballerina, leading with a pointed toe, an arched foot, as if she was treading across the stage to begin a performance, and he expected she was. As she stepped over his bent legs, the toe of the non-leading foot slid across his calf, an intentional caress. She put the mask on his face, leaning forward to ensure the placement of the nose and mouth holes. The fabric stretched, allowing adjustment. Her hair fell onto his shoulder as she bent over him, and he lifted his hand to stroke a thick strand of it, drawing it out straight.

She was lacing the back of the mask. As it tightened over his forehead, the bridge of his nose, around the corners of his mouth, it reminded him of the hood of a diving suit. He had a picture of himself in one of those, without the diving mask that usually went over it. His sister had told him it looked like the coif a knight wore beneath his mail.

That shit had no place here. He'd intended to release Janet's hair, let it ease back into its natural wave. Instead, at the thought, his grip tightened.

Janet's hand overlapped his, held. "Put your hand at your side," she said unobtrusively. "It's all right. This will make you feel things, Max. It always does."

He'd question how she could tell things had taken an odd turn for him, but he expected it was the same way snipers did it. He'd done some of that in Iraq. He wasn't the best at it, not his go-to skill, but every SEAL knew how to perform adequately at five hundred yards. He'd watched and improved from the guys who had a natural talent for it, and quickly discovered an exceptional sniper was about more than marksmanship. From hundreds of yards away, they would gauge the intent of a potential enemy from his body language alone, determining if he was carrying a bomb on the back of his bicycle or just pedaling groceries home to the family. Every movement meant something.

He put his hands at his sides, focused on how she felt, her hands working along the back of his skull, her leg pressing against his side. When she was done, she spread her fingers over his face, let them whisper over his blindfolded eyes, his cheeks, tease his lips. He kissed them, brushing his mouth over her polished nails. She lingered there, let him keep nuzzling her knuckles, take nips of her flesh. She pressed her body closer against his back, telegraphing her elevated response. The mask was like a second skin, the thin barrier and the removal of his sight ironically increasing his sensitivity to her lightest touch on his face.

"On your feet. I'll guide you into the bedroom."

She hadn't let him see the bedroom, so he was entering unfamiliar terrain. It had her scent though, that female mix of the things she wore. Lotions, lip gloss. He also smelled apples. She'd taken his hand as he got to his feet, and stayed at his side, her other hand on the small of his back, their bodies overlapping to get through the door. She remained that close as they entered the room, likely to keep him from running into anything. He was reminded of the one or two ballet productions he'd seen in his life, where partnered dancers crossed the stage in such a way. One technically guiding the steps of the other, one to lead, one to follow, but that could reverse in a heartbeat, if the dance required something different. SEALs could both lead and follow, adapting to change as needed.

She guided his hand to a carved wooden post. "This is my bed. The clothes I wear to class are lying on it. You must dress me in each piece, and get it exactly right. When you're done, I'll remove the mask. Unlike your instructors, I won't be timing you, but you will get points for style."

The comment came with a faint trace of humor and sexual tension. It made the room seem warmer, closer. Having no ability to see increased his focus on her voice all the more, but in a way it was no different than when he had her in the back of the limo with Matt or one of the other men. Max listened to the rise and fall of her voice, the emotions knitted into every sentence. Humor, exasperation, admonishment. Her intelligence and insight during serious discussions. It was how he'd figured out she had no accent, no tell that placed her in a particular part of the country.

There was a riveting quality to her voice as well. Until now, he hadn't been able to clearly define what it was, but here it was unleashed and obvious. A sharp sexual confidence, capable of drawing a man to her like the laces drawing the mask tight against his face. It was also potent enough to keep a man at arms' length when needed. *I can give you your fantasies, but only on my terms,* was what that voice said. *And only if you beg.* Something about that voice made a man want to beg, sure that what she offered would be worth it.

She didn't ask him to beg, but he suspected that was because she sought something different from him. Maybe they were both in uncharted territory.

"Do I have the pleasure of undressing you first?" he asked, turning in her direction.

"It will be difficult to dress me without doing so," she confirmed. "You may begin."

First he explored the bed, finding the clothes. He identified each piece by recalling her pictures downstairs, as well as any movies or TV shows where there'd been ballet classes. They wore the things that were like one-piece swimsuits, but with sleeves. A leotard. He recognized that by the stretchy fabric, intrigued in a typical male way by the snaps at the crotch. The next thing took more time to identify. He lifted it, sifting it through his fingers. The silky fabric felt like an apron, with long string ties. Then he found the slit in the waistband and realized the ties would thread through, forming a short wraparound skirt. The next item gave him a chuckle.

"Even women have trouble putting these on themselves," he complained amiably. It was a pair of filmy tights. He found no underwear or bra. "Are questions allowed?"

"Only a couple, and only if I think they're relevant. So ask wisely."

"Do you wear panties or bra under these?"

"No. Modesty panels are built into the leotard, and I'm too small-breasted for the support to be necessary."

"Your breasts look just fine to me."

"So says the blindfolded man. Thank you, but I wasn't criticizing myself."

"Sorry. Forgot I was dealing with a miracle—a woman happy with her body. Glad we share that opinion." It was a truth he hadn't considered before. In the time he'd known her, he'd never seen or heard her demonstrate self-deprecating behavior about weight, age, hair. She put herself together well and had a straightforward confidence about that.

"I'll let it go this time."

He found a pair of worn canvas slippers that he expected were ballet shoes, given the feel of the soles, and the elastic bands over the top of the foot to hold the shoe on. Running his hands all the way up to a plethora of pillows, he found nothing else, but was thorough about it, moving to the end and then working his way around the bed to the other side. She'd moved out of range, for she was no longer at the end of the bed, but he could sense her presence in the room easily enough. Her scent, the slight catch of her breath, was to his left, so she was by the door.

He noticed she had a king-sized bed, a lot of mattress for one woman, and it was impossible not to imagine sharing it with her. Did she ever invite that kind of intimacy with a man? Not likely, since her sex life seemed confined to the club. Until now. What would it be like to wake up draped over her, her soft ass against his groin first thing in the morning, that perfect small breast cupped in his hand?

When he reached the bottom of the quilted spread on this side, he hit something small. Jewelry. He caught the ball-shaped earrings, perhaps pearls, before his big fingers sent them popping off the cover like grasshoppers.

"Woman, you are evil."

"I'm disappointed. I would have loved to see you on your elbows and knees, hunting for my earrings."

He snorted. "I'll bet."

There was a necklace, a chain with a charm on it. The charm was too small for him to discern the shape. He wouldn't waste a question on that, since he'd find out once the mask was removed. Of course, now that he knew he had to get her into tights, he had a feeling it might never be removed.

He went someplace in his head he usually preferred not to go. He thought about dressing Amanda for church. Okay, tights had that toe seam, and a tag in the back, like underwear. Unless his diabolical tormentor had removed it. Thank God, they didn't come with the seam up the back of the leg like the nylons Marcie preferred to wear. She worked for Savannah's company, Tennyson Industries, but whenever she came to the office to meet Ben for lunch, that provocative look could make any man with a pulse walk into walls.

"I said no time limit, but our time is not unlimited."

He straightened. Circling the bed, using the posts for guides, he moved toward her voice. She was standing approximately three paces from the bed, but she stopped him at two, her hand grazing his chest to bring him to a halt. His brow creased beneath the mask at her silence. Was she just studying him? "I wanted to be sure I knew what and where everything was before I undressed you," he explained his thoroughness. "Didn't want you to stand there being cold. The necklace and earrings were a good trap."

"I wasn't sure you'd find them."

Okay, that gave him a clue. There was an odd note in her voice that made him reach out. She lifted her arm again, but this time he wasn't put off, following her wrist down to her elbow, then to her upper arm, closing the distance between them. He fingered her earlobe, locating the gold teardrops he remembered she was wearing, then moved down her throat, to the simple strand of pearls. He wouldn't remove the earrings until he was ready to insert the others, using them as a guide.

"The necklace, it has meaning, doesn't it?"

She said nothing, and he let it be. Instead, he put his hands to her waist, unbuttoned the suit jacket she wore. It was a pretty thing that weighed almost nothing. As he slipped it off her shoulders, feeling the welcome silk of her skin since she wore a sleeveless shell, a wave of that strawberry smell, mixed with some vanilla, reached his nose.

"Are you wearing that perfume between your legs? Because I'd love to taste it there."

She put her fingers on his lips, an admonishment, but he felt the promising quiver in her fingertips. "No more talking, sailor. That's an order."

"Roger that." Her body shifted under his hands, her arms lifting so he could pull the shell from her waistband, take it over her head. Her breasts, the weight of them pressing against the lacy cups of her bra, brushed his shirt front. He imagined the stretch of her body, the tilt of her rib cage. He couldn't wait to watch her dance. He couldn't wait to do a lot of things.

Putting his arm around her waist, holding her there with a palm on her ass, he bent to drop a kiss between the cleft of her breasts. To avoid rebuke, he multitasked, unhooking her bra at the same time. The straps tumbled down her shoulders, sliding over his knuckles where he'd moved his hands to her upper arms. He took the opportunity to press a more insistent kiss on the rise of her right breast. He knew the nipple would be pearling up into a tight point, so close to his mouth. Before she could reprove him, he backed toward the bed, keeping his arm around her waist so she moved with him. He laid the bra on the bed, then felt for the side zipper of her skirt. A whisper of cloth, and the lined garment fell to her feet. Dropping to one knee, he put her hand on his shoulder. "I've got you. Just step out of it."

When she did, he folded the skirt and set it on the bra. He followed her leg up to her thigh, then prayed for restraint as he found she was wearing lacy thigh highs. The bloody woman was standing before him in a scrap of underwear, no bra and thigh-high stockings. Everything in him wanted to pull out his knife, slice off the mask. His cock was already hard and he was sure quite visible against the hold of his khakis. Her fingers slid over his shoulder, along the side of his neck, those lethal nails scraping, conveying her need. He wasn't the only one affected. His blind state was arousing her as well, her breath becoming more erratic.

If he stood up now, captured her mouth in his, would she call it game over, let him take her on that king-sized bed, plow into her wet folds, get lost in it with him? But this was part of it, wasn't it? For as impatient as he was now, what would it be like when he had his task completed, mission accomplished, proving he could do as she desired? He would be nearly insane with lust, her body would be willing and wet. Even so, he already anticipated she would make them wait until after her class. Because that was the game for her. Denial and teasing, until the power of it would overwhelm them both. It could result in a quick violent fuck, but he expected once drawn out to a certain point, such mutual arousal would reach a level where the culmination would slow down, having become too excruciatingly powerful to rush. Like this.

When she worked men at the club, there was a clean line to the power exchange, everything resting in her hands, her shaping the sub's reaction like a sculptor. At the end of a session, he could tell she was satisfied by her work of art, yet she was still separate from it, washing the clay from her hands before she returned to the real world. She was testing different waters with him. At the end of their night, there would be no separation. He was going to make damn sure of it.

He wanted to inspire lingering feelings. When she was at work, he wanted her fingers to still on her keyboard as she thought of his mouth, his touch, the way he thought of hers, the maze behind her dark eyes. Instead of being washed off, the clay would dry on their skin, making them both part of the sculpture.

He knew she had concerns about that kind of closeness. When it was managed well, fear guided a man or woman, helped him or her make wise choices. She was a woman who managed her fear quite well in that regard, but he still sensed it there. He wanted to bring her to the point she understood he didn't have to be a sculpture at all, but a living, breathing part of her own soul.

Wow. That was unexpected. He stopped, taking a breath. She was right. Wearing the blindfold took the mind into some unlikely places.

Hooking the top of one stocking, he slid it down her gorgeous leg, taking advantage to liberally caress the length of it. He pressed a kiss on the inside of her thigh, right where the lace had held the stocking fast. She gripped his shoulder as she shifted her feet, let him pull the nylon free. "Your coat." Her voice was strained. "I want it off."

He nodded, shrugged free of it. She took it from him, turning away but staying within touching distance. He realized she was draping it over something behind her, probably a chair.

"I'll let you keep the gun. In case you feel the need to defend yourself."

He pressed his lips together at that, merely removing the other stocking the way he had the first. Only this time, with her back to him, he had the pleasure of letting his thumbs slide down the tender crevice of her knee. She held on to the chair to balance as he pulled it free.

He held both delicate pieces in one hand as he rose. Her buttocks brushed the front of his slacks. With his greater height, he let the stockings slide along her shoulder, the side of her throat, then down her back. As she stayed still, her body vibrating with sensation he could feel, he trailed the fabric down her arm, to her wrist. When he began to wind it around that slim target, she tensed.

"No," she said. But she didn't move away. Her hand balled into a fist beneath his hold, the wrist flexing. Though he couldn't see her face, he felt that tension that had emanated so strongly from her twice. In the hospital and then again at the club.

Someone had hurt this woman. Hurt her badly, violently. And though it was ironic that it called up related feelings inside him, a fierce desire to visit on her attacker threefold whatever had been done to her, he had the self-awareness, and the understanding of her state of mind, to yoke it back so it couldn't interfere with this moment. Any more than it was already doing.

"No," she said again, her fingers flexing against the light hold of the nylon. "That's not part of this."

The same thing she'd said about the picture in the hallway. Her boundaries were bold black marks in the sand. Despite himself, a twinge of resentment caught him. It was all right to blindfold and impede his senses, but not to restrain her? But then he remembered Thor. As tough a Mistress as she appeared to be, she didn't bind him. He'd never seen her bind anyone, except in a symbolic way. A light wrap or easy-to-break cuffs. The illusion of restraint. Of course, she was so good at this, that was really all she needed, wasn't it?

When he did another wrap around her wrist, her tension increased proportionately. "Max," she said more sharply.

He pressed closer, slid his arm around her waist, fingers drifting to the waistband of her panties. He took his palm in a slow, easy glide over her mound, resting his fingers on her upper thigh. "I don't believe I'm braver than you are, Mistress."

The honorific came easily to his lips. She stilled as he spoke it, her focus now on something else. He shifted, slid his hand down her other arm in a reassurance before drawing it behind her. She quivered harder as he put the two wrists together with a simple twist tie. It wasn't tight at all. She could get out of it in a blink, far quicker and more easily than he could free himself of the mask.

"It's just for a moment. I want to imagine you tied like this, even if I can't see you. Your shoulders drawn back, your breasts thrust out. The flush on your cheeks, your hair falling over your body, dressed only in your panties. And I want to do this."

Kneeling behind her, he put his hands on her hips. He bent over those tied hands and put his lips on them, kissing her palms and curling fingers. He cruised over her ass, tongue teasing the seam between her cheeks through the silk as she shuddered. He went lower, explored that sweet crevice where the buttocks and thighs met, revealed by the high rise of the undergarment. When he nuzzled the sensitive intersection point, his tongue pressing briefly against the perineum, she let out a soft noise. Then he drew back, his thumb caressing the crotch of her panties before he hooked his fingers in the sides and took the last garment to her ankles.

He kissed the backs of her knees, her upper thighs, moving around her so he was on his knees before her. He kept his hands on her hips and lifted his face, nostrils flaring and all senses tuned for her reaction. Her focus was fully on him, he could feel the heat of it, and she was tight as a drum beneath his hands, as if she'd turned all that quivering energy inward.

When he straightened, standing on his knees instead of resting on his heels, he caught her loose hair in his hands, twisted it. "Kiss me, Mistress," he murmured. "I need your mouth."

The heat and wetness of it was enough to make him groan with pleasure, especially when she let out a matching, more feminine sound. Reaching behind her, he untwisted the nylons from her hands and then banded his arms around her hips as she cupped his face, holding on to him tightly as the kiss deepened. He broke it to move down to her breasts, finding her through the curtain of hair to cup those pretty curves and tease them with the heat of his mouth. She brought him to a halt by pressing against his shoulders and stepping back, her breath ragged.

"My clothes, Max. Dress me."

Her tone was determined, even if it wasn't entirely steady. She'd reclaimed the reins. He got back on his feet, with reluctance and some physical difficulty. She noticed the latter, her clever, firm fingers cupping him through his slacks. At her purring sound of approval, he growled. A warning that he could only be pushed so far, especially since, on his knees, he'd clearly scented how hot and willing her body was at this point.

When he turned back to the bed, he almost made the mistake of going for the leotard first. Realizing his error just as he had his hand on the garment, he switched to the tights instead.

"I'm in the chair, Max."

He knew she'd shifted away from him, had heard the give of the cushion, the faint creak of the wood, and followed the sound, touching her knee, the arm of the chair. He knelt at her feet, working one leg of the tights up into a folded circle in his hand. As he did it, he was hit by an unexpected vision, and the flood of emotions that accompanied it.

Child-sized black patent shoes, the strap buckle a tiny pewter flower. *You put the tights on first, silly.* Amanda teasing him, an imperious four-year-old then. She'd asked if she could wear her pink dress to church.

He closed his eyes beneath the blindfold and clutched the tights hard enough he was glad they weren't as thin as the nylons. Else he'd rip right through them. "Can you speak to me while I do this part?"

He needed to hear a woman's voice to remind him where he was, what he was doing. Janet's voice especially. He knew how to manage this kind of memory invasion, but this one was a little stronger than he usually handled in mixed company. He didn't want his shit to fuck things up.

Given how attentive she'd been when she was putting the blindfold on him, he shouldn't have been surprised that she understood and acquiesced without any coy games or challenging questions. He guessed he'd overestimated how much he could scramble her brain with his physical prowess. Of course the woman's self-discipline was legendary. He'd have to work on that. Though at the moment, he was grateful for her ability to recover her composure quickly.

Her fingers slid through his hair. "Matt's noticed us. He talked to me about you."

Max grunted, figuring out the toe seam and working it over her foot. She had trim toenails, expected for a woman he'd yet to see without stockings on her legs. "Yeah. He gave me a 'look' when he left the car tonight. If that's a hint of what Angelica's dates are in for, she'll be lucky if anyone will be brave enough to ask her out."

"I bet a SEAL would be brave enough." She tugged his hair.

"SEALs aren't scared of anything," he agreed, and smiled when she chuckled at him. He noticed her second toe had a swollen joint to it, and there was an unevenness along the outside edge of her big toe, like a scar. When his fingers passed firmly over her arch, he sensed an indrawn breath, a sound of pleasure, and he took an extra moment to massage there, some of his tension easing when she purred, no other word for it.

"Oh…God, you're good at that."

"Is this why you don't wear spiky heels like Alice? Because you have bad feet?"

He detected a hesitation, as if he'd touched on the edges of something more important. "It's very impolite to say that to a woman," she said at last. "But yes. Years of ballet dancing gives many of us foot problems. Which makes what you're doing feel…so…damn…good."

"My pleasure, Mistress."

"You're good at that as well. Knowing just when to call me that so it works for us both."

"I'm a quick study." Reluctantly, he stopped with the foot massage but figured he'd give her a more thorough one, of both feet, after her class. He worked the tights up to her knee, then got the other foot started and up to the same level. Curling an arm around her waist once again, he brought her to her feet. She was completely naked except for that one garment at her knees, and it was a unique experience, to be blindfolded, somewhat at her mercy, even though he was the one fully dressed. She was an artist at what she did, explaining why she had a strong following at the club. But none of those males had ever been here now, in her home. He'd bet on that too.

He worked the tights up her thighs, thought again how few women would be confident enough to let a man be this intimate with their bodies. He had to put his hand inside the tights, find the cotton crotch panel to be sure it was aligned correctly, which gave him the opportunity to brush his knuckles along her labia, feel the moisture there.

Her hand settled on his shirt sleeve, gripping, her forehead briefly pressed to his shoulder as he rose to finish the task, sliding the tights all the way up over her hips. Then he necessarily—and pleasurably—had to run his hands down her body, under and over, to make sure everything was straight and in place, which put him on his heels as he touched her feet, double-checked the toe seams. Perfectly straight, following the bump of her toenails. His instructors would be proud, though he could only imagine their expressions if they knew how he was applying his "ditch-and-don" skill.

Next came the leotard, which was easier, and had the added bonus of requiring him to feel his way around her breasts to be sure the modesty panel was aligned properly. He rubbed his thumb over her nipple, kneaded the breasts until she gave him another breathless admonishment. As well as a gratifyingly reluctant reminder they needed to leave soon to be on time for the class.

That just left the skirt, slippers and jewelry. The first two were quickly done. He worked the earrings in behind the ones he removed, then it was time to do the necklace. She turned for him, putting her buttocks against his hard groin. If she rotated her hips on him, he'd have purred a little himself, but the way she kind of melted back into him, from shoulder blades to the firm ass, was intimate in a different, more moving way, especially when she turned her face so her cheek pressed against his biceps.

She lifted her chin as he guided the necklace around her neck. After he fastened it, he put his arms around her waist to hold her still. Kissing her throat, he nuzzled her beautiful hair again. "Did I pass, Instructor J?"

She didn't respond. She'd tucked her head at an angle that suggested her eyes were closed, one of them pressed into the crease between his shoulder and chest. She'd gone somewhere else, taken there by this moment. He tightened his hold around her. "Janet. Okay?"

She nodded. He stayed silent then, just holding her, letting her deal with whatever had gripped her, making sure she could use the strength of his body and arms to get her through it. She'd become tense all of a sudden, as if fighting something, and he turned her around to press a kiss on her brow, her eye, her nose, finally brushing her lips. Her hands clutched his arms, and she drew a deep breath.

"Yes," she said, her voice normal and even. "You passed."

Chapter Seven
ಐ

"A good beginning for learning lifts is what we rather inelegantly call the fish dive, though if you've ever watched a school of fish dive, there's nothing inelegant about it. They swoop fearlessly toward the ocean floor, with unconscious grace."

Max sat at the back of the class. The community center's room for the dance lessons had a wall of mirrors that sported a long bar for warm-ups. The wooden floor was worn shiny and smooth by the many feet that had pounded, tapped, scuffed or tripped across it. Janet had said it was used for everything from Pilates to yoga to Zumba.

As she'd predicted, he'd been treated to a lot of shy looks and giggles. He expected she was fully aware that such behavior was pretty intimidating to a man, especially when he was the lone male among a pack of teenage girls. Eventually she took pity on him, however, calling the class to order with a commanding tap of a cane. The girls responded with the same mixture of terror and respect that Janet generally inspired at K&A.

They'd done warm-ups, and Janet had groups of three show her how they were doing on combinations they'd learned in previous classes, correcting where necessary with a tap of the cane or demonstration. She was sparse with praise, but as such, a simple nod or lack of correction was enough to make a girl glow. When she showed them a step or movement, the skill she possessed was evident. He thought of the picture of the soaring ballet dancer over her couch. Had she once been able to do that? If so, not any more. As the dance class progressed, the cane she used to tap time or point for correction became a prop for subtle leaning as well. He'd definitely be sure to give her that foot massage tonight.

Thinking about it, he realized even her sheerest stockings had a glimmer to them, the kind of thing that would hide scars. When he'd put on her tights, he hadn't done a thorough exploration of her skin, much as he'd desired to do so. The problem could be joint pain or those foot problems she'd mentioned, but he felt a desire to find out. He was starting to have a desire to find out everything about her.

Bringing his attention back to the class, he found Janet had moved on to the routine they were putting together for a Christmas recital. By the time the dancers were in the last thirty minutes of the two-hour class, they were sweating, but not a one of them slacked off. He didn't think they would dare. At one point, a student had forgotten to turn off her cell phone. When it chirped from the tote bag hung on the back wall, the offending student had practically flown over there to silence it beneath Janet's withering look. "So sorry, Madame, so sorry."

He found that curious, how they all called her that. He didn't know enough about ballet to know if it was a typical address for a teacher or not, but it suited her quite well.

"You've worked hard tonight." Janet stood at the front of the class now, continuing her discussion of the lift. "Once we combine with the male class to bring together our recital routine, several of you will be chosen to perform the 'fish dive'. As such, we're going to spend the last thirty minutes introducing you to it."

There were excited murmurs, the girls catching hands to squeeze and express their pleasure with the idea. Janet gave them precisely ten seconds to settle down, then quelled any further reaction with her look. "You've all noticed I've brought a friend tonight. He's here to help teach the lift, given that he is far better equipped to lift you than I am."

When she glanced back at Max, her lips quivered as the girls giggled. Max did his best not to humiliate himself with a damn blush. The woman was a sadist.

"The first hurdle you must overcome with lifts is your fear of falling. You must have utter confidence in your partner. If you cannot have that, you must overcome that regardless and be like the fish, diving fearlessly, concentrating on the execution of the move itself, stepping outside of yourself. However, tonight I want the confidence portion to be an irrelevant issue, so you can focus on the form." Her gaze swept over them. "As you know, your well-being is always my primary concern."

Despite her strict demeanor, tiny smiles appeared on several girls' faces, some reflecting adoration. It told Max they trusted their teacher, believed in her regard for them. She had that effect on people.

"Max will keep you safe. He has my complete confidence." Her gaze touched him briefly, then moved back to her class. "To assure you of that, he's going to demonstrate the lift with me first. Since I am a heavy old broad, this will prove to you how easy lifting each of you will be for him."

The girls laughed, making faces, and Janet allowed them a small, tight smile. Max shook his head at her but rose, coming to the front of the room.

"He should be wearing proper attire, but being that he is male and therefore entirely stubborn, we shall have to deal with him in this." Janet cast a disparaging look at the jeans and T-shirt he'd donned from the bag of spare clothes he kept in his trunk.

"The only attire you had available were tights," he muttered. The girls tittered and Janet's lips twitched.

"Even so." She set aside her stick and came to stand before him. "To start, you will be in *arabesque en pointe*. No toe shoes tonight though. The ball of the foot will be sufficient. There's enough to think about without making it that complex." She assumed the proper position and nodded without looking at Max. He bent his knee to give added support to the move, just as she'd instructed him during their warm-up before the class arrived.

"He's putting his arm around my waist, just below my rib cage. His right arm goes over and around the right thigh, just above the knee. Now he will dip me toward the ground, arms in this position."

As she demonstrated, reaching out with graceful arms and fingertips, Max lifted her and dipped her to the floor. The girls oohed softly, and he could see the more ambitious ones already imagining themselves in the same position.

"You'll bend the straight leg and touch your toes to your right knee," Janet continued from her suspended pose. "This is the parallel *passé*. Be sure and use your core muscles to pull you upright." She passed her fingers over her upper and lower abdomen, drawing their eyes to that. It seemed like second nature to her to be held nearly upside down, feet nowhere near the ground. "As always, I expect to see clean lines. The arch of your back curves you in toward your partner. The moment you are dancing with another, there should be a romance to the bodies working together. It's what your audience wants to see, and it will draw them into the movement, win their hearts."

When she stopped instructing to show the move, arching back into Max, she looked up at him. Though he knew their sexual intimacy helped, he felt what she was describing, her body fitted into the angles of his, conveying her trust in his hold. As he glanced at the mirror, their position reminded him of the melded sculpture idea that had crossed his mind earlier. It gave him a far greater appreciation for ballet choreography, as well as the strength it required. He felt a brief quiver beneath his hold now, telling him she couldn't hold this pose indefinitely. But her ease and skill in demonstrating it suggested that, at one time, she could have.

"You'll exit the lift by straightening the left leg when he begins to dip you down again. Finish in *arabesque en pointe* as you started. And there we are. Yes, Tasha, we may begin with you."

For the next thirty minutes, he took each girl through the lift, with Janet circling them, using taps of the stick to encourage a lifting of the body here, a straightening of the leg there. From having a teenage sister, he knew how, when it mattered, they could go from an apparent complete lack of focus, giggling and chattering, to this. Though most fluttered and blushed a little if they met his gaze, once they started working on the lift, all of them focused on Janet's instruction.

Thinking of the repetitive activities his instructors had inflicted on him in BUD/S to teach focus and attention to detail, he realized Janet's pre-class clothing exercise might have been to determine if he had the attention span to do this. He had to follow the same form, over and over, and adjust as needed. He felt almost as proud as her students when Janet only had to correct *his* form twice.

By the end of class, he also had a much keener respect for the strength and balance of a male ballet dancer. He'd had the stamina to get through, but he knew it would take someone with his level of fitness to lift and hold twelve different girls in the prescribed position multiple times over thirty minutes. A few of those guys might have what it took to get through BUD/S. Despite the tights.

Over the last fifteen minutes of class, parents started arriving. The way they tiptoed in, lining up against the back wall to watch, immediately checking their cell phones to ensure they were off, it was obvious Janet didn't limit her severe chastising on proper behavior to her students alone.

The last student had hung back until the end. During the class, he'd noted she worked as hard, perhaps harder, than everyone else, though she didn't have the same aptitude for it. She was a year or so younger, maybe twelve, and though she wasn't precisely overweight, she was suffering from the baby fat that could be normal for girls in their early teens. She was hesitant when they got started, but by the time they'd been through the lift several times, she had it, and she positively glowed when he high-fived her. Amanda smiled like that, when she was unexpectedly pleased by something.

"Madame, I felt like a feather."

"You looked like one. Good form. You've been working on your lines, and it shows." Janet put a brief hand on her red hair. "All right, class, that's it for tonight. Practice your recital moves and the new moves I've taught you, with the exception of this one. Until we've performed it a few times here, I do not want you enlisting a male friend to help you work on this elsewhere. Mr. Ackerman received thorough instruction from me. Anyone doing a lift must have similar instruction or they could injure you. They could also injure themselves if they haven't warmed up properly. I know many of you have a great deal of initiative — it's why you are in this advanced class — but I want to hear each of you promise me not to practice this move outside of class."

She waited until each girl said, "Yes, Madame," to her directly, then she nodded. "Very well. Get your things, and I will see you in two weeks. As usual, I will be here for the next thirty minutes if there's anything you need to discuss with me or any other movements you wish me to repeat. To the rest of you, good night."

As several of the girls lingered, obviously wanting to ask her further questions, he touched her arm. "Janet, I'll just hang out in the corner. No rush at all."

She nodded, but one of the girls fixed him with a reproving look. "Everyone calls her Madame while in class. We all agreed."

He nodded solemnly. "My apologies. I obviously need more thorough instruction. I'll just be over here in the corner if you need me, *Madame*."

"Thank you, Mr. Ackerman." The look she flashed him said she'd be more than happy to give him that instruction, and that she might make him pay dearly for teasing her. He hid his grin as he returned to his chair.

As he took a seat, the one girl who hadn't blushed and fluttered when he did the lift with her sat down in the chair next to him. Since the chairs were all pushed together, her hip was brushing his. She met his gaze with a bold stare and inviting smile. Tasha was obviously one of Janet's top students, the first to step forward for the lift and when Janet required proof of their practice earlier in the class. She also had the feline smile and brazen confidence of a barfly. Unfortunately, she had the dangerous looks to go with it. She had jewel-blue eyes and long black hair, which she'd now unbraided and was stroking her fingers through, letting it pour in a silken curtain over her shoulders. Since she was all of fourteen years old, any intelligent man would steer clear, recognizing pure trouble when he saw it.

Tasha's parent apparently had not yet arrived for her. Since his chair was at the end, and there was fortunately another foot of wall space, he scooted his chair out, removing the physical contact between them. Her gaze faltered somewhat, and he glimpsed the uncertain child beneath the wannabe siren. Then the feline smile returned. "I enjoyed our lift together," she said. "You're very strong."

He shrugged. "You don't weigh that much."

Those lips curved farther. She wore too much lipstick. He wondered if he was getting too old, since he found himself wanting to get a napkin and wipe it off, tell her to stop trying to be something she wasn't. The fact she was a kid, on that awkward cusp of learning to be a young woman, gave him patience. Though her next words eroded that considerably.

"You can't say that about Debbie. I'm not sure why Madame lets her stay in this class. It's for serious dancers, and she's obviously not serious if she's carrying around that flab."

The little bitch was fourteen, he reminded himself, and fixed her with a considering look. "You know, Tasha, when I was training in the military, seventy percent of my class didn't make it to graduation. Most of them quit during the first four weeks. And a bunch of those were guys who looked the part, who were absolutely sure in the beginning they had everything it took to make it. Then, when they were faced with the reality of it, they found they didn't have the commitment for the long haul."

Her brow creased. "So? A lot of guys are all talk, no action." Her gaze swept him. "Are you one of those? Because you look like you could do a lot."

Jesus Christ. He didn't want to know how she'd learned to be this brash, but he decided if Matt needed a full security detail on Angelica when she hit puberty, he'd take the job. SEALs were trained to do the impossible, after all.

"The ones who made it were the kind of guys who knew what it was to be knocked down. They knew winning is about a refusal to fail. Until you've been pushed down over and over, and you still get up and dance and give it one hundred percent, don't talk to me about being serious. I'll bet Debbie is here every week, even knowing a lot of you don't think she should be. She practices the steps and works hard for Madame. Which means she's stronger under fire than someone whose natural talent has kept them untested. So if I was putting money on it, I'll bet she's here for graduation, whereas the first time someone sets you back on your heels, you'll run to Daddy or Mommy to have them fix it for you."

Wow, he hadn't expected to go there. Tasha paled. It was actually an improvement over the little-girl-pretending-to-be-a-seasoned-slut routine, but Max cursed himself as she got up and fled. Well, if she didn't come back next week, he'd proved his point.

"Ah fuck, Ackerman. Don't be such an asshole." He would have left it alone if it was fully deserved, but he knew his own shit had driven his mouth, so after a few minutes, he got up and followed her. Several other girls were in the process of heading out, but once they cleared, it left the waiting room deserted, except for Tasha. She stood at the window, staring out at the parking lot, holding her tote bag on her shoulder. It had one of those boy bands printed on it, and a Hello Kitty key chain hung from the strap. He was an idiot.

When he tugged on the strap, she pressed her lips together, crossed her arms over her chest. "Leave me alone."

"I have a sister," he said quietly. "And she was like Debbie. She tried really hard to do everything well. Some things she did great, and others she didn't. You're the best dancer in the class, Tasha. Debbie may not be a prima ballerina, but I expect she'll succeed at something else in life, because she doesn't quit just because it gets hard. That's the kind of person a smart girl would want as a friend. You seem pretty smart to me."

Her lips twisted. "You just treated me like I was stupid."

"Well, you can be smart and still act stupid occasionally. We all do it. It's part of growing up."

She slanted him a glance. "You're already grown up."

"We never stop growing up, Tasha. If we're smart."

"Smart enough to know we're dumb."

He grinned. "Yeah. See?"

She shifted to a hip, tossed back her hair. "Do you have a girlfriend?"

"Working on it." Quickly realizing his error when her gaze lit up with calculation, he nodded toward the classroom. "Madame."

"Oh." Her lips did a pretty pout of disappointment, but then she shrugged. "She's a really good teacher. Strict, but fair."

"I've noticed that about her."

"She can be scary, but don't let that put you off."

"I'll do my best."

A pair of headlights turned into the parking lot, and she adjusted the bag more securely. "That's my mom. Will you be back next lesson?"

"I'm not sure. It will depend if Janet...Madame, needs me to help out with more lifts."

"Well, I hope you'll be back. You're really hot, even if you're old." She gave him a cheeky grin and then darted out the door, hair rippling in the draft.

Some days more than others, he thought. Watching her cross the parking lot, things hurt in his chest. He wanted to grab hold of her, tell her not to treat herself so cheaply, not to let the fact that Daddy wasn't paying her enough attention drive her into looking for a surrogate. He'd also tell her not to mistake sex and acting like an adult for the love and acceptance she truly needed.

Hell. He really wasn't sure how Matt was going to do it. He'd be a wreck.

Turning, he discovered he wasn't alone. The rest of the class had left, because Janet had turned off the lights behind her, only the emergency lights casting a dim light over the wood floor of the main room. She leaned in the doorway, twirling her stick idly, her other arm crossed over her breasts, fingers clasping her biceps.

"I didn't realize I was in the running to be your girlfriend," she noted. "I wasn't informed."

"I panicked," he admitted baldly, and won a chuckle. "I was afraid she was going to leap on me like cake, then and there."

Her expression became more serious. "You had a sister? You were talking about her in the past tense."

"No. I still have her. She's just...she's different now." He debated, not sure whether to open that door, then decided it didn't hurt to open it a crack. It was already hurting, after all. "Something happened to her a few years ago, and she has brain damage. She's in a private facility outside New Orleans. I visit her twice a week."

Janet's expression reflected simple compassion. "I'm sorry. Is she why you left the SEALs?"

That empty place in his gut, a reminder of what was no longer a part of his life, gripped him. "Yeah. She needed me. I'm her only family. The only family who can take care of her, be here for her."

"I'd like to meet her sometime. If that would be okay."

It surprised him, such that he didn't say anything right away. She cocked her head. "That is, if you weren't just using me as your beard to put Tasha off. I assume you *are* working on making me your girlfriend."

"I think that depends a lot on whether you're considering making me..." He hitched over "your boyfriend" because it sounded a little juvenile, but beyond that, it didn't quite fit. She filled in the missing word though.

"Mine." She pushed away from the doorframe, turned away. "I guess we'll see about that. Lock the door, would you? And turn off the foyer light. We'll take the back exit out."

When she disappeared so abruptly back into the classroom, his brow creased. He wasn't sure if he'd done something wrong, but as he complied with her direction and then followed her, he saw she was simply tired. She was leaning on the stick while pushing a stack of yoga mats closer to the wall. As she moved away from them, he noted she was walking stiffly.

"'We'll see about that'," he repeated her words. "Should I treat it as an audition then?"

It brought her to a halt. When she turned toward him, her weariness translated to her expression, her tone of voice. It *was* more than being tired. Something he'd said or done had hit a nerve.

"No, Max. My audition days are long over. You be what you are and I'll be what I am. It's not likely to work in the long run, but I don't count on things for the long run. We've already proven we can be very satisfying to one another in the short term, until the differences become obstacles instead of attractions." She fixed him with a direct look, her back straightening. "When that happens, you won't have to think about a different job or worry about any awkwardness. We'll end it as adults, and friends, with no harm on either side. Agreed?"

"Agreeing to something beforehand and its reality are often very different."

"True. If we have our doubts, on either side, we should probably stop right now and let this be it."

Though she was only fifteen feet away, it was suddenly as if she was behind her desk at work, as remote in that position as she'd been up until six months ago. He could tell she meant it. If he said stop now, that would be it, and tomorrow he had no doubt she'd act as she'd always acted with him, before that day she'd sought him out on the parking deck and sat on the hood of his truck.

She flipped the switch with such calm, it told him two things. One, he'd barely scratched the surface of who she actually was, what she felt about things, and two, a woman with armor that thick had a lot going on below the surface. She'd said a dancer had to have utter confidence in her partner to do lifts properly. He wondered if she applied the same yardstick to opening up in her relationships.

"What's the purpose of having a partner in ballet?" he asked.

"To allow the ballerina to have a greater reach on certain moves," she said automatically. "The ability to float across the stage, rather than merely move across it. To exceed what she can do alone." She arched a brow. "You're a very clever man, Max. But it doesn't answer the question I'm asking."

"You didn't ask a question. You made a statement. But if it is a question, maybe you're the one who needs to answer it." He crossed the floor, closed that distance so he was standing in front of her. "If we do this, I want it to be awkward. I want you to get so deep into me that, if it ends, I'll feel like something has been ripped from my chest. I want to be forced to leave

K&A because I couldn't handle being this close to your scent, your heat, and not touch you, think about kissing you or making love to you." He cupped her face, running his thumb along her jaw. "If you figure out how to put a collar and leash on me, *Mistress*, I'd rather you choke me with it than take it off."

Her pulse was rabbiting under his touch, her eyes burning, her mouth soft in a way that made her seem vulnerable and yet untouchable at once. He didn't give a fuck about her shields right now. Instead, he took the stick from her hand, dropping it to the floor. Thinking about it a bated moment, he dropped his grip to her hips, compelling her to turn so her back was to him. She tilted her head, keeping her gaze on his, trying to gauge his intent. There was a quivering stillness to her. Putting his mouth close to her temple, he directed her attention to the posters over the mirror. "Let's do that one."

It was a Latin dance setting, but he'd already figured out there was a lot of crossover in types of dance, and he saw echoes of ballet form in the lift pictured. The man was raising his partner all the way over his head, and she was arched toward the sky, one leg extended, one bent, arms in a graceful position like tree branches over her head. His part of things seemed pretty simple, but he put his hands exactly where they were in the picture. Janet was ready for him. Despite her tiredness, she bounced into the lift like a bird taking flight.

He had to adjust his stance, figure out the weight distribution. There was a harrowing moment where he nearly had to bring her back to the ground and re-try, but in the end he got it. He found the right groove and locked in, holding her up there for a good ten seconds. In the mirror, he could see her head was back, eyes closed, a look of near peace on her face, as if she was a bird in flight in truth.

When he at last lowered her to his shoulder, her body was curved back against his, her shoulder blades high against his chest, her buttocks pressed to his abdomen. As he took her down farther, her arm hooked around his neck and shoulder, the other hand catching in his shirt and the waistband of his jeans. He held her there with one arm, her feet just above the floor, him bearing all her weight. She wasn't a "heavy old broad" at all—far from it.

He tugged the leotard off the lowered shoulder, baring the round, pale curve beneath. He cupped it, thumbing the nipple slowly, watching her reaction in the mirror. She had her gaze fixed on his hand, and when he shifted his support so he could cup her pussy fully beneath the skirt, she let out an erratic breath, dropping her head back on his shoulder. He swung her body up into the cradle of his arms.

She turned her face toward his neck. "I don't want to leave yet."

"I know." He intended to snag a yoga mat from the stack in the corner, bring it back to the center of the floor, but she stopped him before he could head that way.

"I want to feel the floor beneath me."

Nodding, he lowered her to it. She stretched out on her back, lifting her arms above her head, sliding her fingers along the cracks of the wood. "Where I first learned to dance, I knew every groove in the floor, every worn and polished place, every sanded-down knot. I can still smell the pine. After a dance class, if you laid your cheek on the floor, you could see the scuff marks our shoes had left."

"You loved it."

"Yes. But I was Debbie. I had the passion, the love for it, but I was only good enough to be one of the company, not the star. That was all right though. Since I was good enough to do that, I got to dance on a stage, in front of an audience."

Since he knelt above her, he saw her come out of the past, sharpening on the present. "I want my stick."

He retrieved it, laid it next to her. Then he eased the leotard down to her waist, exposing both breasts to his gaze. Untying the wraparound skirt, he removed it and the leotard fully. The shoes and tights followed. He took his time and she watched him closely throughout. Though her lips tightened, she didn't stop him.

He sat back on his heels. Now, without him wearing a blindfold, without her covering her legs with hosiery, he saw them. Two circular scars on each limb. At some point in her life, they'd both been broken, compound fractures. The age of the scars seemed similar, suggesting they'd happened at the same time.

He understood her enough not to ask, not tonight. Like his sister's story, that was territory they'd have to learn at a careful pace. But he bent, pressed his lips to one of the scars and earned a tremble. She feathered her fingers through his hair. When he lifted his head, he had the pleasure of sweeping his gaze up a lovely female form clad only in her jewelry. The pendant was a charm, a tiny ballet dancer.

He shed his T-shirt. He'd never thought too much about his body from an aesthetic viewpoint. It was a tool, a weapon to keep honed, but he found he responded strongly to how much she appreciated it. Her avid gaze said she wanted to touch, so he came down to her, closing his eyes as those demanding fingers caressed and scraped his upper torso. They lowered to the jeans, tugged on the belt. As he was unbuckling it, she dipped into his back pocket to retrieve his wallet.

Bemused, he sat back on his heels, watched her open it. She flipped past his commercial license, his concealed carry permit, his single credit card. Then she dug into the interior pocket and retrieved a condom, giving him a sultry look she did much better than Tasha—the benefit of true experience. "Always prepared?"

"Always. There are a couple more in my coat." He nodded toward where he'd left it hung on a hook on the wall.

"Hmm. And ambitious. When was the last time you had sex, Max?"

"Not so long ago that I don't need that." He regretted having to say it, but though it had been infrequent, there'd been the occasional hookup with other lonely people. Always protected, but he wouldn't risk Janet for the possibility of error.

She handed the wallet back to him with a reserved expression that made him wonder if he needed to make up for lost ground, but then she dispelled that concern. "Get tested, and you won't need to use it while you're with me. My tubes were tied long ago, and sex..." She paused. This time, he wondered if her imperious look covered something more vulnerable. "You'll be the first in quite a while," she said at last.

"Then I'm honored. Mistress."

He pushed the jeans to his thighs. She didn't object to him not taking everything off, her eyes dark and lips parted, eager. Though urgency beat between them like a bass rhythm, things had slowed down as well. He lowered himself down onto her, and her legs slid around his hips, heels caressing the backs of his knees beneath the jeans. She put her hands on his chest like bird wings, spreading her fingers wide and making him feel like she was learning him, tugging his chest hair, tracing the shallow indentations between ribs as she worked her way downward.

He took care of the necessary evil of the condom, but he was going to do as she'd said. He wanted to feel her without that barrier. When he guided himself to her wet cunt, he led with two knuckles, rubbing against the labia, feeling the slick give before he moved his hand out of the way and pushed inward, lifting his gaze to focus on her face.

She was staring at him. In that hushed silence, his gradual progression into her body, he felt something indescribable. With every inch he sank into her, it was as if he'd found something he'd lost. She'd unclipped her hair and it waved around her face, softening it. It gave him a momentary pause, her parted lips, the yearning expression. Then he was all the way in and her eyes closed, her body lifting up toward him in reaction.

He caught the back of her head, bracing his weight with his other hand as she moaned softly against his lips. The feminine noise set him on fire, the hushed moment giving way to something more edgy and dark, needy. He parted her mouth with his own and plundered, taking over with tongue and teeth. He lifted his hips, partially withdrawing, but only to increase the friction, push into her harder. This time when his eyes opened, hers did as well, and he saw the challenge in her gaze. He dove back into that kiss.

She reached for the stick, sliding it across his upper thighs to grasp the other end, notching the length of it into the crease between his buttocks and thighs. When she tightened her grip on it, he surged back into her, plunging deeper, harder, feeling the insistent pressure of the bar as it pushed against his ass, urging him on.

"Fuck me," she muttered against his ear, taking a sharp bite. He caught his fingers in her hair, tightening enough to pull on the scalp, and her nails dug into his flanks. He plunged forward again as she met him, impact for impact. Pressing his mouth against her temple, he pinned her down with his body, working himself in her like a man determined to stake his claim. He had no idea when the need to possess her had taken root in him, but now it was here in full, raging glory.

He kept kissing her even as he thrust and she urged him on with the pressure on that stick, but then her mouth broke away. "Stop," she whispered.

Complying with such an outrageous request was like sawing back on the reins of an eight-horse stagecoach heading full tilt toward a cliff. He was enough in tune with her that he managed it, however, pushing his body up off her with one arm, breathing heavy, everything tight with lust. When she lifted a hand to his face, he sucked on her fingers, kissed them, nipped.

"After you went down on me in your truck, did you jack off?"

"No." He adjusted deeper, not a thrust, but a response of its own. When she swallowed, he locked on to that reaction. Did it again.

"Stop," she said, a bare whisper of reproof. "Have you given yourself relief since?"

"No." He could tell that surprised her, because he wasn't what she was used to having, and she'd expected him to act according to his nature, not hers. But just because he wasn't a sub didn't mean he didn't understand what she wanted, needed. "I wasn't going to come until I was inside you."

"What if I commanded you to pull out now, tonight, before that happened? What if I don't want you to come inside me until there's no condom between us?"

"I'd say you're a sadist." His cock pulsed inside her, rebelling against the idea quite adamantly. A quiver ran up his arms when she slid her hand over one of them. The edge of the stick now followed the back of his thigh, to his knee, his calf. She tapped him there, lightly, then harder, making him flex in reaction.

She let it roll away with a clatter, replacing it with her hand on his ass, her nails scraping him. "I'm imagining you being flogged while you're inside of me," she whispered, her pupils dominating her dark eyes. "A Mistress is standing behind you, striking on every thrust, the strands of the cat sliding off your gorgeous back and ass. It would be a barbed cat, but I know you wouldn't even feel it, Max. You'd only feel my cunt, squeezing down on your cock. You wouldn't notice the people watching, everyone in the dungeon coming to watch this magnificent, muscular male animal fucking his Mistress."

He dropped back down on her, elbows on either side of her face, his fingers curling into her hair to hold her. He worked his hips in deeper, earning a parting of those glossed lips, a tiny, shuddering breath. "Does that idea excite you?" he rumbled, teasing between them with the tip of his tongue.

"You know it does. The question is, does it excite *you*?"

"Yeah. Because while you were talking about it, your pussy rippled around my cock and your nipples got tighter, harder. I want to see you fucking mindless, Janet. If being a Mistress gets you there, sends you flying, I'll take that trip with you. But it's you, everything about you, that gets me hard." He paused, locking gazes with her. "And if it keeps you from doing it with other men. Fair warning, I'm moving into that zone. I'm not the sharing kind."

"You want to see me mindless? Then pull out of me and take that thing off. I want to see you jack off over me."

He shook his head, moved his mouth down to her throat. "No. I want you too damn much like this."

Janet let out a cry as he covered her breast with his lips, pulling on the nipple hard, even as he thrust into her again, underscoring the point. He could take over a woman's senses. He was good at it, could overwhelm her, take her flying, and he wanted her helpless, screaming his name and raking his back with her nails.

That had been the goal with every woman he'd ever had beneath him. Giving them both what they wanted. At least for that one moment.

As that thought sunk in, he let go of the nipple, but gave it a teasing lick before he lifted his upper body once more, bracing his other hand on her hip. Her skin was flushed, breath rapid, but her eyes hadn't changed focus. She wouldn't fight him. She understood that this was a give-and-take game between them, not the prescribed boundaries she had at the club. But his expanding knowledge of how her mind worked in moments like these, what she might truly want, was a potent form of self-restraint.

Still, he had his own desires, and he wasn't yet ready to withdraw. Sliding a hand beneath her waist, he put a palm on her buttock and brought them into a sitting position, her straddling his lap and him still inside her. It changed the angle and thrust, winning him another gratifying gasp, a lovely shudder through her toned body, but he forced himself to focus, cupping her face.

"How about a compromise? You want to use that stick on me, I can tell. How about you do your worst with it, and then you can sit me down on my sore ass in one of these straight chairs, and ride me until you climax."

She arched a brow. "How about you?"

"My Mistress says she wants me to come inside her without a rubber." He lifted a shoulder, gave her a tight smile. "Sounds like I won't be coming tonight then."

"And if you do anyway? If you can't hold back?"

"Then she gets to dish out another punishment sometime in the future. That'd be a win-win for her."

Janet managed a wry chuckle, but when he tightened his arm around her waist, holding them even closer together, her face folded into a more serious expression. She wrapped her arms around his shoulders, pressing her face into the side of his where he couldn't see her face. Brow creasing, he cupped her skull, holding her with cock throbbing but heart tilting at the sudden desperate measure.

"You're a rare combination, Max," she whispered. "You're caring for me, even as you offer to serve me. Protector and servant both. You're a new experience."

"Same goes, Mistress."

She smiled against his temple. "You're also the first man who's ever called me that as an endearment instead of an honorific. I can tell the difference, you know."

"Is that a bad thing?"

"If it was, I would have told you. I'm not shy."

"I've noticed that." Turning his head, he caught her lips, drawing them both into a slow, spiraling kiss, working himself inside her until she was making those lovely feminine noises of distressed pleasure. Her arms were locked around his shoulders still, their hearts thundering together. When she pushed him away at last, hands flat against his chest, her eyes were sparking with fire and challenge.

"Deal. I'm getting up now."

While they'd been kissing, she'd folded her legs beneath her, so he had to let go of her hips before she could lift off him. As she started to push herself up, he saw the grimace she tried hard to cover. He put his hands back on her waist, taking over so he lifted her onto her feet. She nodded with aplomb, then pointed to one of the straight wooden chairs along the wall. "Get rid of the condom and take that chair to the center of the room."

* * * * *

Janet was shaken and energized at once. She hadn't been kidding. He was such a curious mix, and a very arousing one. She'd barely had the willpower to stop them. Actually, during that last kiss, the desire to let them both go over had been so strong she almost hadn't. Except the Mistress in her loved the power of denial, for herself as much as her sub. Yet Max wasn't her sub. At the moment, she'd call him a woman's deepest fantasy. He'd understood her need enough to resist that overwhelming compulsion to completion as well.

Though a Domme loved a sub, many of her sisters in that nature loved the idea of teaching a strong, non-submissive, alpha male the pleasures of surrender. It was a treasure rarely discovered, let alone offered, as Max had offered it.

He'd placed the chair in the center of the room as she requested. Now she retrieved the stick she'd released. It wasn't flexible, not appropriate for what she wanted, but he'd correctly recognized her desire to leave marks on him.

"Take off the rest of your clothes. Then lean over the back of the chair until your stomach touches it. Grab hold of the seat with both hands. Spread your legs shoulder width."

She circled him, response from her pussy trickling down her legs, not only from him being inside her but from the vision he gave her as he worked off his shoes, shucked off jeans and briefs. He was utterly mouthwatering. She saw more scars, nicks and remnants of serious injuries, but nothing that marred the sheer beauty of a male body honed to warrior fitness. She'd have to join him on one of his workouts, see what he did to stay looking like this. She had a feeling she'd likely need a golf cart or boat to keep up.

When he complied with her order, spreading his legs, she moved behind him, licking her lips at the heavy testicle sac, the curve of the aroused cock that disappeared to brush his belly. She could see it when she shifted to view his profile. Very nice. His buttocks were taut, begging for teeth, strap, tongue.

She dipped to pull the belt from his jeans. When she moved close enough to trail her fingers down his spine, he lowered his head, that attractive quiver going through him again.

"You'll tell me if it gets to be too much."

"I had to go through interrogation training, including waterboarding. Do your worst."

"The physical isn't what can get to be too much." Not for someone like him. When her meaning sunk in, he nodded.

"You're beautiful," she said. "I could beat your ass all night long."

He gave a half chuckle. "Is it crazy that I understood that?"

"No. But don't talk anymore until I say so. Feel."

She rolled the stick over his ass a few times, let him feel that. She thought about sliding it vertically between his buttocks, making him tighten those luscious cheeks and hold on to it while she strapped him, but in the end she put it aside. She liked keeping it simple. Plus, if the muscles stayed loose, the nerves were more sensitive. She rolled her shoulder, let the belt dangle from her hand then folded it over, tucking both ends into her palm.

The first several strikes were to get him used to the feeling, but then she started ramping it up. She loved the red prints left by the strap, loved knowing he'd put the belt back on tonight but never look at it the same way again. He shifted and flexed from the blows, but otherwise held still. When he started lifting to them, she knew he was responding to her obvious arousal, the way she passed her hand over his tortured flanks, cupping his balls and squeezing, pressing her thumb deeper between his ass cheeks, against his rim, teasing him there so he jerked. But he didn't say anything, didn't warn her against that part of him, an intriguing potential.

He was right. He had an enormous capacity for discomfort, but she saw the body language change as he got deeper into his head, letting go of whatever analysis he was doing of what was happening between her and him. Lust started rising up, hot and hard, his cock getting stiffer, the tip getting glossy with thick fluid. The rippling of his back and ass muscles made her hungrier and hungrier, and she started hitting harder and faster, ignoring the ache in her arm and back, shifting on her tired feet, willing to go on until they were stumps.

When she circled him, he lifted his head to look at her. She was completely naked, sauntering around him with the brazen sensuality of a siren. She stopped in front of him, cupping her own breast, idly fondling it as she considered him.

"Come here," he growled. "I'll suck on that for you, Mistress."

She allowed it, coming close enough her knees brushed his knuckles, locked on the edge of the chair seat. Then his mouth was on her nipple, his hands remaining in that restrained position, his ass available for more punishment. She was glad she'd had him take off the condom, because the floor was marked with the drip of his pre-come.

Her cunt clenched hard at the skillful touch of his mouth and she tested herself, giving him the other one as well, until both nipples were glistening and plum-colored, tight points. Then she drew back enough to pivot. Cognizant of the lion in the cage once again, she slowly bent, arching her back in a sensual tease, lifting her ass in front of his face. "My pussy, Max."

She'd gauged her distance so he had to reach for it. He chose a devastating tactic to bring her closer though. He lifted his head, nuzzled between her buttocks to tease her rim with his tongue, sending a wild spiral of sensation through her that made *her* drip on the floor. She arched her back farther, and his tongue slid down over her slick labia, teeth nipping at her clit. The rocket of response through her cunt was so strong she knew she'd come in no time, so she stepped away and straightened, giving him only a taste.

She made a tsking noise, pointed at where her arousal had dripped on the floor. "You should have caught those drops. What a mess you're making." She sauntered around behind him once more, prepared to punish him properly for his carelessness. He watched her in his peripheral vision, and she shivered at the glitter in those gray eyes, the promise and threat of when he'd no longer restrain himself, no matter the strength of her will.

Thwack, thwack. Again and again, as her body shuddered as if he were thrusting into her with each blow, his ass lifting and falling in the rhythm as if he were imagining the same. When she won a grunt from him, she changed tactics, landing several stripes in a diagonal line from shoulder blade to rib cage, like flogging a gladiator before he entered the ring. That change in stroke brought his head up, and his fingers dug into the chair, making it creak.

He was powerful, could turn and take her to the ground in a moment. A weak, crazy part of her wanted to taunt him, tell him to take her down, fuck her the way they both wanted to do it, without a condom, hard, visceral, a branding of her cunt with his seed. She'd never been a Mistress who'd wanted a possessive sub, the very idea a turnoff. It made her think of her unexpected thoughts about owning him, that night at the club. She liked the idea of him considering her his far too much. And that was new, scary territory for her. Because she'd been a man's possession before.

She pushed away the darkness before it could rise up and interfere with this. It was time to go a different route. He hadn't flinched, hadn't once done anything that would shield himself. She heard both of them breathing, rasping for air for different reasons.

"Turn the chair away from me and sit in it," she commanded. "Put your hands behind you, hold on to the lowest rung in the back."

She watched him do it, how he had to fold his elbows almost into a box position since it was a small chair and he had long arms. Though his ass had to be sore, he didn't hesitate to press those choice buttocks into the wooden seat. He didn't look back at her, obviously realizing that was part of it. A form of blindfolding, following her commands without sight.

After retrieving another condom from his coat, she moved around to his front. He carried three, a man with confidence…and stamina. She held the belt in her other hand. His chest expanded and contracted, eyes molten steel, lips tight. Her gaze moved down to his cock, thick and hard.

"Fuck…Janet…" He muttered it. He had his attention on her face, which she was sure showed her keen pleasure at his display. Opening the condom, she bent forward, slid the thin latex down over him. His eyes closed, all those muscles bunching in impressive restraint. Then she put her hand on his shoulder, steadying herself to straddle him. A more reverent oath tore from his lips as she positioned herself, slid down on him slowly, clutching her muscles on him as she descended.

When she got to the hilt, her cunt started quivering. She was so stirred up it would take very little to drive her to climax, and what she was clasping inside her wasn't little at all. Nothing about this man was small, inside or out. She slid the belt over his shoulders, put the tongue through the buckle and tightened that noose briefly around his throat, keeping three fingers between it and his windpipe as she held on to it, used it to rise and fall on him, a slow, torturous movement that caused both of them to shudder. She moaned, her pussy convulsing on him. Damn, she didn't want to go so fast, but it was going to happen. Her thighs trembled, her legs running out of strength, though if arousal alone was needed, it could carry her through a triathlon.

"Game over, Mistress." Letting go of the chair, he cinched his arm around her, pushed her down hard on his cock, making it pleasure and pain both, stretching and filling her. She continued to hold on to that belt, but he gave her his strength, thrusting deeper into her, increasing the power of the movements, which pounded her clit against him. The undertow started to drag her out, her body flushing. He was close as well, she could tell, but she remembered his vow. She wanted him to break it, wanted the chance to punish him again, but she also wanted to feel his seed spurt inside of her. She wanted it all. Wanted everything from him, wanted to do everything to him.

"Come for me, baby," he muttered. "Trust me."

Had he sensed that as well? It didn't surprise her at all, but as he worked himself up inside her, she clutched his shoulders and took the leap, arching back to scream, the room echoing with her passion as her cunt milked his cock, trying to force the issue. Every muscle stood out on his upper body as he resisted it, as he gave her every pleasure and held back his own.

Let me punish you again, Max. Give us both that pleasure. It was so fervent a thought, it was almost a prayer, a plea, and then that prayer was answered.

He went over with a roar, thrusting up into her so powerfully she had to cling to the belt and trust him to hold her. With brutal, blissful finality, they drove one another home.

Chapter Eight

She liked tormenting a guy, that was for sure. After that pretty fucking incredible night, Janet made it clear she'd be the one who initiated another date. She'd said no texts, no flowers, no chocolates, no temptations. He'd grinned at that, but he'd decided to respect her need to hold the reins. He had some intel gathering to do after all, a big part of which was why, two days later, he was standing inside the kitchen of a tiny house in a crappy New Orleans neighborhood. One about a step up from where he himself lived.

"Dale, where the hell are you?"

"I'm back here, Ack Ack."

The response came from somewhere at the back of the house, so Max moved through the four-room box of less than eight hundred square feet, discovering the voice had filtered through the back screen door. The man he sought was standing in the open doorway of a potting shed, which took up most of his postage-stamp backyard.

Dale gave him a look. "Fucking pathetic. You've been ten feet under water at o-dead-hundred in the middle of the night, found a single boat in a marina overflowing with them and yet you can't find one crip hanging out on his own property?"

"It was a warning, bro. Can't believe you leave your door standing open in this shitty neighborhood."

"A SEAL looks to get a workout where he can. The bastards just won't cooperate."

"They probably know a guy who plays with flowers and looks like a brick shithouse is a fucked-up mother with an assault rifle under his mattress."

He'd come to see Dale before he started the rest of his day, so it was barely past sunrise. Dale didn't seem surprised he was here, but then it was that way with them. Even when they were no longer in active service, SEALs often anticipated one another. Dale had been one of Max's BUD/S instructors and then later his MCPO, Master Chief Petty Officer.

Despite the house being barely more than a matchbox size, it was clean and neat, well tended. As he'd driven down the street, Max had seen improvements in the houses around Dale's, evidence of the assistance he was providing to his neighbors, building some community pride. Flower boxes with Dale's carpentry style hung on porch rails, and there was less garbage in the yards. A whole gaggle of kids had been playing in Dale's front yard, waiting for the school bus. It didn't matter whether it was in a questionable NOLA neighborhood or in Iraq, kids gravitated toward those they knew could keep them safe.

When he'd gotten out of his truck, a little girl had shown Max her knockoff brand Barbie doll, dirty and scraped up. The doll wore a homemade dress made of a paper napkin colored with crayon. Pretty creative on the kid's part. Where there was a will, there was a way. Two young boys had been playing some form of baseball with a stick and rocks. Max hoped they didn't brain her by accident.

"You running a daycare now?"

Dale snorted. As Max came to the doorway of the shed, leaned on it, the man looked up from his task, sharpening a set of pruning shears. Dale's workbench was built so he didn't have his back to the door. More evidence of why Max had made sure to call out when he entered the house. Dale would verify it was him regardless before pulling out the Glock he had strapped beneath the bench, but they both understood the courtesies.

"They're good kids. They help me with small jobs here and there, and it gives them a little cash. Need some coffee?" Dale nodded to the pot brewing in the corner. His weathered face creased in a smile when he noted the case of beer Max had brought. "We can chase it with the beer later, if you stay that long."

"Yeah." Max put the case on a clear spot and picked up a mug hanging from the pegboard. As usual, Dale had a few projects going. He was building another flower box, repairing an old transistor radio and had a stack of magazines waiting to be read.

"You haven't been around much these days," Dale observed, handing over his own coffee to be topped off.

Max shrugged. "Been busy. K&A's had a lot happening lately. Amanda had a few bad days, so I've been seeing her a little more often. Twice a week instead of once. She's getting back to an even keel though. I also drove down to Houston and hooked up with Donny to take Jenny and Gayle and her kids to the Gulf for the weekend."

"Did Lewis or Charlie get a text from the neighbors, telling them their wives were stepping out with two good-looking young guys?"

Max grinned. "Within twenty-four hours. They've got a good community watch in Gayle's neighborhood. Charlie sent me a note, said I better have satisfied his wife, because she was a demanding wildcat in bed. I told him he didn't need to come back. After having me, she considered him superfluous."

Dale chuckled. "I'm sure he had some choice words for that. They okay?" Setting aside the shears, he slid his left hip on to another stool, braced his right foot. He kept his salt-and-pepper hair that had once been black cropped military short, which emphasized the strong planes of his face, the deep-set eyes and rock-hard jawline. He was in his late forties, the grooves of his face carved by water, wind and a whole lot of other things. Dale was a retired SEAL, having served his twenty-year stint. His direct blue-green gaze said he had all his shit together, and then some.

He'd made the shift to the stool smoothly enough, but Max knew there was no leg from the knee down on the left foot. His prosthesis was good enough that only someone looking for it would detect a difference in his more casual movements.

"Yeah, they're okay." Max sobered. "Gayle knows the drill, and has figured out how to cope with the months alone. Jenny's having a harder time. She's pregnant with her first. Lew got called down range right after they found out."

"That always sucks."

"Yeah." Max sipped the coffee. "But everyone's been rotating through when they can to help out, and there's a core group of six wives in that area that meet regularly. Gayle's pulled her into it, a support group."

"Their own Seal Team Six," Dale noted, his lips curving. "Gayle will take care of her."

"Yeah. She's about seven months along and doing well, but..."

"But after your experience with Savannah Kensington, you're hyperalert about it. Nothing wrong with that. As long as Jenny doesn't tell Lewis the guys are stalking her."

"If they can be detected in the bushes outside her house or while shadowing her at the grocery store, they deserve to be busted." Max tapped his mug to Dale's. "As you said, you get your practice where you can."

"You never know when you'll be called to serve." Dale gave him a considering look. "I know you love me, but I'm thinking you're here for another reason."

"Still a Master Chief," Max snorted. "Even if you won't let me call you that."

"I have to know my place in this world. The other can be like a drug, you miss it so much. But if you slip and call me that every once in a while, it doesn't hurt my feelings. Ack Ack."

"Yeah." Max's lips twisted at the nickname his fellow operators had given him. He knew all about that feeling Dale was referencing. It was something hard to explain to others, how much he missed those days. Days spent freezing cold, tired, on edge. Adrenaline cycling through his veins like coke, even as his core stayed dead calm, focused, doing everything necessary to flush out, hunt or bring down the target. But Dale got it. "Thanks, Master Chief."

A grim smile touched Dale's mouth. "What's up, Max?"

"I'm getting involved with a woman. And she's a Domme."

"Hmm." Dale took a swallow of his coffee. The guys sometimes called him "Merman". With his odd blue-green eyes, the name fit, but the real reason was because of several missions where circumstances had forced him to deepwater dive in his rebreather gear, well beyond its twenty-five-foot rating. And he'd survived.

He and Max shared the distinction of having graduated BUD/S at one of the youngest ages allowed, seventeen, though of course Dale was a decade or so ahead of Max when he got there. He'd served with Dale on missions and trusted him entirely, and Dale returned the favor, but Dale was right. It was more than the desire to visit with him that brought Max here today.

Dale was a sexual Dominant, a Master in the same vein as Matt Kensington and his executive team. Dale occasionally used his membership at Club Progeny, but most of the time he hung his whip, so to speak, at a smaller, nonprofit membership club in the area. Though Max had never had the opportunity to see him operate in that capacity, he expected Dale brought a psychological intensity to his sexual Mastery that Janet would appreciate greatly.

"You're no one's boy toy, Max." Dale gave him a serious look. "Are you trying to convince yourself you are, just to get what's behind her whip and boots? That doesn't work."

"You can't see me in collar and leash?" Max asked, arching a brow.

Dale snorted. "Yeah right. Sorry, man. I had to ask. There are a few mistresses out there who are convinced every guy wants to be Dominated, and if a guy says he doesn't, he just hasn't met the right Domme to do it. That's not the case, any more than every woman I meet wants to be my sex slave, more's the pity. However, those kinds of Mistresses can be pretty convincing, especially when her target is thinking with his dick. Which, admit it, happens to the best of us."

Max inclined his head. "She's more than that to me."

"Okay then." Dale sat back with his coffee. "So what do you need from me?"

"I've seen her work out with subs at Progeny, and she's pretty tough, has her hands firmly on the reins. But with us, it's more of a give and take, like we're figuring out how to dance with one another. With each meet, it gets more complicated. Like starting with the waltz and moving into the tango. Without giving specific details—"

"Please God don't."

Max grinned. "She does make me feel like doing things I normally wouldn't consider doing with a woman. It's the way she gets lost in it, aroused by it...it's fucking mesmerizing." He took a breath. "So, sight unseen, and given there are a lot of variables, does it ever work, if it's in the blood of one, but not the other?"

Dale considered the question. "I've seen it happen, yes. But it's different for every pair and—I won't lie to you—often it's only a short-term success. Some crash and burn when they approach it for the long haul, because if she eventually needs you to go deep, and you can't do that, that might be a problem. Unless her reasons for going deep are mixed with other factors, things you can satisfy without that dive. This isn't a linear thing. It's more like a maze, and we all find different paths. You'll be able to find the answer for yourself, good or bad. Just keep all your senses open and follow your instincts. What do they tell you about your chances with her?"

"It pays to be a winner, right?" Max gave the maxim from BUD/S training with a serious expression. "If I want her, I make it work. I don't accept defeat."

"Hoo-yah. Unless she puts out a restraining order on you."

Max snorted. "If I became that much of a problem, she wouldn't want the cops involved. She'd handle it herself, with extreme prejudice."

"I'm already liking her. Bring her around sometime." Dale set aside the coffee, rubbed his knee. When Max glanced at it, he shrugged it off. "Damn humidity. Works it up a little."

"You'd be better off in a less tropical climate."

"Yeah, but who'd watch after your dumb ass, kid?" Dale kicked him lightly with the shoe covering the prosthesis. Though he looked amused, Max felt a twist of guilt, knowing that there was some truth to it.

"You don't have to stay around here, Master Chief. I can clean my own house."

"Did I say you couldn't?" Dale asked, pleasantly enough, though Max recognized the don't-bullshit-me-unless-you-want-to-do-a-thousand-pushups edge to the tone that had made him a scary and effective SEAL trainer. "I have plenty to keep me here. Swing sets to build, flower boxes to make. I'm also watching after Eddie's dad and his dogs, over at the junkyard."

Max smiled, though his gut twisted, remembering the day they'd lost Eddie. How they'd brought his personal shit home to Ed Sr. "Is he still doing good?"

"Yeah, but the cancer's catching up to him. He doesn't give a damn. Keeps a cigar clamped in his teeth like a Rottweiler with a bone practically twenty-four hours a day and says it just means he'll get to see his boy and wife all the sooner."

"Now I know where Eddie got his stubbornness."

And his bravery. He'd thrown himself on a grenade to save three other team members.

Dale shifted, bringing them back to the present. "As far as this woman goes, do I know her, or do you prefer to keep her anonymous?"

"You might have seen her, though she usually wears a mask on the public floor." Max hesitated, but it wasn't due to concerns about Dale's discretion. He was anticipating his reaction, which meant he was being chicken shit. "She's my boss's secretary."

"Shitting where you work, Ack Ack. Problematic."

"Yeah, but I've already run through worst-case scenarios. I'll be the one to clear out if it goes sour. I won't let that be an uncomfortable place for her. I know I tend to be protective, but..." He shook his head. "She's a tough woman, but K&A, the club, the life she has here, it's been carefully constructed and reinforced. I see Matt watching me a little bit closer these days, and not just because he's a protective son of a bitch when it comes to the women he considers part of his world. It's like he has intel about her he can't share, and he's gauging whether I'll be able to handle it when I figure it out. And I think I've already figured out a piece of it."

"Well, preparing for the unknown is something you're trained to do. Sounds like you're already pretty deep with this woman."

"Not fully. Still playing in shallow waters, a couple quick trips to the deep end. But I'm ready to go deeper. I want to go deeper." Max met the other man's gaze. "She calms something inside me, even as she also stirs it all up. I didn't expect that to happen, not with Amanda and everything else, but I'm pretty sure she's going to be significant, wherever this goes."

Dale pursed his lips. "Okay then. For what it's worth, I'm not getting any alarm flags from what you've told me. If you need me, I'm here."

"Thanks." Max rose, his mind already resting easier from the simple reassurance. "Have to head to work, but I'll come back this weekend. Help you build that swing set before the gangbangers run off with the lumber you have stacked out here."

"Sounds good. Tell Matt he can't hide behind his wife's pregnancy anymore. I expect him back for poker third Thursday. He better bring a healthy wad of cash."

Max grinned. "Cut the man some slack. He's got two demanding women in his life now. And God knows, one is more than enough."

"I've seen Savannah. If ever she gets too demanding, I'll be in the front of the long line to pick up that slack."

"Yeah, and you'll lose that other leg." Max waited a minute, saw Dale's blue-green eyes sharpen. The Master Chief knew what he wanted to ask. Max always asked about it. But Dale still waited for him to voice the question.

"The other thing…anything new on that?"

"I'd have told you first thing if there was any verified intel."

"Yeah. Roger that." Max lifted a shoulder. "Just got a funny itch lately."

"Might want to get that cleared up before you and your lady get more involved. They don't tend to appreciate that kind of thing."

"Suck me. Respectfully." But it was an absent comment as Max lingered in the doorway. Dale cocked his head.

"You heard anything from the teens at Dana's church?"

Max volunteered regularly there, helping out in the soup kitchen and with maintenance. It had been a natural evolution from his job as Dana's primary driver, but it was also a strategic position to form bonds with the kids who inhabited that rough area. Dale's neighborhood rubbed edges with it.

"Nothing yet, but if he ever surfaces and comes back, I'm feeling pretty sure they'll be the ones to find out about it first and let me know."

"Good. The other guys are keeping track of things in Mexico and Colombia. He's been buried deep for all these years. He's either piss-scared of you, acquired a new identity better than we can detect, or he's dead. Drug dealing doesn't lend itself to longevity."

"Yeah." Max nodded. "Thanks, Dale."

"Keep your head and ass down." The man opened the case of beer and threw him one. "Take this for a snack later. It's New Orleans, after all."

They parted amicably enough, but Max could feel Dale watching him cross the backyard. Fucking intuition could be contagious among those who'd served together, and he'd probably just raised Dale's antennae. He'd meant what he said though. He appreciated Dale helping him with intel, but that's where he wanted his Master Chief's involvement to end. When he finally paid this debt, it would be his ass alone on the line.

* * * * *

As Max held the door for Dana, ensuring she was comfortably situated in the limo, his phone beeped. Closing the door and moving up to the driver's door, he called up the message.

Since you passed the first evolution, I have another for you. If you're not planning to DOR yet, come to my house after work today. There will be pizza. -J

For some reason, a T-shirt logo spoofing the Star Wars movies came to mind— *Come to the Dark Side. We have cookies.*

Max shook his head at the note. An evolution referred to an event in the SEAL training schedule. He needed to get her away from the Internet. That thought led to a pleasing idea, one he mulled over as he took a seat behind the wheel. Dana shifted onto the padded seat behind him, curling her fingers into the shoulder of his coat, playing with the hair at his nape. "Are you sexting while on official K&A business?"

"Since when are you official K&A business? You're the punishment for my many sins." He flicked at her nose with a finger and she wrinkled it at him, swatting his fingers away.

"So I hear you and Janet are seeing one another."

He shouldn't be surprised. He wasn't sure anything happened at K&A without the five-man team mysteriously and instantly knowing about it, which in turn meant their wives knew about it.

"She's just using me for sex."

"I fully support that. I just wish I could see video."

He chuckled. "Do you ever behave?" When she gave him a smug smile he caught in the rearview mirror, he pulled into traffic. "So how did things go today?"

"Pretty good. We're set for Tuesday's spaghetti dinner, and the revival at the end of the month should be a great event for the community. Reverend Morris is still doing cartwheels over the fact the Godspeed Players will be performing for it."

When he braked at a stop light, she brushed her knuckles along his cheek. It was an unexpectedly tender gesture that drew his gaze back to her. As she usually did when she wasn't at home, she wore sunglasses that concealed her obvious blindness, but the bemused curve of her lips gave him an indication of her mood.

"You deserve to be happy, Max. You do realize that, right?"

That was a loaded question, one that twisted things deep in his gut. His mother had deserved happiness. Amanda had deserved it. Who decided who deserved what? Maybe it was just all a big game to that faceless deity.

A SEAL was trained not to fail. If he experienced a setback, he figured out how to turn it into a win. He never quit. But how did you turn your mother's brutal murder and a gang rape that left your sister brain-damaged into a win? He'd been halfway across the world, playing the hero, thinking home would always be there. In the course of one bloody afternoon, home was gone forever.

The bitterness, the grief, broke him. He couldn't go back to being a Navy SEAL because of Amanda, but it wouldn't have mattered. During those first horrible months, he'd no longer been fit for duty. Though fellow SEALs like Dale tried to get him back on track, he pushed them away with a vicious anger. It was Matt Kensington who broke through, by proving to him that it wasn't his fury poisoning him — it was his fear.

Maybe Dale had spoken to Matt, instigated the job offer. However it happened, Max needed employment in the area and Matt Kensington offered him the limo job. At first it had been simple, straightforward — just get the guys in their fancy suits to meetings with other guys in fancy suits. No problem. Then one day Matt told him he was going to have a new responsibility, chauffeuring Peter Winston's fiancée.

Dana was a decorated Iraq veteran who'd been blinded, scarred and had her hearing nearly destroyed by a bomb stuffed in a plastic soda bottle. Cochlear implants had improved the hearing and Peter's unlimited financial resources had fixed a lot of the scarring, but that didn't matter. Max hadn't wanted the job. He didn't want to be in a situation where he had to protect someone that vulnerable. Not now, not ever again.

With Dana's slim hand on his shoulder now, Max remembered the first day he took her to her church. Peter had helped her into the car, so the first time Max actually touched his new charge was on the curb in front of the building.

When he opened the limo door for her, a shaking had started deep in his belly and moved out to his arm, affecting the hand he extended to her. The episode came on him so suddenly, his body was drenched with sweat in a blink.

He was about to jerk back, close the door in her face, try to pull his shit together. Hell, forget that, he was going to radio Wade and tell him they needed to send over another driver.

He'd just lean on the door until his replacement got there, no matter how much she beat on the window. Before he could do anything as absurd as that, Dana had reached out, looking for his hand. Her fingertips brushed his thigh, an intimate touch that might have sent another woman recoiling with a stammered apology. Instead her palm flattened on him, registering how he was shaking.

In the next blink, she'd slipped out of the car. He caught her arm by reflex, keeping her inside the shelter of the door and his body. To anyone looking, he would look like the protective one, but his hand was clammy, fucking trembling. She gripped his upper arms, her fingers surprisingly strong.

"It's all right," she said. "The first time's the hardest. I had awful panic attacks when I started walking around with just my cane. In zero to ten seconds, I looked like I'd come out of a gym, my clothes just soaked." Her fingers plucked at his shirt sleeve, registering the way it stuck to his skin.

Despite that, she clasped that arm, turning him away from the car, guiding them both out of the track of the door before she nudged it closed with her hip. "I don't blame you a bit for freaking out over a church social. They can be terrifying. You just stick close to me whenever you see one of those church ladies coming your way. I'll tell them you're my boy toy on the side when Peter's too busy for me, and that'll keep them from matching you up to their daughters and granddaughters. Unless you see Vivien LeCheau coming toward us. You can't miss her. She's a cross between a cougar and a viper. If she's coming at us, get square behind me. I'll put one of May Clark's potato salad spoons in places the sun don't shine."

She knew it wasn't the social that had him acting like a pathetic idiot, but of course the teasing helped. He would have cut his own throat if she'd coddled him.

"What does Miss Vivien look like?" he managed. "Hot cougar?"

"Boy, you better watch yourself. That kind of temptation comes with bad day-after consequences. Glenn Close and her boiled rabbit look like Cinderella and her house mice in comparison."

"Yes ma'am."

"There you go." Dana had tucked her fingers into his elbow, setting him into position to lead her up the church walk. The top of her head barely reached his shoulder. He kept looking in all directions, as if he was escorting POTUS himself in the middle of an L.A. gang fight. He couldn't do this. He fucking couldn't.

"Just one step at a time." She tightened her grip on his tense biceps. "One breath at a time, one step at a time, and then you're moving forward."

But never away. He was always afraid he was moving in a circle, right back to the beginning.

Coming back to the present, he felt the old surge of resentment, bitterness. Did being deserving really mean anything?

Though he held it back, Dana picked up on his mood. The woman could pluck things out of one touch and silence that most people couldn't if they were given a ten-page action report.

"Some wounds don't heal fast, or at all. But you learn to manage them as things go on. You're managing, Max. Is she good for you? I'd think she would be."

"Yeah. She is."

"Good. You'll be good for her too. You don't have to turn your back on the past as much as figure out what place it needs to hold in your life so the present can come in, give you a future."

"You use that in your sermon?"

"No, just thought it up right now, but I'll jot it down for future ones." She flicked his neck. "Wiseass frogman."

"Dumbass supply grunt."

God help him, but he loved Dana as if she was his own sister. A sister who often flirted outrageously with him and took way too many opportunities to grope him. She was the type of submissive who sought punishment. He didn't like to call it bratting, because it made the reasons she did it sound petty. It was clear she had a need to assert her independence as a fierce affirmation that her injuries hadn't defeated her. Peter's punishments were the balance, the safety net that evened it all out.

He guessed he had internalized more about the BDSM world than he'd thought. He'd picked up a lot just by being a witness to how the K&A men and their wives experienced it. Thinking about his behavior with Janet, those complex exchanges with her Mistress side, he wondered for the first time if he was seeking answers to some of his own needs within her desire to Dominate.

He'd indicated something like that to Dale, hadn't he? It had a different feel and flavor to it, for sure, but when he and Janet were playing their intense, complicated games, things stilled in his head and heart, eased in his gut. Things he'd gotten so used to feeling and enduring, they'd become a chronic kind of emotional pain.

Because of that, and so many other things, he found himself looking forward to tonight.

* * * * *

He parked his truck in the alley alongside Janet's house. It was raining, the sky a white-gray cloud cover hiding the sun. Humidity percentages had fallen, such that it was cool enough for a light jacket, a ward against the dampness. The rain was the gentle, constant kind, though, encouraging a couple to stay in bed for a lazy afternoon of lovemaking and watching old movies. With that in mind, he'd brought a small grocery sack of options for her to consider. He'd debated whether to bring flowers and settled for a single rose, something unique he'd picked up from the florist. The petals were a swirl of vanilla-white and dark-red color. He expected she'd appreciate the irony.

He was starting toward the front door when his phone buzzed with a text. *Come around back, Max. I'm on the porch.*

He let himself through the privacy fence, circled to the back stairs. The walkway flagstones were slick and dark with rain. Hearing a change in the tempo and density of the water, a smile curved his lips. She had the hot tub bubbling.

Imagining the things that could be done there had his blood simmering as well. When he opened the screen door to find her already in it, that reaction intensified. She had one arm stretched along the edge of the tub, the other bent to hold a wineglass. With her shoulders and the rise of her breasts exposed, it was obvious what he could discern through the concealing froth of bubbles was bare skin. The pair of robes hanging on a screen nearby confirmed it. All her lovely dark hair was piled on her head, damp tendrils curling on her neck. She wore the ballerina charm she'd worn the other night, the one she'd seemed hesitant about.

"I've never had an evolution start quite like this," he said, reminding them both of her earlier text. "It's a hell of a lot more inspiring than boat drills."

"I hope so. What's in the grocery bag?"

He placed it on the sidebar. "Gourmet hot chocolate, if you want to keep it simple. Whiskey, sugar, milk and honey, if you'd like something stronger."

"A hot toddy. What a perfect idea for a rainy day."

He pulled out an envelope, held it up, then set it on her sidebar. "My test results. All clear."

In the blink it took her to digest the significance, her expression became something different. Her lips parted, doing that subtle little moistening gesture that made his cock harden. She nodded demurely, however, extending her hand for the rose.

As he placed it in her grasp, he covered her fingers with his, sliding them down to caress her wrist. He wanted to cup her jaw, kiss her with all the hunger the envelope unleashed between them, but something held him back, as if that chain only ran out so far before it pulled him up short. It was a correct instinct, for she drew her hand away to bring the flower to her nose. Toying with it, she considered him.

"During your training, you have to prove you can swim a certain number of meters without taking a breath. You also have to descend to a prescribed depth without gear, and then come back up, swimming no faster than the bubbles you're blowing out."

"Yeah. Else you'll get the bends." He sat down on the edge of the hot tub, trailing his fingers in the water. It was toasty warm, the moistness on her neck a result of the steam where it hit the cooler air. "Did you have a good day, Mistress?"

Her expression flickered. "Yes," she said after a pause. "Mostly."

"Me too. Mostly. As in I mostly thought about you."

Her lips curved in a small smile. "You're good at this."

"With you, I work at it."

"I'm glad. Because what I want you to do will likely require some effort." She brushed the rose over her cheek, dragging it along her throat as she closed her eyes, lifted her chin to experience the petals along her skin. It made him hunger to put his mouth on the same track, taste the rose-scented flesh.

"I want you to go down on me under the water, Max." She fixed him with her dark gaze. "You get to surface three times. But before you need a fourth time, I expect you to make me come."

He rose from the edge of the pool, shed his jacket. "What kind of dive gear do you want me to wear?"

Her eyes sparkled, appreciating him. "Nothing more than the dolphins wear."

"If I was as well hung as a dolphin, I'd go naked as well."

"I'm not in the habit of providing reassurances about the obvious, but you need have no concerns in that department, Max."

He grinned. Stripping off his shirt, he tugged his belt loose, opened his jeans.

"You didn't ask what happens if you don't do it in three tries," she said.

"Don't need to. Failure's not an option. But if it did happen, I'd just try, try and try again, however long it took me to succeed. Or until I run out of breath and die, captured between your lovely thighs." Glancing at the sidebar again, he picked up one of the bottled waters there and leaned across the hot tub to place it on the ledge next to her shoulder. "To hydrate yourself, Mistress. You're going to be losing bodily fluids."

She caught him, tangling her fingers in his chest hair. Max closed his eyes, caught in the sensation as she teased a nipple, then brushed her knuckles down his sternum. "I've wanted to feel your hands since our last date," he said, opening his eyes to stare into hers. "I was about to break protocol and take the initiative. Ask you out again."

"You realized I have a protocol?"

"Yes ma'am. Right now, you want to be the one calling the shots, saying when we'll get together. You also don't really like to be touched unless you give permission, but there are certain moments when your body language tells me it's okay." Proving the point, he touched her temple, traced one finger down her cheek bone, moving over for a brief touch of her moist lips. She was motionless, her left hand resting on his chest while he did that, those intriguing eyes watching his face.

"I've been doing a little studying of my own," he added. "Being a SEAL is a way of living, 24/7. You don't switch it off when you're back from a mission, and it doesn't even really turn off when you leave the Navy. From what I can tell, that's the kind of Domme you are as well. You breathe it, feel it, know it in your blood. I've watched folks at the club, and it's not like that for everyone. But you're also not really the boots and whip kind of Domme, though those boots you wore with Thor that night, the ones that fit like a second skin, were pretty hot."

He grinned at the purse of her lips, her arch look. "You have a psychological mastery thing going that everyone near you feels, from a club submissive to the UPS guy who drops off packages at your desk. You don't have the desire to exercise it in the conventional ways. What you do at the club seems more like a gym workout to me. It's not the end goal. You're using it to stay in shape for rock climbing, a run on the beach, a dangerous mission." His gaze held hers. "You prefer places where the scenery and what you encounter might not be what you expect, so you have the challenge of adapting. But you haven't really found anyone that works for that, someone compatible with it. Someone willing to take risks, but who will also take care with your heart. Someone who won't turn on you."

He saw the change in her expression, the thing that told him he'd knocked on a door she hadn't expected him to find. Whether she'd open it or not was up to her. But he'd told her he knew that door was there.

It was time to ease back, turn his attention to the test she'd given him. Just like BUD/S, he expected he had to pass it to proceed to the next evolution, God help him. If she'd somehow gotten her hands on the whole BUD/S training manual, she'd be putting him through her version of interrogation torture and live fire combat training next.

Rising, he toed off his shoes, pushed the jeans and boxers off, got rid of the socks. He was already erect, no help for that with a beautiful naked woman so close, but her reassurance about his size made him feel pretty good on that score. His typical male reaction to that would probably make her laugh, but he didn't tell her right now. Their conversation had woven a sexual tension between them, given her a pensive look his intuition told him not to disrupt. He wanted to keep her focused on the humming needs of her own body, the obvious visible desires of his.

Chapter Nine
ಐ

Janet broke the seal on the bottle, took a sip of water as she watched him. His analysis of her as a Domme was on the mark, though she herself couldn't have said she was seeking something like him until he showed up on her radar. Her gaze coursed over the exceptional musculature of his upper body, the jutting power of his cock. The heated water swirling over her skin was just an extension of the arousal between her legs.

"Three times," she reminded him softly.

He stepped over the wall. The water came to his waist, because she'd let the pool fill to its maximum height. The spa had three levels of benches built into the side, and she was on the most elevated one. He should be able to get down on his knees below the water line, reach her with his mouth by bending to an approximate forty-five-degree angle. She'd given it a lot of thought.

Putting the bottle of water aside, she settled herself, sliding her arms along the ledge of the hot tub, curving her fingers into the handholds provided for entering and exiting the pool. They were also designed for tying a man's wrists to them. Though she'd never brought a man here, she was a woman who planned for future contingencies.

He dropped to his knees, an act that never failed to elevate her heart rate. In the water, it was a drifting motion, an anchor settling. It was clear this was a familiar element for him.

"Do you swim to keep in shape?" she asked, thinking about her earlier thoughts of keeping up with his workout by boat.

"When the water's warm." Humor creased the lines around his eyes. "You spend so much time in freezing temperatures, both in training and on missions, you never go into cold water unless it's a mandate. Fair warning—if the power goes out during a hurricane, I won't take a shower until I can get a hot one. I'll smell like a junkyard dog first."

"I'll make a note to chain you out in the backyard, something I'd only do to a man, not a dog."

He chuckled at that, then his gaze intensified. "Spread your legs for me, Mistress."

It was a clever combination, serving her will and yet issuing it like a command, the challenge unmistakable. She tilted her head. "I expect you to give me a good reason to open them, sailor."

His eyes sparked in answer, and then he sank below the surface. His fingers slid over her thighs, and then his mouth was on her knees, tongue tracing the seam, up, up, up... She could be a steel bitch when needed, but she wasn't going to make the task impossible. Plus his tongue felt so good, sliding along with the swirl of warm water he stirred. She let her legs part. His hands slipped beneath her knees, caressing the backs before he hooked his fingers under her thighs. Janet's head fell back on the ledge, her breasts rising to the cool touch of the air as his mouth found her pussy, the silk of his hair brushing her upper thighs. He teased her labia, tongue dipping inside her for a long, strong lick of her channel, gathering her cream. He dragged his tongue up to her clit, the pressure sending arrows of sensation shooting all along the insides of her thighs, her lower abdomen.

The water made everything soft, pliant, aiding his intent, but the man had obvious skill in this area. Lucas, the K&A CFO, was reputed to have legendary oral skills, and Janet had heard enough to know he'd coached the other four men, such that all their wives gained the benefit. Now she wondered if he was conducting classes for the rest of the K&A male personnel. She couldn't think of a better use for company time.

Of course, with Max, she expected he simply excelled at everything he undertook. Or practiced it religiously until he did. She gripped the handles harder, her heels resting on his upper back, her legs on his shoulders as his head worked between her thighs. With her eyes closed, her mind lost in blissful sensation, she imagined his tongue replaced by his cock, the water sloshing over the edges as he drove into her. He wouldn't have to wear a condom tonight. He'd brought test results, presented them in a matter-of-fact way, but with a direct look full of erotic potential.

He suckled her clit, plunged his tongue into her cunt again, rotating it around, then stroked the top of the vaginal channel, coming back out to the clit again. She groaned at the stimulation, a needy female response, and his fingers tightened on her legs, as if he'd registered the vibration through the water.

How long had he been under there? How long could the man hold his breath while swimming underwater? Or when doing something perhaps less physically exerting but requiring even more mental concentration? His large hands gripped her thighs, thumbs pressed on the inside, keeping her open for him. His shoulders held her up, so she was floating free beneath the water, only her handholds above the surface keeping her in place. The buoyancy was an amazing feeling as her body undulated in response to his stimulation.

"Max..." She let herself say his name while he was under water. "Max. Oh..." A guttural sound wrenched from her throat as he did something else, a pinch to her clit, then his tongue worked all around it, pushing against it, making it throb. Then he was pulling back from her, his hands sliding along her legs, a reluctant withdrawal. It added to her arousal, his obvious wish to stay where he was, no matter the needs of his lungs.

He surfaced right in front of her breasts, his aroused attention covering both before she let go of one handhold to grip his nape, cover his mouth with her own. She captured his exhalation, taking his breath into her body and giving him back the same, her lips teasing, her tongue tangling with his. When he lifted his head, it was to brush a kiss on the top of her breast, draw several breaths, then he submerged again, leaving her bemused and wanting more of his nearness.

He took up right where he left off, and she was impressed by his lack of apparent urgency. He was accomplishing a mission, but it was the type of mission that couldn't be achieved by racing a clock, no matter the critical time factor involved. She lost herself in it, the only thing grounding her to reality being an awareness of how her ankles rested on his lower back. She made sure they were loose enough he could easily get free of her if he needed to surface. Otherwise she had no concerns, immersed in those lovely whirlpools of feeling he had swirling up from her core.

The heat of the water bubbled against her skin, his body pressed up between her thighs. She dropped her head back to the concrete again and drops of water rolled into her mouth. She wanted to wrap her lips around his cock, suck and suck and suck until it convulsed and gave her his seed. But she wanted his seed in her body. She could have both, could have it all. A man who could do this would be more than capable of serving her several different ways in the same night. Three condoms that first time, right?

She was gasping, working herself in rhythm against his mouth, those spirals getting tighter, closer. His fingers dug into her, shoulders pushing her up so he could change his angle. As he did that, he broke the water's surface for only the key moment to draw a breath, so quick she nearly missed it, her eyes opening briefly to register his second breath before she was lost in hazy arousal once again.

"Oh God..." she breathed. "Oooohhh...fuck." She wasn't one to curse, but she wasn't sure it was a curse, more like a need to say the word that she desired to do with him, her deepest need at the moment. To fuck and be fucked, by this man. It wasn't an ugly word, not when spoken like this. It was the word that fit the primitive needs of her body, mind and soul, her heart pounding like a crescendo of tribal drums.

That intense ripple, the precursor to a dense wave, caused her pussy to clench, her hips to thrust up. As the feeling spread out, his mouth worked her with the steady constancy she usually associated with a vibrator, only this had the added benefit of being flesh and blood, an insistent, demanding male, wanting to give her pleasure even as he took the triumph of pulling it from her, a delicious mix. She thrashed like a caught mermaid in his grip. Her screams vibrated against the wall, the water, such that she could feel the reverberation against her flesh, and knew he could as well.

She had chimes hung from the ceiling, ones that had been making their bell noises from the light breeze stirred by the rainfall. That music joined the flashing lights in her vision, the smell of the rain, the heated water, the dampness of her own skin, to carry her spinning on a sensory experience unlike any other she'd had. It was lovely, intense, mind-numbing, and she wanted it to go on forever.

His hands spasmed on her body, and she had a sudden awareness of other issues. Pulling herself back to reality was a struggle, but she managed it, letting go of both handholds to take a full seat on the underwater bench and catch his shoulders, tugging on him urgently.

He surfaced with a large breath, chest heaving, eyes closed. She realized he'd likely needed his third breath when she began to orgasm. He'd chosen not to break her moment, letting her ride it to the end. Until she brought him up.

She guided him to the bench next to her, shifting in the water so she was resting on his knee. As she pushed his hair back from his face, it reassured her that his arm went around her waist, holding her there, fingers closing over her hip. Despite his being out of breath, the look he gave her when his eyes opened won a smile from her.

"Three breaths, Mistress."

"Actually," she said, trying to sound cool and unaffected, "I meant you could surface three times before you finished the job. Not that your third time had to be at the very end."

He blinked at her, then gave a half chuckle. "Well, my instructors said that nothing fucks you up like not following direction. On the other hand, that means I exceeded expectations."

"Hooyah," she responded, and he laughed outright, though he started coughing. She slipped an arm around his back and rubbed, moving more fully on to his lap. As she did, she realized her nearly drowning him hadn't diminished his own lust at all. His cock was a substantial weight against her leg. Her pussy, still caught in delicious aftershocks, contracted in reaction once more. She wanted to straddle him then and there, let him spend himself as his reward for a job well done, but an out-of-breath man having a climax in hot water was a sure recipe for unconsciousness. Since he was easily two hundred pounds of heavy muscle, there was no way she could drag him out if needed. "Safety first" could be a pain in the ass.

Smiling a little at the thought, she kept stroking his hair away from his face. When he decided to put his head down on her breasts, she allowed it, closing her eyes as he began to nuzzle her with his lips, his hand coming up to cup the left curve, stroke.

She rested her temple against his crown, letting the languorous aftermath of her climax take her over. "What kind of date were you going to suggest?" she asked. "When you were thinking about breaking protocol."

"Camping."

She lifted her head, blinked at him. "You want to take me camping, where there's no indoor plumbing, no place to plug in my hair dryer, no mirror or light for my makeup?"

"You'll have to rely on me to tell you you're beautiful." He settled back farther into his seat, holding her even more firmly. Catching a tendril of her hair, he let it slide between thumb and forefinger, then released it to spring back into a damp curl. His gray eyes passed along her throat, down her breasts, to the rest of her beneath the water. "Easy enough."

She rolled her eyes at him. "If I ever agree to do such an unlikely thing, I'll demand quid pro quo. You'll have to do something you're not entirely sure you want to do."

When he didn't immediately agree, she raised a brow. "A Navy SEAL is worried about what one woman can inflict upon him?"

"Absolutely. We abhor situations without proper intelligence."

Shaking her head at him, she leaned in, curling her fingers in his hair to hold him still as she put her mouth on his throat. She nipped at the pulsing artery, tracing his windpipe with her tongue. His hands closed over her back, her thigh, tugging her forward in an obvious desire to have her straddle him. It matched her own desire, and even though she knew they wouldn't finish here, she moved over him, locking gazes as he positioned himself at her opening, fingers digging into her as he slowly slid her onto his length. She was tight, tissues slick and yet also sensitive from the climax, but he moved slow, working into her, cupping the side of her neck as she gripped his shoulders, letting out a murmur as he pushed into her.

"Fuck, you're heaven," he said with reverence.

"Don't move," she said, a command she reinforced by digging her nails into his shoulders. She wanted to hold his climax out of reach, and not just because she wanted to exert control over him.

"I can take care of you," he said, reading her mind. "I'm fine." To prove it, he lodged himself deeper, his jaw set with a look of male determination that sent butterflies fluttering through her chest. And Janet Albright wasn't a fluttery person in any way.

"I know. Take care of me by serving me at my pleasure. When I demand it. For now, just feel." She tightened her muscles on his delicious length and savored the torment she gave him, making him stay still. His fingers would leave bruises on her fair flesh. He groaned, thighs twitching beneath hers. "I could make you come like this," she purred. "Milking you with my pussy, not allowing you to move until you couldn't help yourself. You're so very disciplined. It tempts me to do all sorts of things."

"I can tell." He gave a desperate half laugh, but then, when she did it again, he gripped her nape, ran his thumb along her jaw, giving her a decidedly more dangerous look. "When I have you under me, I will fuck you unconscious, Mistress."

"Promises, promises." She caught his thumb in her mouth, bit down, sucked on it as she worked her muscles on him again. His breath caught in his throat, even as his eyes got more feral. She was pushing the wild animal to the forefront, and loving every moment of it. "What if I fuck you to unconsciousness first?"

Max's other hand curved around her buttock, fingers teasing the seam. His mood changed, the edgy game they were playing becoming something else as he looked at her. His eyes were moving over her face as if seeing her for the first time. "Let me come inside you, Mistress," he said. "I want that. And so do you."

He brought her to his lips, starting the kiss slow and devastating, his fingers burying in her hair, mouth opening farther to seal over her lips, tongue working against hers. Her pussy clenched again, but this time in reaction to his emotional seduction. He cinched his arm around her waist, where no movement at their joining point was possible for either, just that deep penetration, her muscles working against his length, her clit pressed against his hard abdomen, breasts high on his chest. He kept his attention on her mouth, a never-ending kiss where he teased her lips, tongue and the insides of her mouth to the point the nerves were vibrating like a second erogenous zone, hungry to keep him there, filling her, connected to her.

She wrapped her arms around his shoulders, squeezed down with everything she had, pushed against his hold so he knew she wanted to move. Three strokes and his hands convulsed on her. She would figure out how to get him out of the spa if he fainted, but now she had a feeling it would take far more than that to overcome this powerful man. He was moving forward and taking her with him.

"Come for me, Max."

"You too, Mistress." He held her tight, working her clit against his body as he reacted to her lift and fall with his own thrusts. "Fuck…"

It was a hard, short climax for her, so intense it gave her a series of shuddering waves that prolonged his own. When he released with a groan, she reveled in the feel of his seed searing inside of her. The water would take away any sticky moisture when they finally parted and left the pool. Yet what was inside of her would trickle onto her wet thighs. She might let him lick himself off her flesh. Or maybe she'd let it stay there, a reminder of what he'd given her.

They finished together, wrapped around one another, breathing hard. He had his face pressed to her throat, her arms still around him, and Janet felt a sense of restful peace she hadn't felt in so long. Just holding and being held, the world revolving around them.

Gradually, she became aware of the patter of the rain on the tin roof again, saw the dripping waterfall of it off the eaves. She expected it was a good thing it was raining; else her neighbors on the other side of the privacy fence might have gotten an earful.

"Let's get out and go inside," she said at length, feeling her fingers pruning. "We can lie on the couch and turn on the fire logs."

* * * * *

"If I agree to this camping idea, where would we be going? For all I know, you might be ferrying me to some fringe survivalist camp where you and other ex-military types are plotting to take over the government."

Max chuckled, making her head bounce against his chest. Janet was running her wicked fingernails through his chest hair, teasing his nipple, following the curves and planes of him down to his rib cage, his bare hip, then back up again. She'd wanted him lying on her wide sofa, with her body comfortably draped over him, so that was where they were, lazy as a pair of cats next to the flickering fire logs.

The delivery pizza had been polished off, mostly by him, though Janet had talked herself into three slices. The empty box was under the coffee table. Two empty glasses topside still had the dregs of the hot toddy he'd made them. She dipped a finger in his, tasting the residual sugar and honey, then put that sweetness against his flesh to lick it off. The intimacy stirred him as much the touch. He curved his fingers in her hair, tugged a little, responding to the tease.

"You can hardly blame me for trying to enlist you in our cause," he said. "I've seen you whip giggling interns into ninja assassins in less than six weeks. But since you were whining about indoor plumbing and hair dryers, you may not be as tough as I told them you were."

She pinched him for that, and he fended her off by grasping her wrist. When she gave him that look that said she wanted to do as she pleased, he waited a charged beat before opening his fingers slowly, letting her go. Still holding his gaze, she pinched him again, hard. The sharp edge of her nails left little burning bites along his flesh that made him struggle to stay still. She put her mouth over them, soothing the pain with her tongue and stirring up other parts. Then she got quiet again, laying her head on his chest once more. He stroked her hair again, liking the feel of that, as well as how she lay between his thighs, her body pressed against his cock, which was proving it was capable of whatever she might demand from him next.

"You want to go up to your bed, where there are warm blankets and my feet aren't hanging off the end of the couch?" He had to stay mindful of the side table beneath his heels, where a trio of delicate ceramic flowers were arranged. If she became any more aggressive with her nails and teeth, he might react as if a doctor had hit his knee with a rubber hammer and send one of them shattering against her headboard.

"I'd say yes, but I don't have the energy to get up."

He grunted, levering himself into an upright position and shifting her so he had her supported in his arms. He stood up then, taking her with him. "No need for that, Mistress. All you need is me."

She made a noncommittal noise but crooked her arm around his neck, adjusting so she was deeper in the cradle he provided. It said a great deal about the size of her personality that, until he held her like this, it wasn't obvious how petite she really was. Small-boned, light frame. He thought about those leg fractures and tightened his arms around her, but the way he might hold an egg. Firm and protective, but not crushing.

He took the stairs slow. Halfway up, she touched his face, guided it toward hers for a kiss. He stopped there, holding her securely, even as he was caught by the power of her simple touch. With every gesture, it seemed as if she gave him everything. He'd had an impression that Dommes withheld a great deal, but inside the world she spun, nothing was further from the truth. She made things in his heart swell up, made him want to say unlikely things to her. He thought of the times he'd seen her take a sub to the point he was fervently kissing her shoe, telling her of his love, his devotion to her, but that was the endorphin rush, the mindless drive of lust. This heated kiss on her staircase in a suspended moment of time was something different.

At least for him.

The thought was an uncomfortable one. When he lifted his head, she touched his mouth, but she didn't say anything right away, her dark eyes studying him. He wasn't sure if that helped or added to his concern. "Take me to my bed, Max," she said at last.

He'd only had a brief impression of her bedroom last time, since he'd been blindfolded most of the time he'd been in it. The mahogany tester bed gave him pause, then a wry smile. It looked like it belonged to a queen. The half panel arched over it was lined with velvet, and the headboard had leaf and heart patterns carved into the dark wood. The bed was piled high with thick comforters and pillows, and he could well imagine Her Majesty sleeping, a petite but formidable coil beneath it, her servants coming to wake her in the morning. The wardrobe and dresser matched the bed, but she'd softened the severe furniture with watercolors of Victorian scenes, well-dressed couples strolling in the park, picnicking in a meadow.

Letting her feet down by her bed, he pulled back the covers. As he did, her fingers slipped off his shoulder down to his chest. She liked to tug on his chest hair, give him that tiny pain. As she walked up the steps affixed to the base of the bed and stretched out on the mattress, she released her hair. The thick coil of it wound sinuously over the pillow. Her hand slipped to her breast, molding the curve, thumb tracing her nipple before she parted her thighs, put the other hand there. His chest tightened along with his cock, seeing the slumberous desire in her eyes. She was tired, but she wanted him. Again.

He had no idea what time it was. It must be late, given that he'd come after work, but time had stopped for him once he'd crossed her threshold. Maybe she was as much sorceress as queen. He wondered that Ulysses had ever wanted to leave Circe's island. Of course, there was the matter of his men being turned to pigs...

When he shared that with her, her sinful mouth curved. "Not to mention his wife and child waiting at home. He loved them too dearly to be derailed for long, even by a sorceress's deceptive charms. He was an honorable man."

The shadow through her gaze was unexpected, and he put his hip on the bed, his hand on her face. "You are the best of both worlds," he said. "The integrity and loyalty of Penelope, the seductive power of Circe."

He meant it, but he knew he only had the faith of wishful thinking. He had no true understanding of what was going on in her head, how he really differed from the others, except for location. When he leaned down toward her lips, she put a hand on his chest, stopping him. "What is it, Max?"

Her voice wasn't the appeal of an insecure woman, but a tone he often heard at the office, as she fixed some luckless person with a direct stare that could command truth out of Pinocchio.

"Me, being a dumbass."

She considered that, her touch sliding along his neck, fingers tracing his collarbone. "You broke this once."

"Yeah." He couldn't tell her the where, who, what or why, but how was okay. "Couldn't get out of a blast zone fast enough, timing got fucked. Thrown about fifty feet, landed on something harder than me."

She nodded. "We're playing a game, you and I, but it's an honest game."

"I know." Propping himself on an elbow, he traced a line down her sternum to her upper abdomen, stopping just above her mound to curve his fingers over her hip bone. "You demand honesty from every sub you've driven to his knees, every one of them who's begged you for more. A couple times you've been close enough to me at the club I saw it in your eyes, how you feel when he declares his devotion to you, his desire to serve your every need. It's a game you both understand. At the end of the night, he puts on his clothes, goes back into the world, and that's that. He knows the emotions he expresses to you in that room don't translate to anywhere else."

"We're not at the club."

When he lifted his attention to her face, it was clear she would say nothing else, give him no more than that. Leaning in, he brushed his lips over hers, pressing there a long moment before sliding out of the bed. He pulled the covers over her to her waist, making sure she'd be warm. "It's time for me to head home."

She sat up, bending her legs beneath the blankets to link her hands over them. As he moved to the doorway, he remembered his clothes were still by the hot tub. He should have brought them in, because they were probably going to be damp from the humid air. He wondered if she was going to try to stop him. She didn't. He went down the hallway, past the picture of the young dancer she'd called Nelle, and headed for the steps. *Damn it.*

Going out to the porch, he found his clothes, put them on. As he strapped his watch to his wrist, his mind was rotating. He knew what he wanted, needed. In time, maybe she'd offer that, but he'd forced her hand just now, looking for more of a response. He wasn't sure if it was the right play, but that was the deal. Certain things couldn't be a game for him at all, honest or not. Even so, an ache was growing in his chest, suggesting he was about to close a door that he'd be a fool to shut.

Earlier, she'd trimmed the rose he gave her, put it in a glass on her kitchen table. It made him hurt, seeing that single rose, the swirl of dark-blood and vanilla colors.

He fished out his keys, held them. Shaking his head, he put them back in his pocket, pivoted and headed back into the house. Things were silent. He passed the couch where they'd had their hot toddies, dozed. The blanket he'd draped over her was still rumpled from where it had folded around her. He took the stairs two at a time, paused where he'd kissed her.

During that embrace, he'd thought about her generosity, a thought he knew was at odds with his behavior now.

Now he went up the rest of the stairs, moved down the hall to the bedroom doorway. She'd moved. She was sitting in a chair by the window, her knees pulled up to her chest and feet curved over the seat edge. She'd donned a robe. Her head rested against the cushion, her fingertips tracing designs on the glass. The window overlooked the driveway and his truck, so she'd been waiting to watch him drive away. She hadn't intended to come after him. He wasn't sure how to react to that, but then she spoke.

"I've never been involved with anyone outside a club, Max. Not since my twenties." When she turned her gaze to him, he realized she looked tired. She also didn't look apologetic, but then he wouldn't have expected that. She lifted her chin. "That's all I can give you right now."

There was a chair across from the one where she sat, and he took it, leaning forward and propping his elbows on his knees, making a steeple of his fingers as he studied her. She'd left her hair down, and it curved around her face, the dark, hard-to-read eyes.

"The picture in the hallway," he said. "The girl you called Nelle. That girl is you."

Chapter Ten

Whatever she'd been expecting, it hadn't been that. He saw the flicker of shock in her gaze, quickly masked, telling him she'd learned to conceal any reactions related to that, but then anger replaced it.

"If you think to leverage my emotions by striking at a vulnerable spot, you can go to hell."

"No. Damn it, no."

She'd brought her legs down and stood, obviously intending to exit the chair and probably the room. He caught her wrist, holding her in place. "The only reason I brought it up, the *only* reason, is what you just said. I see things about you, Janet. I notice things. Things I have absolutely no right to know, so if you don't want to share them, that's fine. I just wanted to prove that you can trust me. That if this is all new to you, you don't have to worry about that. We'll stumble along together, but wherever I can, I'll make sure the footing is sure for you."

She gave his hand a pointed glance, telling him she wanted him to let go. Since she'd said he was her first relationship outside a club, he expected it wouldn't surprise her that he wasn't always going to be an obedient lapdog. He tugged her closer, putting his hands on her hips, looking up at her. "Let me do something?"

She gave him a wary look but nodded. He eased her on to his lap, cradling her in his arms as he settled back in the wing-backed chair. She allowed it, though she was stiff. "I wanted to know I was different," he said. "That I wasn't a series of snapshots you delete when you're done looking at them. This feels different to me, and if it's not different for you, I needed to know that sooner than later, to minimize the damage to us both."

"Okay." As she looked up at him, her hair brushed against his shirt front. "Your delivery and timing sucked though."

"Yeah. No argument on that."

They sat that way silently for a while. He didn't feel like she needed him to say anything further, and he'd wait for her cues to see where she wanted to take this next. He hoped it was back to bed, but he accepted that ship may have sailed tonight. For his part, he could make do with this. Just having her willing to be in his arms. The tension in her body seemed to be growing though. He was thinking of a way to alleviate it when she spoke.

"How did you figure it out?"

He touched the ballerina charm where it rested on her sternum. "For one thing, you're both wearing this."

She put her fingers over it. "My mother gave it to me after my first recital. But that's not how you guessed. I could have loaned out the necklace."

He nodded, but with a gentle hand, he opened the robe, spreading it to expose her right breast. His target was beyond it, below her armpit. He touched the faint brown mark, a permanent imprint on her fair skin. "It would be unusual for you and a sibling to have the same birthmark, in the same location. But more than that, when your face softened, right before I was inside you the first time, you became her again." Tracing the planes of her face, he caressed the sculpted lines. "I've been studying your face a lot."

"Yes." She moistened her lips. "I see that." Her face did that softening thing then, but she looked away, out the window. Whatever thoughts she was thinking made it harden once again. He adjusted her robe so it was mostly closed, though the neckline framed the curves in an attractive way.

"Janelle. That was my name then. The last name's not important, save that it's no longer the one I have now. When I was twenty, I was good enough to be in a ballet company, but not good enough to ever break out and be the star. But I had an excellent grasp on technique, and I was good at helping the stronger dancers improve. However, at that point, I still had dreams of being center stage. Like so many women in so many different situations, I ignored the truth and instead believed a man who said he could make my dreams come true."

There was no bitterness in her tone, just a matter-of-fact sympathy, as if she viewed herself at that time as a separate person. "His name was Jorge Mendes. He was in the audience when we performed in Mexico City. To my eyes, he seemed like an important man, with expensive cars and an aura of power an impressionable girl mistook for something real. He flattered me, told me I had an abundance of talent, and if I was willing to stay behind when the company traveled back to the States, he could get me a couple bookings where I would be the headline dancer. It was time for the company to take a summer hiatus, so it made sense, even though friends of mine told me not to do it. I thought they were jealous."

Cold fingers touched his vitals. Her words could unlock a part of him that would take him to another memory, one that would pull his mind away when Janet obviously needed him a hundred percent present. So he steeled himself, resolved not to let that happen. This wasn't Amanda in his arms, not his mother.

"The drug cartels run Mexico. I'm sure that's not news to you."

Though he shook his head, confirming it, she didn't register his response. Her gaze was on that window, the raindrops slipping down it. "He was upper middle management in one of them, I guess. I never saw an organization chart." Her lip curled. "The moment the company left Mexico, I became his possession. To his credit, I did dance in a few performances with a substandard company.

My classical training made me shine, a swan among the ducks. At first I overlooked it, delighted to be the one soaring across the stage, hearing the crowds gasping at the more dramatic moments. I was at last the prima ballerina.

"It only took a few reviews from respected critics for me to realize I hadn't achieved greatness. I'd simply denied the limits of my talent. When I accepted that, I knew my career would go further as part of my old company than as a prima ballerina in Mexico City. I told Jorge I wanted to leave. My fascination with him was dimming in the light of reality, and I was starting to notice things. I knew by then he wasn't the kind of businessman he'd told me he was when we met. When I told him I was leaving, that was the first time he beat me."

Max put his lips on her shoulder, brushed it with his jaw. Her skin was cool, and he adjusted the robe so she was more covered. She tilted her head to him, pressing her cheek to his temple. Closing his eyes, he held that connection, but the images she planted in his brain unfurled an old, deadly rage inside him.

"He didn't do things in half measures. He beat me so severely that first time he broke ribs, but he limited it to what wouldn't show. I was his little china doll, his ballerina on the music box, and he wanted to show me off. I escaped twice, and he caught me both times. He had people everywhere. The third time, he had to make an example of me, because his men knew I was running. This lowly *puta* had defied their boss. He used a baseball bat on my face and legs."

Goddamn him to hell. Max touched her face, brought her eyes back to him. "You don't have to do this," he said.

"I know. But you made a valid point. I can trust you."

Because of the type of person she was, never saying what she didn't mean, the impact of the simple statement on him was tremendous.

"Yes, you can." He cupped her jaw, ran fingers over it. "With anything, Janet. Now, tomorrow, forever. No matter what happens with us."

"I know. Matt seems to attract that type of man. Like Arthur and the knights who flocked to his table. Though I think Arthur might be too moderate for Matt."

Max's lips twisted. "Yeah. Matt's more like a savage Celt king. I can see him drinking the blood of his enemies with no problem at all."

He was rewarded with a faint smile, then she returned her attention to the window. "Jorge put me back together. Imported a European plastic surgeon, paid to have my face reconstructed. My legs were set and healed, but he left those scars untouched, because he wanted me to have a permanent reminder of who owned me. It ended my dance career, of course. There are rods in both my legs. No shock absorbers."

He heard the quaver in her voice, even as she firmed her chin, lifted it. Her hands were gripped together in her lap now, her back rigid where it rested against his arm, as if she'd donned armor against what she was telling him.

"He'd touch my face and tell me that he'd re-created me, just like God teaching Lilith to be Eve, obedient to her Adam." Her lip curled again. "I think it challenged and aroused him as much as it angered him, that he could never get me to submit to him without a fight. Except for the time he used the bat, he always had to tie me up when he beat me, because I fought him so hard."

Which was why she didn't tie her subs down, not so they couldn't get away. He thought of the night he'd asked her about it, the shadows that rose in her eyes. Murder hazed his vision again.

"I would never cower from him like the house staff did, but I got smart. Except in private, I became the dutiful show pony, a credit to his household. And then one day I met Matt Kensington."

*****

She needed a break after that. She rose from his lap and they went downstairs. This time Max fixed them both a straight whisky in shot glasses from her wet bar. She tossed it back and her eyes didn't even water, though he knew how the stuff burned a trail.

"Jorge and he didn't do business together, of course. It was a chance meeting. Jorge was having dinner with his associates, and Matt was at a table nearby. He was so young then, in his twenties like me, but when I first met his eyes, I got caught by that still, raptor look he has. A man in control of things around him. Very different from the illusion of control Jorge had. His was based on a deceptive mix of charm, lies, fear. Matt's was based on intelligence, a keen grasp of the details and his unfailing sense of right and wrong, moral versus immoral. Concepts he never confuses with legal or illegal."

Max felt a vibration on that thread, another thing that connected him and Janet. Matt hadn't had a hand in that "moral versus legal" part of Max's life, but Max knew the K&A CEO was fully aware of it. It hadn't stopped him from hiring Max as a driver. In fact, it was possible it might have influenced Matt's hiring decision.

She pushed the glass toward him. "Another."

He poured it, and she downed it the same way she'd done the first. "As long as I stayed in his line of sight, Jorge didn't care if I sat at the table with him and his dealers while they talked business. I could feel Matt watching me when I moved to the bar, drank my cocktail, stared out into the night.

"After the baseball-bat incident, there were a lot of times I kept my mind blank, because to think was to go mad. I was always watching, though, waiting. Jorge thought my increased interest in his life and business was evidence that I'd accepted his ownership, but I knew my next escape attempt had to work. If it didn't, he'd kill me for sure. At that point, I was ready for that. I would have preferred it to staying with him any longer, but I really didn't want to give him that satisfaction."

She lifted her head, stared at Max. "I never gave Jorge any real power over me. Even now, I think of him in a detached way, the way I'd think of a piece of furniture. To give him more than that would give him a piece of that power, and I refuse to do that. He beat me up because he was stronger than me physically, not emotionally. You understand?"

Max nodded. When she tapped the glass, he didn't suggest she slow down. He'd seen things that a whole bottle of whisky wouldn't even dent, and he had a feeling the worst part of her story was to come, if her desire for the liquid fortification was any indication. Even now, however, her back stayed straight, her hand steady and gaze direct. What would it be like, standing inside Janet's mind and heart, seeing the tides of emotions she'd learned to mask and rein back to be the formidable woman she was? He'd caught glimpses of them, moments he knew were rare gifts. She had a softer side, but not what he'd call a vulnerable one. The Domme side of her was too overwhelming to permit that.

As she'd said, she hadn't given Jorge power over her, a drug dealer who'd nearly beaten her to death. Her will was far beyond a mere physical thing.

She took a swallow of the whisky, put it down. "When Matt came up to the bar to refresh his drink order, he put his business card down in front of him. He was close enough I could see it, and he'd written his cell number on it in large print. He never looked at me, but he spoke. 'Memorize it, and if you ever need a friend, call me'."

She shook her head. "When it was all over, later, I asked him what had made him do that. He said as he watched me that night, he saw certain things in my body language, my expressions, which told him I was in trouble. I was standing on a ledge where I was willing to be free or die, which likely meant I would end up dead. He knew Jorge's connections, knew better than to speak to me directly or give me something Jorge would find on me later. Matt has that canniness to him, you know."

When Max nodded, confirming it, Janet's lips twisted. "Matt said he figured if he'd read me wrong, I'd simply see him as a crazy person and forget the number. Or tell my cartel boyfriend this gringo was hitting on me, and they'd dump his body in the trash."

She sat down on the barstool across from Max, rotated the shot glass in one hand. "My opportunity came about two months later. There was a war going on between competing cartels. I plotted out every detail, had everything ready. Late one night when Jorge was asleep on the couch, I hit him in the head with a skillet until he stopped moving. Then I took a power drill and drilled out his eyes. Used a butcher knife on the tongue. It took a heavy-duty meat cleaver to sever the head. Fortunately, his cook kept one stored in the pantry."

She delivered the words in a flat monotone, but the air vibrated with everything behind them. Max found he had one hand clenched on his knee, the other on his forgotten drink. She lifted blank eyes to him. Those perfect nails tented over the top of her glass, spun it in circles, over and over, like a nervous tic, except all of her had gone so still.

"That's the way the competing cartel was dressing their kills. Jorge had found some of his dealers left that way. I didn't care if they took revenge on the other cartel for what I did, as long as they weren't hunting me. But when I took the head, something funny was going through my mind, like this absurd knock-knock joke. 'What comes back after you cut off its head? Absolutely fucking nothing'."

She nodded in a decided sort of way, finished the whisky. She shook her head when Max offered to refill it. "I broke up some furniture, cut my wrist to leave blood and tore off a fingernail. I wanted it to look like I'd been kidnapped. If they couldn't find me, they'd assume I'd been used and killed, or sold on the black market. Another huge insult to Jorge, selling his woman into white slavery." Her lips curved grimly. "Because I was so free with him, right?"

Max remembered a night he'd slipped into a dingy gasoline restroom, washing gunpowder off his hands as he thought of two weighted bodies, shoved into the river. He hadn't been thinking of the horror of that, but going back over all the important details. All the brass policed and bullets dug out of the corpses, no ID left on them. Yet he remembered the look in his eyes when he'd glanced up in the mirror. He'd seen that look in Janet's face, that night in the hospital bathroom. Because of what he himself had done and experienced, he could reconcile the brutal images she was painting with the woman before him now. A human being was capable of incredible, terrible things.

"I called Matt. I never questioned that was the right thing to do. He really could have been some idiot, living dangerously, flirting with the drug dealer's girl, but I knew it wasn't that. He was back in Texas. He asked me if I could get to the border, and I said I could, but I didn't have a passport, any way to get through. Jorge had locked up my passport, which probably wouldn't have done me any good anyhow, since the picture had been before my face reconstruction. Matt told me not to worry about that, and set up the time to meet me there. I had the cash I'd taken off Jorge, but I didn't take anything else that might connect me back to him. I slipped past the guards he kept posted on his grounds—to keep threats out—and stole a car, which I planned to ditch at the border."

She shook her head. "When I arrived at the border, they made me leave the car and come into their office for further questions. I figured I was about to go to a Mexican jail, where I'd be tortured and killed by Jorge's associates as retribution. Instead, Matt was waiting for me. I assume he bribed whoever needed to be bribed, because he merely thanked the guards as if they were returning an errant, mentally defective relative to him. He took my arm, and I walked with him to the American side. He walked me around to the passenger door of his car, held it open for me."

That seemed important to her. She closed her eyes, her fingers stilling on the glass a long moment before she continued. "He'd brought his own vehicle, no driver. I remember him driving twenty miles without either of us saying a word. I looked at all the empty, flat land around us, nothing significant, but all of it U.S. soil. I looked down at my hands, and saw I still had blood under the nails, staining the cuticles.

"It wasn't until he pulled the car off to the side of the road and put his arms around me that I realized I'd started crying. It took me a couple hours to stop trembling." She lifted a shoulder. "Shock."

She rose then. "I want you to go home now, Max."

What the hell? "No."

"Yes." She met his gaze. "It's not a request. I need the space. You wanted to get a sense of what's going on between us, what it means to me. You needed some kind of reassurance that you're different from Thor, or any of the men I've dominated at Progeny."

He rose as well. "Then don't fucking treat me like one of them."

As soon as he said it, he could have bitten through his tongue. She'd just told him something only one other person knew. But his response wasn't based on that. It was based on his own demons, the empty face of his mother in his mind, forever beyond his reach. There was no way in hell he could countenance leaving Janet now, not when he hadn't been there to protect her, irrational as that kind of thinking was.

But that was obviously what she wanted. She was showing him a window in her soul, then slamming it down on his fingers, shutting him out. It fucked with his mind, twisted in his gut and became something ugly, cutting the intent connection they'd shared.

She didn't say anything, remaining still as a statue. Her expression didn't change, but he could feel a radical shift in the air, as if she'd physically stepped onto a whole different continent.

"Is that what you do?" he asked. "Give them that vibe that tells them they've fucked up, earned your displeasure? It cuts them, slices out their guts and makes them willing to do anything to make it better, right? Don't work me, Janet. I'm not wired that way."

"No," she said. "You're not. I'm not like most women you know, Max. When I let down the shields, I need you to stand at a distance for a while, so I'll be sure you're not going to rush over the boundaries, attack what I'm revealing."

"I won't. But we can't figure out how to make the different pieces of who we are fit together if you won't let me close enough to get a good look at them."

"Do you usually walk into an enemy compound to check things out, or do you survey things at a distance first, moving in closer as you verify the safest approach? The shape of those pieces?"

"I don't see you as an enemy. But maybe that's how you see me."

A muscle twitched in her jaw. "No. But your lack of trust, the way you pulled back earlier, that disappointed me. I do understand trust must be earned, and a lot of this is unfamiliar territory for you. You're adjusting, but I have to adjust too. We both feel it's worth it, because neither of us has backed off yet."

Now she seemed to be talking to herself more than him, but then she brought her attention back to him. "I need you to trust that I mean what I say. Give me space. Go home. I'll contact you when I'm ready."

"Your terms, your way."

"Yes. On that I don't compromise. I'm sorry. If you can't accept that, then it's time to finish this."

Wow, just like that. His emotional radar was screwed up here, things spiraling in a wrong direction that he didn't really understand. He wanted to make it better if he could, but she seemed locked out at all levels, frustrating him.

"Do you have to hold on to all the control? Is it the only way you can feel anything? Can't you let yourself be a normal person for one minute?"

"No. Being a deviant is what works for me. And until now, that hasn't seemed to bother you."

Okay, *so* the wrong tactic. When she gave him a searing look and began to pivot on her heel, he moved to stand in front of her. This time he didn't touch her, but he held up a hand. "Damn it, just wait a second. That's not what I meant. Yeah, being a Domme is real for you, but sometimes it's not. I don't want to make you mad by saying that. But earlier tonight, being a Mistress was something you embraced for your own pleasure, your own reasons. It was real. Now you're using it as a wall, hiding that real part of you. One's your true face, the other's a mask. Tell me if I'm wrong, Janet. *Tell me.*"

Damn it, he couldn't even touch her, hug her like he would any other woman when he acted like an ass. She obviously wouldn't welcome that. All he could do was what she demanded. Which was what the whole Domme thing was about, wasn't it?

Her gaze was frosty, mouth set. "I need you to go," she said, her voice jagged glass. "Now. Don't make me say it again."

Everything about her body language, her eyes, rejected him. It did cut him deeply, such that he realized exactly why Thor and the others were willing to do whatever was needed to stand within the circle of her approval. Even now, he remembered the warmth of her body, her generosity in the hot tub and in her bed. But he couldn't take back what he felt was truth. He wasn't sure what he was seeking from her at this exact moment, but whatever it was, she wasn't in a giving mood.

"I'm sorry," he said. "I'm going. Whatever you decide...I'm sorry."

Picking up his keys, he left her there, standing in the middle of her living room.

* * * * *

He had plenty to keep him busy. He steered clear of "the tower" for a while, what they called the executive offices. Janet cooperated, choosing to update the scheduling grid online and send text alerts to the affected drivers, including himself. When something needed to be couriered, she delivered it through one of the interns, or he delegated another driver to pick it up from her. He was the boss, after all.

Besides that, he had a lot to do outside of work. His visits with Amanda, some time spent with guys at the VA. He helped Dale out at Eddie's place and with building the swing set. While he was doing that, he didn't talk about Janet and Dale didn't push, especially when he realized Max wanted to think the problem through without help.

She'd told him he was different, because he'd been to her home, engaged her in an environment different from the club. In turn, he'd pulled a *Pretty Woman* moment, insisting that was just "geography". Fuck, he really needed to stay away from late night television.

On the day she'd killed Jorge, it had taken her a trip to the border and then twenty miles after that to feel everything that she'd done to escape. She'd planned and committed cold-blooded murder. Then, on top of that, she'd butchered the body. Most people couldn't countenance either act, let alone execute them. He knew up close and personal the difference between taking out a man through the sights of a rifle, and holding him against your body as you cut his throat. Feeling how hard he struggled against his fate, the way the soul slipped away when he lost.

Janet had shared the terrible story with him, a story he assumed no one but Matt Kensington knew. That had been her additional offering to show him he was different.

Yet, in the end, she'd shut him down just like she'd shut down one of her subs. That might be true, but he had no doubt he was the asshole here. He'd basically proven what she'd said. He'd rushed the boundaries, taken advantage of those shields being down. It was an unforgivable breach, he was sure. He'd fucked it up at every level, because he'd wanted it too much. He'd stirred the shark-infested waters, but it was his own demons that had made him crash and burn.

So that was clear enough. But was it the finish line? Was their pleasurable interlude a short-term thing, now over, just as she'd predicted from the first?

If she felt that way, he had no doubt she would have made a move toward closure within twenty-four hours. But five days passed, and that didn't happen. And his feelings toward her didn't dim in the slightest. If anything, they became even more excruciating.

The simple truth was he wasn't done with it, and apparently she wasn't either.

We both feel it's worth it, because neither of us has backed off yet.

The problem was, he had no course of action. No matter from which angle he considered it, he came up with nothing. It suggested the ball was in her court, and he needed to wait her out. She'd said that as well, hadn't she?

He was forced to face the fact he had to do something utterly foreign to his nature. Nothing. He had to wait for her.

At the end of that first week, he sent her a text. *I'm here, Mistress. I'll wait.* And then he hunkered down into his daily schedule, dedicating his energy to not going out of his fucking mind while he waited.

* * * * *

Janet stood on the nature trail, gazing up through the leaves. She should have worn gloves, because her hands were cold, but if she decided to use the park's fitness area, she'd get warm. For now she watched the leaves play with one another in pretty patterns above her head, listened to the birds chirping to one another. She kept her mind still. She really was in unfamiliar waters here. It would have made her laugh, but too much was weighing down her heart, churning in her stomach. She wondered if, when Max went into dangerous situations, it was anything like this. Every detail planned, yet if one small piece went awry, all of it could fall apart, such that he had to be ready for any contingency, adapt as the circumstances changed.

He came down the trail at an impressive clip, given that she knew at this point he'd already run five miles that took him through the marsh, by the river. Though he was in that mental workout zone, she was wearing a red fleece pullover and black exercise leggings. The red caught his attention, as planned. His gaze touched on her, probably expecting she was another insanely early jogger taking a break, then he locked on, recognizing her.

She'd only seen him at a distance for four weeks, and not that often. They'd both managed it that way, and she'd been impressed by his understanding of the nature of their détente. *I'm here, Mistress. I'll wait.* A pause in their chess game, but possibly not an end to it. *Game* sounded too frivolous, especially given that the word had launched their argument, but *battle* was too much the other way.

She watched him slow to a walk. His hair was damp on his neck, and he wore T-shirt and sweats on the body she knew intimately. With his gray eyes fixed on her, the plans she had unraveled. And not just because she couldn't hold it together in the face of how much she felt, being alone with him again at last.

Initially, she'd been angry with him, with his typical male, overinflated testosterone reaction to her wanting him to back off. But then, as she was able to settle the waters of her past to a deceptive placid surface again, she'd thought a lot more about the scenario, things they'd both said and felt. And she'd known there was some truth to his words, but beyond that, there'd been an elusive and unexpected weight in her chest, a sense of regret and guilt she couldn't define.

The moment his gaze met hers, she couldn't have said what it was in his expression that helped her find that meaning, but she did. She finally pinpointed what he'd been seeking from her that night. He hadn't been able to properly express it either, and, as often happened in an argument when emotions were so raw, things had gotten blown out of proportion, truth lost in anger and hurt.

She'd given him the story, yes, which seemed a huge concession, but if she'd been asked to report it to a police precinct, she would have delivered it the same way. And then she'd asked him to leave. In her world, the men who attracted her were managed, enjoyed, but never truly trusted. While it might have been unreasonable for him to demand that much from her so soon, she realized he hadn't been looking for all or nothing, just a step in that direction. Something spontaneous, unplanned.

From his expression, she thought he might be pleased to see her, but he was wary as well. Maybe he thought she was going to call an end to it here. Was that what he wanted as well? She quelled the despised insecurity. He hadn't made that move in four weeks. Why would he want it now?

He stopped, two feet between them, and didn't say anything. She looked up at him, the rise and fall of his chest as he adjusted to the change in exertion, the dark-blond hair rumpled and spiked. He'd likely rolled out of bed and gone straight into his workout.

"It's a little early for a woman to be hanging out in the park alone," he said at last. "Ma'am."

It was the *ma'am* that did it. As she let out the breath she hadn't realized she'd been holding, he gave her a faint smile, though his eyes remained serious.

"I have it on good authority this is where a Navy SEAL does his morning workout," she managed. "I wasn't worried." Reaching out, not sure what she was doing, she curled her fingers into the fabric of his T-shirt. Then she'd latched on with the other hand as well. As she stepped closer, his hand rose, rested on her hip, drawing her in. She pressed her face to his chest, inhaling his scent. In a heartbeat, she was overcome with a sense of well-being so strong she shuddered with it. She'd missed him. Really, really missed him. And she had no words to convey that. Touch seemed inadequate, or at least she thought it might be, but when his other hand cupped her skull, she reconsidered.

"I'm sweaty and nasty," he said.

"Yeah, you are. I tend to like my men that way."

He offered a tight chuckle, then his grip around her grew stronger. "You're not here to end things, are you? Because that would be a shitty way to start my day."

"Well, I was, but since it doesn't fit your schedule, I guess I'll do it another time." The band in her chest loosened further at that mild comment, which drove away any worry she'd had that he wanted to go that direction. "Max..."

"I'm sorry. Fuck, I'm sorry in so many ways. I pushed too hard, too fast. You got deep inside me, quicker than I expected, and I reacted like a kid having his fucking ice cream cone taken away."

She shook her head against him. "No. You don't need to say you're sorry. You followed your gut, and your gut wasn't wrong." She took a deep breath, tilted her face up to meet his eyes. "Sharing that was very difficult for me, but I lock things down when my emotions are involved. I let you in, but I shut you out at the same time."

"It's an impressive skill. Very effective. Like being thrown on a bed of railroad spikes and being told you can leave as soon as you can get up." He sighed, stopping her response to that. "Look, when bad shit happens, and it often does, I've learned not to get stuck in that moment; I use it to do better going forward. From what I see of your life, how you live it, you would have made a hell of a SEAL. If you weren't a girl."

She made a face at him but then sobered. "I haven't been a girl in a long time."

He touched her cheek then, stroking her hair. "The girl in that picture is still there. I know, because sometimes she makes me feel like I'm seventeen again."

He'd said she'd gotten deep inside him, but he had no idea how words like that could drive him into her soul, far deeper than she'd ever allowed anyone, even when she was naïve and innocent. Of course, the soul tended to lie at the bottom of a well, its depth determined by experiences, loss and regret, things that happened over the course of a lifetime.

He cupped her jaw, his thumb stroking it as well as her throat. Tipping up her chin, he pressed his lips to hers, taking it deeper, deep as her soul itself. Her body melted into his, leaning into it in a way she'd never remembered herself doing. It was a surrender of sorts, no physical or mental part of her held apart, just a capitulation to that kiss, to the potential of what was between them. As the kiss deepened, she put her hands under his T-shirt, and he jumped like she'd hit him with a Taser.

"Christ, woman, did you stick your fingers in ice?" He laughed against her mouth and everything became better, such that she chuckled as well. He hadn't tried to remove her touch, merely reacted to it, and now she spread her fingers out wide, absorbing his warmth through her palms and digits.

"Poor baby SEAL," she teased. "Doesn't like the cold."

"Trust me. The one thing SEALs avoid is the cold, because of all the times we can't."

"So if I decide to move to Alaska, this relationship is over?"

"So over. Of course, I've endured a lot of crappy weather to serve my country, and you're at least as important as that."

His fingertips slid into her hair, caressing the sensitive back of her neck. The sensation spread over her throat, her jaw, sending pleasurable signals to everything below those points. She slid her cold hands from the small of his back into his sweats, tunneling under his boxers to enjoy his muscular ass, which flexed beneath her grip.

Banding his arm around her waist, he hiked her up his body, still keeping up with that kiss, teasing her lips with his tongue, a nip from his teeth. She curved her legs around his waist and hips and found herself solidly seated on a growing erection. She gripped his broad shoulders.

"Yeah," he muttered against her mouth. "That's all for you, baby. Now. I need you now."

In answer, she took the kiss to a more violent level, biting his lip. His mouth opened to her so she could delve deep, taste him. He tangled his hand in her hair, pulling her back just enough to survey their surroundings. Going off trail, he hiked swiftly up an incline. When he went over the rise, they were standing on a slope leading into deeper forest, the ground covered with leaves and moss. They were hidden from the main trail. When he laid her down on that natural bed, she was sure it would leave mud stains on her exercise clothes, but she didn't care.

He laid himself down on her and took up where they left off on that kiss. From her way of thinking, he could have stripped off her leggings right then, pushed down his sweats and plunged, since her pussy was already wet, but he gave her this. Jorge had wanted to be on top most of the time, reinforcing his power, so it wasn't a position that captured her fantasies. Until Max. Rather than feeling suffocated, this felt as natural as the earth beneath her. The earth was penetrated by a tree's roots, yet the earth was also the thing that kept the tree strong.

He moved to her throat, then down, unzipping her jacket and cupping her breasts under the stretch yoga top. It had a built-in bra, no padding, so he was able to nuzzle her, let her feel the moist heat of his mouth as he suckled her through the fabric. She moved restlessly against him, wrapping her legs high on his hips again. When she rubbed her needy core against him, he responded by pressing his hardness against it.

"Too many clothes," she whispered in his ear. "I want you inside me, Max."

He worked his way down her body, impressing her with the way he caught her waistband in his teeth, ran his tongue beneath it, stimulating her further before he pulled the leggings down to her ankles. He left them there, her shoes holding them on as he shifted his body inside that closed triangle, his calves beneath the stretch of her leggings holding her ankles together. He guided her thighs back up around his hips again, so now her shoes, leggings and the limbs they contained rested against the backs of his knees. It was as if her legs were bound, but with him inside that space, she had him captured as well.

She was impressed by his cleverness, but they were both in too urgent a state to waste it on words. Putting her hands on his ass again, she pushed the sweats down, thumbs under the boxers, and he helped, getting the cloth past his turgid cock. At the first touch of the heated steel organ against her, she reached between them to close her hands on it.

"On your knees above me, Max. I want to see you."

She wasn't consciously issuing an order, the desperate desire in her voice driving her. She had to look at him. He complied, her thighs widening to give him room to stand up on his knees, his knees pressed against the inside of hers, his cock jutting up. She stroked the shaft, fingernails scraping over the testicle sac, watching all of it respond to her with a convulsive movement.

"Shirt...if you're not too cold."

He removed it, and her gaze coursed over the skulls-and-trident tattoo on his side, then back down that arrow of hair to the groin. His fingers whispered over her thighs, her knees, then they drew back. His hands opened and closed, as if he was warring with something. Her gaze lifted to him at the moment he decided. Lifting his hands, he laced them behind his head, burning gaze fixed on her face. He'd just given her total access to him.

She swallowed, pushing herself up on her elbows to press her mouth against his hard abdomen, his hipbone. She kept one hand wrapped around him, finger rubbing over the damp slit, grip tightening as she slid up and back down. She could smell that heady scent of semen, male arousal. When she turned her head, tasted him, sucking on just the head, working her tongue around the rim, he let out an oath. His thighs trembled, but he held fast as she moved back to his stomach, let her other hand roam over his chest, down his sides, back to his hip, knuckles brushing the delectable ass again.

"Marking your territory, Mistress?" he asked in a husky voice.

He was encouraging her possession, something she hadn't expected from him. Looking up at him, hands behind his head like that, she knew there was only one answer to give.

"Yes."

His eyes flamed hotter in response. She eased herself back to the ground, letting her other set of fingertips trail down his thigh. When she released his cock, she gave him back the same gift. Deliberately, she laid her hands over her head, shooting him a look of raw need and challenge wrapped together.

"Now you do the same."

His hands dropped. One braced him on the ground at her shoulder while the other gripped the base of his cock. He guided himself into her, measured, deliberate, keeping his gaze on her face the whole time. So she knew he was seeing the pleasure that suffused her features, the way she bit her lip, how her hips lifted to his, taking him in deep. Wrapping her legs high on his hips again, she tightened them, drawing him in farther. She got lost in his gray eyes as he settled on her, elbows on either side of her head, and began to pump his hips into her. Slow, steady, a rhythm that she met with her own body. As her arousal built, the lift of her hips became more demanding. And then he really began to thrust hard.

She let out a groan at the painful pleasure of it. "Max," she gasped. *Mine. Mine. Mine.*

Remarkably, she was already spasming around him. She hadn't let herself come these four weeks they'd been apart, though in her bed at night her body had burned for him, recalling him there, in the hot tub, on her couch. She'd even fantasized about taking him on the hood of his truck in the parking deck. She'd open his jeans, straddle him as he leaned back against his windshield. His fingers would dig into her hips, eyes hidden behind the sunglasses but jaw rock-hard, reflecting his absorption in their shared lust. Randall's eyes would have popped out of his head, she was sure.

Their gazes locked. "I missed you," he said, the fierce truth of it in his voice.

She reached up with trembling fingers and he kissed them, bit them when she lingered there, then she curled her hand over his shoulder. The feeling was building higher, hotter. "I missed you too. I won't do that to you again."

"Damn right. I'll come sleep under your window."

The challenge sparked her own. She reared up to capture his mouth as she squeezed down on him, savoring and pleasuring them both. His arm banded around her like steel, his other arm and her stomach muscles the only thing holding them both up, the anchor point in a spinning world. The smell of damp leaves, earth and forest mingled with Max as she prepared to let herself go.

When she went over that precipice, she managed to make her own demand. "Come for me, Max." *Come for your Mistress. The one who wants to own you.*

She let out a glad cry as he obeyed, every muscle of that fine body beneath her legs and hands hardening, rippling, his face going concentrated and even fiercer. He groaned out his release, hips pistoning strong enough to push her into the earth. She let her head fall back, careless of the dirt and leaves. Cognizant of who else might be in the park, though, she turned her head to his forearm, pressed her mouth against it, her screams vibrating against his flesh.

As he started to come down, his other hand slipped from her waist, cupped her jaw, strong fingers caressing it as well as her throat as she offered those cries to him. He kept going until she was all done, carrying her through every aftershock until she wasn't sure she'd ever felt so sated. So...loved.

It was an unexpected but not unwelcome thought. As she finished, she used the pressure of her hands to bring him back down to lie upon her body fully again. He complied, though he held himself with an elbow to keep his full weight off her. They were breathing in tandem, his fingers laced with hers to her right, her other one curled over his back. "See?" he murmured into her neck. "I told you that you'd like camping."

She bit his ear. "This isn't camping. I interrupted your workout."

"I'd say you enhanced it. Want to help me finish it? I usually go through the outdoor fitness stations before jogging home."

Her heart was still thundering, her limbs loose and body languorous, so as she looked up and saw he was serious, she didn't know if the energy and virility gave her heart an amusing feminine leap or made her hate him.

"You're bluffing. Your legs have to be noodles. Every man has to have a post-coital nap. Women have counted on it for centuries, to give them that precious moment to slip a knife between the ribs of their Viking captor, or an overly ambitious king."

"If she's slipping him the knife, sounds like she's the ambitious one. Also sounds like a really good reason to keep one eye open around a woman." Max pressed his lips to hers, a long, sweet denouement to ease the loss as he slid out of her, moved back up to his knees. He adjusted his sweats, then moved off her to help her pull her leggings back up to her hips. As he did so, he dropped a kiss here and there. Her knee, her thigh. When he slid an arm around her back to help her to a sitting position, she crooked an arm around his neck as well. He surprised her, lifting her off the ground entirely as he rose to his feet.

"I can walk to the fitness station."

"I know. But I haven't been able to hold you for four weeks. I'm taking advantage."

Well, that definitely caused a feminine leap to her heart.

* * * * *

It continued as he went through each station to work out his upper body, legs and back. If he was trying to impress her, it worked, but she could tell it wasn't that. This was a part of his day he took very seriously. He was no longer in the SEALs but he still trained like one. She thought of how he'd driven Savannah through traffic, demonstrating the skills of a man who'd served as personal security for high-risk dignitaries visiting occupied zones. Probably another reason Matt liked having him on staff, since all the drivers had some form of law enforcement or military background. Though it wasn't a regular job requirement, Max, Wade and some of the others had accompanied the K&A men more than once to do the driving for them when they were scoping out new plant locations in Central America.

Her radar detected something more to it than just force of habit though. She wondered if he was staying prepared for something specific. The thought was an uneasy one, taking her back to the roof and Matt's warning that Max had his own demons.

A mystery to puzzle over and unravel another time. Today, she had no desire to open a new can of worms. It was much more pleasurable to float in a dreamy haze of lust, watching him working out his upper body on the push-up stand, pommel horse, parallel bars and horizontal ladder, then showing off his climbing skills on the integrated fitness station. He finished up with the bounding bars and floating balance system, testing his agility.

"You know, if you *really* wanted to impress me, you'd fuck me three more times after doing all this. And still show up for work on time."

He flashed her a grin as he came off the last station. He'd left his shirt off, bless all the gods. She tilted her head back for the kiss, but he gave her that and more. Snaking an arm around her waist, he lifted her off the balance beam and put her up against the tree beside it, one fluid motion. As he pushed his body between her thighs, her still-damp pussy responded to hard male demand, her tissues quivering. His gray eyes got that heated look that suggested they might end up in the leaves again. It was insane.

"Exercise turns you on?" She had to gasp it out, no help for that, though she laid a quelling hand against his chest. "Now I really hate you."

He put his mouth on her throat, one hand gripping her ass, fingers sliding along the seam. "Just answering the challenge, Mistress. Wouldn't want to disappoint you. Christ, I can't get enough of you. What is that scent you wear?"

It would have made her laugh if she didn't feel so swept away by him and bemused by her own reaction to it. "At the moment, it appears to be male sweat."

He chuckled against her skin. "True enough. But something else beneath that. You put it on your thighs as well, because I smell it when I'm eating your cunt. It gets me hard during the day, thinking about what you put between your legs."

She tried to get her legs down, slip his hold, but each time she did, he countered it, caught her to him again. It moved them to the grass, and now she tried twisting inside his grip. That just gave him the opportunity to cup her between her legs, send a ripple of pleasure through her core. She was laughing through her frustration and tried to drop out of his hold. He countered that as well but brought their play to a halt, releasing her enough to let her step away, though he held on to her hand.

"You're trying to break my hold the wrong way," he said. "Everyone thinks you fall back against your attacker, and instead you fall forward. Look."

Now serious, he turned her so her back was against him again. "This time, lunge forward, not back against me. I outweigh you by nearly a hundred pounds. That's like shoving back against a tree. If you lunge forward, I have to grab at you, and I'm off balance for a vital second. It might give you the chance to duck under my arms."

She did it, found he was right, though of course she was sure he modified his response to show her how it worked. When she did the duck, she balled up her fist, hit him in the side, albeit not too hard, but he had a correction for that too.

"Better to hit below the sternum with the heel of your hand. For a girl, tiger claw is better than the full fist." He took her hand, curled it so the knuckles pointed out, fingertips pressed to the top of her palm. Running his finger over the knuckles, he had her do the same with her free hand. "See how hard and sharp that is? You get that on either side of his windpipe, or hit his temple, you've really landed a blow. Plus, those beautiful nails of yours left some great marks on my back, but they make it hard to form a tight fist."

"Show me the marks," she demanded, and he smiled.

"You were ogling me close enough to see them, Mistress. You haven't seen me in four weeks. They've faded. You'll have to give me new ones."

She narrowed her eyes at the ogling comment, but he dropped a kiss on her knuckles, his tongue teasing the crease between two of them. He also wasn't done with his lesson. "Your best shot is a kick that takes out someone's knee. Or if you can get your hands on the back of his neck, pull him down, put a knee in his diaphragm. Women have much more strength in their legs. Even the average guy has two-thirds more upper body strength than you do, so you play on your strengths. You should take some Tae Kwan Do. You'd be good at it. You already have the confidence part down, and that's the hardest part for a woman."

Her brow lifted. "And why is that?"

He shook his head. "I'm not insulting women. When it comes to fight or flight instincts, men are more socially conditioned to fight, with women conditioned to flight. Which makes sense if you think about it, because women usually have the kids. They run to get children out of the way while men hold the line to give them time to do that."

Then he rolled his eyes. "Okay, let me correct that. Men *used* to be more socially conditioned to fight. Now they're momma's boys who play non-competitive sports and duck the ball at baseball games so it hits their girlfriend."

As she smirked and shook her head at him, he continued. "Anyhow, the thing most women have a hard time doing in Tae Kwan Do is standing toe to toe to spar with someone, accepting and giving blows. But learning that skill is vital, because when it comes to some scumbag chasing you, nothing's harder than to stop and wait for them to come at you. However, if you're at the end of a blind alley, that's all you can do."

He touched her face, bringing her eyes back up to him, "From what you told me about Mexico, I think you've learned that. You don't run, Mistress. That's why I said you'd make a hell of a SEAL."

"For a girl," she added, more moved than she wanted to reveal.

"For a girl," he agreed. He dodged her attempt at the tiger claw. Chuckling, he caught her to him, but when he did, he sobered, hands cupping her face so he could press his forehead to hers.

"We good now? Because I don't want to go through four weeks like that again."

"I can't promise. You're my first relationship outside those club doors, Max. Sometimes I need space to deal with that."

"You could have at least sent flowers. A card."

"Really? What were you saying about momma's boys?" Laughing, she broke free and dodged around the balance beam, letting him chase her down and catch her at the horizontal ladder. He pressed her against it, kissing her deep, freeing her hair so it rippled down her back, tangled around them both.

"Will you come visit my sister with me this week? I'd like for her to meet you, if she's up to it."

She lifted her head, studied him. His expression said he wasn't sure what had made him go down that road at this exact moment, but she had a distinct feeling he'd been thinking about offering her the invitation for a while. And that made her feel a variety of ways, not unpleasant.

"Yes," she agreed. "I'd love to."

All in all, it was a perfect morning.

Chapter Eleven

෨

They'd showered at his place, which he'd warned her wasn't much more than a hole in the wall, but the small size of the shower had proven to be a benefit beyond measure. For one thing, he knocked another pin out of the challenge she'd issued about impressing her. He'd taken her up against the wall, driving them both to orgasm. The water tattooed against her face, her throat and against his back where her hands gripped him. Within only a few moments, the shower had echoed with her cries, his guttural sounds of release.

Afterward, while he was occupied in the kitchen, pulling them together an omelet, he encouraged her to look around. He was right. His house was no more than a box divided into four rooms. The neighborhood was close to Dana's church, so it wasn't the safest area of NOLA.

It was military neat, such that she considered bouncing a quarter off the smooth bedding. There were few personal items in the house. Given how likely robbery was in this neighborhood, that might explain it, but he didn't even have an old television. Just a radio, an assortment of old paperbacks on a shelf, his toiletry items and clothes. The suits he wore for more formal assignments with K&A appeared to be the most expensive things in the house. That and the gun safe bolted to a central support beam in the bedroom wall. Standing in his closet, she ran her fingertips down the sleeve of one dress shirt. There was a precise inch of space between each garment, all pressed and clean.

Max, you're a little scary. Turning to the shelf behind her that held a small assortment of dress shoes and two pairs of running shoes, she found a picture propped up behind them. His mother and sister obviously. They were laughing, at some kind of birthday party. His mother had dark eyes and hair. His sister had the dark hair, but Max's gray eyes. The dark-blond hair and impressive size must have come from his father, but there was no picture of him.

He'd talked about how intoxicating her scent was, but she felt like if she slept anywhere in this house, it would be here, where she could inhale the various scents that were all him. Of course, if he was in that bed, that was where she could inhale the drug direct from the source. She thought about waking him in the morning by putting her lips around his cock, a slow, leisurely, dragging suck up the hard length. He'd wake to find his hands tied loosely to the headboard with her robe tie, and she'd bring him to climax that way.

Of course, she suspected he was a very light sleeper, so more likely she'd order him to put his hands above his head and do as she pleased while he watched her with those heavy-lidded gray eyes. His fingers would clench in self-imposed restraint, body bowing up to her mouth.

"In here stealing or snooping?" He spoke behind her.

"I was told I could look around. You didn't put any limits on it."

"No, I didn't." Two steps to cross the room and he put his arms around her waist. He drew her back against him to nuzzle her throat. He was bare-chested, wearing only a pair of flannel shorts. His skin was still damp from the shower, hair scented with the fragrant shampoo. "Breakfast is ready. You smell like my soap. I like it."

"You don't have a picture of your dad?"

"No. He left before Amanda was even in school. Mom did it all, so he didn't earn a place on my shelf. A guy that cuts out on his family like that isn't a father. He's a sperm donor."

It was a trait she liked about Max, and one they shared. There was no self-pity in the flat statement, nothing to suggest he nursed the specter of an abandoned kid who wished daddy would care more. If the incident defined him at all, it was likely in making sure he was the antithesis of what his father had been.

He also made a good omelet. Returning to his kitchen, she sat at his little table, which she expected had been pulled off someone's curbside trash and repainted. There was a crack through the middle that had been caulked and sanded before the paint was put down. "You know, I could talk to Matt about your salary. If this is the best you can afford, he deserves to be horsewhipped."

"I get paid well enough, as I'm sure you already know. This just suits me. I don't spend much time here."

"No, you don't. You're usually at work, or apparently doing an insane fitness regimen. What demons are chasing you, Max?"

He kept his eyes on his plate, didn't answer. Reaching across the table, she touched his face. When he caught her wrist, she didn't withdraw, just met his gaze. "I asked you a question, Max."

"I don't have any demons chasing me."

She studied him. "No. That's true. You're the one doing the chasing, aren't you?"

The dangerous flicker in his gaze confirmed it, but he merely squeezed her wrist and let her go to scrape up another bite. "When you're done eating, I'll give you a ride to your place, make sure you get to work on time. Don't want Matt chewing your ass for being late."

"He's not that brave. As many times as I've stayed past midnight or worked from home to make sure they have what they need the next day, I'd like to see him try."

"And I'd like to watch that. Bet it would make a great YouTube video."

"Max." She folded her hands in her lap, stared him down. "After what I shared with you four weeks ago, you're really going to dodge this? Quid pro quo."

"That's emotional blackmail. And in all fairness, you put me through hell these past four weeks. So I'd say slate's balanced."

"Probably. But you've given me a bad feeling, and I don't like it. You don't work out like you're addicted to exercise. You work out like you're staying ready for something."

"I don't want you to be a part of that." The set to his jaw said the topic wasn't negotiable. He sat back in the chair, wiping his mouth with a napkin. "When it's done, it will be done, and I'll never revisit it again."

He shook his head at her look. "I'm not shutting you out, Janet. I'm trained in OPSEC, operations security. The demon I'm chasing, I view it the same as I viewed any mission I took with the SEALs. I don't divulge any information about it, because it's classified, and it's going to stay that way, to protect everyone around me as much as the mission. It's like when a SEAL is married. It's just separate from what he is with his wife. She has to figure that out and accept that to accept being with him. It's not an ultimatum or a fucked-up power play, I swear. It's just the way things in my world work. Understand?"

She pursed her lips. "Not an easy thing for a woman used to control to accept."

"Not an easy thing for anyone to accept from someone they love," he said seriously. "That's part of why SEALs have an eighty percent divorce rate." Then, as if realizing how the statement might be taken, he shifted in the chair. "Not that I'm saying that you love me, or have given marriage any thought…"

He shook his head as she lifted a brow, her lips quirking. "Yeah, you're just sitting there holding the shovel, aren't you?"

"Well, it's much more fun to watch you dig the hole with your bare hands."

He snorted, picked up her empty plate and dumped them both in the sink. For the next few moments, she watched him efficiently wash and rinse, stacking their plates and cups neatly in the dish drainer. Then he dried out the sink with a towel, polishing the faucet.

God, she was in trouble if just watching the man do dishes could make something in her stomach yearn, her heart soften. Rising, she slipped her arms around him, pressing herself against his back. She didn't say anything, just held him, and he put the towel aside, closing his hand over her linked fingers.

"Something is happening with us, Max. Today was a breakthrough moment, and we both see it. If you agree this isn't a casual thing for either of us, and you believe not only in being prepared, but in preparing those around you, then it needs to be talked about."

She had him there, because tension thrummed through his muscles. She rose on her toes to put her lips against the back of his neck, then slipped down again, still holding him to her.

"I think there is a difference between chasing a demon 'down range' and chasing one in your own backyard. It might require a different level of disclosure at some point. If you get hurt, and I was close enough to stop it from happening, I'm going to be extremely angry with you. I gave you a sign of my trust four weeks ago. I didn't do it well, but I did it. Can you give me something?"

He sighed, the broad chest lifting and falling beneath her touch. He turned in her arm span, putting his hands on her hips and leaning back against the counter, stretching his legs out on either side of her. "My mother was killed as an example to those in the neighborhood who stood up to the gangs, Janet. She was beaten to death. My sister...they raped and then beat her as well, only she lived. In a way. She had brain damage, part of it psychological, a lot of it physical. All of it apparently permanent. While I was away on a mission to keep our world safe, they weren't safe. Not even close. If you've been doing your SEAL research, you saw the movie where they said that a

SEAL is always trying to get home, that home's the whole point of it. But my home was gone when I came back."

"And the men who did it?"

"There were three of them. Two are no longer an issue. The ringleader went underground."

She studied his face, the calm stillness of his gray eyes, the set of his jaw. The same way he'd understood never to use her real name, she knew not to speak aloud the possibility of what had happened to those two.

"I expect the police will eventually find him."

"He's a cold file at the bottom of a stack of files, because he left the country. Went underground, lost in the network of Mexican cartels. And even if they do luck out and find him, I know how it works. His mommy won't have held him enough, he was poor and misunderstood, it's racial profiling...whatever bullshit they want to concoct to excuse his actions. There's right and wrong, and there's the law. Sometimes they agree, but a lot of days they don't. You know that as well as anyone."

Yes, she did. She touched his face. "There's this peculiar thing that happens, Max, when a Domme gets attached to a sub. She considers him hers. Her property, and she expects her property to take very good care of himself."

His hands slid up her back. He pressed her close as he wound his hand in her hair, clipped back in a tail now so when he caressed the strands, he tilted her head back, his lips coming so close to hers they hovered an inch apart when he finally spoke.

"What about the sub? What if he considers her his as well? Does that happen?"

"All the time. Though some are more blatant about it than others." She liked the strength of his arms, the determination in his expression. She wanted everything about him, even the things they'd just discussed that disturbed her. They were all part of who he was. "So take me to work, and promise me when I'm not around to do it, you'll guard that fine ass of yours."

"Sounds like my fine ass is yours, not mine. Mistress." He spoke the last word against her lips. The way it vibrated through her body told her, amazingly enough, he was going to prove he was more than capable of taking her once more before they headed to work.

In some ways, the man truly was a god. But in some very harrowing ways, he was all too mortal and fragile.

* * * * *

There were physical repercussions to doing all that on a work day, but she knew adrenaline could carry her through until quitting time. What she hadn't expected was how thoughts of the past several hours could utterly destroy her focus. Her skin bloomed with heat whenever she thought of him, her heart rate elevating like a tiny mouse scurrying up her chest wall. She'd laugh at herself about it, but there was a poignant ache in that same vicinity. She'd started down a path from which she couldn't return. She was falling for him, and she was pretty sure he felt the same way.

Her mind kept revisiting the morning in delicious detail. That first touch, curling her fingers in his shirt, moving into his embrace, the two of them simply holding one another. Max's smile. Him calling her "ma'am" in that slow, sexy way. How he'd lifted her up so effortlessly against the shower wall, his body flexing inside the clamp of her arms and legs, the powerful urgency in his expression. The unsettling issue of him pursuing the last man responsible for his mother's death.

She'd been in a situation where she couldn't rely on the police to save her from a violent criminal, and she'd employed macabre measures to handle it. She couldn't throw stones. Beyond that, she worked for a man who clearly felt the way Max did. If anyone ever harmed Savannah or Angelica, Janet had no doubt the last thought on Matt Kensington's mind would be calling the police. The perpetrator would die wishing that the police had had time to get to him before Matt had. And every man of his executive team would help him, because they shared that same code.

"Janet, can you read back that last point?"

Speak of the devil. She shook herself out of her thoughts to find Matt gazing at her from the head of the boardroom table. Though his expression was bland, she sensed something quivering beneath the surface. Amusement? Whatever it was, Peter, Jon, Ben and Lucas seemed to have a dose of it as well, because their body language and expressions were almost identical to Matt's.

She glanced down at her shorthand. "Production in Costa Rica is up fifty percent. Peter anticipates that trend to continue while handling the Porter account, justifying the equipment upgrade—"

"I win," Ben pronounced. He stretched across the table, collecting the five poker chips that had appeared in the center of the table as if by magic. As he pocketed them, he gave Lucas a grin. "You were close, but I hit it dead on. She tuned us out four bullet points ago."

The K&A lawyer glanced over at her, his green eyes twinkling. "You completely missed our plans to hire tranny prostitutes for the Johnson reception."

"And the policy change that requires all female employees to wear string bikinis whenever the predicted high is over eighty," Peter put in helpfully.

An unprecedented flush climbed up her cheeks. "I apologize," she said stiffly. "I—" She cleared her throat. "Did I miss any action points? *Real* ones?"

"No. We were generally discussing the direction for South America, but it was more brainstorming than anything." Jon offered the information kindly, which was almost worse than Ben's teasing. He studied her with his serious midnight-blue eyes, enhanced by the fall of dark, silken hair around his sculpted face. "Nothing concrete."

"I apologize, sir," she repeated to Matt, but she directed her next words to all of them. "It won't happen again."

Matt nodded. Straightening, she put her pen to paper. "Now, how many tranny prostitutes will you need?"

The men chuckled, easing her embarrassment, though she felt Matt's scrutiny lingering. A few minutes later, they concluded the meeting. As the other men rose, heading out of the boardroom to start their respective schedules, she wasn't surprised to see Matt motion to her to stay.

Ben brought her a napkin that held three mini-muffins and a cup of coffee. Since she never ate during the monthly staff meeting, the men always saved her three of the muffins that Ben baked himself. She saw the chocolate chip, blueberry and raspberry flavors she preferred, while Ben put down a fresh black coffee next to it.

Giving her a nod, he added, "Go with a baker's dozen on those prostitutes. It'll take that many to give Johnson's attorney an apoplexy, and I'm looking for a full-on drop-dead stroke so he's no longer a thorn in my ass. See if you can get us a group discount."

"I'll work on that," she said dryly.

He gave her a wink. When he left, he closed the door after him, so she and Matt were alone. Rising, she moved to the head of the table, taking a seat at Matt's right. It wasn't unusual for him to have her stay behind to dictate additional notes or correspondence, but she knew that wasn't the case today. She folded her hands in her lap. "I am sorry, Matt. I know I'm distracted today."

He sat back, his shoe braced on the table leg beneath to rock him on the chair's axis, giving his legs more room. "Janet, you could take a nap through every staff meeting we have for the next five years, and only then would it balance out all the times you've been right on top of everything we need, right when we need it. I'd be a poor boss to snap at you for taking fifteen minutes. But I know you well enough I'm going to ask. Are you all right?"

She pursed her lips. She really didn't know how to answer that question, and Matt Kensington was not the type to take a generic "fine". "How do I seem?" she ventured.

Very few things mattered to her as much as how she presented herself when she was representing K&A and Matt's interests. If she was in uncharted territory, she trusted Matt to give her an evaluation, direct and to the point. He didn't disappoint, but it still startled her to hear it said aloud so baldly.

"You look like a woman falling in love. Happy, anxious, thoughtful. And you have a stubble burn on your lovely jaw. I threatened to skin Ben alive if he brought it up."

"Thank you." She thought she'd covered that with enough concealer, but apparently she needed clown makeup with these men. She wanted to be horrified, but she'd known them too long...especially Matt. "I told him. About Mexico."

His gaze flickered. "He won't abuse your trust."

"I know. Else I wouldn't have told him. I've also learned that he and I have some things in common. Only that chapter in his life, unlike mine, isn't yet closed."

Not many people could read Matt Kensington, and even she had difficulty at times, but this time she caught it. "You know."

Matt nodded. His thigh muscles flexed as he rocked the chair back, his fingers tapping the table surface in a meditative fashion. "I do. I wish it was closed, that he would close it, but I also understand enough I can't stand in his way. He won't allow me or anyone else here to help him with it. SEALs share a very close bond. His teammates helped with...the first phase, but he's kept them limited to intel, making it clear they have other priorities he expects them to put first. They've had to be satisfied with that, which means not satisfied at all, but it is what it is. He's one of the most quietly stubborn and unshakably honorable men I've ever met."

Quietly stubborn and unshakably honorable. The description fit Max well. There was no flash to him, no sense that he ever had to be the center of attention, and yet he commanded confidence, a sense of safety, with the strength of his presence. It was that steadiness that drew her, that perhaps called to something in her she'd always sought, a gift for herself. And Max was offering it to her fully, making it irresistible.

"I've never contemplated a long-term relationship with a man who's not a sub."

"I don't think you've ever contemplated a long-term relationship with one who is." Matt tapped her hand, winning her smile. "You've been waiting for the right combination. You'd never settle for anything less than everything you want, and women are so intuitive, they often don't know what that is until they feel it, deep in the heart and soul. The day you and Max brought Savannah to the hospital and I thanked him...there are some things about that day that passed in a blur, but others that stand out in sharp relief."

He shifted to an upright position again, lacing his fingers on the table and leveling his hawklike gaze at her. "When I walked back up the hall, I saw you, watching us. Watching Max. It wasn't the first thing on my mind, but when I thought about it later, I knew something was going to happen between you. You've been looking for a man all your life who matches your strength, Janet. One who understands your passion, your occasional savagery and glorious darkness, and your tremendous capacity for love. Most importantly, you've been looking for a man who is not deeply terrified of you. That number is few."

She chuckled at that. Matt smiled. When he rose, a subtle hint their tête-a-tête was over, she gathered her tablet and cup of coffee. Matt picked up the napkin of tiny muffins in his large hand, handling them like a bird's nest as he followed her.

He deposited them on her desk, but before he turned toward his office, he touched her hand once more, drawing her gaze to his serious face.

"You've earned a great deal of vacation and personal days in the years you've worked for me and K&A, Janet. And Max pretty much lives on the clock. If either of you wants to take some time off these next few weeks, I will support that."

"What if he and I want to take the same days off?"

His eyes twinkled, appreciating her. "Wiseass. Call Rosalind and have her on standby. She always appreciates the extra money, and she knows your job well enough to cover things adequately for a day here and there."

"Plus she's not terrified of you." Janet tucked her tongue in her cheek. "Also a very small number."

"I'll have to work on that. She could spread the word that I don't actually decapitate incompetent employees in my office. I'd have to sacrifice one or two to debunk the rumor."

"Like you would ever hire an incompetent employee," Janet scoffed. "But if you decide to sacrifice Ben to prove the point, I'll pay for the extra roll of plastic to keep the blood off the carpet."

* * * * *

She'd told Max she'd go visit his sister with him Wednesday afternoon. Just to prove she had some willpower, for the next two days she didn't go home with him or invite him to do the same, though he sent her some fairly provocative and suggestive texts. When she responded with a threat to sic Human Resources on him, he started sending her lines of poetry. Everything from e. e. cummings to Edgar Allan Poe. She responded he was going to have to do better than steal one-liners from a *Best of the Poet Masters* desk calendar.

You're a tough crowd. Take a break this afternoon. I'll give you a foot massage.

Maybe.

But at two p.m., she decided to do just that. The moment she saw him stretched out on his truck in that sexy, deceptively somnolent pose, arms crossed over the broad chest, long thighs and groin accentuated by the crossing of his ankles, she thought visiting him on break might become like a crack habit to her. As she crossed the parking lot, he sat up and slid off the hood, meeting her halfway. She was carrying a meatball sandwich left over from a lunch meeting and a napkin full of cookies, both of which she extended to him. "I thought you might enjoy these."

"What are you having?"

She chuckled, enjoying him. "I had my lunch in the meeting, but I expect you to share at least one of those chocolate chip cookies."

"I'm not sure our relationship has progressed that far."

Giving her a grin, he set the food inside the front seat of the truck, then guided her around to the truck bed. Intrigued, she saw he already had the tailgate down and the thick quilt folded there as a cushion. He put his hands to her waist and lifted her on to it, the same way he'd done the day this had all started. Only this time she kept her hands on his shoulders, letting her fingers whisper over his neck, curl in his T-shirt, bringing him closer. The skirt she was wearing was short enough she could spread her knees and bring him inside their span. He put his hands on her waist, drawing her against him so core met core. The kiss was hot, deep, and kept them both holding to one another, even when he finally drew back with a regretful look.

"More than that, and I'll compromise your reputation on the security cameras. They're only catching our head and shoulders in the corner of the screen, but even so…"

His eyes were sparkling though, aware of the significance of her encouraging the act where it would quickly become public news they were seeing one another. "So this is no longer bound by OPSEC?"

She punched his shoulder. "Unless you tease me about it."

"Stopping the teasing immediately, ma'am. At least that kind." He amused her by pinching the hem of her skirt on either side and working it back down her thighs. It restored her modesty for the grainy resolution of the security feed, if the camera could see her legs. From what he'd said, she suspected not. She noticed his truck was at a different angle and realized he'd likely checked on the scope of the video camera in this corner of the parking deck. A wave of pleasure washed through her, thinking of him protecting her privacy that way. It was exactly the type of thing he'd do.

Then he turned his attention to her feet.

Apparently, there were reasons other than the camera angle that had him placing her on the tailgate instead of the hood. More pleasant sensations swirled through her chest and lower abdomen as he dropped to one knee. He glanced up at her as he did it, making clear it was deliberate. He removed her shoes, setting them neatly on the tailgate next to her before clasping her stocking-covered feet in his magical hands. As he began to rub her arches, working her toes between his strong fingers, massaging her ankles, she was hard-pressed not to moan like she did during sex. She struggled for something to distract herself.

"You'll be happy to know Matt gave us his blessing. Not that I need his blessing for anything I do, but he did. He told me I could trust you, and that you are one of the most honorable men he knows."

Max stopped at that, looking up. "His opinion carries a great deal of weight with me," she continued, "but he didn't tell me anything I didn't already suspect."

"He's been…" Max lifted a shoulder, then looked down at her feet, his fingers tightening on them. "I trust him."

She knew he couldn't give a greater compliment to another man, and she made a note to share that with Matt sometime, return the favor.

Max didn't say anything for the next few moments. She figured he was focused on her feet, trying to inspire an orgasm through her arches. He was pretty damn close to succeeding, enough that if she ever saw him with his hands on another woman's feet she'd probably shoot him for infidelity.

Wow. Getting a little possessive there, girl.

"You know," he said slowly, keeping his eyes on his task, "I earned a punishment that day, when you told me not to come until you said so. Remember?"

"Yes, I do." Her gaze coursed over the strands of his dark-blond hair, the angle of his face she could see. She could almost hear the gears turning in his mind, the decisions being made. That coil in her lower belly became even sweeter.

"So I was thinking that maybe it…the punishment, could clear a few things up. If I joined you at the club this weekend. As your guest." He cleared his throat, lifted his face to her. "As yours."

She prided herself on being able to anticipate a man, enjoyed the pleasure of being a step ahead, but he'd taken her by surprise on that one. As a Domme, she was intuitive enough to recognize a situation where a sub was pushing himself where he didn't really want to go, just to please a Domme. The signals for a non-sub doing it would be similar, but she didn't see that in his face. The reasoning became clearer as he put his hand on her knee, fingers toying with the hem of her skirt.

"I trust you, Janet. I not only want to prove it, I want you to believe it." His gray eyes held hers. "It's like me going to the ballet class with you. I'm not a dancer, but you included me in it, because it was something important to you, a passion. You didn't leave me on the sidelines as a spectator either. You helped me understand the steps, let me lift you, even knowing I'm not going to be leaping around in tights. The way you brought me into it like that...something in me responded to your love of it. I want to have the experience of sharing this other part of you the same way. I trust you to know what I am and what I'm not."

As she considered that, his fingers curled on her leg. "It's a lot like foreplay," he added. "Women always need more of it than men, but we like what happens to you when we're doing it with you. That gives us an incentive to keep doing it."

Only to a man who understands the rewards of generosity of spirit, she thought. Matt had essentially told her she was a different kind of Mistress, that she'd been looking for a rare combination in a prolonged relationship. Max had said it more directly. She didn't need him to be her typical sub. Just hers.

"All right. How about Saturday night?"

He considered that. "Can you do Friday? I'm supposed to fix a friend's plumbing and eat pizza with her Saturday."

She didn't have a jealous bone in her body, but suddenly her entire skeletal system turned green. "Her?" she asked, deceptively mild.

Rising to his feet, Max cupped her face and kissed her again, making it last even longer, to the point she hoped he was right about those cameras and slid both hands to his ass, gripping hard and pressing him closer against her. He responded with a growl and cinched his arm around her waist so his thick erection was against her abdomen.

How was it that they'd had sex multiple times this morning, and she wanted more? Of course, he obviously felt the same way.

"She's married to a SEAL buddy," he said, his voice not entirely steady when he lifted his head. "We watch after each other's families. You can come with me if you'd like, but it's in Houston, so I'll probably stay overnight. I bet Gayle would love to meet you. I just didn't think to invite you because you seem to like skipping a day or two between our meets. You're seeing my sister Wednesday, and then if we're doing Friday... I figured it might be more than you want to do."

"On the flip side, if I see you three times in the same week, I can get you out of my system, cast you aside. Then I can move on to the next dime-a-dozen, bounce-a-quarter-off-his-ass honorable man with special ops military training and a sex god's stamina."

He grinned. "Stroking my ego?"

"Just telling you the standards I expect you to maintain," she said loftily.

From his expression, she could tell he understood the significance of her agreement. Not only was she seeing him three times in the same week, she was agreeing to meet people he considered his family—both blood and chosen. And speaking of *quid pro quo*, in that same week he would be submitting to her, in a formal club environment.

It was an exchange of worlds, to see how they did in both. Maybe it was a little much all at once, but to be honest, Matt was right. She was falling in love, and like any woman in love, in the first throes of that breathless passion and fascination, she wanted to be with him every minute. The possessive grasp of his hands, the look in his eyes, the demand of the lips he put back on hers now, told her he had the same overwhelming desire.

So fuck it. Go big or go home. And she didn't want to go home unless Max was with her.

* * * * *

Amanda Ackerman was a permanent resident at a private, top-of-the-line psychiatric home. Located on the outskirts of New Orleans, the main building of the property was an old plantation with graceful pillars and a verandah. The grounds had extensive gardens, a pond and peaceful nature trails. Brick annex buildings housed the medical facilities, so that such ugly necessities didn't intrude on the living quarters. In the main house, the thirty permanent residents had their own rooms and were watched over by an ample full-time staff. There were several solariums, an indoor and outdoor pool, a recreation area and more.

Another annex was being built. As they passed it, Janet read the construction sign. *Future Site of the Clinical Neurological Studies Center.* Beneath that, she noticed the building would be dedicated to Angelica Kensington. It confirmed a couple things for her. One, Matt and Savannah Kensington deserved every blessing they received in their lives, precisely because they never forgot how blessed they were. Two, Matt had probably used his not-insignificant negotiating skills to convince Max to let him help get his sister into the facility. While military benefits could be good, she suspected they were not this good.

Max was not the type to accept charity, but she already knew he'd swallow an ocean of pride to give his sister the best of all things. Just as she knew Matt would never hold it over his head to influence Max in any way. The people who were loyal to Matt were loyal because of the man himself, not because of what they owed him. She knew that firsthand, didn't she?

When they arrived in the lobby, the nurse told Max his sister was in the west garden. As they moved in that direction, Max squeezed Janet's hand. "If you want to have a seat on a bench when we get out there, I'll bring her over to introduce you, if she seems in the right state for it. If she's not, I'll give you a signal, and you can go do whatever you'd like while we visit. I hate to do that to you, but—"

"You already explained this to me three times, Max," Janet said with gentle reproof. "I completely understand. If things aren't right, I'll just be another person sitting in the garden, one she doesn't have to meet. I doubt I'll get restless watching you two together, but if I do, there are plenty of walking trails. Plus I have my tablet, so I can catch up on my email. Don't you dare think of rushing your visit on my account."

He nodded, leaned down and brushed her lips with his. "It's stupid that I'm nervous about this. I want her to like you, even knowing that's nothing that I can control, and it doesn't have any significance if she doesn't, because of how she is. Mother Teresa could walk in there and Amanda might react to her like Jeffrey Dahmer, because her eyes are the wrong color, or she has an age spot on her hands."

"No matter how she reacts to me, it will be okay." Janet reached up, touched his face. "I will love her." *Because I'm pretty sure I love you.*

He held her gaze as if she'd said the words out loud. Lifting her hands, he pressed his mouth to them. Then he gave them one more squeeze and stepped out the door.

After he was about ten paces down the garden path, Janet slipped out as well. She picked a bench set on a concrete pad encircled by a lovely rainbow of flowers and sculpted dwarf shrubs. As she settled, she watched him move toward a young woman in a blue dress, her dark hair cut to her shoulders. When she turned, Janet saw the curious vacancy in the gray eyes turn to a different kind of light. The way she walked toward Max, jerky and somewhat unbalanced when she got too fast, the listlessness of her left arm, showed the evidence of the brain damage, but the enthusiasm in her face was like a lit candle in darkness.

"Max," she said. "Max Max Max."

The tightening in her throat was unexpected, the sting of tears in her eyes. He'd said he saw her twice a week, and Amanda acted as if she hadn't seen Max in months. Janet wondered if she always reacted that way. But it wasn't that alone which caused the emotional reaction. Three men had held this beautiful child down, brutalized her, beat her. Janet remembered what it was like, being down on the ground, Jorge whaling on her with the bat, blow after blow. If he'd hit her head just the right way, she could have been this. Only she wouldn't have been in this beautiful facility. She'd have been tossed in a hole somewhere, left to die.

She closed her eyes, fighting the surge of unbalancing emotions. She couldn't do this here and now. Not if Amanda wanted to meet her. She had to pull herself together. Damn it, she should have predicted his reaction.

"Sad girl. Sad girl. Max."

Janet snapped back to the present. She always lost time when this happened, and a quick glance at her watch told her about ten minutes had passed. Amanda was standing right in front of her, those gray eyes so much like Max's fastened on her face. Amanda was handing her something. A tissue.

"Sad girl." No, she wasn't handing Janet the tissue. Amanda was bent forward, wiping her eyes for her, dabbing at the tears. She sat down next to Janet, pressed the tissue into her hand and put an arm around her. Then she rocked the two of them back and forth, making a crooning noise. "It's okay. Max is here. Max makes everything okay."

Janet looked up to see Max watching them. The concern on his face pierced her heart even more deeply, particularly when he dropped to his haunches before them, laying a hand on Janet's knee as well as his sister's. As he looked up at them both, her with her reconstructed face, his sister with her obvious neurological issues, Janet saw regret in his expression, his realization of the connection.

She firmed her chin. She wouldn't let this visit take that turn. Covering his hand with her own in reassurance, she put her other one lightly on Amanda's, hoping it wasn't the wrong move. Amanda's head popped up, her gaze locking with Janet's.

"Thank you, Amanda. I feel better now. Thanks to you and Max."

"Amanda, this is my friend Janet. She wanted to meet you."

Amanda gave her a perusal that was the equivalent of a visual strip search. She touched Janet's hair, then began to pluck out the bobby pins. Max made a move to stop her, but Janet shook her head, a slight movement telling him it was okay.

"Ooh. Pretty. Doll hair." As it unraveled down her back, over her shoulders, Amanda stroked it, touched Janet's face. "Okay. You'll take care of Max. Max needs someone to take care of him." She made an expression so remarkably like a smug little sister Janet smiled. "He's a big dummy."

"Better a big dummy than a priss pot," Max returned. He pinched Amanda's knee and she swatted at him. Then she settled against Janet's shoulder, tracing the patterns on her skirt. Max sat down on the other side of his sister, and the young woman took both their hands and began to hum. As Max cupped the back of her head, stroking, Janet saw the strain on his face.

She couldn't imagine how hard it was to do this, to see his sister forever caught in the state of a young child. Amanda was in her late twenties, perhaps even thirty. She overlapped their hands, so that they were holding each other as well as Amanda.

"Do you play checkers?" she asked Janet.

"Yes, I do."

"Will you play with me? And then maybe read me a story with Max? He got me the Nancy Drew set, and he's reading them to me. Then it will be time to eat. I'll share my snack with you."

"Thank you. I'd love that."

It all went well until the snack. In almost every room and even out in the gardens, signs clearly and emphatically indicated all cell phones were to be turned off, but one visitor had ignored the signs. The cell tone that blared forth was a rap song. Before it reached its first stanza, Amanda transformed from a playful child into a ferocious banshee who screamed at invisible attackers to stop, stop, *stop*. Max refused the orderly's help, holding his sister against him, arms banded across her upper torso, until the nurse injected her with a sedative strong enough to make her mercifully insensible in a matter of minutes. As she faded away, she was repeating it over and over. "Stop hurting me. Stop...hurting...me."

Max lifted and carried her to her room with the nurse in the lead. Janet trailed after him. When he laid her down in her bed, as tenderly as if he held an infant, he excused the nurse, telling her he'd care for her. Apparently the sedative would keep her out for hours. Janet joined him, helping him undress Amanda and put her in a cotton nightgown. She wondered if he'd picked it out for her. It was warm and rabbit fur soft, with pretty embroidery on the hem and neckline. After they tucked her in, he sat at her bedside, stroking her head and murmuring to her. When the nurse returned a half hour later, he brushed a kiss on Amanda's forehead and nodded to Janet, indicating it was time to leave.

As they walked out the front door, he seemed to be setting a straight course for the parking lot, but Janet took his hand, tugged him toward a bench surrounded by the flowers and foliage of the front landscaping. When she pressed him to a seated position, she sat on his lap, wrapping her arms around him. He said nothing for a moment, stiff and rigid, but she said nothing either, simply putting her head on top of his. He sighed, his head sinking down to her breast. As his shoulders began to shake, her heart broke.

Letting a new person bear witness to a wound that could never possibly heal could bring forth such emotions. Hadn't she reacted in a volatile way of her own when she had told Max her story? She held him, letting those bitter, silent tears mark her shirt. He banded his arms around her, rocking them both.

"It's okay. I'm here. I'm here." She ached for him, and also understood fully why he wanted every single person responsible for this dead. In his shoes, she'd hunt and exterminate them like the vermin they were.

"When I don't come every few days, she lapses into that state," he said at last, lifting his head. He would have wiped at his eyes with typical male self-consciousness, but just like Amanda, she did it instead, taking the tracks away on her fingers, caressing his jaw. "It's like she uses me as a touchstone, cycling around it. When I'm gone, the cycle breaks, and she gets pulled into the center, back into the nightmare. Once, we tried having me stay away for a month. Though they warned me she might forget who I was, they thought it might alter the nucleus of the memories, make things better. Instead, it got so bad she almost died. Wasted away to nothing. I had to stay here for a couple weeks, hand-feeding her, and if I left the room at all, she had to be sedated. We eventually got her back to this."

Thinking about the toll of doing this, she could comprehend why Max was so quiet, so steady. Or perhaps it was a chicken or egg thing. The calling that had put him overseas when this happened must be the same one that gave him the strength to deal with this week after week.

He turned his head, looked at her, and she saw the stark desolation in his gaze. "I know it would be better if she had died. Why was I in the right time and right place for Savannah and her baby, for so many missions, and not for my mother and sister? What kind of God fucks with you like that? You can make yourself crazy with the questions. Even if He couldn't stop it, why would He let only a part of her mind survive it? Why not be merciful, take her life?"

She shook her head. "I don't think it works like that. I never have. I don't think God, whatever It is, is like some kind of movie director, on top of every action and reaction. I think it's much more high level than that."

"As a SEAL, you learned it was all up to you and your team, and you don't quit until the mission is accomplished, no matter what goes wrong. That's the way life is. You don't give up, you don't quit." He sighed. "Superman. That's what Amanda called me, because of the jaw." He gestured to it wryly, the square cut that defined his strong face. "But it didn't matter. I was trained to be the best of the best, but it means nothing if I'm not there at the critical moment I'm needed. I wasn't there. That's nothing you can predict, change or help. Completely out of my control. It makes no sense. I felt like God was fucking laughing at me."

Janet stroked his hair, touched the handsome jaw. "I've done that too. Thought about the moment Jorge said the right combination of words, the things that made me decide to stay with him instead of going home with my dance company. I think of a hundred ways I might have noticed this or that, chosen differently. But I didn't. Maybe in some alternative universe I did, and as a result, I became a different person. Maybe a less strong, less certain person than I am now. But when this happens to an innocent, one who was given no choices at all in her Fate, there seems to be no clear answer."

He nodded, a bleak look in his gray eyes. She put her lips to his temple, spreading her fingers between his shoulder blades. "In this situation, you can only love her," she said softly. "Help keep the pieces together. That was the lesson I learned when I crossed paths with Matt, and he helped me pick up my pieces. If he hadn't been there, it's very likely I would be in a far worse place than I am now. Each of us has this sense that we're somehow divinely touched, a chosen person, but the reality is we're no different from any other creature struggling to survive. We try to find moments of peace and contentment, ways to enjoy the life we've been given, because this life is the only sure promise we have. You've given her the very best option she can have, and she has you."

Janet touched his face, drawing his gaze up to hers. "I can tell you that if I was reduced to nothing, but you were a part of my life, I'd still feel blessed. The fact that girl's eyes light up at the sight of you says she knows it too, even if she knows nothing else. You're her peace and contentment, Max."

He stared at her. She'd never been gladder for her hard-ass, no-nonsense bitch reputation, because it meant the sincere words had the power to startle him, shock him out of the dark place his mind had been trying to take him. And she did mean it. It even shook her up a little, given that her words weren't much different from a declaration of love. Perhaps even more significant than that.

"Thank you." His voice cracked a little. He cleared his throat. His arms had slipped down into a loose coil on her hips, his fingers curved over her buttocks. Not as a sexual tease, but more as a resting place from where they'd fallen, loose and tired. She kept her arm around his shoulders, stroked the hair at his nape, encouraging him to lay his head back down on her breast. *You can rest for a little while, Max,* she thought to herself. *I've got you.*

Even a warrior deserved a port in a storm. Maybe especially a warrior.

"My mom and I were really close," he said, his breath warm on her flesh. "Like partners, as I got into my teens and could bring home some money. We were in such a crappy neighborhood, broke, barely making it. I wasn't great at academics, but I had such self-discipline and determination, the school guidance counselor suggested I look at the SEAL program. Mom encouraged me in every way possible to do it, and kicked my ass if I even looked toward the riffraff in our neighborhood that wanted me to go a different way. She was so proud when I graduated from BUD/S, both her and Amanda."

That was where he'd acquired his deep respect for women, Janet realized. He'd experienced firsthand the power of a tough, loving mother. "I was worried about leaving them in that neighborhood, but I sent them home money, which she could put away to get them into a better place eventually." He swallowed. "There was this one op...I can't tell you much about it, but basically for a short time we had our hands on a shitload of drug money, confiscated on a raid. It was just us six guys watching over it, guys who knew everything about one another.

"One of my buddies joked about grabbing a handful before the politicians had their hands on it. They even did the Mel Gibson impersonation. You know, from *Lethal Weapon II*, where Murtaugh is thinking about taking some drug money to put his kids through college, but then puts it back, saying it's fucking drug money. And Riggs says, 'So? Do some good with it'. That haunts me now. If I'd taken one fucking fistful of that money home, my mom and sister could have moved out of that neighborhood. That's a stain I could have borne on my soul."

She considered that. "But it would have been different, wouldn't it? You wouldn't have known then you were saving them from that fate. You would have been just some guy who did something immoral, going against everything the SEALs stand for. You would have taken the easy way out to give your mom and sister a better place to live, and if your mom's the type of person you say she is, she wouldn't have wanted you to do that. She would have donated the money to some charity, and kicked your ass seven different ways."

His lips twisted. "Yeah, she would have. Dale—he's a buddy of mine—says the same thing you do, that the only sure thing we know is that we have this life. That the code we live by says what and who we are. Nothing else matters, everything different is just an excuse. You'd like him. He's a hard-ass like you. Metaphorically." He gave her a discreet squeeze. "The actual ass feels pretty good."

"Mine or Dale's?"

"I've never felt Dale's. Never had the urge and he'd probably shoot me in the balls if I did, but my guess is yours feels better."

"At least you didn't say it was soft," she sniffed.

"Only in the exact right way."

"Good answer." Janet sighed, put her head on top of his.

"There's a part of me that knows it wasn't in my control," he continued. "Within a few years of me serving in the SEALs, Mom could have moved them out of there. But Amanda had graduated high school, was working a job. She'd been in ROTC, was thinking about enlisting, and they both...Mom had friends in the neighborhood, and so did Amanda. They ran a community watch, were trying to make things better. And they both had this attitude of 'this is our home, and no one's going to make us leave it'. The fucking irony is that's why they were targeted. The bastards wanted to make an example out of the ones who stood up to the monsters, who refused to be broken by them."

"The what-ifs can put you on a lifetime-numbing dose of Xanax, trust me. There's what-is, and that's that. You live your life based on the what-ifs, and you'll never live." She touched his cheek, trying to change the direction of his thoughts. "Tell me something wonderful you remember about being a SEAL."

He shifted, propping his chin against her shoulder. "Underwater dives in tropical waters. It's a different kind of garden, but still a garden. There are so many things that glitter at night. Particles, the trails that fish leave. You don't expect it. In some ways, you want to stay down there forever."

He remained silent in her arms for a while. "Dale was with me when I got home, had to identify my mom's body and figure out what to do for Amanda. Mom was always so strong, and seeing her broken like that... I wanted to die. I couldn't imagine anything worse. Dale got me through, he and a couple of the other guys. Matt was connected to them, and they introduced us. He helped me find this place for Amanda. The guy who founded it, he was a doctor who had a son in Vietnam. The kid came back with PTSD, killed himself. When Matt told him about my situation, he worked out a payment plan I could afford, probably a tenth of what it costs to be here. He died a year after that happened, but even left it in his will, that Amanda could always be here, no matter my income level."

He shook his head. "It's things like that which don't make much sense. How some people can be so good, and others can be so bad. My SEAL buddies checked in on my mom when they were home and I wasn't. One of them talked to me about moving them into the adjacent unit of his duplex when the renter's lease was up. It wasn't too far from where Mom and Amanda were living, but it was a better area, and would have been safer. And Eric's wife and kids lived in that other side. Mom was killed two months before the renter moved out. Eric felt so bad about it, but I told him Mom wouldn't put up with him feeling like that."

She felt his lips curve against her, a painful grimace. "She always said she had her hammer and her pepper spray, bars on the windows, and I'd taught her to use a gun. But she wasn't able to get to it, they cut her off. Everything was the wrong timing, too fucking late."

Some things worked out perfectly, other things went so wrong it was hard to imagine how they could have been any worse. And like he'd said, it was good and bad. A person just had to learn how to appreciate the one and survive the other.

"How about I buy you some lunch, sailor?" she murmured. "That sandwich place off the highway looked pretty good."

He chuckled against her, lifted his head. As he did, she put her hands on his face, her thumbs passing over the dried tear tracks, her heart twisting anew at the sight of them.

"That's what my mom always said, if I came home upset about anything. There was nothing that a good meal couldn't cure."

"For a teenage boy, I expect that's true. And even more so for a big, strapping man with a healthy appetite. Just keep in mind I have a secretary's salary."

Max squeezed her, then lifted her to her feet. "Can't fool me, ma'am. You're Matt Kensington's secretary, and he pays his people what they're worth."

"So the truth comes out. You're after my money."

"Nope. Just the sex." He looped an arm around her waist, gave her a smile with a few less shadows behind his eyes, making her own heart lighter.

"I'd like to come back here with you. Whenever you and Amanda would like my company. Maybe I can teach her some ballet. Does she like to dance?"

"She always wanted to take ballet and jazz. We never had the money. I bet she'd love it." They'd reached the truck and Max opened the door for her, put his hands to her waist to lift her into the passenger seat rather than her having to use the step. Once there, he held on to her, putting the two of them eye to eye.

"I love you, Mistress."

Chapter Twelve
ಬ

He hadn't said anything else, just closed the door and crossed around to the other side. It had been an emotional afternoon, but Max didn't strike her as the type that led with emotion for a declaration like that. He felt things strongly, that was clear, but he thought things through before he spoke. He hadn't seemed to need her to say the words back, hadn't followed up with her on it, but the words surrounded her heart, held them, made her feel...wonderful. Still, happy, flustered...anxious.

One of Gayle's kids had come down with the flu and so they had to reschedule their visit with her for the next weekend. But Friday was still on the books. She had forty-eight hours to clear her mind and think about it, about him coming to Club Progeny as her guest.

Thursday she didn't get to see him because he took Matt and Jon to Baton Rouge, but in the late afternoon she received an intriguing text, probably while he was out in the parking lot waiting on them.

Any special instructions for tomorrow?

Yes. Shave off all body hair and paint your nails hot pink. I've shipped an I Heart Justin Bieber T-shirt to your home. Wear that with jeans. No underwear of course.

Sorry. Urgent mission. All SEALs being recalled to active duty, Friday night only. Crisis in Tahiti involving a shortage of sunscreen on swimsuit models.

I'd rethink that mission, sailor. Doubt you'll get out of that one alive. A not-so-friendly fire incident.

Love it when you're possessive, Mistress.

That had made her smile. It wasn't a bad feeling, thinking of Max as hers exclusively, especially when he seemed to reciprocate.

No special instructions. Just bring yourself. If you can find time to brush your teeth and put on deodorant, that would be appreciated.

Check. No sweaty man smell or spinach between my teeth.

No disagreement on the spinach, but she found she actually liked Max's sweaty man smell. She'd prefer to cause that state, however, and planned on it for Friday.

Putting her cell phone away as the elevator opened, she was surprised to see Dana. Using her cane, the minister navigated her way efficiently to Janet's desk.

"Janet, you wear the prettiest scents. Still making your own?"

"Always. I have a new honeysuckle and lemon verbena combination that's lovely. I'll send some home for you with Peter. Was he expecting you?"

"Not at all. With Max off in Baton Rouge, and everything wrapped up at the church early today, I had Wade bring me back here. Since I have some class tapes to review, I figured I could park in the back lounge area where I'll be out of everyone's way until the end of Peter's work day. If that's okay."

"It's a pleasure to have you here, as always. Can I get you a soda or snack?"

"No, I can check the break room. I'm not here to interrupt your work."

Belying that, however, Dana lingered, parking a hip on the desk and fishing through Janet's candy dish. She always knew which of the wrapped selections were chocolate. Of course, Peter's wife had enhanced senses on many levels, as she proved now.

"So I hear you're putting moves on my other man."

Janet lifted a brow. "Surely you don't mind sharing? Peter and Max are more blessings than any one woman deserves."

"I've been so good, I deserve all the blessings that come my way." Dipping her head so Janet could see her eyes over the edge of the sunglasses, Dana gave her a wicked wink. "Can I get raunchy? Are we all by ourselves?"

Janet chuckled. "Yes. Nearest occupied office is Lucas', and he can't hear us from here, unless we're shouting. Plus he and his accounting team are working on quarterly taxes, which means he has his doors closed so I can't hear him lavishing creative and vivid curses on the government."

"Bless the incompetence and greed of our government then. Seriously, Max is a good man. I was delighted to hear the boy is getting some. I was beginning to worry he'd retired that dick altogether, and that would be a sin, with a body like that."

"And being a minister-in-training, you are an authority on sin."

"Peter calls me the cause of original sin. He's so sweet." Dana unwrapped one of the chocolates and extended another to Janet. Deciding to roll with it, Janet took the candy, enjoyed the taste in companionable silence. Dana didn't make a habit of wasting anyone's time, so Janet expected there was more she wanted to say. While the woman was mulling it over, she decided to take advantage of the information source.

"Max has been volunteering at your church, hasn't he?"

"He's a godsend. Does a lot of heavy lifting, maintenance, plays basketball with the boys. They love him, though they've nicknamed him White Boy Can't Jump. CJ for short. I tell them to give him a break, because they know they have a genetic advantage on him. He claims that's racial profiling. I tell him it's just the sad fact of why black people have taken over professional contact sports." Dana smirked, but then sobered. "I love him to death, Janet. He's tough as nails, but try not to pulverize his heart. I don't think he's offered it to a lot of women in his life. If he has a mind to give it to you, treat it with care, even if you decide to give it back."

"He wants me to take him to the club on Friday night. As mine."

Dana, about to rise, shifted into Janet's guest chair with a decided thump. "Say again?"

"Yes." Noting the concern on Dana's face, Janet settled her hands on her desk, clasped them. "Do you think that will be a problem?"

She hadn't intended the cool edge, but it was there. Dana didn't take offense. "I wasn't meaning anything against you, Janet. I just…he's not a sub."

"No, he's not. I do know that. But he wants to show that he trusts me, and he wants to experience that side of me. It's a gift, but I intend for it not to be one-sided." She couldn't really explain something so complex further, but fortunately, it seemed to make sense to Dana. She was as much a part of that world as Janet, only on the submissive side.

"That fits him. And you." She hesitated. "Are you looking for advice?"

Janet felt her hackles ease. "I would welcome any, yes."

"All right. I have a friend who's married to a SEAL. She says the best way to turn them into basket cases is park them at a table in the center of a place that has about a dozen different exit and entry points. It's like watching a bunch of cats in a roomful of rockers. Doesn't matter that they know they're on civilian ground. They're trained and trained and trained until these things are like breathing to them."

"So what would you suggest?"

Dana's full, moist lips pressed together, considering. "Do your session in a private room. Let him see it before you blindfold him. If it's at Progeny, the rooms only have one exit and entry point. Show him that it's coded so that he knows once the door's locked, the only one who can come in is a staff member with a master key override, and that only happens if there's a safety issue. Even so, he's not going to be able to handle being restrained to the point he can't get loose. I know nothing's more tempting to a Domme than seeing a man that fine bound and helpless, but it will make him edgy, nervous, and you don't want to put a SEAL in that state."

"Do you think he would do it, if I asked, despite that?"

"Yes," Dana answered her bluntly. "But don't make him do that, Janet. Please."

She reached over the candy bowl and found Janet's knuckles, tapped them. It was a plea and admonishment both.

"BDSM is so intense, it's kind of crazy to call it a game, but it is, at one level, where the pleasure comes into it. Tying him up so he can't get loose…that won't be a game to him, and there's no way you'll be able to make it one. From what I understand from Peter, I think he'd pretty much do anything you wanted him to do at this point. Until he realized it was a mistake."

Max had told her he loved her, which had been a shock to her system. She knew Max well enough to know he wouldn't have shared that with anyone else, so hearing that the men she worked for had already detected his feelings was an additional surprise. Not necessarily unpleasant but…unsettling.

"No unexpected loud noises. We all hate those. I still can't stand hearing kids play those dumbass war video games. If you go the way of blindfolds and light restraint, do a lot of physical contact. Keep connected to him by voice or touch, so he knows where you are in the room. You'd be amazed at how much control a SEAL has. He could pull up the nose of a gun a hair before a civilian pops out of the woodwork in front of his target, but he's still trained to be a deadly force weapon. He wouldn't be willing to do this unless he trusts you and himself enough to keep things safe, but you can help him do that."

Janet digested that. "Understood. How about anal?"

"Hmm. A strap-on might not be out of the question. You'll have to figure that one out. Hasn't come up in our daily conversation." She gave Janet a cheeky grin. "But I can tell you right off, don't touch him with an actual cock. That boy's as straight as Pat Buchanan on a holy roller tour. Some poor guy would lose their most vital appendage."

Janet chuckled at the image, even as she remembered how he'd handled Thor, so casually intimate, but firmly distancing himself from any sexual implications to it. "All right. Anything else?"

An expression of feline pleasure wreathed Dana's face. "Yeah. I'd probably sell my soul to be able to see this go down. You're one lucky woman. Why don't you plan to come to our girls' night this month? I bet everyone would be willing to offer major bribes to hear you rattle off a play-by-play."

"I'm never averse to bribes."

* * * * *

For the third time, Max checked himself in the mirror. This was getting ridiculous. He wore a belted pair of stressed jeans and a black dress shirt. He'd seen the things Janet did with her subs, and he was starting to think he was crazy, imagining himself in similar positions. One night, she'd led a poor bastard around the club on hands and knees. He'd been buck-naked, except for a cage-like thing around his cock. What if any of the K&A men were there? He cut the vision of Matt seeing his limo driver being led around by a cock leash right out of his head, because the mere thought would make Max break out in hives. It would probably make Matt break out in hives as well.

He hadn't thought about any of that when he offered this. He'd had some vague sense of her hand upon him, him being on his knees, close enough to put his mouth on her sweet-smelling skin, rub his cheek against whatever sexy concoction she'd wear to drive him crazy. So basically his brain had disengaged and his cock had done his thinking.

Except it hadn't been his cock leading him, but his heart. He should have remembered his heart had no more of a brain than his cock did, and they'd both left his head out of it. Idiots.

Okay, he was turning his internal organs into a community forum, so he was not in a good head space right now. His date was waiting on him. If he waited five more minutes to leave, he'd run the risk of being late, not a good start to the night. Fuck it.

No. He drew a deep breath. It wasn't his date waiting for him, but his Mistress. He liked the way she reacted to that, her eyes sharpening but her mouth getting a little softer, the silky brows arching in an interested way. It would be all right. Either way, he'd agreed to do it and he wasn't backing out. No sense chewing on it any more. Grabbing his keys, he headed out.

She'd told him she wanted to meet him at the club, not be picked up, so as he drove that way, he wondered what she'd choose to wear. Leather, corset...those awesome boots and gloves that fit like a second skin. No, he bet she was going to be more unpredictable tonight, though if she showed up in sweats and running shoes he'd still be hard as a rock for it. Yeah, he had it bad.

His mind moved to thoughts of their day together with Amanda, then to what Janet had done when they left the facility, guiding him into the garden and putting herself in his lap. She hadn't coaxed or chased his emotional reaction. She'd demanded it, in a way that had resulted in a purging of the pain. He'd broken down after his mom, sure, but by himself. In the early days of dealing with it, he'd almost lost it a couple times in Dale's company, or with the other guys, but their way of handling it was letting him walk it off, protecting him from interruption until he collected his shit.

Maybe it just wasn't in his makeup to accept from a guy what Janet had offered. When she took charge, instead of swallowing it down, he'd let it swallow him up. Everything he'd needed to do since he first saw his mother's body had risen out of his heart and taken over. He couldn't remember the last time he'd cried about anything, but if a man couldn't cry about losing his mother and the death of his sister's future, then he supposed he had no tears for anything.

He pulled up to Club Progeny. Fortunately, Matt and his guys mostly preferred the slower weeknights. Since that meant they likely weren't here, that was a plus, but seeing the profusion of people coming and going, Max felt an unfamiliar shot of uneasiness through his vitals, something perilously close to unmanly fear. He was familiar enough with this stuff to know there were safe words, limits. He could tell Janet what was a no-go for him. But of course that caught in his craw, because it clashed with his determination to be the big alpha guy who could handle anything.

"Fuck it. Get the hell out of the truck and do it." *Trust her. That's what this is about, remember?*

As he strode up to the club, he was aware of calculated glances. When he brought the limo, he had an obvious role as a staff person delivering a club member. Tonight his status was up for speculation, an unknown quantity. Dom? Sub? Curious voyeur?

Trinity was the hostess on shift tonight. She was a gorgeous blonde with glossy pink lips and a lot of soft white breast displayed up high in a blue satin corset with black lacings. He'd had cordial dealings with her before, had even brought her a cup of coffee one night when she couldn't get away from the desk and he was waiting on Ben and Marcie to finish their session.

"Mistress Janet told me you'd be coming as her guest," she said with a smile. "Glad to have you with us as a player tonight, Max. Will you give me your wrist, please?"

When he complied, she put a rubber bracelet on him. It had been stamped with dark letters. *Exclusive property of Mistress Janet.*

"No one will offer you any proposals while wearing that," she said as he studied it. "She said you'd be most comfortable that way."

When he glanced up, Trinity gave his hand a quick squeeze, fingers whispering over his palm. "Don't worry. They're just people. No one's going to try to eat you alive, though we can't keep people from fantasizing about it." She chuckled. "She's waiting for you in room D, second level. That's a private room."

Though he should be embarrassed that his anxiety was that obvious, some of it eased at the information. It underlined what he'd thought when he got out of the truck.

Janet knows you. You can trust her.

The club really was hopping tonight, music booming on the dance floor, the bass accompanied by the bounce and twist of a lot of bodies showing plenty of bare skin. In the public play rooms, several scenes were happening on the suspension beams, with the St. Andrew's Crosses and spanking benches at full occupancy. Though he usually enjoyed watching from the safety of his coffee spot, he decided keeping his eyes averted tonight was the wise move. On the first HALO jump, he'd found it was better not to lean out of the plane and see how fast and far the guy who'd jumped ahead of him was falling. But he remembered the rush of adrenaline when he followed him, the *oh fuck, what the hell did I do*, followed by the glorious sense of *I'm fucking flying. When can I go on this ride again?*

This was going to be like that, because that's what he wanted to happen, and it was what she wanted to happen. They were in it together. He was being a fucking pussy. He'd gone through buildings that were a maze of blind turns obscured by concrete dust and darkness, fire crackling at his heels, the possibility of an insurgent's gun or an explosive device directly ahead. He could handle one D/s session with a petite, beautiful Dominatrix who already had most of his heart in her hands.

Room D. He started to turn the door handle, then stopped, knocked. The security light over the door turned from red to green, a beep inviting him to enter. He noted a security card was needed to get in, unless the person already inside unlatched the door. Secure and ultra private.

Out of habit, he glanced through the crack as he opened the door, checking behind it, and then his gaze swept the room as he stepped inside.

It was a simple rectangle with a lavatory closet built into the far left corner, that door open to show a polished silver sink, commode. A built-in cabinet along the same wall displayed an array of items assembled on the counter's surface. Velcro cuffs, a flogger and a sturdy cloth bag whose contents were concealed, but he expected there was more of the same inside it, since he'd seen Janet bring it to her sessions before. The floor was painted with concentric circles, a chair bolted on the bull's-eye. One wall had several different options for restraining a body against it. The opposite wall had some of those options as well, but they were obscured by an image being projected from the video equipment embedded in the ceiling.

It was the ocean. Just a continuous, panoramic view of a mild surf breaking and then rushing to shore. The sky was a pre-dawn marmalade. The projector provided sound, matching the image flowing from the wall onto a foot of the floor. He digested all of it in a second, and then found his Mistress. She was leaning against the opposite wall, watching him.

The things he'd imagined her wearing—boots, corset, tight pants—were things he'd seen her don for this type of play in the past. Things that made any man's imagination run to hot, wet dreams. Her outfit tonight definitely met that requirement, but it wasn't something he'd seen her wear before. It was as if she'd worn it specifically for him.

She wore a bikini top, the sides shaped so the garment lifted her small breasts and made them swell out and over, her cleavage deep and tempting a man's tongue to tunnel there. The pale-yellow color showed the dark smudge of her nipples, the silky, thin fabric molding the points. A sarong wrap was tied at her hip, so her leg appeared bare all the way from waist to ankle. She wasn't wearing anything under the sarong, unless it was a thong so small the strap was hidden beneath the knot of the fabric.

She was barefoot, her hair down, curled around her face. She was wearing makeup, but it was different from the office or what he'd seen her wear here. This was so natural, he might have missed it, except for the gleam of the lipstick, the scent of her gloss. Some kind of musk he expected was injected with pheromones, because it pulled him across the room to her like she'd wrapped a chain around his cock.

"Stop." Her eyes were half slits, her head leaned back as if she was on the beach, listening to the waves. "Go to the wall, Max. The one with the ocean."

When he hesitated, those dark eyes opened fully. "This is your punishment, yes?" Her voice was a sultry purr. "Which means you follow your Mistress' commands. She knows what kind of discipline you need."

They were the type of words he didn't expect to arouse him, make him harder, but they sure as hell did. Nodding, he moved to the wall. She watched him, that mysterious gaze following his every move.

"You won't speak unless I give you permission to do so. Face the wall and grasp the handles that are closest to the full stretch of your arms."

He could see the flicker of the video as he obeyed, his body becoming a part of the wave images. The handles were just above his shoulder height, and she'd accurately predicted his arm span. The set at the full reach of his arms had already been locked down in their tracks.

"Spread your legs shoulder width." She'd moved closer. When she curved her hand over his tense shoulder, let her fingers glide down the center of his back, over his shirt, his nerve endings reacted to that touch like a drug. It helped him deal with the fact he had his back to the door, making him twitchy.

"That beep you heard when you entered happens whenever the door unlatches. There's a five-second delay before it opens. Once it's coded by the user, the only one who can come in without me unlocking it from the inside is a staff member with an override. Even with an override, there's that beep and five-second delay. All right?"

He nodded, another concern dissipating. "Yes ma'am."

She moved away from him, over to the cabinet on the adjacent wall. As she studied her options there, she pulled her hair over one shoulder, so his gaze was caught by what was drawn on her back. He'd seen enough of her body to know she had no tattoos, but this temporary wasn't a cheap sticker. Her skin was the canvas for a monarch butterfly, wings stretched out and curved over her shoulder blades. The lower set of wings were pierced by a trident, the eagle with the bowed head along the base of it, across her lower back.

The butterfly was a fragile creature, but so beautiful its beauty had an indelible strength. And it had been pierced, captured, by a modified form of the SEAL trident symbol. Whether she'd intended the meaning or not, the idea of it swamped him, giving him courage and a willingness to handle whatever this was. As well as risk additional punishment by speaking without permission.

"I like your ink."

She looked at him over her shoulder. "I didn't know about the eagle, why his head is in that position. I liked that."

The SEALs were the only armed services division whose symbol showed the eagle's head bowed. It was done that way to honor the fallen. Seeing her honor it on her flesh made him want to put his lips there, follow the trident up her spine, kiss every inch of the butterfly's wings. His neck was getting a crick, looking at her at the strained angle, but he didn't care.

"The artist said he'd enrolled in SEAL training once, when he was much younger," she continued. "He made it to the third week, and had a tremendous appreciation for SEALs. He also said, and I quote—'those are some of the craziest motherfuckers in the world'."

"We take that as a compliment."

"Hmm. I figured as much." Now her lips curved. "Look at the wall, not at me, Max."

She'd pulled something from the bag but was keeping it concealed in her hand. As she returned to him, she touched his nape. She leaned against him, her breasts pressing against his back, and he felt silk against his cheek.

"I'm going to blindfold you, Max. You'll be able to hear my voice, and I'll tell you what I'm going to do before I do it. You may wish I didn't," that seductive tease was in her voice again, "but I'm counting on that brave, alpha, all-guts-and-balls side of you to take your punishment like a man. Can you handle that? It's just a day on the beach…and you know just how punishing that can be, don't you?"

Even his missions hadn't been as tough as certain parts of BUD/S training, so she was right about that. As she guided the blindfold over his eyes, she spoke again. "Tell me about Hell Week. What do you remember about it?"

"Everything hurt. There was nothing but cold." God, every SEAL remembered that fucking, unbelievable cold. "But when you reached a certain point, your brain shut down. All you did was follow the instructors, trusting them and the guys around you to get you through. You weren't going to quit. No…it wasn't even that conscious. You passed exhaustion, left it way the hell behind. Everything was stretched past breaking…it was broken, and yet you were being remade too. You'd keep going as long as the instructor said you had to go, until you dropped and died."

"You gave everything over into his keeping," she said quietly. "The most difficult and yet most complete moment of your life. The mind no longer involved. Just the effort, the goal, the instructor's commands. That was everything."

"Yeah." He hadn't ever really thought of it that way, but he guessed that was true. She'd made the blindfold snug, using a Velcro strip in the back, something he could rip off if needed. Her nails slid across his back, and then her touch was gone, leaving only the rush of the waves. He couldn't hear her footsteps.

"Janet."

"I'm here."

He didn't know if he should call her Mistress, but her name was what came to his lips. Ironically, he realized he called her Mistress when he felt in control.

"I was getting these." More cushiony fabric brushed his left hand, wrapped around his wrist. "These cuffs are going to hold your hands to the handles." After she put another one on the right arm, a wider piece brushed his throat. "This is a collar. I'm going to put a short tether on it, attach it to a clip embedded in the wall. All of the connectors are plastic snap locks, which can be broken easily by a powerful man. But you won't break them. That would displease me. You will restrain yourself, follow my commands. Do you understand, Max?"

He got his cue this time. "Yes, Mistress." They could be broken. It didn't make his gut tighten any less or make his throat less dry. Though the cuffs made him feel peculiar, they couldn't hold a candle to his reaction to the collar. Maybe it was how she lingered over it, stroking his throat, tugging on the strap in a way that told him that putting it on him seriously aroused her. His cock, which had diminished some while evaluating the uncertainties of the situation, came back to life. When she rose up on her toes to hook the tether, keeping his face within a foot of the wall unless he pulled against the leash, her body pressed against the side of his.

"I like the outfit. You dressed up for me. Nice jeans, black shirt. You even shined your shoes."

"Yes ma'am. My mother always told me to look my best for a lady."

"Ssshh. No more talking unless I ask you a direct question. If I have to remind you again, I'll gag you."

Her tone was firm, calm. A reminder of consequences. She hadn't snapped the cuffs to the handles yet, but he figured out why soon enough. She wanted to undress him first. She ran her hands down his back, like a police officer searching a suspect, only her touch was far more provocative, teasing, molding to his sides, his waist and hips, cupping his buttocks in the jeans, then slipping her fingers into the back pockets. She took out his wallet, his keys, fingers caressing his groin through the pointed reach of the front pocket. The waves continued to make their rushing noise. Some sort of air filter was adding to the hologram, because he could smell sea air.

Her hip bone was against the lower part of his buttock as she reached around him to tug his shirt out of his jeans. She worked open the buttons from bottom to top, palms sliding over his ridged abdomen, his chest, fingers tugging the curling hair there, then the shirt was fully open. When she slipped the buttons on the cuffs, her nails scraped his wrist pulse, then trailed down the opening of the sleeve as far as it would allow.

"Lift your hands from the handles and put them behind your back."

As he complied, she slid the shirt off his shoulders, slow. When she got it to his elbows, she shifted her grip so she was pulling on the collar only and putting her other hand directly between his shoulders, palm against his heated flesh, nails scraping as she pulled the shirt free. Her fingers lingered on the tattoo on his rib cage. She seemed to like touching that one quite a bit.

He only had the one, representing a mission where he and his team had taken out three high-level insurgents. They'd also lost three men of their own that day; hence the three prongs of the trident for the three lost men, and the three skulls for the three enemies removed. He had it on a mission patch, but while he'd been in the SEALs he'd never marked his body, since tattoos could reveal his branch of service if he was captured. But when it was clear he would never return to the SEALs, he'd needed the connection. It had been the last mission he'd done.

Now he thought about what she had inked on her back. Maybe he'd put that design on the opposite side of his rib cage. A symbol of the mission he served now, the one he might want to serve for the rest of his life. Would she like that? It would be an ownership mark of sorts, wouldn't it?

"Put your hands back on the handles." She snapped the locks so he was held to those handles by the cuffs, his body kept close to the wall by them and the one-foot tether to the collar. Her fingers traced his belt. "I liked using your belt on you, that first night. Did you look at the marks on your ass the next day, in the mirror?"

"Yes ma'am."

She cupped one buttock, squeezed it hard through the fabric, and his cock ached, imagining her hands on both of them, kneading hungrily as he thrust into her wet pussy, serving her pleasure.

"How did it make you feel?"

"Owned."

No use denying simple truth. It was the word that had come to mind when he'd stared at those fading marks. In a totally different but similar way, it was like carrying a picture of his mother and sister with him whenever he'd been able to do so. That invaluable sense of belonging, of connection, no matter how far from home he got. Which was probably why he was having that crazy thought about the tattoo.

"A nice answer." She put her mouth between his shoulder blades and worked down his spine with heated lips and moist tongue. Her hands curved around his waist, following the line of the belt until she reached the front. She loosened the tongue, unbuttoned the jeans, worked the zipper down, her body still against the back of his. Her leg hooked over his thigh and she rubbed her mound over the seam of his ass, making him harden, his muscles tighten. He had to quell a desire to thrust forward, show her what he wanted to do for her. Then she shifted, bringing both feet back to the floor so she could slide her hand into the open jeans.

"No underwear. You're a tease, Max. Who would have guessed? And the area around your cock so smooth and neatly trimmed. You really did make yourself presentable for a lady. You didn't pick up that tip from your mother, did you?"

He strangled on a half chuckle. "No, not that one."

She gripped his cock in a loose curl and slid upward, working the velvet skin along his shaft. A wave of sensation rushed up through his balls, following her touch. She kept doing it, up and down, showing a skillful knowledge of a man's body. He tried not to thrust into her hand, but it required tightening his buttocks so the muscles were hard steel. She rubbed herself against them, her scantily clad breasts pressed to his bare back. Her nipples had turned into aroused stiff points as she used the friction between their bodies to arouse herself.

Releasing him, she worked the jeans off his hips. She untied his shoes, had him lift each foot so she could remove them. He could have toed them off. He didn't like the idea of her having to bend down like that. He bit it back before he spoke though. He didn't want to be gagged. He was doing well with the blindfold thing, better than he'd expected, but he was still tense enough to know he wouldn't maintain as well if he lost another perceived freedom. The more he capitulated to her as a Mistress, the more he suspected that would happen. He needed to control the pace as much as possible.

While she was down there, she wrapped cuffs around his ankles, attached tethers of the same length as the one at his throat and snapped them to hooks in the wall as well. Now he was naked except for collar and cuffs. She straightened, her nails trailing over his ass. One finger tunneled between his buttocks, despite his reflexive tightening there.

"Open up for me, Max. Relax."

He recalled what he'd thought about in the car. Ground rules, safe words. Janet had done none of those things with him, relying on their innate understanding of one another, the trust he was attempting to grasp. He could call a stop to it now, but he didn't. For one thing, she changed her mind about her direction, stroking his flanks briefly before stepping away, leaving him there.

He couldn't hear her footfalls over that wave score, but a moment later he heard the cabinet open and close, the clank as she likely went through what was in that velvet bag. His fingers flexed on the handles and he shifted his weight.

"Oh that was nice. Do that again. You have a superior ass, Max. Dana's right about that."

He grimaced but obeyed, feeling a little foolish until he heard her hum, a note that made him think of a cat eyeing cream. Or in Janet's case, a lioness eyeing a bull calf.

When she touched his back again, his muscles eased a fraction. She noted it, pressing her fingers more firmly into his flesh. "I'm here, Max. I'm not leaving the room. I promise."

"I know that." He didn't mean to sound impatient with her. He didn't want her thinking he was weak, nervous. He just wasn't great with being blindfolded and that damn wave track masking noise. The speakers must be embedded in this wall. "Don't worry about me. I'm fine."

"Yes, you are. More than fine." She stroked his buttock again, nails scraping his flesh. "If I had my way, I'd put you just like this against the wall across from my desk. Of course, there wouldn't be a K&A female employee who'd get any work done that day, and that would include me, since they'd all be making excuses to come to my office."

"Not to mention what Matt would have to say about it."

"We'd do it when Matt and the others were traveling. It would be a girls-only day on the executive floor. Maybe I'd invite Savannah, Dana, Cassandra, Marcie and Rachel for lunch. Strap you down on the boardroom table. Do you know the new one converts to a St. Andrew's Cross of sorts? Designed by Jon, of course. I'd blindfold you like this, and they'd tease, taste, bite. Feed you bits of their lunch. Perhaps I'd talk to Peter about it beforehand, so I could order Dana to wrap her lips around your cock, make her suck you to orgasm but deny her one of her own, punish her for taking liberties with you."

"It's not like that. She's just... It doesn't..."

"Mean anything? No, perhaps not. Until you belong to a Mistress. And then it's a serious infraction." Her palm slid down his side, over the trident and skull tattoo, down to his hip, then back to his front, stroking his groin, his stiff cock, fingernails tracing the corona, thumb pressing against the slit as she took hold of him again like the gear shift of her Mustang. "She and I will have to talk about that."

He groaned as she eased under his arm, bringing her body between his and the wall. A scraping noise, like heavy plastic, and then he realized she'd brought a small footstool, because when she stepped onto it he felt the touch of her breath on his brow, meaning she was a couple inches taller than him. Unhooking his tether, she wound it around her hand so that he felt the pull of it against the collar when she rested the point of her wrist on his pectoral. She allowed the strap enough slack to turn her back to him, put it over her shoulder, tugging upward so he lifted his jaw. A moment later, she rubbed her ass against his abdomen.

His immediate desire was to thrust his cock up between her legs, because he could feel the brush of her thighs against his aroused sex. He suppressed the desire, having enough sense to know that was going to be a punishable offense. A warning tug on that tether reinforced it. However, another second of that delectable ass against him and he might go for it.

She put her hands over his on the wall, rubbed her ass in a slow circle against him, making that little teasing purr in her throat again. "The tie to my bikini top is in front of you, Max. Pull it loose with your teeth and you'll get a reward."

As he leaned forward, she caught his cock between her thighs, squeezing down on it and making him thrust involuntarily. Fuck, she felt good. She chuckled, a dangerous sound.

"Behave, or you'll wish you had."

First, though, he pressed his lips between her shoulder blades, where the drawing was. He could smell the faint scent of the ink. "I really like this."

"I really like you."

The simple, whimsical response made him smile. He tugged the tie loose, grateful for that slippery fabric that made bikinis easy to remove when dry. She started to turn, so he leaned back, but not very far. He knew just which part of her anatomy would be within reach of his mouth on that turn, and he wanted to be ready if she gave him that reward.

The beep of the door made him stiffen. He jerked back reflexively, forgetting he was bound, and the cuffs pulled against his wrists, the tether holding him like a dog on a short leash.

"It's all right. It's a staff volunteer. I pressed a button requesting a few minutes of assistance. It's Rita. You know her."

"Mistress Janet." At the female voice, he didn't relax, but he did stop pulling. He didn't like this. He hadn't heard the door close. The wave sound emitting from the speakers above him might have drowned it out, or it might be standing open.

"Turn the soundtrack off. Right now."

"I will in a minute if you want me to do so, but think it through. It's just you, me and Rita. The door is closed and locked, I promise. Can you trust me, Max?"

He set his teeth. That was the point, he got it. But as much as he might trust her, there was no way he could relax like this. He couldn't pleasure her the way he wanted to do it, not with half his mind caught up in the vulnerabilities of the environment. But every environment had vulnerabilities. Hell, a well-placed sniper could take out half the tourists in Jackson Square on any given day, and he could have a cup of coffee there without freaking out. The restraints and unfamiliar scenario had shifted him into a defensive mindset, but this wasn't a third-world country, and he wasn't here as a SEAL on a mission. He was in a BDSM club in the middle of New Orleans, with a beautiful Mistress demanding only one thing from him. Trust.

"I was promised a reward," he managed. He sounded sullen. A little mean.

"Yes, you were." Her fingers buried in his hair, pulled his head forward. His lips brushed her nipple, and he needed no more invitation than that to latch on and suckle, tease, nip. He licked her breast all around the tip, wanting to arouse every inch of her. He rubbed his face between them, attacked the other one, giving it the same treatment, rough, aggressive, demanding. She dug her hands into his scalp, her body arching into his. His cock pressed between the seam of her thighs, but that was as far as he could get. She had his ankles cuffed to the floor. He couldn't angle his hips to drive into the naked, eager pussy under that barely there sarong.

"Rita is going to touch your back now." Janet's voice was satisfyingly strained, breathy. He pulled on the right nipple so strongly she cried out in pleasure and discomfort at once. Her foot had hooked around his left thigh again. She liked to hold on with her legs. It made him think of that ballet pose where the ballerina stood on one toe, gripped her partner with her other leg like that while he turned them both, their bodies melded together. He'd like Janet to teach him that one.

Rita's fingers slid down his back to his ass. Janet rubbed her mound against his body, shifting to brush against his cock, teasing him with the hint of her pussy.

"I want to fuck you," he growled against her breast.

"You will. When it's time. When I say. Please me, Max. Let me lead you where we both want to go."

Rita's fingers were now between his ass cheeks. She had something slippery and warm on her fingers, something that heated his skin and tingled on contact. She teased his rim, stroking. His attention zeroed in on that, but then Janet's cunt brushed him again, this time the wet lips sliding provocatively over the head of his cock. He jerked, and in that moment, two of Rita's fingers slid inside him. His head came up like a startled stallion, buttocks tightening.

"No. What the hell is she doing? Stop." He twitched, trying to get away from her, but she simply moved with him. As she did, a not-at-all-unpleasant sensation thrummed out from the point where her fingers were. "Fuck."

"Many straight men enjoy anal stimulation, Max. It's a mind-blowing experience, I promise you." Janet's lips brushed his cheek, that musky gloss scent so near his mouth he reached for it, but she drew back, denying him, teasing him. "Rita is going to strap a dildo inside your ass. Once she does that, I'm going to command you to fuck me. When you bring me to climax, the dildo and my pussy will make you want to come. But you're going to resist until I give you permission, unlike the other night when you misbehaved. And when I finally, finally say you can come, it's going to feel better than anything you've ever felt."

Her voice was that mesmerizing croon, like a succubus fucking a man straight into hell and making him long for the fire. She'd push him beyond his limits, because she had that quality to her, but he'd been trained to be pushed beyond his limits, hadn't he?

Let me lead you where we both want to go. This wasn't something he'd ever fantasized about, but he admitted that sensation Rita had coaxed from his ass had been unexpected. Maybe the biggest hurdle was getting past the idea of it, that he was bound to the wall, being topped by a woman. He'd known when he agreed to it that the night could go this way, though he'd avoided imagining the details. What had been more important was the intention. He was willing to hand that power over to her tonight, to show her what she was beginning to mean to him.

He understood the blindfold now. That scrap of cloth could help him do something he might not be able to do if he saw himself reflected in her eyes. Accepting the unexpected in oneself was easier without sight, existing in a formless world where she was his one point of contact.

"My nipples are feeling neglected." She didn't ask him if he was okay with what she'd just laid out, but how he responded to that simple statement would guide her. It really was like a dance, wasn't it? He expected she saw it that way in her head, and it was probably why she could lose herself in it. She'd brought him on stage with her, to be her partner.

"What do they look like?" His tone was husky, uncertain and demanding at once. Her fingers slid back through his hair, a caress this time, her fingernails scraping the sensitive skin under his ear.

"You've made them swell to the size of cherries. They're deep, dark red, the flesh around them glistening from your mouth. My breasts are swollen, just like my clit and cunt. I want your cock inside of me."

He put his mouth back over her left breast, took as much of it as he could, and began to gently suckle. His cock jumped at the sound of her pleased moan. Rita's fingers were busy, working more of that oil into him. It was an odd sensation, but still not unpleasant. Just disturbing. When she at last pulled out, she lingered to massage more oil into his rim. His hips bucked at the stimulation, his cock spurting pre-come against his Mistress' thigh. Janet's hand slid along his length to the point of contact and collected it. When her arm brushed his shoulder, he knew she'd put it in her mouth, tasting him.

The firm rubber head of what he assumed was the dildo was placed against his rim, Rita gripping his buttock.

"Push out against her, Max. And try to relax everything else. Just let it slide in."

It wasn't the easiest command he'd ever followed, but he managed it. It wasn't excessively thick, thank God. Janet was merciful enough to go easy on his virgin ass, but his balls drew up, his cock convulsing as Rita seated the dildo and then strapped it around his thighs and hips, cinching it into place. But on top of that, she also cinched something tight around the base of his cock. Something that made him groan and quiver.

"That will keep you from going off before I command it."

"I would have held out until your command, Mistress."

"Even so. I like the way your cock looks, all bound up like that. It makes me wetter. Squeeze down on that dildo, Max. Imagine I'm wearing it, thrusting into you."

Not an image he ever would have imagined with a woman. He liked to be doing the thrusting, but there was no denying his cock was thick and pulsing, liking whatever that dildo was stimulating. When he squeezed down on it, it got more intense. "Fuck."

"Thank you, Rita. Please leave us now and close the door after you."

"Yes, Mistress."

This time he heard the snick, because he concentrated hard enough on the sound, anticipating when it would happen. Then he turned his attention to better things. His Mistress had brought his head back to her nipples again. She really liked his mouth there, making little whimpering noises to prove it.

"Janet. You're driving me crazy. I want to fuck you."

"Show me. Show me how much. I want to feel your strength, Max. Prove how it can take me over, even as it serves me."

He didn't stop to think what she might mean. He simply acted. He broke the plastic connections to the wrist cuffs with one fierce yank, released one of the ankle cuffs with another sharp snap of his leg. Catching her ass in one hand, he lifted her up against the wall as he put the other behind her head and neck, making sure he hadn't shifted her on to the metal hook that tethered his collar to the wall. Then he found her mouth and plunged with teeth and tongue, pushing her skull back into the cup of his hand.

Both of her legs curled around his waist. With the side slit of the sarong all the way to the hip, there was nothing in the way of his other plunge. He'd been right. She wasn't even wearing an indecently tiny thong under that thin fabric. He'd seen the provocative shadow of her ass, the seam between her buttocks when she left him to go get the blindfold, and now he worked his hand under the fabric so he was clutching flesh when he drove into slick, hot wetness.

He let out a reverent oath, mirrored by her guttural moan, and he was pounding against her, reveling in the sound of her body hitting the wall with sensual impact. He showed her his strength, how it could serve her, just as she said.

That thing in his ass was making things even more crazy intense than they already were. He'd gotten impossibly harder, and the cock ring was starting to cut like a son of a bitch. He wasn't going to be able to come with it there, an agony that would serve his Mistress to the nth degree, since he was staying titanium hard.

"Your punishment, my pleasure, Max," she whispered against his ear, his Mistress inside his world of darkness. "I'm going to come, and you're going to listen, and beg me for the same privilege. But I'll make you service my pussy with your mouth until I come again, before I even consider it. With that dildo still inside, I'm going to flog you, make your skin burn fiery red. Then, and only then, I'll let you come. I'll play with it, push it in and out, and you'll come into a condom. Your punishment. You get your Mistress' pussy after that. If you can still get hard at that point."

"Count on it, Mistress." He said it between clenched teeth, everything in him worked up, like a battle rage but different, everything driven by the need in his cock, by her scent, by the taunt in her voice that was all seductive cruelty. She wanted to wear him out, wring every ounce of sensation from him, turn him into a mindless fucking machine. Make him let go of his will and serve her with everything he was. Exactly like his instructors had done during Hell Week.

He was going to give it all to her, even more than he'd given to them. And he thought he'd given them everything.

* * * * *

When he'd pulled his cuffs away from the wall, he'd used enough force that one of the metal handles had cracked the sheetrock. She'd pay for that damage, of course, but it had been worth it, on so many levels.

Now she sat on the bull's-eye chair, studying him. He was on his hands and knees in the middle of the floor, condom rolled onto his aching cock, wrists still in cuffs, locked to each other while he clasped a metal bar embedded in the floor. She'd ordered him to spread his knees and was studying his gorgeous ass, the quivering of his flanks. He'd just come into the condom, and his head was down, forehead pressed to his knuckles. She held the cock ring in her hand, working it around two of her fingers like a tiny hula hoop. It was slick from the sweat off his balls, the lube that had slipped out of his ass, the semen trickling from his cock.

He'd come while she was flogging him. She'd used a medium-weight flogger, knowing his nerves were aroused enough that the slap on his tender inner thighs, the crease between legs and ass, the muscle layers of the upper back, would intensify the sensations as if she was using a heavier weight. She'd driven him to the finish like a drover over a team of wild horses. Reaching down between strokes, she worked off the cock ring, squeezing the thick base of him with deep pleasure, and then started flogging the upper back again.

With the other hand, she'd started to work that dildo in and out, in and out. If she'd tried to fuck him with it earlier, he likely would have frozen, but at that point it was all about the physical sensation. She'd worked him too hard, too relentlessly, for a little macho hang-up like his concerns about sexual orientation to get in the way. He'd convulsed, bucked, his face contorting, and managed to strangle out the words he'd instinctively known to reach for.

"Mistress...I need to...can I..."

From a true sub, she would have demanded, *May I come, Mistress?* Maybe even made him hold out a little longer.

Instead, she stopped flogging him and bent over his body, wrapping her arm around the great chest, pressing her hips against the curve of his buttocks, giving the dildo a firm push with her pelvis. "Let go for me, Max."

He'd roared with it, overpowering the thunder of the waves she expected he'd forgotten during that key moment, though he'd stayed intensely aware of his surroundings far longer than she'd expected. She'd wanted him to lose focus, to see if he could trust her that much, if she could overcome bone-deep training. Arrogance on her part, an unreasonable demand, but it was a female thing she wouldn't deny herself.

She couldn't say for certain he'd completely let go of that control, but he'd joined her on the beach for certain. She could live with that.

Rising from the chair now, she eased the dildo out of him, wrapping it in a towel and moving to the sink to leave it there. She found a bottle of cold water in the mini-fridge and came back to him. Folding down on her knees beside him, she touched his face and brought it up, curling her fingers in the collar he wore. She didn't ever want to take it off him. She wanted to make him a permanent one, something with steel links that she could toy with, twist in her fingers to tighten it when she drew him down to her for a kiss, that would mark his flesh when he slept in it.

She'd put him in the zone, but she was deep in there with him.

She told him to release the bar and straighten. She didn't unlatch the cuffs from each other, so his bound hands rested on his thighs as she brought the bottle to his lips. He drank from her hand as she stroked his face, his sweat-dampened hair. He'd worried that he was like the others, that he was no different, and she wasn't ever going to allow him to think that. She loosened the blindfold, letting it fall away so he could see the rapture she knew was in her expression, the sheer bliss shining out of her eyes.

"That was stunning, Max."

He was...dazed wasn't the right word. He was too self-aware for that. But he was definitely in what was probably the SEAL version of post-subspace. Breathing leveling out but still deep, a quiver in all his muscles. Everything riveted on her, body and mind caught in a curious stillness, no words to say. He turned his head to kiss her hand, mouth working over her fingers, moving to her wrist, down her forearm. He brought his bound hands up to hold it, then drew her forward, his knees spreading to bring her as close as the restraints allowed. He captured her mouth, his fingers still wrapped like a manacle around her wrist.

"Mine," he muttered. "My Mistress."

She closed her eyes, captivated by his power over her senses. She clasped his shoulders with her free hand, deepening the kiss, but he was through letting her take the lead. When he broke the hasp between the two cuffs, she had to suppress a curse. He'd gone through a fair half dozen clips tonight. It didn't matter though, not in the face of more important things. He wrapped an arm around her waist, pulling her against his body so she straddled him there on his knees.

"Take off the condom," he said against her mouth. "I want to feel your pussy when I shove into it."

As she reached down between them, she found her fingers were shaking. He hadn't been boasting. He was recovering fast, and she was more than happy to help, tossing the used condom to the side and closing her hand over him to caress his cock. He caught his hand in her hair, tongue lashing hers, every muscle in his body showing his demand, his need for her. He worked her against him, kneading her ass, rubbing his shaft with devilish skill against her swollen clit as he got stiffer.

"You must take Viagra," she gasped.

"That's what your cunt is for me, Mistress. It makes me hard just to think about it." He tugged her head back, arching her throat, and then he was biting and kissing her there as he continued that massage between their bodies. Janet writhed on him, working herself over him. With a primal sound of demand, he used that impressive strength to turn her away from him, put her on her hands and knees. In one shift, he was behind her, his cock still stimulating her clit, only now he was erect enough he could do it with his pelvis flush against her ass, hips working as he rubbed the ridged head against her pussy.

She'd never done it like this. Not since Jorge did it to obviously dominate her. Which was what Max was doing, but in an entirely different way, with entirely different responses. *I'm yours...but I can do this to you, because you're also mine...*

That was the message, and it overwhelmed her. With him, she accepted it, didn't resist either side of that coin, and relished both.

He draped himself over her, taking her to her elbows with the gentle pressure of his body. He fastened his teeth on the back of her neck where her hair had fallen away, exposing the nape. He licked her there too, still moving his hips against her, and she was lifting up to him. One large hand cupped her breast, squeezed and she let out a soft gasp at the pleasure that shot from the pinched nipple to her core.

"Can never get enough," he muttered, biting her shoulder, then kissing it. Pain followed by a soothing caress, and she was so caught up in those sensations his penetration took her by surprise. One lift of his hips and he'd slid home like he'd slide his sidearm into its holster, sure and straight, powerful and strong. Strong enough that it plowed her deeper onto her elbows and he banded an arm around her waist, holding her close to his body, breath hot on her neck.

"Want to fuck you forever, Mistress. Make you come all over my cock, make you scream my name."

She closed her eyes, the pleasure of his demands and desires sweeping over her. The passion gripping him now had as much to do with what she'd stirred in him while he was her captive as with her being in his arms now. Cradled like an egg even as he vowed to shatter her universe.

She pushed back against him, challenging him with her answer. When she tossed her head back, he caught her jaw, fingers pressing into it to turn her face to him. Sealing his mouth over hers in a powerful, deep plunge, he began to work his cock inside her. When his hand dropped from her face to slide beneath her, she bucked her hips, reacting to his clever touch upon her clit. The man had multiple talents while fucking, thank the gods.

He growled in satisfied response to her moans, driving into her harder. His fingers bit into her hip as his other hand pinched, stroked, worried her clit until she was rotating against him, slamming back into his cock over and over. She could have squeezed down on him, tried to take over the pace of the climax, but there was nothing now but the wild, rushing whitewater ride of their pleasure together. As she went over that pinnacle once again, she screamed out his name, just as he'd desired and threatened. And he called out for her as he joined her on that fall.

*****

They'd been quiet for a while. Max was idly stroking the line of her back as she lay on his chest, her thigh draped over his. Janet was glad she'd booked the room for the night, as she wasn't sure she'd have the strength to get up anytime in the next hour. She was...well, sated might not even cover it. This was like a human form of paradise, everything so utterly right, so perfect, that there was no desire to move. Hadn't there been a *Buffy the Vampire Slayer* episode like that, where Buffy and Riley were caught in a euphoria where they didn't want to come out of a bedroom? Of course they were magically ensorcelled and bad things were eventually going to happen as a result. Unlike this situation, where she felt everything that should be right with the world was here in this room.

She shared the Buffy part of that thought with Max, won the lazy, devastating smile she'd hoped to see, to verify he was feeling the same way. He was a big, replete male animal, and she wanted to simultaneously devour and lie upon him like this forever.

"I didn't figure you for a Buffy fan."

"Marcie was, as a teenager. When Cass and Lucas were on their honeymoon, we were taking shifts, staying at the house at night so she'd have an adult to help out with the younger children. She and I did an all-nighter, watching a marathon of Buffy episodes. She talked me into it."

Max grunted. His fingertips whispered over her buttocks, circled, came back. She couldn't remember when she'd last relaxed in a lover's arms, both of them naked like this. Or when she'd last given a lover total access to her body, the permission to touch implicit with every breath, every heartbeat, rather than a formal structure. This was beyond issues of rules or restrictions. She needed his hands on her, wanted him to touch her however, whenever he wanted to do so. And she wanted to do the same.

"How was it?" she asked.

He tilted his head down to hold his lips against hers in a lingering touch. When he pulled back, just enough to break the connection, he touched her face, fingers sliding along her jaw.

"I think it was everything we both wanted it to be. I've no regrets, Mistress. And any time you want to do something like that again...I'm game. As long as it's just with you."

"Damn. I had the Miami Dolphins' cheerleaders all lined up to jump you, but since you're going to insist on being monogamous..."

Laughter vibrated through his chest as he lay back again. "Well, maybe I spoke too soon. I *can* be more open-minded with the right motivation. How about if the cheerleaders were jumping you?"

She glanced up at him. "You'd prefer that?"

He shrugged. "Yeah, probably. I'd love to watch you get it on with another woman. Maybe even more than one, though a whole cheerleading squad might get too chaotic. But as far as I'm concerned...I just want you, Janet."

"You are either an incredibly good liar, or you're..." Her words drifted off as she looked into his steady gray eyes.

"You can say it," he said. "I told you that day, with Amanda. It's still true. Fuck, I've pretty much known since that day at the hospital."

She swallowed, sat up. "Yet for six months..."

"I did nothing. Yeah. I'm chickenshit, what can I say? I wasn't sure if it was one-sided."

"No," she decided. "You weren't afraid. You were waiting."

He gave her hair a tug. "You're a hard woman to bullshit. Like your boss. Were you two created in the same alien pod?"

"Actually, we exploded from the same chest, complete with teeth." But Janet put a hand on his lips, tracing them, her thoughts whirling. "Why did you wait?"

"I knew you were the type who made the first move. My job was being ready with the right second one."

She smiled at that, but his expression became thoughtful. "What we just did…it wasn't exactly like I expected. It took over until it wasn't clear who was what, if that makes sense."

"If done right, that's exactly where you hope to get." She lay back down on his chest, slid her fingertips through the light mat of hair there. "When Matt first took me to a club, introduced me to things, I was still in a very resistant phase. Jon was there too, and he sat with me for a while. While he was keeping me company, he drew my attention to a couple. The man was tied to a frame, and she was whipping him. For the half hour we watched, she used a variety of emotional and physical means to shake him up, break him down. When I first started watching, all I saw was the bondage, the pain, but Jon made me look at their expressions, their body language.

"In time, I saw what he was seeing. The Mistress was as wrapped up in things as the sub. There was a thread between them, so vibrant and strong that it quivered every time one of them uttered a word or made the slightest motion. His body was gleaming with sweat, and I could see the marks she'd left on his back and ass. When her fingernails glided over them, he quivered as if he was being touched by a Goddess, totally enraptured by her will. But I also saw her expression when he reached that state, the softening of her mouth, the way she gravitated toward him."

She shifted, propping her chin on his shoulder. "Are you familiar with the yin and yang symbol?"

"The little black and white circle decal a lot of kids put on their cars?"

"Yes, that's the one. Though adults have been known to put those on their cars too." Janet pinched him, but she settled deeper into the curve of his body, fingers tucked under his shoulder beneath her, her other arm stretched out so she could stroke his bare hip the way he was stroking her back. She traced a line to his upper thigh, shifted her knee so it rubbed with sensual idleness against his testicles.

"Jon said that when a session starts, it's like the black side of the symbol, with the small white spot in the middle. The Dom is the black, surrounding the sub, making her feel small, safe, like a cat in a box. Have you ever noticed how cats like to do that, get into a small box, as if being contained by that limited environment makes them feel safe? The Dom takes over, takes control. Psychologically, physically, giving the sub a limited world within his commands. If they're doing it right, eventually the sub lets go of control, surrenders. When the session progresses, something amazing happens. The other side of the symbol. The sub's energy grows and surrounds the Dom, the white taking over. The Dom becomes the black speck, like a sorcerer in the middle of an energy cloud, amazed by what's been unleashed by their interaction with one another. It's a form of rapture, for both. Yin and yang. A circle and balance both."

"That sounds like Jon's kind of thinking." He smiled against her forehead.

"It's the kind of truth you can hear, but until you reach it yourself, you don't feel it, believe it. And then it feels like it came straight from your own soul, even if someone's already said it."

"Yeah." She could feel him thinking that through, so she stayed silent until he worked it out, spoke. "I think you've got it right...based on how it felt to me. When we first started talking about this, I admit I found it hard to understand. Especially after you told me about what had happened to you. It seemed like the last thing you'd want to do is take away someone else's power, give them pain."

He tightened his arm around her back, preventing her from drawing away. "I get that it's not the same thing now, but when you were on the wrong side of that coin for so long, it seemed odd to me that you'd stay so close to the line, even on the right side, if that makes sense."

"It does." She pushed down her automatic defensiveness. "People come to this for so many different reasons. There's no one single motive for it. When Matt and Jon showed me that side of things, I realized what a profound difference there was between it and what Jorge did to me. Such that every session I did with a sub was a big black line on the universe, underscoring that difference. I was saying *this* is what holding power over someone for mutual pleasure is. The power of that synergy, of that yin and yang, is so much more than Jorge ever found imprisoning me the way he did."

She hesitated. "Another part of it was confirming to myself that I wasn't him. That though I did what I did to get away from him, it wasn't the same. I can hold control over others, and I don't cause harm. I don't take without giving back in equal or greater measure."

She tilted her chin, met his eyes. "I'm self-aware enough to know that might be a coping mechanism rather than truth, but if you can find an illusion to bring balance to your reality, it makes every day possible, manageable. Right?"

"Yeah, it does. Other things do that as well. Moments like this."

She had no disagreement with that. She laid her fingers on his lips. "I guess we need to be thinking about clearing out."

"Yeah." But neither of them moved. She studied him, pondering, then realized there was nothing to think about. She simply refused to let go of him. "I want you to come home with me, Max. Share my bed tonight."

His gray eyes kindled with heat, telling her they'd be doing more than sleeping. Probably several times. She was going to need some painkillers in the morning. That was fine — she'd gladly swallow down a bottle of Advil to pay for a night like that.

"Yes ma'am."

Chapter Thirteen

He stayed until Monday morning, something she hadn't expected herself to offer. But he helped her prune and trim the shrubs, edged the walkway. They took strolls around the district, ate at small holes-in-the-wall restaurants that offered better food than opulent ones. When Saturday night came and they were sharing takeout on her living room floor, watching television, it seemed natural to invite him to share her bed once again. Especially when he carried her up there and gave her a memorable bedtime story.

On Monday, he offered to take her to work, if she didn't mind going by his place that morning so he could pick up clean clothes. She didn't mind. She hadn't minded waking up with him curved around her body, the smell of him on her skin, the lingering stickiness of his seed between her legs from the couple times they'd come together in the night. Her designer pillows had spent the weekend scattered about the floor of her bedroom like a flock of colorful sheep. There hadn't been room on her bed for them and a sprawling, large man like Max. She liked the new look.

Showering with him had been an indulgence that almost made her forget it was a workday. He'd given her sore back muscles a thorough massage under the jets. When he'd moved down to her lower back and hips, she'd let out a noise that he observed sounded close to orgasmic. He'd also knelt and sponged off her thighs, cleaning in between while she watched him, bemused, threading her fingers through his wet hair.

He placed an almost chaste kiss on her mound, her clit, her labia, then suckled beads of water off her skin, tongue making slow, heated circles beneath the spray that had her gripping the wall bar and her thighs loosening. His hands slid up behind her buttocks, supporting her as he worked her up to a slow, decadent climax that sighed out of her body. He hadn't asked for anything after that, simply standing to give her a kiss, letting her taste herself on his wet mouth.

"Later," he'd murmured, though he'd been hard against her abdomen, enough she rubbed against him, teasing. He'd turned away with a glint in his eye that promised he'd want to get back at her later for that. "We better get to my place if I'm going to have us to work on time."

When they arrived at his house, he parked her at his scarred kitchen table with an excellent cup of coffee they'd picked up at the corner, from a store with bars on the windows and graffiti on the outside walls. She sipped it, studying the dismal backyard he had, neatly mowed but otherwise devoid of flowers or even a decent shrub. No cover for an approach, she realized. He had a clear view of any of the neighboring houses, small shoeboxes like his own. He might have grown up poor, but she expected his mother in Texas had had at least a flower box, little touches to make even a poor house a home.

Ah well. Inside his safe, all his guns, grenades and rocket launchers were likely arranged with the proper *feng shui*.

She smiled into her coffee, then heard the sound of a vehicle stopping out front. From the roar of the diesel engine, she guessed an old pick-up truck. When she heard a door slam, she assumed a neighbor was picking up a carpool companion. However, a moment later, a large man strode into the backyard and onto the broken concrete walkway, headed toward the back door. While he moved confidently, she noted a hitch in his step, a slight limp.

It was more than the clean-shaven jaw and close-cropped dark hair, handsomely peppered with silver, that told her this was one of Max's brothers-in-arms. He had the same alpha-male-capable-of-handling-anything expression. She wondered if they ran them through a press at BUD/S graduation, stamping it on their faces.

She was sitting in the corner nook, not visible until he opened the door and stepped in, but his eyes went to her immediately. She'd surprised him, she could tell, and she expected that didn't happen often. "Sorry," he said genially. "I didn't realize Max had company."

"Not a common occurrence?"

An amused look crossed his rugged features. "Honoring the bro code, I'd say that's need-to-know, but you have eyes. What woman would come to this dump willingly? He didn't kidnap you, did he?" He bent to look beneath the table. "No chains, but if you want to make a dash for my truck, I'll get you to safety—and to a place that doesn't have lingering eau-de-crack-house, what this place used to be."

When she chuckled, enjoying him, he offered his hand. "Dale Rousseau."

"Janet."

The pressure of his fingers and the direct look telegraphed another quality, one she'd seen often enough for her to guess she and Dale had something else vital in common. She decided to throw out a line and see if she was right.

"So, did Max come to you for advice on how to deal with someone like you and me?"

His slow smile told her she'd hit the target. "Lots of differences between a Master and Mistress. I hopefully told him enough not to get his ass chewed off. How'd he do with the information?"

"He exceeded expectations."

"He always does."

She ran her gaze over him, a thorough appraisal of the broad shoulders, the fit body that looked solid and unstoppable as a Mack semi. When he shifted, the tilt of his head, the hitch in his step, brought the whole package together, and she realized he was familiar to her. She was almost certain he was an occasional regular at Club Progeny. Though he was always masked, his public sessions with submissives were memorable enough that Janet had watched more than one of them. He was thorough and overwhelming, an artist of their craft.

She didn't ask if he recognized her as well. With the level of detail Max brought to every encounter, if this man was of the same stripe, the decorative mask she wore for public play wouldn't hamper his ability to pick her out of a crowd. "Would you like to share my coffee? I still have half a cup. I'm sure I can find a mug here to split it."

"There's nothing in these cabinets except roach powder, though he usually keeps a supply of paper plates for takeout. Since he mostly swigs beer and bottled water, paper cups aren't a priority."

She hadn't gotten as far as snooping through Max's cabinets, but when Dale crossed the spare couple strides to the nearest one and opened it, she saw he was right. Even to the roach powder. Her brow creased.

Everything about Max's house was neat, clean, well-ordered. But as she'd noted on her earlier visit, except for his clothing, a pocket change jar and a file cabinet for some paperwork, there was nothing personal in the house. Even the blankets on his bed looked like they'd been picked up from an Army-Navy supply store.

"In all fairness, given the neighborhood and the fact he's here so rarely, he doesn't buy things that can be stolen. He doesn't lock his doors, so he doesn't have to worry about repairing broken windows." Dale shook his head at her expression. "Don't judge the boy too harshly for it."

"His mother and sister were his home," she said.

After a pause, during which he was clearly evaluating how much she knew about their common subject, Dale inclined his head. "Not sure he knows how to make one without them."

"Besides which, he's still down range, isn't he? Still working the mission."

Dale's eyes sharpened on her. She leaned forward. "Are you helping him find the last one?"

"Are you going to tell me he shouldn't be doing that, that he should be moving forward with his life?"

"What do you think?"

He sat down across from her. When she pushed her coffee over to him, he took a sip, handed it back to her. "You take it strong. No cream or sugar?"

"I don't like diluting the full strength of something meant to be strong."

"I'm liking you better and better. You won't be able to talk him out of it."

"I get that. But did he try other options? The police?" She knew the hypocrisy of pointing it out, but she cared enough about him she asked anyway.

Dale grunted. "Max has a healthy respect for the law, the Constitution—the real deal, not the crap that people and politicians twist to serve their own purposes. But he gets there's a difference between justice and the law sometimes, and justice gets served first when we have the ability and choice to make the call. This call is his choice. No muss, no fuss, no drama. He's not going to talk about it, but I guarantee it takes up about a third of his brain space every day." He cocked his head. "I expect the other two-thirds is probably about you. So you still have the majority of his brain cells, if that's a comfort."

"Competition is not my major concern, not when it comes to this." She met his gaze. "Why do you limp, if it's not too personal to ask?"

"Amputation below the knee. Lost it during an explosion."

Her gaze swept downward, and now she noticed how one pants leg seemed to crease differently below the knee. At her look, Dale reached across, closed his hand on hers. He rested it on what felt like a plastic cuff molded to his knee joint beneath the denim. Continuing downward on her own, she felt the solid metal shaft he had instead of a leg. He wore hiking shoes, such that except for the slight limp, she wouldn't have guessed it.

She looked up. They were almost eye to eye. He gave her a faint smile, nodded and straightened.

It affected her peculiarly, feeling metal and plastic where a firm calf should have been. She moved her touch to his other leg for comparison. It was intimate, forward behavior, but Dale didn't object. She gripped the calf as he flexed beneath her touch and offered her a somber wink. When she sat up, sat back, her stomach was doing an odd flip-flop. That could have been Max. Or instead of losing a limb, he might not have come home. His sister would have been all alone in the world, and Janet would never have known him.

You might as well say it. I've known since the hospital... She hadn't said it. Unlike him, she wasn't ready to accept the strength of his feelings, let alone her own. This moment didn't really leave her a place to hide from that, did it?

She reclaimed her coffee, took a bracing swallow. "You know what happens when you break them down, break them open. You understand who and what they are. There's no compromising that. I wouldn't want to compromise what Max is, but I have a real problem with him doing anything that would take him away from me, by death or imprisonment. I'm a selfish bitch that way."

"Well, God bless you. Hope that he starts to see things your way." Dale fished a card out of his pocket, slid it across the table to her. A phone number was handwritten on it. "My cell," he said. "In case you ever need it."

Janet lifted her gaze, held his. He had unusual blue-green eyes, but in them she saw a clear message. With a nod, she slipped the card into her pocket, took another sip of coffee.

"You know, sound carries through this house like a megaphone," Max said, arriving in the doorway.

"Don't kid yourself, Ack Ack. These walls are thin enough people could sit in the street and hear you," Dale said comfortably. "Brought you the yard and plumbing tools you wanted for Gayle's next weekend."

"Appreciate it. I would have come and gotten them."

"Eh. I was in the neighborhood."

Janet turned to see Max shrugging into his shirt. Today it was tailored silk and cotton, coupled with slacks. Matt had an important meeting at the Omni Royal, one that called for his driver to wear formal attire to properly impress the attending members. As he buttoned the shirt, Max moved into the kitchen, touching her shoulder before claiming his own coffee from the counter. He didn't seem particularly perturbed by Dale's discussion with her, but from the glance the men exchanged, she realized Dale wouldn't have imparted anything to her that Max wouldn't want her to know.

"So did you check to see if he had a prosthetic ass while you were groping him?"

"That looked nicely real to me," she said without missing a beat. "But I'd be happy to verify."

"Better not challenge this one," Dale advised. "She'll kick your balls into your throat. And then grope my ass while you're curled up like a shrimp on your dingy-looking tile floor. Jesus, buy some cheerful linoleum. Something with little yellow and blue flowers. At least a freaking potholder. I'm getting you a potholder for Christmas."

Janet looked between the two men, amused, but then focused on Max, brow raised. "Ack Ack?"

Max rolled his eyes. "My nickname."

"Kind of like Maverick or Ice Man from *Top Gun*, only a lot less cool-sounding." Dale winked. "It's from an early John Cusack movie, *One Crazy Summer*. There's a character in it who's a mild-mannered Boy Scout. He always comes through in a pinch. Face like a choir boy, heart of a lion and stubborn as hell when he's sure he's right. His nickname was Ack Ack. It fit, on all levels."

Scraping back his chair, Dale rose, giving her a nod and another wink, then directed his parting words to Max. "I'm due at the community center. Let me know if you need anything else for Gayle."

"Thanks for bringing them by."

Dale raised a hand, letting himself out the back door without another word. The minimalist communication of the *Homo sapiens* male, Janet thought. A moment later, they heard the diesel roar of the truck starting up.

She put down her coffee, just in time to have Max lift her under the arms, turn and sit her up on the counter, putting himself in between her knees. He pushed up her short work skirt, his fingers sliding along her thighs under the hem. "You wore stockings just to drive me crazy," he muttered against her mouth. "I need you."

She gave back as good as given on that heated kiss, but then she pushed him back, holding him off. Somewhat. He started on her throat, his body pressed close enough to her core that she felt his erection grinding against her. "I thought you said we had to be to work on time." Despite her protest, she slid her arm over his shoulders, bringing him closer.

"We will be. Need you. Just need you, Mistress. Please."

It was the please that did it. The almost desperate request of a man who always seemed so self-possessed. Maybe her being here, amid the bare evidence of his life outside of his work, had sparked this response. She was real and alive, part of the present and his tentative future. A stark contrast to his past, that poignant desolation provoking a clash between the light and the dark.

She knew that feeling. At particularly bright moments, she still occasionally experienced it, that blot of darkness on the sun, the memory of blood in a bathroom. Hacking through a throat with a meat cleaver. She clung to him tighter and surrendered to their mutual passion, willing to be swept away from nightmares together.

* * * * *

The emotions he'd stirred up there at the end lingered with her, making her feel unsettled. Not wrong, exactly, not after such an incredible weekend, but emotional upheaval was emotional upheaval, and even the good kind could stir the silt at the bottom. The war between dark and light wasn't something that could be shrugged off lightly.

One member of the K&A team knew that better than anyone. Unfortunately, it appeared the condition was contagious this morning, because when she arrived Ben sounded as unsettled as she felt.

She heard him snarling at someone on his phone, then he slammed it down with a creative combination of oaths that could fill a swear jar to the brim. "Alice," he snapped.

Janet dropped her purse and keys on her desk and moved down the hallway to his office. It was in a separate wing due to the confidential nature of the things he handled, but in this mood, he could be heard clearly. "Alice is off this morning. Doctor's appointment, remember?"

"Great. Fucking great." He muttered it under his breath, so she decided to let it pass. He looked tired, telling her he'd been here all night. When his therapy session dredged up particularly difficult things and he got in a foul mood over it, sometimes he came to his couch here, rather than taking the attitude home to Marcie. Janet knew he'd do better if he went home to her, but men could be stubborn about that, especially a man determined to give the woman he loved only the best side of himself. He sometimes forgot that what Marcie wanted most was all of him, good and bad. It made Janet think of her discussion with Dale again.

Ben launched into another tirade. "Somebody down at the courthouse royally fucked up the filing of the Watkins affidavit. Missed the deadline. The asshole judge, who likes to jerk our chain, has rescheduled the hearing for fucking two months."

"I'll call Stacie in the clerk's office. She owes me a favor. She might be able to fix that."

"Fine," he snapped. "Fucking do it then."

As Janet patiently waited, he stopped, closed his eyes. Pivoted away from her. She could almost hear him counting. He didn't turn back toward her, but when he spoke, his tone was more even. "Sorry, Janet. No excuse for that."

"No, there's not. It's just a piece of paper or two." When he glanced over his shoulder at her, she kept her expression neutral. "Are you all right?"

"She made me agree to marry her. This spring. I was going to let them know this morning, before the Omni."

"I assume you mean Marcie."

"No. The hooker on the corner who gives me insider trading tips. Yes, Marcie."

It made sense now, what had dredged up the same attitude he had after a bad therapy session. Despite the fact he likely wouldn't welcome it, she crossed the room and touched his arm, drawing his green eyes to her. "You deserve her, Ben. You belong together. She loves you tremendously. And you staying here on the evenings when you can't make it all make sense? It's stupid and wrong, and it hurts her, shuts her out."

He gave her a narrow look. "You finally decide to put down the whip and see a guy without a leash, after how many years, and you want to talk to *me* about shutting people out? Sounds like you're the real expert on that. *Mistress.*"

The derision in his tone was intended to cut, and it did. It was ironic that she recognized the tactic so well, exactly because of what he'd just pointed out. They weren't all that different. Except she could step back from this and see his misery. His fear.

She dug her nails into his wrist, right above his insanely expensive Louis Vuitton watch. "Ben O'Callahan, you're being rude and cruel. Do it again, and I'll slap your ear through your head."

His jaw tightened further. "I didn't ask you to come in here. And if you draw blood and get it on my cuff, you're paying for the dry cleaning."

"Stop it," she said. "Ben, think about Dana, and her PTSD. She worked through it, because she wanted to heal, to be the best person possible for Peter. He loves her so much, doing anything less is unacceptable to her."

He stared at her, then his attention shifted to the window. Sensing a similar shift of his mood, she touched his jaw. "What you're doing, trying to heal the scars of the past to be a better person for yourself and Marcie, it would be tremendously difficult for anyone. But you're doing it, Ben. You are a remarkable man. I think you forget that far too often."

When his gaze flickered, she caught a glimpse of what she was painfully aware lay behind the formidable Master, the exemplary lawyer. The younger version of himself, so unsure of his own worth.

"Let Marcie be everything for you that you want to be for her," she said gently. "That's the deal, and as much a part of healing as anything else."

He didn't say anything, but when she dropped her hand to his arm again, he glanced at it. "You're such a pain in my ass," he said gruffly.

"Yes. I love you too." The worst had passed. She squeezed him, moved back toward the door. "I'll take care of the affidavit with Stacie. You get ready to tell them your good news. They're going to be thrilled."

Coming out into the office area, she saw the insulated bag with her homemade lunch on her desk. She'd left it in Max's truck by accident, but of course her SEAL had noticed, brought it up for her. The gesture cut some of the tension the confrontation with Ben had provoked, but not as much as she would have liked. She rubbed her forehead, rolled her shoulders.

At least when she came around her desk, she noticed the light on her phone that indicated Ben's line was engaged. It stayed that way for nearly ten minutes, telling her it was likely that he'd called and talked to Marcie. Either way, when he emerged from his office and came toward the boardroom for their pre-Omni Royal strategy session, he looked easier.

She sat in on that meeting, but she was relieved it would be a short one. Ben's turmoil had obviously pushed a few of her own buttons. What she deserved, what she wanted. The silt everyone brought into their relationships. She felt like the lid of a kettle, sitting on a building pressure.

Ben's good news would help distract her. She hoped. As Matt concluded the meeting and they all shifted, preparing to rise and head out, Ben cleared his throat. Absently, she noted all of them looked so handsome today, dressed in their power suits and ties. Any female attendees of the Omni Royal meeting were in for a treat. How in the hell did Jon's dark hair always look so gorgeous and silky, feathered back from his brow, the tips brushing his shoulders? Rachel swore he didn't wear any hair product, which simply confirmed that God was female, and She liked looking at men more than women.

"There is one last discussion point, though I don't want it recorded, in case it comes back to bite me on the ass, which I'm sure it will." Ben shot Janet a significant look. "Marcie and I are getting married. In the spring."

"You aren't already married?" Peter lifted a brow. "You've been so pussy-whipped since you hooked up with that girl, I figured it was already a done deal."

"So says the guy who gave his wife a clone of himself as a limo driver."

Dana had always been very flirtatious with Max, part of her M.O. as a hardcore sub who liked to brat for punishment.

Even during her earlier discussion with Peter's wife, Janet hadn't reacted personally to that aspect of their relationship. But now Janet thought of what she'd said to Max about Dana, in their intense session at Club Progeny. He'd taken that as part of the scene, but given the twinge she felt now, Janet wasn't so sure she hadn't meant it.

Had Peter ever shared Dana with Max? It wouldn't fit with the K&A men's usual code of keeping everything within their circle, but there were certain areas she didn't delve into too deeply for specifics.

Really, she was going to go there? She needed to do her own personal therapy session if she was getting bogged down in things she normally understood quite well.

Lucas grinned. He came around Peter to embrace Ben as the K&A lawyer rose. "Congratulations. Don't ever forget what a lucky bastard you are. Or I'll be forced to personally beat your head into a wall to remind you."

"Like Marcie wouldn't take it off with my restaurant-grade meat cleaver if I forget."

"It won't be your head, my friend. It—"

She'd been reaching for her coffee mug. It slipped out of her fingers as they jerked in reaction. She grabbed for it, a mistake, because it was already tilting. She managed to turn a simple spill into a spinning arc of coffee that splattered her tablet, her chair, the carpet, and the front of her pale yellow suit, one of her favorites. As well as her wrist, and it was still quite hot.

"Damn it all."

The men reacted like a well-oiled machine. Peter brought a damp cloth from the sidebar and pressed it to her arm. Lucas retrieved the cup from the floor as Jon dropped a towel on the floor to mop the excess out of the rug. Their quick jump to her rescue made her eyes sting with an appalling emotional reaction.

Ben brought two additional wet cloths, one for Jon to soak the stain on the carpet, and another for her clothes, which he handed to Peter, since the operations manager was still holding the compress to her arm.

Peter considered her thin blouse, the coffee making it stick to her skin, then extended the cloth to Janet. "I'd do it," he teased, "but you might file a harassment suit against me."

"If it was one of the others, no," Ben said dryly. "But due to your well-known obsession with women's breasts, your ass would be nailed."

As the men grinned at her, she tried to smile back. That was when her body betrayed her yet again. Two of the threatening tears made the leap, started sliding down her face. "Damn it." She snatched the cloth from Peter, started wiping the front of her ruined suit. Her fingers were trembling.

A hand gripped her arm, lifted her out of the chair, putting her against a solid, reassuring male chest. Of all the people she'd have expected to step forward at that moment, it was both the biggest surprise yet the most inexplicably suitable choice to find herself in Ben's arms. Heedless of what the coffee might do to his clothes, he held her close, letting her take shuddering breaths against a wall of muscle as she fought for control. "It's all right," he said against her hair. "Falling in love sucks, doesn't it?"

She couldn't help it, she laughed, a broken sound. Then, before she could get uncomfortable about the intimacy, he'd turned her toward Matt. With that exceptional intuition they all had, Ben knew Matt was the one man she'd trust with her raw emotions for more than a few seconds. However, Ben's hand remained on her shoulder, massaging. Peter clasped the other shoulder, Jon squeezing one of her hands as Lucas stroked her hair. Matt held her other hand against his chest while he rubbed her back.

As part of her rather extensive classified personal knowledge of the team, she knew the men had more than once worked together to sexually dominate and give a woman the erotic experience of her life. Each of their wives—or intended wives, in Marcie's case—had been the recipient of that enviable experience. As amazing as that idea was, she wondered if any of them had ever thought of calling on the five of them when the woman in question needed a good cry. The fortress of protective male reassurance was like being inside a warm comforter on a rainy day, with a bottomless thermos of rich hot chocolate at hand. It was as overwhelming an experience as an erotic one.

She and Matt had a special connection through her bloody past, but it was the first time she realized the K&A men—all of them—saw her as one of theirs, her family when she had no other. They'd closed around her, sheltering her from the world.

"You're going to be late for your meeting," she managed. Matt squeezed her fingers.

"I'll make an even grander entrance if I'm late. Send the message that my ass is the most significant one to kiss."

She lifted her head. She'd left tiny dots of moisture on Matt's white shirt. Her tears, she realized. She glanced up as Matt used his handkerchief to dab at her face, then closed her fingers around the cloth before she could fuss at him for the babying. He gave her a faint smile.

She took a couple deep breaths. Steadied. When she did, he nodded, touching a brief finger to her cheek in approval.

"I'm sorry for yelling at you, Janet," Ben said. When she turned in Matt's grasp, the lawyer brushed her arm, another reassurance. "I'm a total prick."

"You know that wasn't it." Gathering her courage, she met each of their gazes, accepted the same thing she'd seen in Matt's expression. Caring and understanding. "Thank you, all of you. You've made it better. Now please get the hell out of here and let me go back to being me."

Lucas brushed the tender line of her throat with his knuckles. Peter handed her the damp cloth he still held. "Run some more cold water over your arm. There's some topical in the first-aid kit if you need it, but usually air's the best thing."

She nodded. They exchanged glances with Matt, then, based on that unspoken communication, the other men filed out, leaving her with her boss.

"I really am fine. I know you'll be angry if I say I'm sorry, but you know how mortifying I find something like this."

"I do." His serious dark eyes twinkled. "But you've given us verifiable proof you're human. We've had a standing bet about it for some time now."

"Oh?" She sniffled, trying not to well up again as he pressed his large fingers over her own, reminding her that she was holding his handkerchief. "Who won? Or is that information going to piss me off?"

"Probably, but I'll tell you anyway. I did." He winked at her. "In the beginning, Jon thought you were a very sophisticated robot and Peter agreed. He said you were a top-secret prototype I was demo'ing for the military, trying you out as a potential sleeper assassin. Ben's money was on you being Satan's mistress. He told us we'd have to forward his winnings to him, since he couldn't provide verification until he died and ran into you in Hell. Lucas and I were the two who believed you were human. The bet was for how long it would take to indisputably prove your humanity or lack thereof. I beat Lucas' estimate by about a year. Of course, I probably owe a portion of my winnings to Max, since you might have held out until Lucas' projected date without him."

"If you tell Max about any of this, I will put you in the industrial shredder in the basement."

With a smile, he leaned forward, pressed his lips to her cheek, his hands closing on her shoulders once more. "We love you, Janet." He spoke against her temple, making her close her eyes, her heart aching. "Tell me what you need, you'll have it."

"You gave it to me, all those years ago. And you haven't stopped giving since. Now please, at the risk of repeating myself, get the hell out of here. I need to deal with the carpet and my suit."

"Both of which you will charge as company expenses. Don't let me find out you paid for it, or I'll transfer you to Ben's area for the next six months."

She snorted. "I'm not scared. You couldn't survive that long without me."

"You'd be surprised what I'll do to prove a point." His fingers tightened on her. "Janet, I mean it."

"Oh fine." She shrugged him off irritably. "Shoo."

He chuckled, stepped back. "I leave all of it in your capable hands, as always. But you know where we are if you need anything."

"That's my line, thank you."

"Yes, it is." He dropped one more kiss on her forehead, his lips curving when she shrugged him away with an irritable noise. "See you this afternoon."

He strode toward the door, relieving her with his matter-of-fact acceptance that she was back at the helm. Given how intuitive the five men were, it was unlikely they'd even mention it again...unless they felt it needed mentioning, and she'd make sure it wouldn't.

She surveyed the carpet, already thinking of the local vendor K&A used when the carpets required deep cleaning. First, though, she'd better spot treat her blouse and coat until she could get them to the dry cleaners at lunch. She had a spare change of clothes here, for the occasional all-nighter required by some of K&A's more ambitious projects.

As she moved to take care of that, her office area quiet with all her men gone, she saw her cell phone had a text, not a surprise. Picking it up, she read it.

How about we make it a long weekend in Texas and do some camping? I promise it will be fun. I miss you already, Mistress.

She closed her eyes, pressing the screen to her forehead. After another moment, she replied.

If it isn't, I'll tie you to a rack and give you a full body wax.

She'd found the number for the carpet cleaning company when her phone buzzed again.

The rack part sounds intriguing. Pass on the wax. You like my manly body hair.

She pursed her lips. Yes, the rack did sound intriguing. And the fact he gave her the idea he'd be okay with it made it even more tantalizing. But camping…hmm.

She sighed. Matt had said to let him know if she needed anything. She wished he could erase the last member of that gang from Max's mind. She wanted to attribute her uneasy feeling about it to echoes from her past making her paranoid, but she didn't think so. Dale had told her. *I can promise you it occupies one-third of his brain…* And yet it had happened years ago. What if they found the man in Mexico, or South America, and Max went after him? Or if he went after him here, and was caught or injured? Or killed?

She firmed her chin. She wasn't some swooning heroine, waiting for Fate to trample her. It was obvious Max's only real fear was that of being less than the man he felt he was supposed to be. So she would figure out how to deal with this. The way any Navy SEAL's wife, girlfriend — or Mistress — had to figure it out.

* * * * *

Ben checked his watch as he came out the front door, saw Max and the limo waiting. Peter, Jon and Lucas would be following in about an hour, because only Ben and Matt were needed for the first agenda items. Matt wouldn't push it too late, but he'd make sure Janet was okay. Even so, Ben had a few minutes to kill. He could duck into the back and arrange some documents…

Or not.

Max stepped in front of the passenger door, blocking his entry. Sometimes he did the door-opening routine, usually if Matt needed to appear impressive, though for the most part Matt didn't waste a lot of time on that kind of shit. But Max's intent wasn't to open the door for Ben. From the expression on his face, Ben thought it more likely he was considering Mel Gibson's *Lethal Weapon 2* maneuver, hammering Ben's head *in* the door.

"Problem, Max?"

"Yeah. I brought Janet's lunch up to her. She'd left it in my car."

"And?"

Max's cool gray eyes fixed on Ben's. "I get that you and she lock horns sometimes, and that's part of your deal. But it's time you stop talking to her like that. Period."

Ben's kneejerk reaction was to set aside his briefcase, step toe-to-toe with the tight-assed, muscle-headed bastard and ask him who in the fucking hell did he think he was talking to. Then he thought about the tears in Janet's eyes—something that had scared the hell out of all of them, frankly—and what he'd do if he'd seen some guy being a foul-mouthed ass to Marcie. Well, fuck.

"Yeah. You're right." He saw the brief flash of surprise in Max's eyes, then it was back to that ice calm, I-can-break-your-neck-with-my-mind look. Ben might have grinned at the thought, except the man code required that he keep his hackles up the requisite amount of time. "Can you get your ass away from the door? Don't worry. I won't ask you to open it for me."

"That would be smart."

Unlike Ben, Max wasn't posturing. He was obviously still pissed.

Ah hell and Jesus. *Therapy is making me such a pussy.* Ben sighed. "If you ever tell her this, I'll kill you, but there's something about her... Sometimes it's like she's a mom, the kind I can snap at, but she'll love me anyway, even as she'll bust my balls for mouthing off, and I'm looking for the ball-busting, you know? But mom or not, she deserves way more respect than that. I've heard you. Okay?'

Max considered that, nodded. "I don't think of her as a mom at all."

"Relieved to hear it. Else I'd park you on the shrink's couch with me and tell *you* to stay the hell away from her."

This time Max answered with a tentative curving of lips, but Ben saw the conflict in his eyes. He stepped closer, put a hand on Max's broad shoulder. Jesus, the guy was built like a fucking tank. They should put bets on him and Peter mud wrestling one night. Though it would be way more fun to see Marcie and Dana go at it. In thongs. He'd rather not entertain that visual of Peter and Max, though Marcie and Dana would probably love it. Even if Dana only got the visuals through Marcie's description.

"I get it. She's your girl, and you're going to kick my ass if I don't treat her right. Good. She deserves that. Though if I tell her you think she needs defending, she's going to kick *your* ass. Keep that in mind."

With a wink, Ben got into the car.

* * * * *

Yes, she'd completely lost her mind. *Camping.* Showing the depths of her insanity, she would have given him the whole week if he wanted it, but she understood now that five or six days was as long as he could be away before Amanda had problems with his absence. She took Monday and Tuesday off, with the plan being they'd return on Tuesday night and he'd go see Amanda on Wednesday.

They were headed for the Rio Grande area, but as he'd indicated, they broke up the trip with an overnight in Houston to visit with Gayle Kirby and do some chores around the house for her. Gayle's husband Charles was currently deployed. As a matter of course, SEALs like Max or Dale, as well as SEALs not currently on active missions, tended to keep tabs on SEAL families when their men were gone, to help out where needed.

It made her think again about Eric, the SEAL who'd hoped to get Max's mother and sister to move into a duplex. If all SEALs had the same commitment to personal responsibility, she imagined the guilt had weighed heavily on the man's mind, likely as much as Max's. But from what Max had said, Janet expected her SEAL had helped Eric accept that some things were beyond a man's control, no matter how bitter a pill that was to swallow.

Her SEAL. She liked the sound of that.

Gayle had three rambunctious boys, ages four to nine. Max quickly employed them in the yard work, telling Gayle to take a couple hours to rest her feet. Watching from the front bay window, Janet smiled at the sight of the four-year-old carrying small, mostly ineffectual handfuls of leaves to the wheelbarrow while Max pruned, trimmed, mowed and had the two older boys weeding and dragging cut limbs. He had an easy way with children, direct and not patronizing. His authoritative, no-nonsense attitude commanded the children's respect and attention.

She could have watched him all day, but she turned her attention to giving Gayle a hand with the breakfast dishes and getting some laundry started so the mother could have a portion of those couple of hours Max had indicated.

Gayle was also watching over another SEAL wife, Jenny Reid. Jenny lived up the road, but she was seven months pregnant with her first child, so she was now staying with Gayle until the baby came. She was a baby herself, barely twenty years old, and though she smiled and shook Janet's hand, and was cordial to Max, Janet could tell the pregnancy was putting her through a rough time. After she and Gayle got the mother-to-be settled for a nap on the patio lounge chair in the back, they sat down to share an iced tea on the sun porch, where they could watch over her. Max and the boys occasionally came into view as they dumped bagged leaves in a compost heap in the side yard. Gayle's property seemed to encompass a couple acres.

"It's a blessing and a curse," Gayle noted, watching the boys wrestle with Max. He picked up the oldest one, tossed him into the leaves, then had to do it to all of them, though he was of course far more gentle about it with the four-year-old. "They never stop missing their dad, and when any of these guys come through, it gives them that sense of him. Which is wonderful, but it makes me miss Charles all the more."

"I can't imagine how difficult that is." Janet thought about Max's text from the other day. *I miss you already.* She knew it was the stage of their relationship, that heady, falling-in-love feeling where no amount of time was enough, but even so, she wondered if, for a couple truly in love, that feeling ever went away.

She'd never considered herself such a romantic, but the feeling hadn't waned in the slightest between Matt and Savannah, and they'd been married the longest of the K&A team. Not so long really, but she'd seen the same thing between elderly couples sitting together in the park. Perhaps time and maturity taught a couple how to manage it, tone it down in public, but they couldn't hide the fact they felt complete only when they were with one another.

At least, she hoped and suspected that was the way love was. The kind of love she might be willing to consider with Max in the long term. That was an even scarier thought than camping.

"No, it's not easy, but you figure it out." Gayle sobered, glancing toward the lounge chair. Jenny shifted, but from the slackness of her wrist, the fact the book she'd been reading was now pressed to her belly, it appeared she'd drifted off into a doze. "I'll have to have Max take care of her swollen ankles. He gives a hell of a foot massage."

Thinking of the back massage he'd given her in the shower, Janet shivered. Catching it, Gayle nodded. "Yep, you can thank me for that, sister. I taught him how to give a proper massage when I was pregnant with my second one, but you can't train anyone to have those kinds of hands. A strong man massaging your feet... Oh my God, there's nothing like it." She took a bracing swig of tea. "And getting one when he's not expecting sex out of it—or rushing it so he can get sex out of it—that's pretty much God's miracle, right there."

She gave Janet a devilish grin. "Of course, I sort of had the opposite problem with Max. I was in my second trimester, when all you want to do is have sex all the time, and here's this gorgeous guy with a body like they all have. I wanted to stick my husband's face on him and have my way with him. Poor Max is lucky he made it out with his virtue intact."

It startled a laugh out of Janet. Gayle grinned even wider. "I don't usually talk so plain, but you seem the type to appreciate it."

"I do."

The women glanced back toward the patio as Jenny turned away from them, put a pillow between her knees. Her book had been set aside.

"I'm not sure if she's going to make it." Gayle shook her head. "SEALs have a pretty high divorce rate."

"Eighty percent," Janet recalled Max's words.

Gayle lifted a shoulder. "The reasons are kind of obvious. But when you're so young, like Jenny, it's hard to put it together in that first phase. You've met this alpha, no-holds-barred, high-testosterone guy who can face down anything. The swooning damsel inside all of us just melts. What you don't realize until you're in it is your alpha hero is going to be out saving the world most of the time. He's going to be gone for months at a time, leaving at the drop of a hat, returning God-knows-when, so he's only going to get to be *your* hero for limited periods of time.

"While he's off somewhere, you have to become the hero of your own life—handling all the crises with kids, bills, family, the car breaking down. On a good day, you get really mad about it, thinking he's out there playing with his guns while you're sorting laundry and dealing with colic. On a bad day, you think he might be shot, captured...that you may never see him again. Each of those reactions comes with their own kind of stress. But then you see him standing in the door, and you have this little good death, seeing him there. When you have your arms wrapped around him and the kids are grabbing hold of any part you don't already have, you want to hold on to that one moment forever."

Gayle blinked, laughed as Janet handed her a tissue. "Yeah, thanks. Don't tell Max I welled up. I'm the supreme SEAL wife, the example for all the others. But I get what Jenny's dealing with. At a certain point you pass the 'all clear' sign, so to speak. You've figured it out, intuitively, and you know the two of you will make it, because you've worked it out in your head, accepted what is. But until you reach that point, it can be a tough road. I've told Charles it's the wives' version of BUD/S, only it can go on for years for us, rather than just a few months. Even now, I sleep on his side of the bed when he's gone, as if it's how I can be the closest to him."

She pursed her lips. "Sorry. God, listen to me. I'm talking too much."

Janet shook her head. "If you're the supreme SEAL wife, I'm thinking you don't get to talk about the way *you* feel too often. Beyond using it as a tool, an example to help other women."

Gayle's expression shifted from mild embarrassment to a warm gratitude, and she touched Janet's hand in simple solidarity. "In my own defense, you have a great listening ear. Not to mention an obvious strength to you. It's nice to be around."

Given the fact Gayle was dealing with Jenny's fragile state and three demanding children, Janet expected being around another independent woman was like a bracing shot of whisky. Like Gayle, Janet was viewed as a mentor by most of her women friends, probably because she had no patience for the self-pitying, wallow-in-trumped-up-personal-baggage that seemed to be the norm these days. She was usually quick to shut down any female who was carping about issues that any woman could handle if she'd merely stop whining incessantly about it and take responsibility for her own life.

She decided she liked Gayle immensely. "Same goes," she said, winning a warm smile, another press of that chapped hand.

It was like her feelings toward what had happened with Jorge. She'd done it, she couldn't take it back, and she couldn't make herself regret it. So she'd moved forward with her life. She refused to stay in that blood-soaked room in her mind when her body hadn't been able to get out of there fast enough.

"Max seems to appreciate strong women," she observed. "I like that about him."

"Me too." Gayle beamed at her, poured her more tea. "As they mature, a lot of the SEALs realize it's the strong women who can handle a relationship with them for the long haul. Because reconciling yourself to his absences is only part of it. You also have to understand his bond with other SEALs."

She shook her head. "It's indescribable. Impenetrable. Did you know, when one of them falls, his fellow SEALs will each hammer their Trident into the top of his coffin, signifying he's taking a part of them with him? I've had to see Charles do that twice, and both times, I prayed I'd never have to see them do it for him. But that's the terrible, beautiful part of their connection. The other side of it is the one that can really test a marriage.

"If he's just gotten home from a thirteen-month absence, but something comes up with one of them, he's going to invite his buddy over, or take him a six-pack to help him out. That's pretty tough. It makes a wife feel like she's less important to her man than those guys, but if she pays close attention to the way he looks at her as he comes through the door, that hunger in his eyes, that sense that yes, there is something in the world worth fighting for, she'll get it. He doesn't look at anyone else the way he looks at you or his kids. You're his anchor, you're what he fights for, what he lives for. They may be adrenaline junkies, but they're also human beings. When they're in the thick of horrible violent stuff, the one thing they hold in their heads is getting back home. And you're home."

She looked over her shoulder at the young pregnant woman. "The problem is, that's not always enough for a woman. I hope they make it. We try to help each other through. But that's what we all do with those we love, right?"

"You aren't in here telling her bad stuff, are you, Gayle?" Max opened the screen door, stepped onto the porch. "I'm counting on you to be my wingman, convince Janet how lucky she is to have me and all that."

"I'm just astounded someone's putting up with you. If she's hit the two-week point, she deserves a medal."

"No doubt." He picked up Janet's half-full glass of tea and drained it. He'd stripped off the shirt and had been sweating. He also had a leaf stuck to his lower back. Janet plucked it free, twirled it by the stem so he could see it. He grinned. "We had a wrestling match in the leaf piles. The boys are now re-raking what we messed up. I'll go get you some more tea."

He moved into the kitchen area, raising his voice as he disappeared around the corner. "Gayle, I took care of the stopped drain upstairs, but is there anything else you need me to handle while I'm here? I don't want Chuckles to think I'm slacking off."

"Well, I need to be serviced sexually, if you can work that in. And I'm sure Jenny wouldn't mind a go if you could handle her as well." Gayle winked at Janet at the sound of the glass hitting the sink. "He wasn't expecting me to tease him like that in front of you," she murmured. Janet bit back a smile as Max returned, shooting them both a narrow glance.

"Women," he pronounced, putting a full glass down for Janet and topping off Gayle's. "One is trouble enough. Get a pack of them together, and a smart man steers clear."

"Damn straight." Gayle toasted him. "If you can come back in a couple weeks, I'm going to have a barbecue for all of you guys that have been helping us out so much. Bring Janet, if she's still putting up with you."

"Absolutely," he said. His gaze moved to Janet, a warm, lingering look that made her want to take her tea glass and slide it along the slick ridges of muscle on his abdomen, down to those belted jeans. She'd hook her fingers there and feel the intimate flesh beneath. Giving her a slow grin, he bent to brush his lips over hers, a promise.

"Got to finish the job," he said. "Don't believe any terrible things Gayle says about me."

As he left the sun porch and headed back toward the front, they heard him roar. The boys had apparently planned an ambush, if the stray leaves that spun by on the light wind were any indication.

"At this rate, they'll be raking for the rest of the day," Janet observed. Gayle laughed.

"Most likely. But the main point is him spending time with the boys, letting them have male role models in their life as much as possible. For that, I'm happy to let those leaves pile up like snow drifts."

She sobered then. "In a way, I'm glad you found Max after he was out of the SEALs, because you won't have to deal with a lot of this, but unfortunately, he'll figure out a way to find trouble. A lot of them go into law enforcement or related fields. It makes sense, doesn't it? You don't train to be a rocket scientist, work for NASA sending up rockets, and then find contentment as a cable guy. They have to live on that edge somehow. Except Max has a different scenario. His sister is his mission now. That helps, having the mission."

Janet felt an uneasy ripple, once again thinking of her conversation with Dale in Max's far-too-bare kitchen.

Seeing it, Gayle reached across, covered her hand. "All that aside, here's what's important. They're all infuriating in their own way. They all have their code, their set way of doing things, and that's pretty immovable, but Max is a very good man, in every sense of the word. If he gives a woman his heart, he'll treat her right, whether it's today or fifty years from now. If you realize *that's* what matters, that the rest doesn't, then you'll find gold."

Chapter Fourteen

She thought about that, as well as a lot of other things. They left Gayle's early the next morning. Though Gayle had given them a bedroom to share, Max fell asleep in the living room with two of the boys sprawled on him, having indulged them in a horror-movie marathon. When they left in the morning, both women were up to see them off. Jenny even kissed Janet's cheek, pressed her hand. The young woman looked in better spirits this morning, but as she gave Janet an intent look, she murmured, "You're lucky to get one after they're out of it."

Max was standing behind Janet, giving Gayle a big hug, but she knew he heard it. When he turned to say his goodbyes to Jenny, he drew her to him for a warm embrace, holding her an extra moment, hand cupped over the back of her head. He said something to her, something that made her fingers tighten on his broad shoulders, then he eased back, touched her nose. "When I come back for that barbecue, you and me will go to the mall. We'll snag one of those portable wheelchairs so I can zoom you around and your feet won't get tired. I'm a trained chauffeur, after all."

"And a combat driver. I have firsthand knowledge," Janet added helpfully, making Jenny smile.

"Yep." Gayle linked arms with Jenny. "Then when Lew gets back, you'll tell him you expect him to do mall shopping just like Max does."

Jenny snorted. "He'll think of a reason to stay away for another six months if I tell him that."

"No." Max held her bleak gaze. "As soon as he can be back with the both of you, he will be, no matter how much mall shopping he has to do. I promise you that."

When they were in the truck and well on their way, Janet looked toward him. He seemed a little tired from his late night with the boys, but otherwise content. He had her hand in his grip, lifting it to his mouth to brush a kiss over her knuckles. "What did you say to her, when you hugged her?" she asked.

"I told her it didn't matter what corner of the world he's in right now, all he's thinking about is being back with her."

"But don't you think that raises the question 'then why does he go away at all?'"

Max glanced at her. "Yeah. It's a tough one for a lot of the women."

He didn't try to explain it. Perhaps he knew it was like what Gayle had implied to her. If a person didn't intuitively understand it, they never would.

Sliding across the seat, she laid her head on his shoulder. Max shifted his arm around her, driving the deserted two-lane highway one-handed. The sun was rising, and the coffee Gayle had made gave the cab a pleasant aroma.

"Have you ever tried seeing how Amanda reacts to Dale, or one of the other SEALs?"

"Dale's been to see her, and she likes him well enough. Aaron went with me a couple times as well. He lives up near Baton Rouge, but comes into New Orleans regularly to visit his mom when he's here." He squeezed her. "What are you thinking?"

"I'm wondering if you've ever tried to let one of them visit her without you, to see if she'd be okay with them as a substitute, if you stayed away for a slightly longer period, like a week or two. That way, if you wanted to go somewhere for a week's vacation, you could do it."

"It doesn't work that way," he said. "It's me she looks for."

"Because you're the only one who's consistently visited her. If—"

She stopped. He hadn't said anything, but he'd become more focused on the road, his fingers tightening on the wheel, despite the fact there was no traffic. Though he still had his arm around her, it was like she was leaning against a board. If there was one thing she recognized, it was a male shifting into defensive mode.

"You know her better than I do," she said lightly. "It's just a thought. Would you like to listen to some music?"

"Yeah, sure." His shoulders eased a fraction. Straightening, she moved back to her side of the truck to fiddle with dials, scrolling through his satellite radio options until she found a station that played a good mix of contemporary, alternative and oldies. Slipping her feet out of her canvas sneakers, she drew them up on the seat. She linked her fingers over them and glanced out the window at the passing scenery. The silence drew out, but she decided to let him be the one to break it, since the wheels of his mind were obviously creating a cacophony in his head.

"Okay, let me have it," he said at last. "I know you're thinking something I'd rather not hear."

"It's really none of my business, is it?"

"You're kidding, right?" At her blank look, he gave a half laugh. There was a trace of irritation in it, but something else as well. "Janet, I haven't had a relationship since I left the SEALs. Hell, I've barely had sex with anything other than myself since then. I'm taking you camping. I'm introducing you to the wives of guys I've served with. I'm letting you into my life because I want you to be a part of it, and not just as a passing thing. Maybe I'm scaring the shit out of you, saying something like this when we've been together less than a couple weeks, but in my mind it's been a lot longer. I—"

"You don't scare me, Max Ackerman." She was glad to see the rueful tug of his lips in response. Reaching across the seat, he closed his hand on hers, a firm grip. Then he released her.

"All right. If we're going to have our first fight, let's make it a memorable one. Spit it out, woman."

She nodded. "I mentioned Amanda to Rachel. Not just her condition, which I don't know a great deal about, but also about the role you play in her life. I didn't do it to betray your trust. I spoke to her in confidence, as a medical professional, since she has access to a lot of doctors at the hospital where she does PT."

He shook his head. "I don't worry about that with you, Janet. I know you're discreet, and I also know Rachel. She's top quality in that department."

"Yes, she is." Janet paused. "She was told it's very common for the primary caregiver to convince themselves that no one else can do what they're doing, for fear that the person they love will not get every bit of the care they deserve. Yes, Amanda reacts badly if she doesn't see you every few days, but then again, other than you, it sounds like she doesn't see anyone else from the outside. Gayle mentioned the way the SEALs support one another. I noticed how you and Dale have a very similar demeanor, and I'll bet other SEALs carry that same feel to them. You're like an intense extended family. Wherever Amanda is in her head, I wonder if she would pick up on that intuitively."

She pressed her lips together, not seeing any change in his expression, but he was at least listening. "I don't expect you'd ever want to stay away from her longer than a week or two, but having the flexibility to do so would let you have a vacation, give yourself a breather. And you'd be an even better caregiver for her as a result." She reached out now, touched his arm, briefly drawing the gray eyes to hers. "You're wonderful with her, but it tears your heart out, Max. I can see it. You've put yourself on a short tether, perhaps too short. It's also kept your focus on her situation, and the cause of it, in a way that may not be healthy. You've put your life on hold."

The last two sentences snapped them back into sticky territory. His shoulders and mouth tightened. "No," he said. "That focus is going to stay front and center until it's settled."

"Because it's the one thing you can change about what happened? You can punish those who did it? Your mother won't be less gone, your sister—"

"Dead," he ground out. "She's not gone, Janet. Not like she fucking went to Atlantic City or on a trip to see relatives. She's dead, beaten to death by three guys because she wouldn't move out of the way and let them rape her daughter."

"And your single-minded determination to kill all of them may make you just as dead when all is said and done." Janet refused to back down. "Where does that leave Amanda then? Where does it leave me? You've invited me into your life. 'Hey, look at me, I'm this amazing guy who might be everything you'd ever want'. But because you have this fucking code of honor, I might get to identify your corpse before I ever pick out curtains with you."

She'd proceeded calmly, rationally, but his anger unleashed the same in her, a barb festering from the conversation with Gayle, Dale's visit in Max's kitchen, what she herself was feeling about the man himself. He'd been so straightforward. *I'm letting you into my life because I want you to be a part of it.* Most men shied away from that, or if they said it, they hadn't really thought it through, a passion-of-the-moment kind of thing. She'd been unbalanced by it, the fact she knew he meant it, had likely considered it from every angle. But the real shock was knowing how much she wanted the same thing. He hadn't been with a woman, more than a one-night stand, for several years. She hadn't had a relationship since getting away from Jorge.

"That's the deal with me," he responded, fire in his eyes, a hard set to his jaw. "I laid it out there for you. I can't change it, and I didn't take you for the kind of woman who would run from something like that."

"Stop the truck." The ice in her voice was pure Mistress, pure ball-busting admin of Matt Kensington. Max gave her a look. She knew he wasn't any more afraid of her than she was of him, but he did respect her. Whatever he heard in her tone had him pulling off the highway, on to a side road that made a straight shot into the endless flatlands, going all the way to the horizon and disappearing.

Pushing open her door, she slid to the ground. She collected her purse, her water bottle and an opened bag of crunchy Cheetos that she'd carefully rolled closed to keep them fresh. He'd bought it for her at a gas station on the way to Gayle's. She started to walk.

She could sense him watching her, probably trying to figure out what the hell she was doing. She had no idea herself.

Separated from the side road by a split rail fence, the land to her left looked like a field that might be tilled for some purpose at another time of year, or was being left fallow for this season. The early morning sun wasn't hot, but it wouldn't have mattered. She needed to walk.

She'd gone perhaps a half mile before she thought to stop, look back at the truck. She expected to see him leaning against it, or still behind the wheel, keeping tabs on her progress, prepared to come pick her up when she was ready. Instead, he was about twenty paces behind her. So caught in her whirl of thoughts, she hadn't heard him. He wasn't letting her get out of his immediate range in this unfamiliar area. He was watching after her, even as he gave her space.

Fuck, she was so in love with the fucking idiot.

At her look, he lifted a shoulder. "You like keeping men on a short tether. I was just obliging."

She stared at him. Something eased in her stomach, and she shook her head. "Ass."

"Bitch." But the tone of his voice made it a warm caress. He tilted his head toward the split rail fence. "I think this is someone's long-ass driveway. Which means we're trespassing. Want to sit on the fence until they call the cops?"

"Yes. But I don't want to be on the fence with you. Metaphorically."

"I got that. I get a lot of things with you. It's like being around Dale and the others. I almost knew the things you were going to say before you said them, but they weren't things I wanted to hear."

"I got that," she responded in kind, and now it was his turn to smile. When he held out his hand, she closed the gap between them.

Lifting her by the waist to sit on one of the rails, he leaned on the post next to it. "I'll stay on the ground. I'm pretty sure my heavy ass would break it, and then they really would call the cops."

"Yeah, you need to work on that one hundred percent muscle mass. It's getting out of hand. I think it's crept into your brain."

He touched her face. "I have thought about it," he said quietly. "My whole life revolves around what Amanda needs, Janet, and that's the way it should be. But this was a man who raped a teenager and beat a woman to death, and he's still out there. What kind of man am I, if I don't do my damnedest to make sure he doesn't do it to anyone else's mother or sister?"

"Dale said he and the others would help."

Maybe one of them didn't have so much to lose—a sister relying on him, or a woman in love with him. She didn't say it, knowing how unlikely and unfair that was, but the twitch in his jaw told her he probably understood where her mind was going on it.

"What I'm doing is against the law, Janet. I'm not pulling any of them into that beyond intel, no matter how much they say they don't care about the risks. This blood debt is mine to pay."

She put her hand on his, holding his gaze. "You invited me into your life, Max. Do you understand what that will do to me, if something happens to you? The only relationship I've had outside the club sessions is a drug dealer who kidnapped me when I was in my teens."

It was the first time she'd told him so baldly. It wasn't just during the time he'd known her that she hadn't had a real date. His gray eyes digested it, showing the brief surprise, then a more emotional reaction. His jaw tightened, even as his hand closed over hers.

"I have to finish it, Janet. It's not up for any kind of debate. I'm sorry. I don't want to hurt you with that, but I have to be honest about it. I don't want to lose you over it, Christ, I don't." She saw the anguish rise in his gaze. "Even if you think it's too soon, I mean it. I'm in love with you, head over heels, whatever you want to call it. Wherever you are during the day, I feel this connection between us, a pull, like a..."

"Tether?" she suggested. His eyes crinkled at the corners.

"If you like." He took a breath. "But you're right. It's not fair. If you need to end it between us, so you don't get in any deeper, you say the word. I'll turn around and take you home right now. It'll rip my fucking heart out of my chest, but I'll leave you alone until it's done. If you still want me when it's over..."

If he was around when it was over. She caught his wrist, held it tight in her grip. "What I'm worrying about is something different, Max. I need you to hear me."

He twisted his wrist gently, catching her fingers in his. "I hear everything you say, Mistress. You know that. I just don't always obey."

She grimaced at his wry expression, suppressing the desire to box his ears. "Getting away from Jorge was extremely personal to me. However, while I was planning for it, even doing it...it was like I was an entirely different person, because the environment, the focus, it was all about that goal. Your life is more than that now. K&A, Dale, Amanda…me."

"I know that."

She shook her head. "But do you think about how it makes *you* different? I expect when you did missions, there was a certain detachment. Even when you went after the first two men, you were still close enough to that part of your life that you probably shifted into the protocol you'd been trained to follow. It kept you detached, focused. In control. But think about all the time that's passed since then. Despite your appalling lack of home décor, you're living in a different world now. This is your life, not a mission environment."

His gaze became thoughtful. "You think I'm too close to this. I've made it too personal, and I could make mistakes."

"Yes," she said bluntly. "I understand you feel you have to go after him. But promise me you'll think about that."

He nodded. "I will. I promise."

He would, and it wouldn't change a damn thing about his course of action, only how he approached it. But maybe that would help keep him alive. She had to hold on to that. Seeing a person who'd been violently murdered was something that never left the mind, and it was far too easy to put Max's vacant staring eyes, his bloody face, on Jorge's body. She closed her eyes, folded her hands in her lap, even as she continued to lean against Max to keep herself balanced on the rail.

"Promise me you'll also think about what I suggested, about Amanda. If you feel you must do this and something does happen, it's not a bad idea to make sure there are others in Amanda's life to take up the slack. She made a connection with me. I'd be happy to be one of those…" Her voice cracked, thinking of seeing those gray eyes in Amanda's face, but never again in Max's. She stiffened as he lifted a hand to touch her. "Don't," she said sharply.

He put the hand down, his face now expressionless. She'd hurt him, but he was hurting her. It was only fair.

"But I think it needs to be a handful of people. It might be better overall for her. Also, even if nothing happens to you...sharing the load helps share the pain."

They studied each other silently. "Do you want me to take you home?" he asked at last.

"No." She looked down at where her hip pressed against his side. Despite not wanting him to touch her face, her body had betrayed her true desires, maintaining that contact. Sighing, she slid her fingertips down a fold of his shirt, feeling the heat and solidity of the man beneath. "There's nothing more pointless than running away from someone because you think they're going to break your heart."

He closed his fingers over hers, his thumb passing over her wrist. It was a tentative touch for both of them, full of things unsaid. "I'm going to try like hell not to do that, Janet. I promise."

She nodded, tracing his knuckles. A few more moments passed between them, then he reached out with the other hand, tapping the opening of her purse where the bag of Cheetos was visible. "Care to share some of those?"

Janet gave him a look of pained amusement. "Do you never stop thinking with your stomach?"

"I'm a growing boy, and they're right there and everything."

The air had shifted between them, the anger gone. What would be, would be. She rolled her eyes, pulled the bag out and withdrew one of the crunchy pieces, lifting it to his mouth. As he took it, he put his lips on her fingers, drawing them in. His hand closed around her wrist so that even when he let them go, he held on to her.

"You turned my fingers orange," she accused, giving him a frown. He licked the powder off, then wiped her fingers on his T-shirt. She snorted at that, tried to pull away, but he held her, his other arm sliding around her waist to ensure she didn't pull back too vigorously and topple off the fence. It was literally impossible to stay furious with the man.

"I've seen some of the Mistresses in the club do that," he said, nodding to the bag. "Feed a collared slave at their feet. You've done it a couple times."

"Yes. It's very moving, to have a man take food from your hand. Wine from your mouth." Retrieving the bottle of water, she took a drink of it, then curved her other hand around the back of his neck, bringing him to her lips. Mouth-to-mouth intimacy wasn't something she encouraged with her club hookups, but she did well enough now to transfer the water to his mouth without spillage and still get a nice taste of Max and the lingering flavor of the Cheetos.

He curled his fingers into her hips, pulling her closer to him, and then he abandoned the reserve of the past few moments. He took her off the fence, hiking her up his body so her legs wrapped over his hips and he had her propped against the post to brace them both. The functional exchange of food and drink became a deep, needy kiss, a reminder they hadn't had carnal knowledge of one another since they left New Orleans, an interminable amount of time. He made the kiss demanding and more than a little possessive, as if he was verifying his claim on her despite the near miss. In return she was a little angry, biting at his mouth, digging her nails into the bare skin beneath his collar.

He didn't retreat from it an inch, taking everything she inflicted and giving her back his desire, pushing himself firmly against her core. When he finally pulled back, his gray eyes were molten.

"We need to get to that campsite," he said.

They hadn't made any decisions or resolved anything, at least not in words, but the kiss was the answer. Frustrated, stubborn, passionate and yearning all at once. Breaking it off with him wasn't going to be an option for her. Not anymore. It might nearly kill her, losing him, but it was as Gayle said.

There was a point past which it was no longer on the table. Somehow, they'd already passed that point.

*****

When they reached the park, Max shouldered a backpack, which contained their tent as well as a few other items they'd need for their overnight, and hoisted a cooler on his shoulder. Then he took her hand with his free one. In that manner, she experienced her first hiking-to-a-campsite experience. She looked over her shoulder toward the more populated area, which also included a bathhouse, but he just gave her that charming smile and told her being at a more remote location would outweigh the perk of a communal shower.

She wasn't so sure about that, but the walk was beautiful, taking them across several bridges and open natural areas. It wasn't overly strenuous, and yet he refused to let her carry anything except the small tote containing her toiletries and a change of clothes. "Just enjoy the scenery, Mistress," he said, giving her a wink. Since there were times when the trail narrowed to the point that he preceded her, she couldn't argue with the advice. Watching him bear the cooler on his broad shoulder, the shift of thigh and ass muscles under his jeans as he navigated the terrain, wasn't a hardship at all, though it made her even more eager for them to get to their campsite.

The spot he'd picked out was in a birch forest. The trees were spaced widely enough to allow them a tent, and there was an appealing hushed tranquility. She was still thinking about that bathhouse, but seeing the location, she was more willing to give him the benefit of the doubt.

She learned how to put up a tent with his help, observed with fascination while he made them a campfire. He was as comfortable living out in nature as she was in her colorful bedroom with its many comforts. He'd provided a rollout foam mattress for the tent, complete with a couple pillows. When he camped alone, she suspected he was fine sleeping on the hard ground. Then she remembered his aversion to the cold and rethought that, noting he'd brought three tightly rolled blankets.

She didn't think staying warm was going to be a problem, however. Not with the intense gazes they kept exchanging and that aura of heat she felt between their bodies, even on the trail. More than once she savored the memory of him wandering around shirtless doing Gayle's yard work. That kiss on the fence was still branded on her brain.

A freshwater stream gurgled less than fifty feet from their site, and while he went to fill a jug with water, she knelt on the foam pad in the tent, ran her fingers over it. She remembered that first night Max had slept at her place. In the morning, he'd gotten up to go do a run. She chose to sleep in, trying not to hate him for his self-discipline, but when he left the bed, she automatically shifted into his spot, absorbing the heat he'd left, his scent. He'd paused over tying his shoe, head lifting to watch her.

Thinking of what Gayle said about sleeping in her husband's spot, she wondered if that was a common thing for SEAL wives. For military spouses, period. Had Max known about it, explaining his oddly pleased and touched expression?

She was having a hard time dealing with the mere possibility of him going after a gang member. She wasn't sure she could be as strong as Gayle, dealing with her man being gone for months, not knowing if he was alive or dead, or what kind of things he was facing. But it helped her understand Gayle's patience with Jenny, as well as Max's compassion. Max hadn't been married, but he'd know the toll his absences took on his mother and sister, even before the attack.

"Hey." He was squatting in the tent opening, looking rugged and far-too-appealing in his jeans and T-shirt, his hiking boots. He ran a hand down her back. "All right?"

"Yes." She turned so she was folded on her knees, facing him. "So, what do you propose for dinner? If you plan to kill something that I have to de-fur or de-scale, I will take your truck keys and head for the nearest hotel."

He grinned, reaching over her shoulder to capture her braid. She'd plaited her hair this morning, assuming it would be the easiest style to manage for camping requirements. "But I have this mountain man-squaw fantasy, and you already have your hair done right for it."

"Give me your keys." She made a lunge for his pocket and he caught her about the waist, holding her closer to him with a laugh.

"Gayle packed us meals. It was the deal I worked out with her in exchange for my extensive manual labor skills." He winked. "She's a great cook. Tonight it'll be her lasagna. She also put a couple salads in the cooler, and I brought a bottle of wine. You prefer red, right?"

"Yes. How did you know that?"

"I noticed it at the Christmas party."

A party that had been months ago. She shook her head. "If you're trying to impress me, it might be working." But when his arm loosened, thighs tensing as if he intended to leave the tent, probably to go check on her dinner, she hooked her fingers in the collar of his T-shirt. "What I want right now isn't food. Not exactly." She tilted her head toward the foam bed. "I want you to stretch out there. No clothes. Now."

He met her gaze. "How about you in no clothes?"

"Maybe. If you please me."

Another weighted moment, then he inclined his head. When she released him, he backed out of the tent so that he could stand, pull the shirt over his head. No more questions, no hesitation. It fired her blood, made her wet her lips, especially when that muscular terrain rippled before her avid gaze. He unbelted the jeans, opened them, then bent to untie the hiking shoes. He toed them off, gaze returning to her as he got rid of them and then the rest of his clothes, dropping them in a pile on the shoes.

"Stand there, just like that."

There was a pure beauty to a man in superior physical condition. Not bulges of muscle, but hard curves meant to support stamina, endurance...combat conditions.

"Do you keep in the same shape as you did for the SEALs?"

"Pretty much. It's a good routine. Makes me feel connected to them."

It also kept him in condition for what was ahead. But she didn't want this moment to be about that. "Turn around. Face away from me."

He complied, hips shifting. As he turned, her gaze drifted over the skull trident, then slipped back down to his fantastic ass, the muscular thighs. Rising to her knees, she put her hands on his buttocks, molding her palms over them. She slid her thumbs down to his thighs, causing him to widen his stance at the implied command. Making a noise of approval, she slipped her fingers between his legs to caress that sensitive joining point of the balls, then cupped them to squeeze. Leaning forward, she teased the seam between the cheeks with her tongue, nipping at him as he suppressed an oath. She suspected he would have turned then, but when he made to shift, she tightened her grip.

"Unh-unh. All mine." She whispered it against his flesh. "Mine to do with what I want. And what I want is you to keep this fine ass still."

He strangled on a half chuckle, and then his back muscles tightened as she kept idly tracing that line. She was aware of the responsive nerve endings she'd find deeper in the intimate crevice, around his rim. But to access that she'd need both of her hands, and she liked holding his testicle sac in her palm, her fingers closed firmly over the solid weight. Well, there was no need to limit herself. She had a pair of hands at her command, didn't she?

"Reach back and spread your ass cheeks for me."

It took another bated breath, but then he complied. She was touched and delighted to find he'd shaved his manly hair, at least in that region. It suggested he'd thought about some of the things his Mistress might want of him, and what would please her. He might not be a sub, but he anticipated as well as one of the best.

He'll treat her right, whether it's today or fifty years from now...

His fingers clenched on that delicious tautness as she ran her tongue over the crinkled area of his rim, then delicately pushed into his anal region, making him groan. He was going to leave bruising fingerprints on his own ass, and she had no problem with that. She'd love adding her own marks over them. She continued to knead his testicles, run her thumb along the base of his cock as far as she could reach, while she teased his anus. His feet were pressed into the earth, his thighs like cement columns. She slid her free hand up over his right one, caressing his fingers on his ass cheek, then she drew back, a clear message that she wasn't inviting contact. Not yet. When he turned a hungry gaze on her, her libido growled in sympathetic response.

"Lie on the mattress. Face up."

She shifted out of the way so he could duck into the tent opening. He squatted at the base of the foam pad, moving into a very tempting position on his hands and knees before he turned and stretched out on the mattress. His cock was a stiff soldier, making her wet her lips again. She was still dressed, and that was the way she was going to stay, for now.

"Legs spread so your ankles are as wide as the tent entrance. Arms above your head. Grab the back tent support, and don't let go. Not unless I say so."

The expression he locked upon her was the one that sent his power rolling over her, giving her that titillating feeling that she was in command of a wild beast who could overwhelm her with his strength in a heartbeat, but wouldn't. Not if she managed that delicate play of power exchange perfectly. He complied, body stretching to accommodate her desire.

"Good boy." Though there was nothing boy-like about the body she was appraising, or the rigid planes of his concentrated face. She knelt between his legs, running her nails up his thighs. "Your obeying my commands pleases me, Max. And you know about obeying commands, don't you?"

His eyes lit with flame, suggesting she was challenging the fighter in him further. But he was also very disciplined. His fingers tightened on the tent pole. "I can give you pleasure, Mistress, if you'll let me."

"You are giving me pleasure, Max. I want to take, on my terms. Your only job is to comply with my desires."

She closed her hand around his cock, began to slide up and down, working him in her loosely wrapped fist. It was a method and rhythm sure to get a response, and she did. His hips flexed, and when she bent to put her lips on his head, slide down his length, he jerked, his fingers tightening even farther on the tent pole. She didn't think that metal shaft could be any harder than the one in her mouth, and it was getting harder, blood filling and thickening it so he pressed against her tongue and teeth.

"Jesus," he muttered. "Janet....Mistress."

She dug her nails into his thighs, and he drew in his breath, shuddered. When she moved her hand to his stomach, she scratched him there as well, enjoying the score marks. She was tempted to draw blood, to put proof of her ownership on him. He said he was falling in love with her, and she viewed that declaration as synonymous with ownership, a giving of himself to her utterly.

The new part, to her, was considering such possessiveness a two-way street. She'd seen it happen with each of the K&A men. All of them hardcore Dominants, yet each man had found that one woman who spoke to his soul and captured his heart. Perhaps she wasn't much different.

Max may have bided his time waiting for her to initiate, and she had taken that time herself, deliberately, but now, on this side of it, she realized they'd both known it, felt it.

She would have liked to ease a finger up his rear passage to heighten the intensity of the climax she was going to give him, but her nails were too long. She didn't want the sharp edges to give him the wrong kind of pain. Even the toughest guy in the world had delicate anal tissues. She'd keep that thought to herself though, since men like Max didn't like to hear that any part of them was less than battle tough. But the fragility of those tissues was also what made the rear entry so deliciously responsive.

She increased the suction of her mouth on his cock, the rhythm and flow of her grip, so he was bucking up against her like a bull in the chute, waiting to be let loose. She reveled in the sight of all that power, his arms stretched above his head at her command, him gripping the tent pole such that she hoped it was buried deep enough that he wouldn't yank it loose. But the idea of that, the canvas floating down, blinding them to anything but the physical sensations they were giving one another, wasn't unappealing.

The vein under her thumb made a hard convulsion, telling her he was there. "Come, Max."

She spoke against his flesh, her mouth full of him to the throat, but he understood her. He let go with a harsh, needy sound, shoving hard between her lips. She held him taut at the base, reveling in the pump of heated fluid. She swallowed down the salty thick taste, letting some of it escape to lubricate his shaft further, wetting her fingers and giving him a full measure of the climax. He kept shuddering and jerking in her grip, every nerve ending oversensitized by the strength of his release. She brought him down slowly, squeezing, sucking, running her tongue over him, polishing and collecting every last bit of the climax she'd commanded from him.

His hand landed on her shoulder, then the other, and he was pulling her up his body to lie fully clothed on him. He gripped her buttock, long fingers pressed intimately into her crotch, and held her tight against his cock, letting her feel that pulsing aftermath. Then he had her by the wrist and was cleaning her hand with his mouth, caring for her. Her throat tightened and she stroked his thick, soft hair with her other hand as he suckled each finger, licking her palm, her knuckles. "Max," she murmured, a consecration. "Dear, sweet man."

Dangerous, loving, generous... His gaze turned to her then, his task done, and she saw all those things in his eyes as he put his hand in her hair, pulling loose her braid so her hair spread over her shoulders.

"What about the squaw fantasy?" she asked softly.

"This is part of it," he said, studying her every feature so she felt worshipped by his regard. His gray eyes moved to lock with hers. "That's what he'd be thinking about, when he was out hunting, checking traps..."

"Doing whatever mountain men do."

His eyes sparked with sensual humor. "He'd be thinking about getting home to her. How she'd have a meal ready for him, and then at night, he'd unbraid her hair, brush it for her. He'd spread it out beneath her as he laid her down before the fire."

So many times she'd thought about cutting her hair, realizing that such long hair wasn't necessarily fashionable for a woman in her forties, but his expression when he saw it tumble down her shoulders, or fall against his bare chest as it did now, made her glad she'd never given in to that impulse.

"I want you under me," he rumbled. "I want my cock plowed so deep inside you..." He left that hanging, but that was the only image needed. Her body, already charged with arousal, her panties soaked, wanted that too. It wasn't a denial of her Mistress side, simply an understanding that she could be anything she wished with him. Like dancing with the perfect partner, who anticipated the flow of her movements with his own. No choreographing necessary, as if they shared the same soul.

She was getting fanciful, like the romantic girl she'd once been. Only this was far more real, far more certain, grounded in the reality she was experiencing with him, not what she imagined the relationship to be.

"I want that too. Whenever you're ready."

He rolled them, his arm banded around her waist, putting her under him with that effortless strength that could steal away the most cynical woman's breath. She wondered what all those who knew her would think of that. Janet Albright, Satan's Mistress, out of breath, her heart tripping like...a woman in love. For the first time in her life.

She managed to smile at him with her eyes, the weight of her heart too full and momentous. When she put her hand to his face, he turned his mouth to it, holding his lips against her palm. "You might need a little recovery time, sailor," she whispered.

"I'll find a way to pass the time," he promised, with a look that sent heat searing through every part of her that would benefit from that delay.

He started by opening her shirt, one button at a time, nuzzling her breasts over the lace of her bra, showing his appreciation of the delicate, thin fabric with a pleased murmur. He traced the curves, let his tongue dip into one cup to find a nipple, curl around it. The pressure of the bra added to the intense pleasure of the sensation. He released the front clasp, replaced the cups with his hands, and she was mesmerized by how it looked, his large hands cradling her, his thumbs passing slowly over the nipples. She watched the way they gave way beneath the pressure, then became tighter, more rigid under the stimulation. Her breath was making little catch noises in her throat, and he was registering all of it.

Moving down her body, he removed each of her shoes, fingers caressing her arches, then he opened her jeans, slid them off her legs, leaving her panties on, a match for the filmy bra. He could see the outline of her pussy beneath the undergarment. As wet as she was, the silky fabric had to be glued to her labia. Moving back up, he put his hand high on her thigh, thumb passing over that exact spot, so she arched into his touch with a sigh of pleasure.

"I love seeing you wet for me, Mistress." He cupped himself then, cradling his testicles for a moment before running his curled fingers up his shaft, his cock starting to rouse before her eyes as he masturbated himself, looking down at her, the bra open, panties wet. Her pussy contracted at the stimulus, her thighs quivering in reaction to the convulsion, and he logged it all, the SEAL who wouldn't miss a single detail.

Now he shifted again, bending so he could place his mouth on the damp area of her panties. She moaned, and his hands slipped beneath her, gripping her ass, kneading the curves as he suckled her, licked the fabric, a dragging friction that made her undulate harder. She was already so worked up, she wanted him inside her now. But she also wanted this gradual unfolding of pleasure to never end, so she said nothing, seeing where his clever mind took them both.

He pulled the crotch of the garment to the side to plunge his tongue inside her, and she cried out, locking her legs on his shoulders, heels pressed into his broad back. He took his time, settling down to play and tease until she was making helpless noises in her throat. Then he ducked out from beneath the hold of her legs. Before she anticipated what he was doing, he'd turned her onto her stomach. He pressed his chest against her back, curling those powerful hands around her wrists, gently tugging her arms until they were out to either side of her. The stiffening evidence of his cock was against her buttocks, his thighs between hers, spreading her open to accommodate him. He kept the majority of his weight off her, letting her feel just enough of it to make her feel sheltered, pinned in the right way.

He kissed the back of her neck, the sides. He spent a great deal of time on her throat, the sensitive flesh beneath her ear, the line of the major artery, pumping fiercely beneath his heated mouth. Then he moved to the bump of spine at the nape, pushing her hair out of the way so he could tease the two slender bones that ran all the way to the base of her skull. He kept his hands on her wrists, thumbs caressing her thundering pulse. Now he was flexing against her ass, a teasing, coital rhythm that had her rising up against him in matching response, feeling him get harder, thicker, more ready.

She had her eyes closed as he moved to her cheek bone, her jaw, and she tilted it up to give him access to the soft skin beneath. "You are everything, Mistress," he murmured against her flesh. "Beautiful. Fearsome. Perfect…"

There was a word hanging in the air there, something she could feel him wanting to say. However, even in this charged, enchanted moment, he was mindful of her past, caring of her feelings. When two were cuffed, not just one, it made the possession even more powerful

"Please say it, Max." She trembled, hard, and he laid his cheek against hers.

"Mine," he murmured. "My Mistress."

He'd said it spontaneously the first time. This time, she'd requested it.

"Yours," she agreed, closing her eyes. His hands tightened on her wrists, then he let go of one of her hands so she could turn it to meet his, palm to palm, fingers twisted together.

"And I'm yours too, Mistress. Always."

He let her go then, but only to slide that muscular arm around her waist, bringing her up to her knees as he tugged her thin panties down to her thighs. He came back down over her, pelvis flush against her ass, cock pressing against her tender flesh as he shifted his hold so his forearm was banded above her breasts. It allowed her to rest her chin on his forearm, press her cheek to his shoulder. He guided himself into her, sliding in slow. She moved her hips, accommodating, adjusting to his thickness and length, and made a tiny feminine noise as he came to a stop deep inside her. His free arm was braced next to her, the anchor point for them both as he began to move.

Usually, she needed some clit stimulation to come in this position, but her whole body had become an erogenous nerve center, ready to detonate. Plus, when he started to move with more demand, his testicles began to hit her clit with each stroke, the stretch of her labia to accommodate his thrusts sending little frissons of sensations to that rich nerve center. She curled her hands around his arm over her chest, wanting, needing to hold on to him as he took them both somewhere she'd never gone before.

The climax was almost unbearably pleasurable, coiling up tighter and tighter, like the moment before a dancer bounded upon the stage in a dramatic *grande jete*, a leap for the heavens.

"Let me hear you come, Mistress. Make my cock harder."

The words were like the stage manager in the wings, that dramatic whisper.

Go.

She made that leap, pouring all her energy and desire into it, breaking loose of every restraint, every binding and fear of the past to give him all of herself. To soar.

She cried out his name, mixing it with screams of pleasure as he kept thrusting, taking her over that cliff and sending her flying, a *grande jete* with no end, so she reached the heavens in truth. She bit his arm, and his fingers tightened on her shoulder, holding her with bruising strength now. He understood—she wanted to feel his lust override his gentleness. Everything was primitive yet euphoric, animal demand meeting a profound, mind-numbing experience.

Toward the end, he came again as well, a tight, intense release that shot her into a series of rippling aftershocks. She reveled in his male groans against her ear, the jerk of his hips as he spilled his seed inside of her. *Yes, yes, yes...*

When the carousel came to a stop, they were clinging to one another, chests rising and falling in rapid counterpoint. His mouth was against her throat again, hers against his arm. She squeezed him inside of her and won a half-chuckle, half groan. "Jesus, that feels good." So she did it again, and a few more times after that, enjoying his grunt of response each time, but then she was out of energy.

He shifted them so he was curled behind her, giving her his heat against that Texas post-sundown coolness she was only now beginning to notice. He wrapped both arms around her, holding her close. She didn't feel a need to talk and apparently neither did he, the two of them listening to the night sounds outside and the slowing rate of their thundering hearts.

She remembered what Gayle said. *Many of them eventually go into law enforcement, security, things where they can indulge that craving, the edge they need...*

She closed her eyes. Whatever would be, would be. Maybe she couldn't bear it, but she couldn't bear being without him either. She'd cope, make sure that side of the scale kept the upper hand. Maybe that was how Gayle did it. Love could be fragile, yet once it passed that "all clear" sign, it became one of the strongest things on earth.

Now she wiggled her toes in the thick hiking socks he'd left on her feet. Her bra had been cast aside, her panties at her knees. "This is a sexy look," she ventured. "I predict the Victoria's Secret models will be walking the runway in their lingerie and knee-high camping socks at next year's fashion show."

He grinned against her jaw, sliding a hand down her belly to tease her mound with his long fingers, then tucked them between her legs, resting them against the slippery petals of flesh. "For the record, I find it a very sexy look. Much sexier than those stupid wings and New York fashion stuff they pile on them to detract from what us guys really want to see."

"Mmm." She tightened her thighs on his fingers, rubbing her ass against his damp cock.

"Stop that," he mumbled. "Christ, you're going to kill me. Take a nap."

"You know, women in their forties are just hitting their sexual peak. You better build up some stamina, sailor."

When he chuckled sleepily, she smiled against his biceps, pressed a kiss there. Then she became still against him, letting him ease into a light doze, content to be held by him as he slept. The current moment was all anyone was ever promised, after all. She wasn't going to waste it on worry about tomorrow.

Chapter Fifteen

ೞ

"What did you do to your fingers?" Lucas asked, touching one of the Superman Band-Aids Janet had on the pads of two of her fingers. "I like those, by the way."

She examined the design. She'd bought them to tease Max, but the way he'd put them on her fingers, kissing them to take the hurt away afterward, had led to a different kind of teasing. "Max showed me how to use a bow when we went camping this weekend."

"Was there video? I'd pay good money to see that." Ben slid a hip on her desk. He peered at the Band-Aids as well, shook his head. "So did you take down a three-point stag? A forest ranger? Other campers?"

"I would never harm an animal for sport," she informed him loftily. "And other campers only if they were annoying. No, we were target shooting."

She'd thought of snipers as men with fancy, high-tech rifles, but she'd learned that high-powered bows were also used by SEAL snipers, to take out targets without the muzzle flash that could give away their position. He hadn't brought one of those, of course, but a basic, decent-quality bow they could use for practice. They'd done that, gone hiking, eaten Gayle's meals and enjoyed gorgeous scenery, special places Max knew from visiting the park before.

On the second night, when they were sitting by the fire, Janet had read to him. She'd brought a couple books, a Douglas Preston and Lincoln Child thriller, as well as a biography of Margaret Thatcher. He'd asked her to read to him from the thriller, stretching out on his side, teasing a lock of her hair, occasionally pressing a kiss to her hip where she sat on a log. When he noticed her shifting from the log's hardness, he changed their positions, putting her between his legs, becoming her chair on the soft forest floor, letting her lie back against his chest while he propped against the log.

He might make her a camper yet. It had been peaceful, in a very different, very pleasing way.

"You will locate no YouTube footage of this trip," she informed Ben. "And get off my desk. I have work to do."

He grinned and rose. "I told Marcie what you said, about helping her with the wedding. She'll probably be calling soon. Why a wedding needs to be planned this far in advance, I have no clue, but I'm leaving it to you women. You all just tell me when to show up."

"I'll pencil it into your calendar," Janet said dryly. "And add a weekly reminder, so you don't plan anything over it."

"Good idea," Lucas snorted. The two men moved into Matt's office for their morning meet. It would be a short one, because in an hour they'd all be at the airport, on their way to South America for the next three days to oversee the ownership transfer of a plant there. Max wasn't on schedule today, and she knew he was going to visit Amanda after dropping Dana off at her church. She wondered if he'd come back by the office to have lunch with her, but Dana might pull him into doing some volunteer task at her place. Or maybe he had some other errands to handle, or something going on with Dale. She'd just spent several days with him, for Heaven's sake. They weren't at the point they were reporting schedules to one another, after all, and she was both amused and irritated at herself for thinking along those lines.

Get a grip, Janet.

Still, when lunchtime came, and the office was quiet without any of the K&A men around, she decided to take the trolley to Dana's church. Ben and Marcie wanted Dana to officiate, so she and Janet could go ahead and discuss some early details. It was a gorgeous afternoon in New Orleans and she'd enjoy the stroll from the trolley to the church, as long as she wasn't mugged in the dubious neighborhood where it was located. The Taser in her purse was there for backup, but usually her direct, icy stare told any idlers she wasn't an easy target.

When she entered the church through the office area, the church secretary told her Dana was in with the minister. "But if you want to wait in the nave, Ms. Albright, I'll send her to you when she comes out of the meeting. Probably about fifteen minutes."

Janet nodded. "Is Max Ackerman here?"

"No ma'am. He was out at the basketball court earlier, but I think Dana said he had to run an errand."

Janet nodded, then followed the hallway to the main body of the church, taking the side door into the cool chamber. As she moved down the aisle between the pews, she absorbed that universal hush, the sense of peace, that all churches seemed to contain. It made her think about their birch forest, how similar the two places were.

She'd never considered herself much of an outdoorsy person, but there was something to be said for camping with a man who knew how to care for a woman, cushioning her from the more unpleasant aspects of outdoor living. He'd had bug spray, toilet paper, wine, homemade lasagna...the man was a treasure.

She slipped into the second pew from the front, studying the altar. The wooden crucifix had been carved by one of the parishioners, primitive and moving at once, the stretch of Jesus' arms, the agony of his lean body, contrasting with the acceptance on his face. If a person chose to believe the story, he'd seen both the good and evil in men's hearts and loved all of them anyway.

She thought of Jorge, the things he'd done to her, to others. The world he'd inhabited had been a world of violence and blood. Yet at one time, he'd been a baby in some mother's arms. Had his mother hoped for good things for him, the way Max's mother had hoped for her son? What would Mary have done if the angel had told her the whole story? Yes, her son would bring hope to the world, but he'd also be betrayed and crucified. He'd die an excruciating death when he was barely in his thirties, because of the message of peace and hope he'd brought.

What would Jorge's mother have done if she was told the baby in her arms would beat a woman's legs into broken kindling, smash her face, all to keep her with him?

Rising, she moved to the altar. While Dana's church wasn't Catholic, she'd suggested the tradition of having candles available so people could light them for loved ones, to add to the strength of their prayers. Peter's wife didn't hesitate to mix religious traditions to capture the interest and needs of her parishioners. Janet picked up the taper, put it in the flame of one of the lit candles. Her hand was trembling, she noticed, her chest tight, but she firmed her grip, took a breath and touched the taper to an unlit candle.

All these years, and she'd spared no thought to Jorge, blocking him out of her mind, trying to get ahead of the horror he'd inflicted upon her, trying to keep it contained. Perhaps they were right, that love opened unexpected rooms in one's heart, because for the first time, she gave an ounce of her compassion to the man he might have been. To the mother who bore him, the hopes she'd harbored for him. She also lit the candle as hope that maybe there'd be a day when every heart would embrace love over hate.

She couldn't go further with it than that, but it was far more than she'd ever given. She also asked forgiveness for taking a life. She couldn't have done it differently, wouldn't have, but she could feel regret over the act itself.

"I'm sorry," she murmured to the still air. Sorry could cover a lot of things, and it felt better saying it, as if a small weight was lifted off her heart. Yes, falling in love could suck. But it could also bring better things.

"Janet?"

Swiping away the small tear that had escaped her eye, Janet turned to see Dana at the entrance to the sanctuary, her fingertips resting on the doorframe. "I'm here."

Dana came down the aisle, sweeping her cane ahead of her, comfortable enough with the surroundings that it appeared mostly a precaution. "This is an unexpected surprise. Were you getting too much work done without them underfoot? You needed spiritual counseling to handle the shock?"

"Pretty much." Janet laughed. "No, I thought it was a nice day to be out, and I figured I'd stop by and—"

"See if Max was here. Since he's not, you'll tell me you came to talk about the wedding so he doesn't find out you're stalking him."

"You know, I'm starting to understand why Rachel pinches you all the time."

Dana grinned, gesturing to the pews nearest them so they could both take a seat. "Max was here earlier this morning, repairing the basketball goal, but he headed out about midmorning. One of the kids said the goal's not fixed yet, so I assume he needed another tool and got tied up with something else. Since he's picking me up this afternoon, he'll likely come back in time to finish the goal and take me home."

"Most likely." Yet Janet glanced down at her phone, her brow furrowing. Max often sent her texts throughout his day. She hadn't had one since he'd left her bed this morning. She'd gotten busy with the guys, had thought about sending him one on the trolley, but figured if she was going to be seeing him... She admitted part of the reason she hadn't sent one was she enjoyed the messages he devised to coax her to text him back.

Quelling the desire to send him a clingy text like *Where the hell are you? I haven't heard from you every hour on the hour, just like a cuckoo clock*, she turned her attention to her very valid reason for being here. Even if it was an excuse.

"I wanted to touch base with you about Marcie and Ben's wedding, to see if you're going to need anything from Ben regarding the ceremony or the vows. That way I know when to start badgering him, make sure he has it done."

"Good idea." Dana beamed. "I spoke to Cass the other night. She's doing the big-sister thing. She isn't really sure if it's good for Marcie to get married so young, but the fact they're waiting until spring helps."

Janet suspected Cass worried that Ben hadn't yet made enough progress in dealing with the debris of his past to make a good husband, but he would be. He was an impossibly strong-willed man, but all five of the K&A men were. They were also incapable of ignoring their primary imperative—the well-being of the women they considered theirs.

"We all expected they'd marry," Dana continued, "but I wasn't sure if they'd be the type to go on for years before making the decision. I expect Ben would have done just that, he's so new to all the relationship stuff, but Marcie probably threatened to date other guys if he didn't marry her within a year of her moving in."

Janet could well believe Marcie would pull such a move. What had Ben said? "She made me agree to marry her", not "I asked her to marry me". Ben was the most hardcore of all of them, a sexual sadist definitely not for the fainthearted submissive, but Marcie embraced and even craved that side of him. "I think she'd better remember he has the resources to create an actual dungeon beneath his house."

"That would only excite her," Dana said, confirming Janet's thoughts. Since the minister didn't wear her sunglasses in the church, Janet saw her pale green eyes twinkle. Then Dana put a finger to her lips, a self-admonishment in deference to their surroundings. "But anyhow, yes, there are a few things you can put on his calendar. They've agreed to a series of sessions to discuss the significance of marriage with Reverend Morris, and then—"

"Reverend Dana? There she is. Yo, Reverend Dana."

Two teenagers had appeared at the entrance to the nave. The one who'd spoken came down the aisle at a trot, dragging a slighter boy behind him. They were both dressed in oversized jeans and T-shirts, a hoodie flopping off the narrow shoulders of the one being dragged.

"Jimmy, slow down. This is a church, not a gymnasium," Dana scolded, but she had her hand out as they came to her. "Who's with you?"

"Terence. He's got something he needs to tell you, right now." Janet saw the slighter boy's cheeks had dried tear tracks. Dana picked up on his distress, because she rose, settling her hands on his shoulders. Despite his age, he was still a few inches taller than her. The other boy towered over them both. "C'mon, man, tell her fast. He don't have time for you to dick around. To waste," he corrected himself, casting an apologetic look toward the altar, much as Dana had when she was referencing Marcie's sexual preferences.

"Your driver, the big dude…"

"Max." Janet spoke before Dana could, stepping up beside her. That faint unease in her gut was suddenly doing a meringue across her vitals. "What about him?"

Terence's eyes slid to her. Dana's hands tightened on him, however. "She's all right. You can trust her. Tell us, Terence. What's happened? Is Max all right?"

"He's totally fucked, is what," Jimmy said, then winced as Dana sent him a searing look. "Sorry, Reverend D."

"He asked me to find out something for him," Terence blurted out. "A few months ago. I almost forgot about it, and I wish I had. But I gave him the info this morning, and he left. But it wasn't…"

He burst into tears then. It shattered the street toughness, made it clear he was barely in his teens. Even so, Janet had to restrain herself from shaking the rest out of him. Dana caught that vibration, because now she had one hand on Terence, one on Janet's forearm. "Some guy gave me money to tell Max something," the boy continued, "but that's just like Judas, isn't it? I needed it for my mom, but when I told her how I got it, she said I had to come tell you, and I know it was wrong, but I can't take it back..."

"Never mind that now. Tell me what happened."

"Max wanted to know if this particular dude came back to the neighborhood. A Mexican guy called Dino. A long time ago, he used to be hooked up with the 9th Streeters, ferrying their shit to them. He hasn't been around in a really long time, but he showed back up. I don't know how he knew I was on the lookout for him, but one of Dino's guys came to me, told me if I'd tell Max he'd be at this one place, he'd give me a grand in cash. But Max couldn't know that we'd talked. It had to be like Max would think *he* was surprising Dino, but that means they were gonna be the ones doing the surprising."

The kid was sobbing. "I knew it was wrong, so I went asking around, but it was too late. He went straight there. I talked to some homeless dudes and they said Dino's guys carried something out in a sack. Something the size of a guy like Max."

Janet's heart faltered, her vision getting skewed, but she dug her fingers into the top of a pew, holding fast as Terence kept talking.

"They're supposed to hold him somewhere until Dino gets in tonight, to deal with him himself, settle some score he has with Max. Nobody 'round there knew where he'd been taken though. He's gonna be dead, Reverend Dana. And it'll be all my fault."

"Where did you tell Max to meet Dino?" Dana asked firmly, giving him a shake to keep him on track.

As Terence relayed the location of a derelict building in the warehouse district, Janet already had her cell phone out. When the man answered on the other end, she took a breath. "Dale, we need your help. Max may be in trouble."

*****

Dale came to the church. Marcie arrived about the same time, with a zippered black duffle bag almost bigger and heavier than herself, but the lissome, athletic blonde carried it easily. Dana had called her right after Janet spoke to Dale. Janet had also called Alice, managing to tell her in a calm voice she'd decided to take the rest of the day off to get some errands done. She'd given her direction on FedExing out several contracts and disconnected. She didn't want Alice involved in this.

"So explain to me why we're not calling the cops?" Marcie asked, putting down the bag. They'd moved to an activity room at the back of the church where it was quiet. Dana had sent Terence and his friend to talk to the minister, so it was just the adults now.

"Beyond the fact we don't have a location at this point, when we do, if the bad guys hear sirens, they'll just kill him and cut out. There are also too many questions that'll be raised about why they took Max in the first place. There's a reason Dino has laid low as long as he has. He knows Max took out two of his buddies and has been on the lookout for him for a while."

Dale spoke bluntly, but Janet had told him everyone in the room could be trusted. The fact he took her at her word meant he'd gauged her character at their one meet and found her to be someone he could trust. Any other time she'd been flattered by it, but all she felt was a pounding urgency to get moving, to do something. But she had to trust him as well.

"That's kept him scared enough to stay in the shadows, but time blunts fear. There've also been some power shifts happening in his cartel, so that's probably why Dino popped back on the grid. He's ready to move back into the limelight with the 9th Streeters, capitalizing on his old contacts with them. Max is a loose end in the way of that." Dale propped a hip on a table. "I've already gone by the warehouse where the kid sent Max. Saw evidence of the scuffle, but no one's there. If they put him on a boat, we'd likely be screwed, but my guess is they're not going to take him far. It sounds like Dino has a vested interest in making the kill here, so he can reestablish his power base."

Janet parsed the words, boxing up "kill" so it had nothing to do with Max. She concentrated on Dale's information, on what needed to be done. Dana had made a good call with Marcie. Though the young woman blinked at the information, pressing her lips together, she held firm.

"I have feelers out to figure out where they took him," Dale said. "Shouldn't take long. Wherever they hold him, it will be a defensible position, with lookouts outside, anticipating any trouble, and more watching him inside. Some crews like the impressive show of numbers, but I'm hoping we'll luck out and it will be more low key than that."

He tapped the cellphone on his hip. "I have reinforcements coming. Four operators are near enough to be called into action. They're on their way. Once they get here, we'll figure out a way to get eyes on the inside, create a distraction, and then make our move from there."

"What evidence?" Janet asked. When Dale's gaze turned to her, she firmed her chin. "You said there was evidence of a scuffle? Blood?"

"Yeah, blood. Broken crates, what looks like a fist plowed into the wall of the warehouse."

Blood. Why had she asked? Max's face, his torso, all those perfect lines of muscle, flashed through her mind. An empty corpse, lying in a pool of blood.

"But no body, Janet." Dale gave her a hard look. "Keep that in mind."

"I'm fine," she said shortly. And she was. Ice was flowing through her veins, a simmering rage. At Max, at Dino, at Dale, at the whole situation. She needed to get a grip on it. She could tell Dale registered her tension, and she couldn't be less than invincible right now.

"I've got surveillance equipment to help with the eyes inside stuff," Marcie spoke. "And I stopped at your house to get the things you wanted." She directed that to Dana. "It was tough to leave the assault rifle behind. That was sweet."

"Yes, but it's hard to conceal," Dana said dryly. "As long as you have the handguns and the Tasers, we're good."

"My guys will come geared," Dale said.

"It's not for you," Dana responded. "You need eyes inside and a distraction, right? If you're right, there's only one thing that's going to get you through the outer perimeter and inside, and it's not a bunch of strapping guys who are obvious military. If you pose as a homeless derelict stumbling into their lair, they'll shoot first and dump the body."

"So what are you proposing?" Dale raised his brow. "If you think I'm taking civilians into an op like this..."

"I believe we called you, so technically it's our op." Dana's expression hardened. If Janet hadn't known of Dana's military background before, she'd have been forcibly reminded of it now, because her expression mirrored Dale's. "I'm a combat veteran, Marcie is MMA trained and has used it—more than capably—for her job in corporate investigations. She also knows her firearms."

Marcie nodded. Her brown eyes were cool, her hip cocked and arms crossed.

"As for Janet," Dana tilted her head toward her, "some of her nicknames at K&A include Ice Bitch and Scybo. It's an acronym for She'll Cut Your Balls Off. Sorry if you didn't know that, Janet."

"No problem. You left out Dragon Lady. HR likes that one."

"Sorry to be rude, but you're blind, soldier." Dale reached out, tapped Dana's forehead with one finger.

"Thanks for the newsflash. The blind have over-developed proximity senses. Consider it like the Force. I could have caught hold of your wrist just now and broken some shit, but didn't want to mess up your trigger finger."

Dale set his jaw, but before he could say anything else, Janet stepped forward. "I get it," she said. "You don't feel comfortable with this. But they're right about the eyes inside and distraction, aren't they? It would be ideal if all three of us had your training, but perhaps that's not what this moment requires. It simply requires the ability to stay cool under pressure, to play a role no matter what stressors occur. The firepower, the strength, the accuracy, the response—that will be your area, yours and your guys. Dana isn't overestimating our abilities. There are women who work as cultural support teams to SEALs, women with military training, aren't there? This is like that."

This was how she accomplished things for Matt. Lay out the facts, the logic. Though she'd never compared meeting arrangements, legal documentation and handling the schedules of five busy men to planning a military op, she expected some of the same advance planning skills and anticipation of contingencies were needed. As well as a cool, level head. She could do that. Because if she looked beyond that, there was terror, trembling...the smell of blood permanently embedded in her nose.

Dale blew out a breath. "Max said you'd been watching way too many SEAL training videos. Okay, soldier," he directed that to Dana, "tell me the plan. But let me make one thing clear."

He swept a hard gaze over all of them. "I *am* in charge of this op, which means you follow my orders from beginning to end. If you don't convince me that what you're thinking is a sound plan and our best chance, then you'll obey my order to stand down and let me and my men handle this. The objective is to get Max out of this alive. You have to trust me to know the best way to do that. All right?"

Dana and Marcie didn't speak. Instead, they looked toward Janet, and she saw Dale did the same. By stepping forward, she'd taken the leadership role, and Dana and Marcie had deferred to her. Though Janet knew she had formidable organization skills, she didn't think that topped their tactical skills. They were deferring to her because they somehow realized she had the most to lose. That terrified place inside her trembled hard, and she clamped down on it like a pit bull. Reminding herself she was the Ice Bitch, she gave a short nod. "Fair enough. Dana, tell us what you're thinking."

When Dana was done, Dale had grilled her twenty different ways on it, tweaking and refining. Janet and Marcie jumped in here and there to add additional details, which seemed to increase Dale's confidence in all of them. By the time he seemed satisfied, the others had arrived. Four strapping men was a good description, though it wasn't because of their size. Lawrence was no taller than five-seven yet stocky with muscle, and Neil had a rangy Jimmy Stewart build. Billy was closer to the size of Dale, and sounded like he'd come straight out of the West Virginia hills. But they all had the same stamp she'd noticed on Max. They were men trained to undertake dangerous jobs and not let anything stop them from succeeding.

The fourth man was Aaron, but rather than having him come to the church, Dale explained he'd sent him to collect intel in the field.

The ticking clock in her head was going to drive her mad. Terence had been clear. They were to take Max, hold him for Dino, and the street intel said Dino wasn't coming in until after dark. It was closing in on five o'clock now. Max had to still be alive, unless something had gone wrong on the snatch, and if that had been the case, Dale would have found his body. She swallowed over a jagged ball in her throat.

"Master Chief?" Neil extended his cell phone to Dale. "Might want to show them our target."

Nodding, Dale turned the picture on the screen to them. "This is Dino—"

"Delgado," Janet finished, staring at the picture. "I know him."

The world had tilted. Dale reached out to steady her, Marcie slipping a hand around her waist. Janet's mind fought through the swimming hysteria. *No. It's been over fifteen fucking years. I am not letting this control me.*

"I was involved with a man in Mexico, years ago," she said. "This was one of his associates. He was very low on the totem pole then, but obviously he's moved up." Probably due to the gap she provided by taking out Jorge.

"So does that help us or harm us?" Neil asked.

"Helps," she said, firming her chin. "It will make our cover more believable. We can adjust the plan like this…"

The initial objections were fierce, because the adjustment put her at the front of the approach, but they couldn't argue with the logic to it, not when she laid it out as coolly as she did, pointing out flaws in any argument against it. After the strategy was mapped out thoroughly with all players, there was a moment of significant silence. Dale shook his head. "Max won't forgive me if you get hurt, Janet."

"I'm not concerned about his forgiveness. He's mine. I'm getting him back. You said if the plan wasn't the best way to go about it, you'd say so. You're not saying so."

The SEAL met her gaze, nodded. "Yeah. It's a sound plan."

He drew his men away, going over tactical issues relevant to their placement outside the potential location. Janet and Marcie looked at one another, Marcie reaching out to cover Dana's hand. "One of us needs to call Savannah," Janet said. "Tell her what we're doing, so if something goes wrong…she'll know what happened and can notify Matt, do damage control as needed. Know how to find us."

Anticipate contingencies, make sure the flow of information was adequate to keep all necessary parties informed. Who knew being a secretary would prove to be so useful on a special op?

"Agreed," Dana said. "She'll bring Rachel into the loop. We might need her before the night is over. She can pave our way into medical facilities with few questions. Unless we're dead, of course."

"Yeah." Marcie gave them her serious smile, though her brown eyes glinted. "On the plus side, if this goes well, Ben is going to be so pissed at me. I can't wait."

"You twisted freak," Dana said with fond exasperation, but then she closed her hand on Janet's, linking the three of them. "Are you okay, honey?"

She'd never been the type of person anyone would call honey. In fact, no one had ever used an endearment on her. Except Max. He called her Mistress, meant it like that. "I can't lose him," she said tonelessly. She felt like an iron furnace, everything locked down yet containing hellfire. "I just found him."

"We're getting him back," Dana said resolutely. "Count on it. You knowing the target is going to be a big plus, Janet."

Marcie nodded, putting her hand on Janet's other arm, squeezing hard. Despite her joke, the young woman's eyes were sharp as a knife blade. She could handle herself in this environment. They all could. They'd all been there, in one way or another. Janet thought of the blood on her hands, running down a sink, and closed her fingers into fists. She'd killed Jorge when she was in her twenties. Now, in her forties, she could endure, handle anything. Except losing the man she'd finally given her heart.

Dale had insisted on a thorough understanding of how she knew Dino. She hadn't told him she'd murdered Jorge, because no one in the world but Matt and Max knew that, but she told him she'd gotten away from Jorge and then heard he'd been murdered by a competitor. All technically true, so she didn't feel it hampered their efforts to leave it like that.

Going after a man who'd been kidnapped, who might be killed, was one thing, and bad enough. Making Dale and the rest of them accessories after the fact to her crime was a whole other scenario.

As a result, she understood why Max had wanted to go after Dino on his own, to avoid putting his fellow SEALs in the position of breaking the law to come to his aid. Yet the day Dale had given her his cell number, his direct look had been a silent, clear message. That was Max's choice, but Dale had the right to make choices of his own. Just as Dana and Marcie had made the choice to be here with her now, the three of them risking their lives for Max.

"Got him." Dale snapped his phone closed, turned around. He met Janet's eyes. "Aaron says they moved him to another abandoned warehouse right off the waterfront. It's a maze down there. Even better, it's the typical rathole where, if the cops ask, nobody sees anything. Got three guys on the outside, four inside. They're part of Dino's crew from Mexico, not locals. That works in our favor as well."

"How is that?" Janet asked.

Lawrence was checking his handgun. When he popped the slide, the stocky man glanced up at her with sharp green eyes.

"Nobody sees anything, that means they don't see us either. Not that we're easy to see anyhow. If they see us, we haven't done our job." He flashed a dangerous smile. "As far as them being from Mexico? Easier to get rid of out-of-town bodies, ma'am. They don't belong here."

At that, Marcie paled a little, and of course Dale latched right on to it. "Dana, I'm going to say it again. Goddamn non-combatants shouldn't be a part of this."

"We don't have time to go over it again. We have a sound plan, remember?" Janet interjected it sharply. Dale shot her a cold look, one she was sure could intimidate a whole platoon of SEALs, but she gave him a stone-cold bitch look right back. "I know what could happen."

"Yeah, maybe you do. You have that look. She doesn't." He jerked his head toward Marcie. "I'm going to lay it out clear, kid. Lives are going to be taken on this op. Max has been hunting Dino for a while, and the guys with him are connected to a cartel. The only way we protect everyone here, and our families, is by not a one of them going home telling the story. Do you get that? You can stay home and no shame to it. I'd feel a hell of a lot better if you did."

This time, Dana and Janet waited for Marcie, since it was obvious her response was what Dale was gauging. The young woman firmed her chin and, though she didn't have Janet's icy look, she met his gaze squarely. "They'll kill Max if we don't go in," she said quietly. "And you're telling me if they aren't taken out, our families are in danger. That's all I need to know."

"We're pretty much Old Testament stock." Dana laid her hand on Marcie's arm, support and approval at once in the gesture, and tilted her head in Dale's direction. "Only we prefer a more proactive approach. Get them before they get us. Let's go take our boy back."

* * * * *

There'd been no further discussion about it after that. It was clear Dale didn't like it, but they were out of time and the plan was the best they had. After that, the men fell into a seamless operational rhythm. Dale stayed in communication with Aaron via phone, the absent man relaying information back to the team at the church to fine-tune what they could tell from the satellite picture they called up of the location. They tweaked the plan accordingly, then turned their attention to ensuring the women were outfitted with the gear they needed.

Dana wore an earpiece inside one ear to hear Dale's communications, since with her blindness it passed as a hearing aid. Janet had both a camera and listening device as part of the pendant she was wearing. The special necklace was one Marcie had used when she worked with Pickard Consulting. It had remained part of her arsenal for her corporate investigation duties at Tennyson Industries. Since then, Jon had helped her re-design the already excellent technology it possessed, so Janet wasn't surprised that Dale pronounced it as more than suitable for their purposes.

Marcie and Dana had done a full costume change for the part they were supposed to play. After examining the choices Marcie had brought for all of them, and considering what she knew of Dino, Janet had decided to go with what she was wearing, making only a few adjustments. Using scissors, she'd increased the back slit six inches, so the snug skirt showed a hint of the lace-top stockings she was wearing. She traded out her more comfortable pumps for a pair of chocolate-brown stilettos Marcie had brought. Fortunately, she and Marcie were comparable in shoe size. The pain of wearing the narrower heel on her misshapen feet was a small matter.

Taking off her cream-colored shell, she exchanged the demure lace bra beneath for a black lace one that had cups a size too small and pushed her breasts almost out of them. She put her suit jacket over it, the pendant teasing her bare cleavage. Taking her hair down, she brushed it out to its full glory. She enhanced her makeup, adding a cream gloss to her lips but keeping it classy.

One high-dollar escort to order, from head to toe.

When she came out of the bathroom, she was mildly gratified by the appraising glances of the four men, and Dale gave her an approving nod. "Sexy as hell, ma'am. Should do the trick."

"No pun intended," Dana quipped. Janet ran her gaze over the other women. In comparison, they'd gone for the cheap streetwalker look, heavy makeup and clothes just this side of the law. Marcie had teased up her hair in a sultry tangle around her face, wearing a miniskirt that barely covered her ass and a low-cut tank long enough to cover the waistband—

as well as the firearm she was carrying there. Dana's likewise skimpy attire was artfully arranged to handle the Taser. Despite her thoughts on choices and free will, Janet felt worry grip her. If either of them got hurt...

She couldn't think like that. They were as prepared as they could be. Max might not want any of them to risk themselves for him, but that was too bad. He was just going to have to live with owing them for the rest of his life, which she hoped would be a long, long time.

* * * * *

The two men hanging around in front of the warehouse gave the dark four-door sedan a studied look as she drove up. Parking it about fifty feet away, Janet got out, making sure they saw lots of leg as she did. She tossed her hair back and sauntered their way, hips swaying.

"Boys." She nodded. "I was told to meet Dino here. Compliments of the 9th Streeters. They wanted him to have a welcome-home gift."

"Which 9th Streeter?" The dark eyes of the taller man narrowed on her, but she noticed the other one was just enjoying an ogle of her body.

"That's not my department, sugar. They called, wired three thousand cash to my handler, told her to give Dino everything he wants. I'm everything any man could want." She took out her hand mirror, checked her lipstick and hair. "I've been in this game long enough to know how to curl a man's toes and leave him smiling. So where is he?"

"He ain't here yet, *puta*. And when he does get here, he's got business to attend. You go sit your pretty ass in the car and wait on him."

"I do love taking care of a businessman." She shrugged. "I can wait in my rental. It's the nicest room in this house, for sure." She cast a disparaging look over their surroundings. "But do you mind if I take care of a ladies room need first? I drove up here from Houston." At their scowls, the protests rising on their lips, she sighed. "I don't care what's inside. Dead bodies, drugs, whatever. I've seen it all and I remember none of it. I used to be Jorge Alvarez's girl, after all. I only want a bathroom."

The man's gaze narrowed on her. "Janelle?"

He'd never met her, but she expected the name was remembered. She nodded. "After Jorge got taken out, I had to split. Ended up with this nice operation out of Texas, taking care of boys on both sides of the border when you have needs. But my preference is still brown skin and those lovely, fuck-me-blind dark eyes." She gave him a feline smile, and his gaze slid down her body, back up again.

"Maybe you take care of us while you're waiting."

"Oh no, sugar. Got to have some professional decorum. You might muss the package Dino's expecting. But maybe if you're around afterward, you could buy me a drink and we'll talk. Bathroom?"

"Hey, bitch!"

Janet turned to see two streetwalkers crossing the road toward her. They were arm in arm, weaving slightly.

"Yeah, you. This ain't your area, bitch, and you need to get your skank ass out of here before we kick it up into your throat."

She gave Dana credit. No one would guess those rasping, vicious words had just come out of the mouth of a minister. Marcie planted her feet about ten feet away and Dana held on to her arm even as she stepped out in front, shook a finger in Janet's direction. "I may be blind, but I can smell that cheap-ass perfume a mile away. Now git."

"You bitches better get yourself somewhere else," the second man said. "This is private hired entertainment."

"Oohhh..." Marcie pursed her lips, gave him a sultry look from beneath her teased fall of hair. "Maddy, I think he just called us common trash. Pussy is pussy, sweet boy. She might be sweeter-smelling, but I'm waaay younger meat." She cast Janet a scornful look. "I can pump your cock better too, even at half her price."

"And leave what crawling on it?" the first man scoffed.

"Ain't nothing wrong with what I'm offering," Marcie said indignantly. "You think high-priced is any cleaner than bargain? Use a glove, and it don't matter no how."

"So you're blind." The other man had stepped forward, and now he caught Dana's arm. She retaliated with a sharp kick to his shin that sent him hopping.

"Yeah, I'm blind, but don't be manhandling me, boy."

"Cunt." He retaliated with a back hand that sent Dana stumbling into Marcie. Janet steeled herself not to move forward, but the black woman straightened quickly enough. Even gave him a sly smile through the split lip.

"I'm also not above playing rough." She sidled toward the man she'd just kicked. "Girl don't need her eyes to suck dick, does she?" Her expression became even more provocative as she rubbed up against him. "In fact, I tend to rely way more on touch, *sugar*. You feel me?"

Janet rolled her eyes, stepped past the first man. "Just tell me where the bathroom is, sugar, and I'll leave you to deal with this trash."

"No she ain't goin' in there. Not unless she want her ass kicked when she comes out."

As Marcie and Dana surged forward, the second man blocked them. The first one threw an exasperated look at Janet. "Fine. Go in that door. Tell Manny that Leo said you were fine and have him show you where the bathroom is. There's an upstairs office where you can wait."

Janet nodded. Slipping into the door, she tried not to worry about the sounds of a scuffle, Marcie's sudden cry of indignant pain as she was likely shoved back or hit, the way Dana had been.

She moved toward the main floor of the warehouse, trying to deaden every facial muscle she had so she wouldn't react to seeing Max. It was a good decision.

Chains were dangling from the ceiling above him, as if they'd hung him there for a while. She could imagine it, his feet a few inches off the floor. She knew how the shoulders could scream in that position, how long before the danger of dislocation loomed. Right now, though, they had him stripped to his shorts and bound in a chair. Blood was running down his upper body, caused by multiple cuts from some kind of blade. There was also bruising, where he'd likely been punched. Given that they were supposed to save the worst of it for Dino, she shuddered to think what Dino had in mind for Max.

The four guarding Max must be the ones who'd taken him at the first warehouse. The stiff way a couple of them moved, the cuts and bruises on their faces, suggested he hadn't gone down easy. She felt a visceral satisfaction at it, though nothing could override the cold clutch in her heart at seeing Max bound that way. She knew he had to be alive, but it was still nigh unbearable, seeing him motionless, his head hanging down, indicating he was unconscious.

At her appearance, the men went on full alert, one of them even drawing his gun. She channeled every ounce of will she had into looking unconcerned about the bleeding man in the center of the room. "Leo told me to look for Manny. I'm a present for Dino from the 9th Streeters, but I really need a bathroom. He said I could wait in an office somewhere?"

"We gotta search you first," one of them said, giving her a leering appraisal.

"Of course," she said, with the bored indifference expected. "Just be careful handling the merchandise, sugar. I'm sure Dino would like his present intact."

At the first word she spoke, she noted a tightening of Max's shoulders, a slight twitch of his head. He was awake then. There was a relief to that, and an opportunity. They'd concocted a couple plans, including one involving his participation. It was on her to determine if he was in a condition to do that. That question was answered easily enough.

When he slowly lifted his head, she was confronted with a steel-gray gaze that said exactly what he thought of her being here. It reminded her of a Hulk movie, only in this case mild-mannered Dr. Banner had embraced his anger with both hands, welcoming the beast.

Hold fast, Max. I'm here because we have a plan.

She forced herself to stay relaxed as Manny nodded to one of the other men. When he approached her for the search, she gave him a scornful look, raised her arms like a ballerina and did a slow pivot on the balls of her feet before he reached her. The move would give Dale a panoramic view of the surroundings, show him where everyone was. She gathered up her hair, twisting the mass of it on her neck so it wasn't impeding the search.

The man was as zealous as she expected, his hands wandering with great familiarity over her breasts, under her skirt, squeezing her ass and rubbing against her pussy, but he was also thorough in his search for weapons. She gave him a teasing look and bumped him with her ass when he got too pushy with his fingers. "You go any further with those, sugar, you have to pay for it."

He gave her a feral grin, but then nodded to Manny. "She's clean."

"In so many ways. Bathroom?"

The next moment, her cheekbone exploded with pain. Manny had closed the three steps between them and knocked her down with the back of his hand. Even as the agony rocketed through her, she knew it had been designed to set her down on her ass, not to do any harm. She'd been beaten by Jorge enough to know the difference between an object lesson and uncontrolled rage.

"Don't be acting like you're more than a whore around us, just because you're some fancy piece sent by the 9th Streeters. Shit, they owe us. When Dino's done, we'll all take a piece of you, and they can consider it a tip on their back rent."

She got to her feet, tossing her hair back. She didn't dare a look at Max, but when she fell, she thought she'd heard the chair scrape, as if he'd lunged against the bonds. Fortunately, no one else had noticed that.

"Sugar, if you're the kind of boy who's into the pain, I can bend you over my knee and have you begging for Mama to give you more."

The other men snorted with laughter. Even Manny's expression eased. As she suspected, it had been a simple dominance gesture, nothing personal to it. "Bathroom's up that way." He pointed to the mezzanine behind Max.

All the better. She sauntered that way, but then she deviated on her track, bending down a couple feet away from Max to tsk him in a mocking voice. "You're having a bad, bad day, sugar, aren't you? Working for Jorge, I could have told you that Dino's the wrong badass to cross."

"Hey, don't be...you knew Jorge?" Manny's gaze sharpened on her.

"Of course." She straightened. "I used to be one of his. I told Leo that. When they cut him up, I came back here. But I wouldn't mind living South of the Border again. One of the reasons this job tonight interested me." She let her gaze pass over all of them. "And why I'm interested in seeing what I can do for Dino to make him appreciate me."

Before they could stop her, she slid on to Max's knee, and ran the tip of her tongue over the blood at his temple. He was still playing unconscious, though he let out a grunt, his head trying to roll away from her as if he was disoriented. She caught his jaw to hold him fast. As she wet her lips with her tongue, she ran a provocative hand under her hair, letting it spill forward onto her breast, taunting him. "Hmm... You taste good, sugar."

She caressed his shoulder, let that hand drop to dig her nails into his bare back, hard enough he flinched, since she found a place they'd already marked. She tightened her grip on his face, turning it so their eyes met. His were in half-slits. "Dino's going to kill you nice and slow for whatever nasty thing you did to him," she chided him. "Shouldn't have done that, you know. Shame. You're a pretty boy. Some mama's going to miss you terrible."

Standing up, she ruffled his hair like a schoolboy's. She licked away the blood on her fingers like cake icing. "You said the bathroom's upstairs?" she asked Manny, her expression bored again.

He shook his head. "Yeah. You're a bit of a twisted bitch, ain't you?"

Janet smiled. She wouldn't have been surprised if there was frost coating her lips. She was made of ice, ice through her veins, even numbing the pain in her cheek. "You have no idea."

She made her way up the mezzanine stairs with lots of hip action sure to draw attention. She heard the men chuckle among themselves, make comments about Dino either being a lucky bastard or one deserving their pity. In her peripheral vision, she could tell Max had lifted his head again. She couldn't look at him. She'd worn the honeysuckle gloss he liked so much, a light layer over her lipstick. He would have smelled it, and she'd left it on his skin, marking him. Hers. He was hers.

When she reached the top of the mezzanine she turned. "Manny, do you mind—"

He looked up at her, and that was when the shot took him straight through the head, accompanied by the plink of broken glass from the window above her left shoulder.

Janet felt time slow down. A stunned expression crossed two of the men's faces in that elongated moment, but the third man never had time to register it. Another shot dropped him. Then things sped up, like a fiery star streaking across the heavens.

Max surged out of the chair, the zip ties on his wrists cut by the short knife she'd given him when she'd trailed her hand down his back, delivering the blade beneath her hair to his waiting hands. He used the blink of time when shock gripped his enemies to cut his ankles free and launch himself. Since the two men were standing next to one another, he hit them like a bowling ball hitting pins. They both went down, but one made a faster recovery. It didn't matter. From where Janet stood, he never had a chance. Max killed him with an eerily efficient blow to his temple. She knew he'd killed him, because when he shoved him away, the man's body fell and rolled face up below the mezzanine. Life died out of his eyes as he stared up at her frozen visage.

The other man bolted, headed for the door. When he got there, it hit him in the face, because Dale bounced the heavy metal off his forehead, dropping him like a stone. Max stopped in mid-pursuit, his expression settling when his former master chief gave him a nod. "All clear. Aaron and Billy took out the guy watching the back entrance."

Janet watched Max brace himself with hands on his thighs, drawing a breath, then he straightened, nodded back. Dale pushed open the door for Neil and Lawrence, who were dragging in an unconscious Leo and his companion, as well as a third man. The man watching the back, she assumed. Marcie and Dana were helping. When Billy and the invisible Aaron didn't come in, she assumed they were continuing to stand watch. Dale confirmed it, touching his earpiece and acknowledging they were in a concealed position outside.

She jumped at the short, crisp puncture sound of three shots, muffled by a silencer, and Lawrence emerged from behind a stack of crates. It was where they'd dragged the three unconscious men. Janet wondered if he'd have done it right there in the open, if "civilians" hadn't been present.

She was feeling intangible, as if her mind was floating above all this. Max was free. She should be running to him. Yet something in her was silent, unresponsive. She stood at the rail, held on to it, stared down at the scene as if she was watching a play.

Dale raised a brow, sweeping a glance over Max's mostly naked body. "You're underdressed. There are women present."

"And one of us can't take advantage of the view, damn it all," Dana said. Though she spoke with her usual sense of humor, her tone was strained. She had her arm around Marcie, and Janet saw Marcie was limping, as if she'd turned her ankle.

"Next time, remind me to wear my hooker Nikes instead of my hooker stilettos," the girl said.

"It was your own fault," Dana snorted. "You just had to be sexy."

"She's got my vote," Neil said. "She looked hot as hell when she throat-punched that guy. Like Kate Beckinsale in latex, only blonder. I like blondes."

"Yeah, don't even try it," Dana advised. "You may be a badass SEAL, but her fiancé is a complete motherfucking psycho. In a really good way, but you still don't want him to think you're hitting on his girl."

There was some more banter back and forth. All with dead bodies lying around them, others executed behind crates. She shifted her gaze back to Dana and Marcie. They seemed fuzzy to her and she focused, harder. Except for the limp and Dana's cut lip, both looked okay, though Marcie was pale and her participation in the banter was more limited. It made sense. The girl was tough, but she probably felt like a rookie cop dealing with her first homicide, up close and personal.

Neil had found Max's clothes, and he'd pulled on the jeans. Dana said something to him, but Janet didn't make out his reply. Marcie reached out to him, touched his bloody shoulder, and he gave her a short, reassuring nod. He was formal, all business though. No time for sentiment or niceties. Not in this place.

"Billy said it looks like Dino's on his way," Dale said, tapping his earpiece. "Boat just pulled up to the dock, and a couple more assholes like these jumped off, tying it up. Looks like he's traveling low key, just him and those two, not wanting to attract attention. He's expecting his reinforcements here. They got him into a car before Billy could pull off a shot, but I figure we don't want to use the sniper option outside this building anyway if we can avoid it. No telling what eyes we got out there. ETA probably five minutes. You want to stay in place, Max, keep him off guard until the last moment?"

Max's eyes were still wild, but Janet could see him pulling it together. It was remarkable that anyone could switch gears that fast, but he did, the muscles across his shoulders rippling as he squared them.

"Yeah, that seems the best play. How you want it to unfold, Master Chief?"

"I think we need to get the civilians, capable as they are, out of harm's way." Dale gestured to Marcie and Dana. "How about you go up there on the mezzanine with Janet? Neil, Lawrence, let's get these bodies up there, prop them up in the office so when Dino first comes in, it'll throw him off."

"Yeah." Max picked up on his line of thinking. "It's a metal building, so he'll think that's why they didn't get his advance call that he'd arrived."

Dale shrugged. "Not foolproof. He may still spook, in which case we have Billy out there, and can go the sniper route. But if he comes into the building, he'll see them up in the office and be ready to hand out an ass whipping, thinking that they aren't watching his back or overseeing the prisoner the way they should. He'll also think the blood on the ground is yours, especially if we go ahead and grab these tarps, throw them down over the worst of it..."

She hadn't thought about phase two. She'd only thought of what would be needed to get Max out of here. But it made sense. It would end here, tonight. Suddenly, she felt sick. Turning, she rushed into the office where Manny had said she'd find the bathroom. Manny who now had a bullet through his head. She made it to the toilet just in time, dropping to her knees over a non-working bowl of dubious cleanliness, but it was better than throwing up on the floor, since that was where she ended up. When she finished, she closed the lid, pushing away from it so she was on her backside against the wall. Hearing Marcie and Dana coming, she scrubbed her hands over her face. *Pull it together. Ice, ice, ice.*

It must be working, since that felt like what she'd thrown up, icy shards gouging out her insides. There was no time for anything, and she hadn't spoken to Max. He hadn't looked toward her. No...no, he had. A quick glance, verifying she was okay. That was all there was time for right now, really. Right? But what if Dino was more prepared than they expected? What if he got off a lucky shot? What if...

"They're coming." Dana came into the bathroom, helping Marcie hop over the threshold. "Dale says we stay down until he gives us the all clear. It should be over pretty quick." She slid down on one side of Janet, Marcie the other, and they each took one of her hands. "Janet, you're so cold, honey." Dana chafed her hand between two of her own, which felt warm as a furnace in contrast. But it was a distant revelation.

"Dana, I didn't talk to him."

"In a few minutes, you're going to have a lifetime to talk to him, and now's not the time. We barely said two words to him either. His head's still in the game. He made sure you were okay, and that's all he's going to process until it's all over. Sshh, now." Dana rubbed her cold fingers some more. "Let me tell you, I wish I'd had eyes to see Marcie drop that piece of shit outside. Hit the ground like a sack of oranges. Girl, you have mad skills."

"Same goes." Marcie squeezed Janet's hand. "Lot of bodies though. I knew...I didn't really expect Lawrence to do that. You know, shoot them like that. I get it, why he did it, but still...too many bodies."

"I know. It's okay. Put it away for now. We deal with it later."

Given how out of it she felt, Janet suspected Dana's firm reassurance was probably directed to both of them. In Marcie's voice, Janet heard what was echoing against her hollow insides. She and Marcie were the only ones not military-trained, and on top of that, Marcie was twenty-three years old. She'd likely never seen a body in her life. Let alone chopped one's head off on purpose.

Janet choked on a giggle that sounded like it should come out of a clown's mouth in a Stephen King novel. She pressed a fist against her lips. *Hold tight, hold tight. Ice, ice, ice.* Like a cheerleader. She'd thought about being a cheerleader in junior high, but dancing consumed her, and she was in a school for the arts before the opportunity presented itself.

Max. Max. Max. She thought of the blood on him, the bruising, the murderous light in his gray eyes. Her hands tightened on Dana's and Marcie's as if she was holding him, but she wondered if imagining it was all she was really capable of doing at the moment. She didn't even feel as if she could lift her arms. Marcie gave her an extra squeeze but then let go, shifting across from them, positioning herself behind the toilet. She had Dana's nine millimeter and cocked it. Though she kept the nose up, her body was angled toward the door. Prepared, just in case.

* * * * *

When Dino came in, he wasn't happy. His gaze flitted over Max, bloody and bound in the chair, barely conscious, the tarps around him spattered with body fluids. That made him feel somewhat better, but his attention shot up to the office where he saw Leo's profile, the other guys bent over a table with him like they were playing cards. Which meant Manny and Javier were jerking off somewhere instead of watching the door. If he didn't kill them, he was at least going to fucking fire them. "Leo," he shouted. "What the hell—"

Max stood, snapping up the muzzle of the gun he'd been holding behind his back. He took out Dino with a tight grouping to the chest, a final one to the head. Dale's shot dealt with the other man. As Max moved to pull the gun from Dino's belt, he sat back on his heels, watched him die. The man gave him a final sneer, but Max saw the fear. Then he was gone. It was done.

Well, the killing was done. It was going to be a hell of a clean-up job. Dale was already on his radio, having Billy and Aaron bring the van to the shipping entrance where they could pull it all the way inside. The scene here would be scrubbed, visible blood washed away, and another layer of grime would cover anything else in no time.

In the meantime, the bodies would be loaded up, taken to the border and dumped where cartel disputes were commonplace. The bullets would be dug out of them. By the time they were found—if they were found—the coyotes would have reduced any forensic evidence to nothing, and it would look like just another dispute between warring drug factions. Maybe it would motivate Dino's crew to take out a bunch of guys from the rival group. A win-win.

"You look like crap," Dale commented. "Way you're moving, I'm betting they cracked a couple ribs."

"Yeah." Even so, Max kept staring down at the body. "I didn't want you all to be part of this. Didn't intend for that."

"Yeah, because you being dead and this POS still being on the loose is a better scenario for everyone. We've saved one another's asses plenty of times. This is just another of those times, bro. The team succeeds where the individual fails, remember?"

Neil nudged Max's haunch with the butt of his rifle while Lawrence gripped him under the arm to give him a lift to his feet. "Don't be such a drama queen, Ack Ack," the shorter man said. "We didn't do it for you. We did it for your hot friends. Too bad they're all taken. Though if you don't stop being such a pussy, the one that's yours is going to start looking at me. I think I already caught her staring at my ass..."

Janet. Oh fuck, Janet. It was like his mind suddenly re-engaged to full throttle, with a painful grinding of gears. He left Dale and Lawrence, was running up those stairs, holding his side to make it as fast as possible. He almost tripped over Marcie at the bathroom door, saw her check the gun with a startled oath.

"All clear," he managed, but he was looking for one person only. Since the bathroom was so small, Marcie did her best to get out of his way gracefully, wiggling past him in the small space to step out into the hallway. Reaching in under his arm, she grabbed hold of Dana's hand, guided her out as Max practically vaulted over the petite black woman to get to Janet.

She was sitting on the floor, looking down at her hands. He remembered that look too well, from the hospital, from the times the past grabbed hold of her and wouldn't let go. He put his hands over hers, covering them. Maybe he shouldn't have, because his had blood smeared on them. Her eyes lifted to his. Held. His Mistress began to cry, but she seemed unaware of it, her gaze so unblinking, tears running down her cheeks, her hands limp inside the grip of his.

"It's over," he said, and he heard the hoarseness in his own voice. Exhaustion would hit him later, along with a lot of pain, because they'd beat on him like a frigging piñata, but for now, there was this. "It's done."

She nodded. "Okay." She started to get up, and when he helped her, he thought she was like a mannequin, stiff and rigid. She shifted her gaze to the door, where Marcie and Dana stood by the mezzanine rail, watching them. "One of you should call Rachel. Tell her we're on our way. Hopefully neither Max nor Marcie will need hospital care, but if you do, we'll figure out what to tell them. Luckily, no one was shot, because the police..." Her voice cracked.

"Janet." Max closed his hands over her shoulders. "Look at me. *Janet.*"

She shook her head, put both palms on his chest. Closed her fingers on his flesh, digging into his chest hair, the chest hair he knew she liked. Then she was tugging, clawing, striking, her face screwing up in pain and rage, like an oncoming tornado.

When Marcie murmured to Dana, and Dana began to step forward, he spoke sharply. "No. Let her go. Get out of here. Let me handle this."

He didn't know how they responded to that, because everything but Janet disappeared for him as she started screaming at him. Incoherent but terrible sounds, accusing, enraged, despairing. She punched at his face, his torso, hitting bruised ribs, but he didn't let her go, kept grimly hanging on as she fought him, hammered on him.

Her screaming became a cry of rage so visceral it reminded him of a savage creature, driven mad by pain. Until one word slipped out. "Why. Why. *Why...*"

Why did she keep ending up to her elbows in blood? Why had any of it happened? Why did he insist on this? He didn't know. All he could do was let her punish him the way she needed to do, until she was sobbing. That one word had broken something inside her. Now he could bring her to his chest, hold her there. Despite the pain she'd just exacerbated, he couldn't imagine any balm sweeter than her body against him, especially as the rage drained from it. But she was still tense, rigid. He held on to her anyway, unable to let go.

"No more, Mistress," he murmured against her hair. "It's done. I'm all yours. I promise. Forever. Long as you want me."

The hard ball in his gut told him there'd be a fuckload of fallout to handle from this night though. He owed all of them, big time. It had been way the hell over a line, even for what SEALs did for each other. And Marcie...Dana. Fuck, Peter and Ben were going to fucking kill him. Matt would take his own piece of flesh for putting Janet in harm's way, no matter that she'd chosen that course herself. To say he was fired was probably going to be the least of it. He might be sharing a shallow grave with Dino.

But she was all right. That was what mattered. His heart had nearly choked him when she'd walked into that warehouse, cool-eyed and calm. It was as if she could put on any mask needed, even that of a sociopathic whore who would taste the blood off his forehead, wiggle her ass against his thigh, while the woman inside that mask, the woman he loved, dropped a knife into his hands.

Now that same woman was shuddering, face pressed to his chest, hands still gripping him there. He wanted to scoop her up, carry her down the steps and out of this place, hold her cradled in his lap until she stopped shaking, but his ribs weren't going to let him do that. He'd probably drop her down the steps, and that was no way to impress a girl.

He'd been in a lot of ops far more intense than this, but this one had been the most personal. She'd warned him of that, hadn't she? But he hadn't expected her to be part of it. They were like two leaves on a thin branch, shaky as hell. Lawrence might be right about the pussy part, at least on Max's side of things. His Mistress had balls of steel.

"Let's get us all to Rachel's," he said. "Though we might have a problem. I think Dana's in the best shape to drive us."

She nodded without a smile, wiped at her nose with her bloodstained knuckles. He pressed a kiss to her forehead, held her close. "You are the most amazing woman I've ever met. And considering the women I know," he thought of his mother, Marcie, Dana, all the K&A women...Amanda, "that's saying something."

She didn't say anything.

Chapter Sixteen

In fact, he might say technically it was the last time she spoke to him. Really spoke to him. Rachel had taped his ribs, recommended an x-ray, which he'd declined. Marcie had a bad sprain, but beyond that and a little bruising that she and Dana had sustained in their scuffle with Leo and his buddy, all was good. When Rachel had turned her attention to Janet, Janet shook her head, that cool look fixed on her face like a vacuum-sealed jar lid. "I wasn't injured."

After a searching look, Rachel had made her tea instead and slipped a warm blanket on her shoulders. She'd also recommended a hot shower and that Janet sleep at her and Jon's place for the night. Janet had accepted the offer with a simple "thank you". Max followed her up the stairs, but at the guest bedroom door Janet turned, her expression anything but welcoming.

"I'm glad you're okay, Max." Though she was staring into his face, he didn't feel like she was connecting to his gaze. It was more like he was transparent, or she was blind like Dana, aware of him but not focused on his features. "But I'll need space for a while. I'll do what I can with Matt."

"I don't care about that. I—"

She shut the door in his face, and he heard the lock turn. He stood there, vibrating with helpless frustration, and turned to see Rachel at the top of the stairs. The blonde with compassionate hazel eyes gestured to him to come back to her, away from Janet's door. "I'll watch over her, Max," she murmured. "I promise. As self-possessed as she seems, she's in shock right now. Overwhelmed. You all saw a lot tonight. Marcie is pretty shook up as well."

"Damn it. Can I—"

"She'll be fine," Rachel assured him. "There's a reason Marcie's a good match for Ben," she added. "The death and killing was new for her, and would put anyone in a tailspin, but she's a Southern girl through and through. Taking out drug dealers to protect someone she considers her family is something she can live with."

But she shouldn't have been put in that position. He understood what Rachel was saying, even agreed with it, knowing what he knew about Marcie. But he also knew exactly what every decent person went through to learn to live with things like that. If he could do it over, he would have made them kill him right off, rather than making her and Dana a part of this. And then there was Janet, who'd been there before, who'd tried to leave it behind... Fuck.

He lowered himself to the top step, not yet willing to be that far from her. Rachel sat down on the step next to him, putting a hand on his shoulder. He felt the strong nurturing vibration in the touch, a woman who was a healer in a lot of different ways, but he was afraid what was wrong with Janet was beyond her influence. "She went through something once, Rachel. Something she got through by locking everything down until it was over. Do you think...can you get stuck that way?"

Rachel's brow creased. "Not knowing her circumstances, I can't say for certain, but if that's what's happening here, you need to give her time to break out of it." She ran a soothing hand down his arm. "I suspect, when things are calmer, she'll come out of it on her own, or you'll have a better sense of how to help her out of it. Tonight is not the night."

"We'd just started..." He looked up toward the closed door and felt the ache of it then. What price had he paid for finally ridding the world of Dino? For settling his need for justice...for vengeance. It had put the woman he loved in the middle of something violent and dangerous, but more than that, he'd put her back into a scenario she'd spent years trying to put behind her, to control her environment and life so bloody chaos wouldn't be part of it anymore. In order for her to get past it again, would he be left behind as a casualty? Christ, she'd been standing right above him when he killed that one guy.

Rachel tightened her grip on his arm. "I know. Give it time, Max. Why don't you bunk down here—"

He shook his head. "I'll go on home. Check in with Dale and see if he needs anything. Truly."

If he stayed, he wouldn't be able to stand it. He'd push, and he remembered what had happened the last time he did that. He knew Rachel was right, even if another part of him howled against it.

He put his hand over hers as she began to protest. "I'm fine, thanks to your nursing skills." He glanced around at the tranquility of the home she and Jon shared. The Japanese maples, the quiet fountains, the clean, simple layout. Clean and simple. Something he hadn't thought about having in so long, and tonight he might have killed any hope for it.

Janet had said he had great intuition. The weight on his chest told him this wasn't just shock for Janet, but something deeper. It brought back the helpless feeling he'd faced when he realized his mother was gone, and Amanda was never going to get any better, barring a miracle.

No. He wasn't losing Janet like that. Even if it had gotten fucked up because of him, he was going to figure out how to fix it.

"I have Dale's truck. I'll take Marcie back to Cass', get it back to him and then head to the office. My vehicle's there." In fact, it was likely he'd sleep in it, unrolling the camo quilt and lulled to sleep by the drip through the parking deck ceiling pipes. Tomorrow was a freaking work day, wasn't it? The guys weren't back until Friday, so it was fairly light duty, unless Janet needed him to run an errand. But he'd lay good money she wasn't going to be back tomorrow either.

* * * * *

She wasn't. In the morning, he decided to go home for a scalding hot shower and half a bottle of aspirin. Headed out of her office, he ran into Randall. The security chief had given the cuts and fist marks on his face a close look, but Max had discouraged questions and the man had fortunately respected his privacy. On the way to his house, Max tried Janet's cell, received no answer. Checking in with Rachel, he found out Janet had gone home about an hour ago. But she'd left him a message — through Rachel.

Jon's wife had hesitated, then delivered the message that even the kindness in her voice couldn't soften. "She asked that you not contact her. For the foreseeable future, she said she needs to go back to the way things were. If she wants to talk to you, she'll let you know."

That weight in his chest became a fucking anvil. He took his shower, sat at his crappy kitchen table, stared out into the yard that was pretty much just bare patches and mowed weeds. Then he wrote up his resignation. He'd said he'd be the one who backed off if the shit hit the fan, right? This was her job, her world. He could make a new world elsewhere, give her the space she needed. And maybe, in time, she'd...

Or maybe not. When all was said and done, he was just a limo driver and a guy who used to be a SEAL. Damn it, he wasn't giving up on her. But all night, when he'd barely slept, he kept seeing her dead eyes, felt her rigid body beneath his hands. He'd done that to her. What right did he have to shove himself in her face right now?

He could have used the resignation as a way to see her, but whatever he decided to do or not do, he knew it was too soon. Instead, he drove out to Matt's house early Saturday morning. He didn't know how Dana and Marcie had spun it, but he understood enough about the Dom/sub thing now, and how deep it ran for them, to know they'd likely told the complete truth to explain the bruises, Marcie's ankle. But honesty didn't always make things better. He'd never lied to Janet about anything, but they'd ended up here anyway, right?

He could have come by Matt's house Monday morning before the K&A CEO left for work, but a soldier didn't dodge his commanding officer, putting off the ass chewing. When he pulled up in the driveway, Matt was sitting in a chair on the side lawn, next to a cup of coffee and the remains of his breakfast. Max didn't see Savannah, but maybe they took turns with the baby's morning routine, letting the other sleep in on weekends. That's what married people did, nice things for each other like that. The way it was supposed to be, right?

Angelica was on a blanket at Matt's feet, playing with some toys. She looked up as he crossed the lawn to them. Matt folded his paper, set it to the side, fixed his gaze on him. No smile of welcome, just those measuring hawk eyes.

Oh yeah. They knew.

Max cleared his throat, extended the envelope. "I'm sorry to disturb your breakfast, sir, but I thought it might be best to get this done first thing. I'm resigning, effective immediately. I brought Wade up to speed on things these past couple days, and I'll be available to him for anything he needs. I know you'll decide who you want in the position, but I figure he's the best to step into my shoes until you do that. He's a good man though. He can handle the job."

Matt put the envelope on top of the paper. Still said nothing. Max forced himself not to squirm.

"Sir. If, at any time, I'd ever thought my presence would endanger a member of your family, I never would have accepted your job offer. I know I should have foreseen it, anticipated it. There's nothing that excuses that lack of judgment, but I wanted you to know it was never an intentional decision."

"I know that, Max."

If someone told Max that Matt Kensington had the ability to laser a man's torso into three pieces with the look he was giving him now, he'd well believe it.

"I'm going, but I need to ask if you've heard from Janet. If she's okay."

Angelica cooed, shook her rattle at Max, but he couldn't summon a smile. Matt took his eye off Max long enough to lean forward, close his fingers gently on the top of the rattle and engage in a playful tug-of-war with her. She beamed at her father, giggled.

Something hard and ugly twisted in Max's chest. He needed to go. He'd find some work in the Baton Rouge area. Amanda's facility was on that side of the outskirts of New Orleans, so the commute back and forth wouldn't be bad. And he was going to take Janet's advice, see if he could integrate more people into her life. Maybe he'd get a nice two-bedroom apartment, talk to Gayle about having Jenny come up and stay with him a couple weeks after her baby came. He could help with the kid, show Jenny a good time around New Orleans and maybe prevent what everyone figured was pretty inevitable, that she didn't have the strength to deal with what her husband was. It wasn't for everyone. But maybe Max could tip the balance, make the impossible seem possible to her.

"Please, sir. I don't have a right to know, I get that, but please make sure Janet's okay. I know you will anyway, but I'm worried this maybe opened up some bad memories for her. She might need someone close to her for a while, and she's not letting me…I'm afraid she won't let me be that person."

It ached like a fucking wound to say it out loud. He wanted to sleep beside her, hold her through the nightmares. Share break time with her, make her smile. Bring that warm flush to her cheeks when he called her Mistress. Give her foot massages that made her moan in that soft, amusing, arousing way…

"Thank you for everything, sir."

He pivoted, a fucking rash burning in his lungs. He'd managed five strides when Matt spoke.

"I spoke to her last night, Max."

Max stopped and turned, heart in his throat. Matt still had the same look, but he was talking about her, so that was fine.

"She indicated that you had no control over their participation—hers, Dana's and Marcie's. Knowing all three of the women in question as we do, we were well aware of that. But she asked, as a personal favor—the second one she's requested from me in all our years together—that there be no repercussions against you, that you keep your job. She also called and spoke to Peter and Ben, making clear what Dana and Marcie, respectively, also made clear to them. That you are not to be blamed for the situation."

"With all due respect, that's bullshit, sir. And I don't hide behind women."

"You'd need to hide behind your SEAL team if I relayed that second comment to them." Though the comment was dry, nothing about Matt's visage suggested humor. "But I agree with your first one. You understand there are consequences to your actions that no friend, foe or family member can exonerate. Which I expect explains this." He put his hand on the resignation, and his gaze sharpened, such that Max almost did feel the laser cut of it across his sore ribs. "You understand our code. That no matter what was outside of your control, three women I consider mine to protect, two of whom also belong to men of my family, were put at serious risk because of your situation."

"Yes sir."

"That, should anything about this matter ever come to light, they are accomplices to murder."

He'd cop to the death of every one of those bodies under oath to take the full heat of that, but that wasn't Matt's point. Max nodded again, swallowing hard.

Matt inclined his head. "I accept your resignation. For now."

Max blinked. "Excuse me, sir?"

"If you accept the consequences of your actions, then you accept responsibility for healing what you've injured. My trust, the trust of my team. Janet's heart. You're used to situations where you go on missions, and then you come back home, two totally different theaters. When you were pursuing Dino, you weren't in that kind of vacuum. You built relationships. Dana, Marcie and Janet all came into that situation because that is what happens when you create a family. They would no more allow you to face what you faced alone than you would have allowed them to do so if they faced something similar."

That same nail, being hammered into his head once again. Hadn't Janet as much as said that to him? *This isn't a mission environment. This is your life.*

"So I understand the guilt you are carrying," Matt continued, "likely far better than they do. You know it was your fault that they were there. However, the answer is not abandoning your family. We know what lengths you'll go to avenge them. Show me what you'll do to keep them, heal them. Now, come shake my daughter's rattle to prove to her that she utterly captivates every person who sees her. I only have a few more weeks to spoil her. Then she'll be walking and she'll have to learn about rules and manners."

Max dutifully came back across the grass. When he squatted by the blanket, he managed a stiff smile as Angelica looked at him with her mother's liquid blue eyes. But the dark hair, the determination in her delicate features, that was Matt. She was going to be a scary heartbreaker. He touched her small hand, and she ended up being the one who shook the rattle at him, which made her burst into another fit of baby laughter that couldn't help but make him smile a little more naturally, despite the ache it increased in his chest.

He looked down at the design of the baby quilt. There was embroidery on every other panel, a mouse and rabbit dancing together in a field of flowers on one, taking a nap together in another, and so forth. Between each panel was a quilted blue square. With all the horrible things he'd seen, it always bemused him that such things existed in the same dimension, let alone on the same planet. He wondered how long Janet had felt like that after Jorge. Probably quite awhile. And he'd driven that schism back into her world again.

"I don't know how to break through, sir," he said miserably. "She's shut me out. It's like an ice wall. I could go beat on her door, force her see me, but I know that's not going to break it." She'd just stand behind that wall of ice and stare at him, tell him to go away. "I know it's only been a day, but I know what my gut tells me. Something's really wrong, something that time's not going to help." Or at least, by the time it got resolved, she'd have him completely cut out of her life. If he wasn't a selfish bastard, he'd accept it, accept she was maybe better off without him, but he couldn't let go of her. He just couldn't.

"I've been around SEALs for a while, Max. First through my father's acquaintances, and then you. The one thing I know is you don't give up. You figure out how to win, and there's no strategy you leave unturned. So figure it out. If you can't break the ice, melt it."

Angelica had hold of one of Max's fingers now and was examining it with great interest. Keeping himself in her grasp, Max looked over his shoulder at the CEO. "Any intel to help with that, sir?"

Matt was totally within his rights to tell him to go to hell, he knew it, but Max wasn't above pressing an advantage. The CEO gave him a cool look. "You know her vulnerabilities, her needs, Max. You know the way in. The question is to what lengths you'll go to get there, what sacrifices you'll make. That's what it's always about. The willing sacrifices we make for those we love."

Matt picked up his paper, indicating their meet was at an end. Giving the baby a brief stroke of her absurdly soft hair, Max straightened. "Thank you, sir."

Matt offered one more of those withering glances before he shifted his attention back to the financial section. "Be aware—at some point, Peter and Ben are planning to subject you to a vast amount of blunt-force trauma. On general principle."

"Roger that, sir."

* * * * *

When gathering intel, there were a lot of routes to take. He made a few test runs, trying to shake something out. He didn't respect her request about contacting her, at least at a distance. He texted her. He left messages on her phone. He sent her flowers, whimsical trinkets. Small gifts and gestures that he hoped she received, because he received no response. Not to any of it.

He was certain the key was in his mind, in what he knew of her. She was a Mistress. Not necessarily the hardcore, whips and leather boots Dominatrix type, but there was a core to her that was about possessing another, winning their trust and surrender. Had he damaged that trust? What had happened that night to shut her down so firmly? Since he continued to volunteer at Dana's church, he learned from the blind woman that Janet was back at work and doing her job as efficiently as ever.

"But it's different. Alice says it's like she's on autopilot. Right smiles, right catty remarks at the right moment, but no feeling. Like a doll. Matt's tried to talk to her, and so have I. She just says she's fine, smiles and squeezes my hand like I'm worrying over nothing, and then Janet-bot goes back to work. Matt would push harder but…"

Dana had paused then, her blind eyes searching for something, but Max filled in the blank.

"He knows that's my job. He's waiting for me to figure it out. Figure her out."

He had plenty enough money to live on for a while, so rather than seeking another job, he'd thrown himself into more demanding projects at Dana's church, helped Dale landscape several of his neighbors' yards, and continued his regular visits with Amanda.

He also took Dale to see her, as well as Lawrence. Janet had been right, no surprise there. Amanda was initially wary, but just as she'd demonstrated with Janet, she seemed to gravitate toward those who had a strong connection to him, almost as if they bore his scent or some piece of his soul. In Janet's case, that was the truth.

He was going fucking insane. He missed her like a vital organ, as cliché and stupid as that sounded. It was still as true as a knife blade plunged in the right place was fatal. No ifs, ands, buts or passing go.

You know the way in...

The purpose of the hellish first few weeks of BUD/S training was to ensure full commitment. To verify that each man had what it took to not only endure but accomplish the missions they would face. They were broken down, subjected to unimaginable levels of physical and psychological hardship. Maybe to get into the head of a Mistress, figure her out, he had to do the same, so to speak.

He knew he had a good body, fit, hard, the kind that drew women's eyes. With the right look and attitude, he could take a deeper step into her world, see if he could figure it out from the inside. She'd taught him the way of it, the mannerisms, the codes.

So Friday night, he shaved and cleaned himself up, slapping on a light cologne. He put himself in a pair of black jeans, a snug T-shirt, boots. Then he gave himself a critical once-over in his cracked mirror—lucky he wasn't superstitious, at least not that way—and took a breath. He was going to Club Progeny. Time to use that guest membership again. On his own this time.

* * * * *

Janet sat out on her balcony, watching the evening dogwalkers go by on the sidewalk. Poodle...English Springer Spaniel...Great Dane. She'd thought about getting a dog at one time, but she had a feeling she and a cat would see more eye to eye on things. For almost a year, a feral tom had been hanging around for the scraps she gave him. Sometimes, in the heat of summer, he'd lain in her bird bath to cool off, the mockingbirds fussing at him from the trees.

She looked at the book she hadn't cracked open tonight, though her hand rested on it with intent. But she knew if she started it, she'd look blindly at the words and not internalize the story. No point. The routine of getting up, going to work, handling things for K&A and the domestic requirements of her house—that was all she was in the mood to do of late.

Yes, something was wrong, but she'd been here before. After she came to the States, after Matt helped her get out of Mexico, she'd been this way for months. It had taken awhile to break out of it, but one day, she had. She'd started to feel, rather than pretending to feel. She'd embraced the pleasure and freedom of that. But she wasn't sure what the catalyst had been then, any more than she could anticipate what would do it now.

When she laid her head back on the chair, closed her eyes, Max filled that darkness. His scent, his body, his steady gray eyes. Camping with her, lying on his truck. Before she could get much further than that, though, she saw chains hanging from a ceiling, his bruised and battered body slumped over in a chair. The distant, cold intent in his eyes when he killed the man just beneath her, his expression when he came to her, to tell her it was over, that it was done. The mission was done. He'd be dealing with that feeling now, what to do, where to go from here.

She'd been there as well. When a goal that big was accomplished, a person died a little death. They had to resurrect themselves to embrace the future. But she couldn't deal with that. She couldn't sustain any good memory to get past the bad one, so it was like Jorge. She had to package it all up, box it away. Put it away. Let it go.

She pressed her fingertips to burning eyes and took a swallow of the wine she'd poured herself. She might need something stronger tonight, and thought about cracking open some of the rich bourbon she had for holidays. Just a shot glass should be enough to put her to sleep.

Her cell phone buzzed. She kept it with her, despite the fact she deleted all of Max's texts without reading them, the voicemails without listening to them. She couldn't go that route, had to box him up with all the rest.

She glanced at it and her brow furrowed. She had an excellent memory for numbers, but she had to stretch to recognize that one, since she'd only dialed it once in her life. Dale. It was Dale. Was Max calling from Dale's phone, hoping to get her to pick up? No, he wasn't like that.

She flipped open the phone. "Dale?" She tried to make her voice sound cordial, pleasant. Detached. Like she hadn't shared an evening of murder and mayhem with him and his impromptu SEAL team.

"I'm down at Progeny, Janet. Max has signed up for a session with Mistress Sue. I called up the form he submitted on himself for Dom review. He's representing himself as a Level Ten. No holds barred on pain, no limits in terms of being shared with other Doms or subs. Male or female."

"Within two seconds of being around him, no Mistress in her right mind will believe that shit."

"He has the training to do and be whatever's necessary to get the job done," Dale said evenly. "And you know no one can stretch a Level Ten like Sue. She'll break him down like a set of Legos."

"If he thinks…"

"He doesn't know I'm calling you. I think he's trying to figure things out about you. Like BUD/S training. Full immersion. So this call is a lot like the one you made to me a few weeks ago. Max may be in trouble. If that concerns you, you have until ten o'clock to make an appearance and do something about it. That's when his session with her is scheduled to start."

* * * * *

She waffled, she struggled with herself. Getting dressed to go to the club almost defeated her. She didn't want to leave her solitude, the comfort of her nest. By the time she appeared in the foyer of Club Progeny, it was quarter to ten. She'd wasted five more minutes debating on whether she was going to get out of the car. She was angry at Dale for calling her, angry at Max for doing this. She was just angry, but in a passive, badger-down-its-hole way. She wanted someone to stick their hand within biting range so she could take off a few fingers, almost as much as she wanted to stay unmolested.

Dale was watching for her in the public sitting area visible from the lobby. She showed her ID to the hostess, barely pausing for the hand stamp before she came to him. He was alone, so to speak. A female submissive knelt on the floor next to him, her head on his knee while he stroked her hair. She was still perspiring from the session they'd shared, the lash marks on her bare back and pretty buttocks visible because she was naked except for a silver collar and leash. She was holding on to his leg as though she couldn't let go. Since she seemed to be spiraling down from an intense subspace, Janet had a feeling his leg was her anchor.

The sight of the girl's devotion, her response to Dale's mastery of her, made things clutch in Janet's throat, her stomach start to hurt. No, she wasn't ready to feel. Was she? Or maybe she should have come here sooner. But not when Max was here. Not like that.

"Public floor," Dale said, nodding in that direction.

"Janet's gaze sharpened on him. "You said ten o'clock. It's not ten."

"I called you at eight. He approached Sue about letting him 'warm up' for her, and she obliged him. She's had him on display for an hour."

Though there was no reproach in Dale's tone, Janet felt guilty. It irritated her tremendously. Max made his own choices. He didn't know she was here. She had no need to rescue him. It wasn't like anything unsafe would happen to him. He was just going to learn that a hardcore Mistress was no one to fool with. To fool, period. If Sue thought he was Level Ten that's how she'd treat him, unless he used a safe word. And the chances of that happening...

Setting her jaw, Janet went toward the public floor. Dale motioned to a slim Goth sub in dog collar and stressed jeans. The young man came over immediately. "Yes Sir?"

"Noah, watch over Debbie for a few minutes. I need to handle something."

"Absolutely." Noah slid into the booth on the other side. Dale shifted his charge across the floor with easy strength, transferring her hands to Noah's leg with tender firmness. Debbie blinked at both of them hazily, and Dale touched her face. "It's all right. You stay with Noah and behave for him. I wouldn't want to have to whip you again."

"No, Master."

Noah resumed stroking her head, just as Dale had been doing. He'd probably be cuddling her on his lap like a kitten when Dale got back. The boy had a wide nurturing streak. He could also use his vibrating tongue stud with diabolical effectiveness. Maybe he'd have Debbie suck him off while Noah lay on his back between her spread knees and took her to the screaming edge of a climax. Dale's focus had been taking Debbie into that subspace zone, rather than coming himself, but a release would feel damn good.

First things first though. Best to stay close at hand to prevent a possible homicide. Max had done something misguided, but Dale didn't think it was a capital offense. Janet might feel otherwise, and he suspected her ire was going to be like an IED — aimed at anyone who tripped her wire.

Janet slid through the crowd. She didn't have to go far to find Max. He was the subject of a lot of attention. Sue had him in a full headmask, only the mouth open to allow breath. That explained the rigid state of his muscles. He was surrounded by people, noises, things he couldn't identify, and she had him bound face forward — legs, arms, torso and throat — against one of the cages.

Inside the cage was a trio of female subs, dressed in strips of black leather and lots of black eye makeup that made them look like a trio of succubae straight from Lucifer's harem. Six hands were greedily caressing his flesh, two of the women on their knees to nip, lick and suck his cock. With his hips strapped firmly to the cage bars, he had no ability to pull back, and his buttocks were flexing in helpless struggle against their stimulation. There was a big ring around the base of his shaft to keep him from coming, but Sue also had a vibrating dildo shoved up his ass, tormenting him further.

Max had never taken anything up his ass but the slim probe she'd used with Rita. What was inside him now had the girth of a well-endowed male, so Janet knew it had to be burning like a son of a bitch, no matter how much lube Sue had used to ease it in properly.

Every visible muscle in his neck, shoulders, back, ass and legs was tense as a board. Not like a sub fighting against the inevitable, but like Prometheus grimly chained on his rock, being disemboweled by an eagle. Could Sue not see it? Of course she probably could, but as long as he wasn't using the safe word, and he was in no physical danger, there'd be nothing to trigger ending it.

The Mistress in question, a voluptuous woman in a short black bob wig and beautifully tailored red corset, was sitting nearby, playing with the cock of a handsome slim man she'd bound onto a wheel while an additional submissive slowly rotated him, Sue had volunteers playing a game of rings with his erect member. Anyone who succeeded was given a prize, little trinkets. Sue was a versatile and creative Mistress. Janet curled her lip.

As Janet suspected, Sue was keeping a careful eye on Max, but she wasn't seeing what Janet was seeing. However, she was a good enough Domme to pick up weird vibes, because Janet noted Sue was keeping that eye trained on him even a little more closely than usual.

Dale had called it immersion, like BUD/S training, trying to figure out what Janet needed. Maybe that was part of it, but as Janet shifted to view Max's profile, she recognized it as more than that. This was penance. Max had put Level Ten because he wanted everything Sue could dish out. When the real session started, Janet would lay money he'd push the voluptuous Mistress until she'd done everything to debase and humiliate him. He was punishing himself.

No one but his Mistress had the right to do that.

Goddamn Dale, goddamn Max and goddamn herself, for this frozen wasteland of her heart. But when Sue glanced at the clock and rose, reaching for her single tail, Janet was already pushing through the crowd toward her.

Sue had just positioned herself on the platform, within range of Max's unmarked back, when Janet stepped on to the platform with her, shifting between the two of them. "You're not going to touch him," Janet said. "Not now, not ever."

Max's head snapped around as much as his bonds would allow, but Janet ignored the reaction, her attention on the other Mistress. She knew it wasn't Sue's fault, that the woman hadn't done anything wrong, but it didn't make the threat in Janet's voice any less vehement, the emotions surging forth in her breast any less violent.

Sue blinked, brought the single tail down. "Mistress J," she said carefully. "I'm sorry, what..."

Dale appeared at Sue's side. Resting his hand lightly on the boning at her waist, he spoke in her ear. Janet stood there, vibrating with...rage, anguish...she didn't know what. She spun around, eyed the three subs in the cage. "Get back. Get away from him. Now."

They complied immediately, lifting their hands like they'd been caught at a crime scene. She shot a glance at the nearest staff member, an assistant to Mistress Sue. It was one of the perks provided to her, since her public scenes were a major draw at the club. "Take everything off him but the headmask and collar. I need a private room."

She didn't know what Dale said to Sue, or what they said to the dungeon master who'd appeared to see what was happening, but after a moment Dale gave her a nod, indicating that she was going to get the private room she wanted. Then a snarled oath, a strangled groan, jerked her attention away from him and back to Max.

When the staff attendant removed the vibrating plug and the cock ring, Max was too close to the edge. Just that bare amount of stimulation pushed him into orgasm.

He caught hold of the cage bars, the force of his reaction driving him down to one knee. His hips jerked as he spewed into the condom that had been rolled onto him. Since he wore the mask, she couldn't see his face, but from the rigidity of his torso, she imagined the rictus of mortification, his embarrassment. All in all, he was a fairly private man. Yet he'd subjected himself to this. The complete moron.

It broke her heart open, and the pain of it nearly drove her to her knees. She moved to stand between him and the crowd, an ineffectual screen but one that allowed her to put a hand on his nape. He shuddered under her touch, and she knelt over him, her lips on his shoulder, her arm over his chest. She sheltered him, told him with the press of her body she was here, and she was the only one who mattered.

When he was done, his head was hanging low, mouth against her forearm, chest heaving. She slid away and he caught her wrist blindly.

"Let go of me, Max," she ordered, her voice harsh. His fingers slipped away reluctantly, his mouth tight.

She took a tether from the staff member, clipped it to the wide collar around his throat. His body was quivering like a plucked bow string. Putting her hand on his chest, she exerted enough pressure to make him rise on shaky legs.

"Follow me," she said.

She took him through the watching crowd, away from the main floor. They'd believe it had been orchestrated as part of the scene, and that was fine. No one knew what was truth or fantasy here except the Dom and sub, and sometimes the staff. But in the end, truth and fantasy always overlapped.

The room they'd given her was a small one, probably the only one available on this busy night. It had nothing but a chair and a sink. A Picasso-style mural on the wall showed a primitive and colorful scene of copulation between whimsically distorted human figures. She guided him down into the chair, unsnapped the tether and stepped away from him, placing herself against the wall. His head tilted, following her movements through the scrape of her boots on the tile floor.

The chair wasn't a good idea, for the moment she saw him in it, she was transported to the warehouse again, seeing him slumped down, sitting under those dangling chains. She could tell his ribs were still tender, but the bruising was gone. The knife cuts were now pink, shiny scars.

"I want to take off the mask," he said thickly.

"You'll leave it on until I say so," she said. "What the hell was this? What were you trying to prove?"

When his lips tightened again in stubborn reaction, her anger surged forth, hot and uncontrolled. It was out of proportion with the moment, but she didn't care. She took a step forward and swung at his face, a sharp slap.

He caught her wrist before she could draw back. He dragged her onto his lap, holding her stubbornly while she squirmed against his hold. He just held her tighter, pressing his face against her flesh. She hated the feel of the mask. Finding the fastener, she unlocked it, unzipped the back and yanked it free of his flushed face, his spiked short hair.

"Let go of me."

"No," he said, holding her even tighter. "No, Mistress. I won't. I can't."

"Stop it." She shouted at him, struggled harder, hitting him wildly like she had that night. He kept his face pressed to her breasts to protect his eyes, so she didn't realize he was answering her until she felt the force of his hot breath through her shirt, the vibration of the words.

"No. Don't. Don't. Please. Janet. Don't do this."

"What?" She jerked his face up with trembling hands. "Do what? What the hell am I doing to *you*?"

He looked away. When he did, the tears he was struggling to keep from falling glinted, driving into her heart like shards of clear glass. "Just don't," he said miserably.

She fought for control, to make some sense of her rage, the storm within her. "Tell me," she said. "Goddamn you."

He closed his eyes, and she couldn't help herself. She gripped his face, pressed her forehead hard against his. "No. I didn't mean it. Tell me. Just tell me."

When he spoke, it was a low rumble, a half breath, like it was cracking his ribs all over again just to say it. She shifted her head so her cheek was pressed to his and he was speaking into her ear, each of them staring at the opposite wall. If there were mirrors, they would have seen endless versions of themselves.

"I came home," he said, "and there was no home. My sister was there, but she was no longer... We'll never be able to connect, love one another the same way. If I ruined that for us, Janet, if you're... I'd do anything to go back to that day."

He drew his head back, stared at her. His gray eyes were raw, tormented, and she found looking at them was like looking at the sun. Too bright and painful, risking permanent damage, but she couldn't look away. "There's this diving term we use. 'Reset point'. It's when you choose a familiar underwater object to orient yourself if you lose direction. I realized — too late — that you're that point for me."

He swallowed. "If I could do it over, I'd say the hell with the code, my need for vengeance or justice. I'd just make sure I never sent you to that place in your head that's beyond where I can reach you. I need you, Mistress. I love you. Come back to me. Please."

Just like that, the catalyst happened. An almost audible snap as everything tore loose, like a dam giving way. She hadn't figured out what broke her out of that self-imposed prison last time, but there was no doubt what had done it this time. Max.

His voice broke. She found herself wrapping her arms as tightly as she could around his head and shoulders, curving her body against his. And he reciprocated, banding his arms around her, rocking them both, because now she was crying too. The ice was thawing, even as it was cutting her, hurting her.

But she was tough, tougher than anyone had ever expected, right? She wouldn't let herself *not* love this man, this man who was afraid he'd lost her. But things were tender, painful, bleeding. She didn't...she couldn't pull it together.

"I couldn't breathe, I couldn't feel, Max. I don't know why...I wasn't trying to punish you. You didn't do anything wrong."

"Yes, I did. I forgot the most important mission. Protecting the people I love, giving them everything they need. Amanda, you." His voice stayed thick, even as he lifted his head so his gray eyes locked on hers. "There's this thing we learn called counterinsurgency techniques—COIN. It's when you learn that taking out a target or kicking in a door isn't always the best route. Sometimes it's getting the village kids candy or playing soccer with them, or helping their moms or grandparents rebuild a door that got kicked in on a raid. You defeat the enemy by winning the hearts of people who have dealt with too much death and loss, show them there's some other way, showing yourself there's another way. I should have seen there was some other way."

"No." She shook her head. "Max, you can't regret something like that. You were right. He won't harm anyone else. That has to be worth something."

"But it's not worth losing you. I'm sorry, Mistress. I won't fail you again. Just don't go away from me like that. It fucking killed me, these past few weeks...seeing you so far away, though you were so close..."

"Stop, stop, stop..." She rained kisses on his eyes, his wet lashes, his nose, his forehead, the strong jaw, and then she landed on his lips and held there, a deep, drowning kiss, filled with soft whimpers and needy moans.

Touch me, she thought, and he put his hands on her back, sliding down to her hips and up again, as if he was trying to touch her everywhere at once.

"I need to be inside of you. Please."

Don't ask, show me. Make me feel how badly you want me. Don't just melt the ice. Turn me into a fucking tropical ocean.

Again, she spoke not a word, but within the first second of the thought, he was out of the chair, holding her by the waist with one arm, his hand plunged into her hair. He held the strands so tightly they pulled against her scalp while he dove even deeper into the kiss. He dropped to one knee and she kept her legs around him. When he shifted, for one breathless moment he was holding her parallel with the ground, her body wrapped around his torso, his one arm and his knees holding them both. Then he'd laid her down beneath him.

She hadn't dressed up, merely donning her last set of work clothes, a modest skirt and blouse combo, a pair of low-heeled boots. He tore open her blouse, doing the same to the bra beneath in one powerful motion.

He descended on her bared breasts, licking and biting, then fell to a deep suckling, as if he was nourishing himself from the contact. She bucked up against him, scoring him with her nails, drawing blood. He put his other hand between them, found her panties beneath her rucked-up skirt and yanked the crotch aside, tearing the seams as he drove into her.

He was rutting stag hard, and she squeezed her legs tight around him, welcoming the deep pain and pleasurable agony as he plunged, thrusting so hard he was moving them on the tile floor. She would hurt tomorrow, but it wouldn't matter. It would be the best kind of aching.

"Don't go away...mine...Mistress..."

"No. I won't. I won't." She made the whispered oath against his flesh, her tears pressed against his skin. He felt them, because he slowed down. Seating himself even deeper, he lifted up enough to frame her face and kiss each tear away with slow, tender precision. Which caused more tears for him to kiss away. Those gray eyes gazed upon her in a you're-everything-to-me way that could melt even a Dragon Lady's heart.

He was finding his center again, that rock steadiness she needed. She was part of that center now. He'd made that clear, and yet he'd become the same for her. She couldn't have found her way out of the ice without him. He'd done it in a shocking, quick and brutal way, exposing himself to this, but that wasn't the miracle. It was how seeing him under another woman's touch, how the first grip of his hands on Janet's body, had simply smashed that ice as if it would never have the power to hold her again. Not against her need for him. She was reeling from it. Reaching up, she touched his face.

What happened when two sides surrendered everything to one another, when the love became more important than anything else? Maybe they found their own special paradise, peace in a sometimes ugly, scary world. She held that thought to herself, even knowing he'd probably agree with it. She didn't hold her next thought to herself though.

"I love you, Max. Endlessly, totally, completely."

As he pressed his face against her neck, a great sigh raised his shoulders. It settled his weight upon her, but she didn't mind. He didn't let it become too much, anyway, lifting up within a few breaths to begin moving inside her again. As he did, he slid an arm around her waist, palmed her buttock so that he handled most of the movement, most of the effort. His eyes glowed with heated pleasure as her cries became more insistent, her body arching to his, her hands gripping his biceps.

"Come with me, Mistress."

She did, going over that edge with him. Even as they fell, she knew they'd find that peace and paradise they'd never expected to find alone. But together, the impossible became possible.

When they got their breath back, were ready to fly again, she was going to kiss every inch of his wonderful muscled skin, every inch she thought she might have lost, and she wouldn't stop until…

Fuck it. She wasn't ever going to stop.

Epilogue
One month later

ஐ

"So if he chickens out of this thing, do I still get to keep the gifts?" Marcie eyed the pile of opened packages for her and Ben's engagement party. "That single-cup coffeemaker alone is worth marrying him."

"I can get it for you at a discount, then you don't need him at all," Lucas advised. Ben shoved at his shoulder.

"Way to have a brother's back."

Janet smiled at them as Ben brought Marcie to his side. The engaged couple enjoyed a warm kiss, followed by a moment of intent adoration. The two of them were so obviously wrapped up in one another it was bound to incite reaction from Marcie's younger brother.

"I am *so* going to puke," Nate said, emulating a gag.

The family gathering was assembled out on the large sun porch at Lucas and Cass' house. Sitting on the foot piece of a lounge chair, Janet felt Max's hand brush between her shoulder blades. She glanced back at him. He straddled the chair right behind her, his knees splayed to accommodate her hips. Her hand rested on his knee. He had a beer balanced on the other one, but his eyes on her were warm, promising.

He knew exactly what he did to her when he looked at her like that.

"Behave," she murmured, trying to look stern. "Or I'll make you go sit in the car."

"Yes ma'am," he chuckled. Leaning forward, he pressed his lips to her shoulder. She turned her face to his forehead as he did it, held there, even realizing the two of them looked no less besotted than the guests of honor. And it hadn't escaped notice.

"Oh God, it's contagious. Now I'm going to puke too!" Ben made the same noises as Nate. The teenager barked with laughter as the K&A lawyer pretended to throw up behind Marcie. She shoved at him and aimed a slap at Nate, which he dodged.

"Keep it up, boys, and I'll take back that single-cup coffeemaker," Janet threatened.

As laughter swept the room, Janet looked around at all of them. Matt and Savannah sat across from them on a loveseat, Angelica asleep at Matt's foot in her portable cradle. Jon and Rachel were next to them, Jon on a chair, Rachel sitting at his feet, ostensibly to stroke and coo at the baby, but also because Rachel enjoyed subtle signs of her submission to him, something that brought her peace.

In fact, in this room, Janet saw many examples of how peace had been found, demons had been laid to rest. Ben probably fought the most in that regard, and yet she'd never seen him look so happy. Lucas and Cass could see it as well, such that the worry Marcie's older sister had held about Ben was decreasing. Ben was going to be okay. Love could do that.

Her gaze shifted to Peter and Dana. The big man who bore a distinct resemblance to Max was sprawled in a large easy chair and Dana was balanced on the wide arm. She'd pulled her bare feet up onto it and crossed them at the ankles, Peter's arm snug around her hips, keeping her steady. It was hard to believe not too long ago Dana had come back from Iraq broken in body and mind, wishing she'd died in the explosion that had taken her sight. Now she was a fully ordained minister, already beloved by her congregation, and of course she did the impossible—reconciled that identity with her need to be Peter's hardcore brat submissive, challenging and loving his Mastery of her.

Janet's gaze went back to Matt, to find her boss's attention on her. She expected his mind was on something similar, because those dark eyes smiled. He lifted his drink in a subtle gesture of affection to her. He was pleased with her happiness, and his regard for her, his care, was obvious in his expression. She swallowed. *Thank you.*

He shook his head at the silently mouthed words and rose, leaving Rachel and Savannah overseeing his daughter. When he bent to Janet, he brushed a kiss over her mouth. His murmured words to her were covered by the animated discussions of the others.

"You deserve happiness, Janet. You both do." When his attention shifted, including Max, her man pressed against her back, his hands lingering on her hips.

"We're all your family here," Matt said. "Don't ever forget that, and you'll never be lost again."

* * * * *

After they left Lucas and Cass' house, Max drove her out to a deserted road that gave them a vantage point to watch planes taking off at the New Orleans airport. Amused, she saw him pull a cooler out from the back of the truck. Flipping it open, he offered her a wine chiller and popped open another beer. Then he laid out a generous display of truffles, cheese and other treats from the party.

"Does Marcie know you made off with these?"

"Only if you tell. And if you eat any, you're an accomplice."

"Hmm. Blackmailer." She picked up a truffle, tasted it, closed her eyes. "My God, Ben can cook. He really should run a restaurant." Then she leaned over, eyes still closed. Max slid the food out of the way so he could bring her up against his side, give her the kiss she was wanting. She tasted the flavor of the beer, enjoyed it with the truffle, the scent of Max wrapping around her.

"So why do you come out here?"

He settled back against the windshield, shifting her between his thighs, cradling her. She rested her hand on his belt, idly tracing it, tugging at his dress shirt. Her ribs were pressed against his groin, and she liked the interested reaction she was getting there. It might be nice to make love here, while the planes went overhead. She wondered if the pilots would be able to see them, though she expected they weren't close enough.

"Sometimes when I close my eyes, I imagine I'm up in the sky, about to do a HALO jump," he said. "I remember the way it felt, leaping out of that plane, seeing the curve of the earth for a few seconds... It's a lot like I feel when you climax around me, when I see you get lost in it."

She tilted her head to look up at him. He had his eyes closed now. "You think about it?" he asked.

"Jumping out of a plane? Or climaxing with you? Hell no to the first, all the time to the second."

He smiled. "Getting married."

She hadn't expected that, and something tilted in a not-so-unpleasant way at the thought. Still, she kept her tone casual. "Sometimes. If some ancient Saudi sheikh asked me, and I could figure out a way to off him pretty fast and take all his money."

He cracked an eyelid, considered her. "You'd probably need an accomplice to pull that off. I'd take a fifty-fifty cut. We could go hide out in Belize together."

"Sixty-forty. I'm the one that has to sleep with him."

"Can I have fifty-fifty if I agree to sleep with him too?"

"Idiot." She looked up as the next plane passed overhead, found his hand. When his fingers curled around hers, she turned her head, let it rest on his shoulder. "Yes. I've thought about it. But only recently. Which means I need a *lot* more time to think about it."

"I'll be around. But just so you know, for you I might even endure a cold shower. You can ask Dale—to a SEAL, that's the ultimate sacrifice."

"I will be asking him, so you better not be lying."

His lips brushed her temple then he touched her jaw, tilted her face up so that he could put his mouth on hers, a slow, deep, drugging kiss that had her sinking into the hold of his arms as he slid both around her. Cradled in his arms, held between his thighs, his heart thumping steadily against hers where she lay against his chest...there was no better place to be.

When he at last broke the kiss, she stared up into his gray eyes, so serious and intent on her face.

"I'm already yours, Mistress. You want to make it formal, today, tomorrow or when I'm as old as that sheikh, I'll be here. You ever want to cut me loose..."

Her fingers were on his mouth in an instant, stopping his words.

"No. I never do. I never will."

His lips curved in that sexy, slow smile. She wasn't one for rash or impulsive declarations, and while this felt like both, the rarity of it reflected her true, deepest feelings. She would marry him. They both knew it, though neither one said it.

She lay back down in his arms. They watched the planes come and go, both of them content to be silent, holding the precious weight of truth...and each other.

Also by Joey W. Hill

eBooks:

Chance of a Lifetime
Choice of Masters
If Wishes Were Horses
Knights of the Board Room: Afterlife
Knights of the Board Room: Board Resolution
Knights of the Board Room: Hostile Takeover
Knights of the Board Room: Willing Sacrifice
Make Her Dreams Come True
Nature of Desire 1: Holding the Cards
Nature of Desire 2: Natural Law
Nature of Desire 3: Ice Queen
Nature of Desire 4: Mirror of My Soul
Nature of Desire 5: Mistress of Redemption
Nature of Desire 6: Rough Canvas
Nature of Desire 7: Branded Sanctuary
Snow Angel
Threads of Faith
Virtual Reality

Print Books:

Behind the Mask *(anthology)*
Enchained *(anthology)*
Faith and Dreams
Hot Chances *(anthology)*

If Wishes Were Horses
Knights of the Board Room: Afterlife
Knights of the Board Room: Hostile Takeover
Nature of Desire 1: Holding the Cards
Nature of Desire 2: Natural Law
Nature of Desire 3: Ice Queen
Nature of Desire 4: Mirror of My Soul
Nature of Desire 5: Mistress of Redemption
Nature of Desire 6: Rough Canvas
Nature of Desire 7: Branded Sanctuary
Virtual Reality

About Joey W. Hill
☙

I've always had an aversion to reading, watching or hearing interviews of favorite actors, authors, musicians, etc. because so often the real person doesn't measure up to the beauty of the art they produce. Their politics or religion are distasteful, or they're shallow and self-absorbed, a vacuous mophead without a lick of sense. From then on, though I may appreciate their craft or art, it has somehow been tarnished. Therefore, whenever I'm asked to provide personal information about myself for readers, a ball of anxiety forms in my stomach as I think: "Okay, the next couple of paragraphs can change forever the way someone views my stories." Why on earth does a reader want to know about me? It's the story that's important.

So here it is. I've been given more blessings in my life than any one person has a right to have. Despite that, I'm a Type A, borderline obsessive-compulsive paranoiac who worries I will never live up to expectations. I've got more phobias than anyone (including myself) has patience to read about. I can't stand talking on the phone, I dread social commitments, and the idea of living in monastic solitude with my husband and animals, books and writing is as close an idea to paradise as I can imagine. I love chocolate, but with that deeply ingrained, irrational female belief that weight equals worth, I manage to keep it down to a minor addiction. I adore good movies. I'm told I work too much. Every day is spent trying to get through the never ending "to do" list to snatch a few minutes to write.

This is because, despite all these mediocre and typical qualities, for some miraculous reason, these wonderful characters well up out of my soul with stories to tell. When I manage to find enough time to write, sufficient enough that the precious "stillness" required rises up and calms all the competing voices in my head, I can step into their lives, hear what they are saying, what they're feeling, and put it down on paper. It's a magic beyond description, akin to truly believing my husband loves me, winning the trust of an animal who has known only fear or apathy, making a true connection with someone, or knowing for certain I've given a reader a moment of magic through those written words. It's a magic that reassures me there is Someone, far wiser than myself, who knows the permanent path to that garden of stillness, where there is only love, acceptance and a pen waiting for hours and hours of uninterrupted, blissful use.

If only I could finish that darned "to do" list.

I welcome feedback from readers - actually, I thrive on it like a vampire, whether it's good or bad.

૭

The author welcomes comments from readers. You can find her website and email address on her author bio page at www.ellorascave.com.

Tell Us What You Think

We appreciate hearing reader opinions about our books. You can email us at Service@ellorascave.com (when contacting Customer Service, be sure to state the book title and author).

Why an electronic book?

We live in the Information Age—an exciting time in the history of human civilization, in which technology rules supreme and continues to progress in leaps and bounds every minute of every day. For a multitude of reasons, more and more avid literary fans are opting to purchase e-books instead of paper books. The question from those not yet initiated into the world of electronic reading is simply: *Why?*

1. *Price.* An electronic title at Ellora's Cave Publishing runs anywhere from 40% to 75% less than the cover price of the exact same title in paperback format. Why? Basic mathematics and cost. It is less expensive to publish an e-book (no paper and printing, no warehousing and shipping) than it is to publish a paperback, so the savings are passed along to the consumer.
2. *Space.* Running out of room in your house for your books? That is one worry you will never have with electronic books. For a low one-time cost, you can purchase a handheld device specifically designed for e-reading. Many e-readers have large, convenient screens for viewing. Better yet, hundreds of titles can be stored within your new library—on a single microchip. There are a variety of e-readers from different manufacturers. You can also read e-books on your PC or laptop computer. (Please note that Ellora's Cave does not endorse any specific brands.

You can check our website at www.ellorascave.com for information we make available to new consumers.)

3. **Mobility.** Because your new e-library consists of only a microchip within a small, easily transportable e-reader, your entire cache of books can be taken with you wherever you go.
4. **Personal Viewing Preferences.** Are the words you are currently reading too small? Too large? Too... ANNOYING? Paperback books cannot be modified according to personal preferences, but e-books can.
5. **Instant Gratification.** Is it the middle of the night and all the bookstores near you are closed? Are you tired of waiting days, sometimes weeks, for bookstores to ship the novels you bought? Ellora's Cave Publishing sells instantaneous downloads twenty-four hours a day, seven days a week, every day of the year. Our webstore is never closed. Our e-book delivery system is 100% automated, meaning your order is filled as soon as you pay for it.

Those are a few of the top reasons why electronic books are replacing paperbacks for many avid readers.

As always, Ellora's Cave welcomes your questions and comments. We invite you to email us at Service@ellorascave.com or write to us directly at Ellora's Cave Publishing Inc., 1056 Home Avenue, Akron, OH 44310-3502.

MAKE EACH DAY MORE *EXCITING* WITH OUR

ELLORA'S CAVEMEN CALENDAR

☥ WWW.ELLORASCAVE.COM ☥

Ellora's Cave Romanticon

Annual convention
for women who
refuse to behave

www.ECRomanticon.com
For additional info contact: conventions@ellorascave.com

Discover for yourself why readers can't get enough of the multiple award-winning publisher Ellora's Cave. Be sure to visit EC on the web at www.ellorascave.com to find erotic reading experiences that will leave you breathless. You can also find our books at all the major e-tailers (Barnes & Noble, Amazon Kindle, Sony, Kobo, Google, Apple iBookstore, All Romance eBooks, and others).

www.ellorascave.com

CPSIA information can be obtained at www.ICGtesting.com
Printed in the USA
LVOW12s2332211014

409818LV00001B/299/P